FRANKLY *in* LOVE

FRANKLY in LOVE

DAVID YOON

PENGUIN BOOKS

PENGUIN BOOKS

UK | USA | Canada | Ireland | Australia
India | New Zealand | South Africa

Penguin Books is part of the Penguin Random House group of companies
whose addresses can be found at global.penguinrandomhouse.com.

www.penguin.co.uk
www.puffin.co.uk
www.ladybird.co.uk

First published in the USA by G. P. Putnam's Sons,
an imprint of Penguin Random House LLC,
and in Great Britain by Penguin Books 2019

001

Design by Marikka Tamura

Set in Melior Com
Printed and bound in Great Britain by Clays Ltd, Elcograf S.p.A.

A CIP catalogue record for this book is available from the British Library

ISBN: 978–0–241–37343–9

All correspondence to:
Penguin Books
Penguin Random House Children's
80 Strand, London WC2R 0RL

For Nicki & Penny & Mom & Dad, all together

contents

before we begin

the fall season of the senior year of the high school period of early human life

frank li in love

shake the world upside down and see what sticks

before we begin

Well, I have two names.

That's what I say when people ask me what my middle name is. I say:

Well, I have two names.

My first name is Frank Li. Mom-n-Dad gave me that name mostly with the character count in mind.

No, really: F+R+A+N+K+L+I contains seven characters, and seven is a lucky number in America.

Frank is my American name, meaning it's my name-name.

My second name is Sung-Min Li, and it's my Korean name, and it follows similar numerological cosmology:

S+U+N+G+M+I+N+L+I contains nine characters, and nine is a lucky number in Korea. Nobody calls me Sung-Min, not even Mom-n-Dad. They just call me Frank.

So I don't have a middle name. Instead, I have two names.

Anyway: I guess having both lucky numbers seven and nine is supposed to make me some kind of bridge between cultures or some shit.

America, this is Korea, Korea, this is America.

Everyone good? Can I go do my thing now?

Good.

the fall season

of the senior year

of the high school period

of early human life

chapter 1

lake girlfriend

Senior year is begun.

Is begun sounds cooler than the more normal *has begun*, because if you say it right, you sound like a lone surviving knight delivering dire news to a weary king on the brink of defeat, his limp hand raking his face with dread. *The final breach is begun, your grace. The downfall of House Li is begun.*

I'm the king in that scenario, by the way, raking my face with dread.

For senior year is begun.

Sometimes I look way back to six months ago, during the halcyon days of junior year. How we pranced in the meadows after taking the PSAT: a practice run of the SAT, which in Playa Mesa, in California, in the United States of America, is widely used to gauge whether an early human is fit for entrance into an institution of higher learning.

1

But the PSAT?

A mere trial, we juniors sang. *What counts not for shit, your grace!*

How we lazed in the sunlight, sharing jokes about that one reading comprehension passage about the experiment testing whether dogs found it easier to tip a bin (easier) for food or pull a rope (trickier). Based on the passage and results in Figure 4, were the dogs

A) more likely to solve the rope task than the bin task?

B) more frustrated by the rope task than the bin task?

C) more likely to resent their human caregivers for
   being presented with such absurd tasks to begin with,
   I mean, just give us the food in a damn dog bowl like
   normal people?

Or

D) more likely to rake a paw over their face with dread?

The answer was D.

For come Score Day, I discovered I got a total of 1400 points out of a possible 1520, the 96th percentile. This earned me plenty of robust, spontaneous high fives from my friends, but to me they sounded like palms—*ptt ptt ptt*—slapping the sealed door of a crypt.

The target was 1500.

When I told Mom-n-Dad, they stared at me with pity and disbelief, like I was a little dead sparrow in the park. And Mom actually said this, for real:

Don't worry, we still love you.

Mom has said the words *I love you* exactly two times in my life. Once for the 1400, and another time when she called after her mother's funeral in Korea when I was ten. Hanna and I didn't go. Dad was at The Store; he didn't go either.

In retrospect, it's weird we didn't all go.

Secretly, in retrospect: I'm glad I didn't go. I met my grandma only once, when I was six. She spoke no English, me no Korean.

So in retro-retrospect, maybe it's not so weird that we didn't all go.

Dad has said the words *I love you* exactly zero times in my life.

Let's go back to that PSAT score.

As a leading indicator, a bellwether, augury, harbinger, and many other words from the now-useless PSAT vocabulary study guide, a score of 1500 would mean I would probably kick the real SAT's ass high enough to gain the attention of The Harvard, which is the Number One Top School in Whole of United States, according to Mom-n-Dad.

A 1400 means I'll probably only ess-ay-tee just high enough to get into the University of California at Berkeley, which in Mom-n-Dad's mind is a sad consolation prize compared with The Harvard. And sometimes, just for a nanosecond, their brainlock actually has me thinking:

Berkeley sucks.

My big sister, Hanna, coined the term *brainlock*, which is like a headlock but for your mind. Hanna lives in Boston near the other Berkeley, the Berklee College of Music.

Berklee is my real dream school. But Mom-n-Dad have

3

already nixed that notion. *Music? How you making money? How you eating?*

Hanna's two names are Hanna Li (character count: seven) and Ji-Young Li (nine). Dad named Hanna Li after Honali, from a popular 1960s marijuana anthem disguised as a children's song, "Puff (The Magic Dragon)." The song had found its way into high-school English classes in Seoul in the 1970s. Dad has never smoked pot in his life. He had no idea what he was singing.

Hanna is the oldest; Hanna did everything right. Mom-n-Dad told her to study hard, so she got straight As. They told her to go to The Harvard, so she did, and graduated with honors. She moved on to Harvard Law School, and graduated with a leap big enough to catapult her above assistants her same age at Eastern Edge Consulting downtown, which specializes in negotiating ridiculous patents for billion-dollar tech companies. She's even dabbling in venture capital now from her home office high atop Beacon Hill. Weekdays, she wears very expensive pantsuits; weekends, sensible (but still very expensive) dresses. Someone should put her on the cover of a business travel magazine or something.

But then Hanna did the one wrong thing. She fell in love.

Falling in love isn't bad by itself. But when it's with a black boy, it's big enough to cancel out everything she did right her whole life. This boy gave Hanna a ring, which Mom-n-Dad have not seen and might never.

In another family perhaps on another planet, this brown boy would be brought home for summer vacation to meet the

4

family, and we would all try out his name in the open air: *Miles Lane.*

But we're on this planet, and Mom-n-Dad are Mom-n-Dad, so there will be no Hanna this summer. I miss her. But I understand why she won't come home. Even though it does mean I'll be left high and dry without someone to make fun of the world with.

The last time she came home was a Thanksgiving holiday two years ago. She was at a Gathering. It was the Changs' turn to host. I'm not sure why she did what she did that night. *So I have this boy now,* she said. *And he is The One.*

And she held out her phone with a photo of Miles to Mom-n-Dad and everyone. It was like she cast a Silence spell on the room. No one said shit.

After a long minute, the phone turned itself off.

Mom-n-Dad went to the front door, put on their shoes, and waited with eyes averted for us to join them. We left without a word of explanation—none was needed—and the next morning Hanna vanished onto a flight back to Boston, four days early. A year later, after six or seven Hanna-free Gatherings, Ella Chang dared utter the word *disowned.*

And life went on. Mom-n-Dad no longer talked about Hanna. They acted like she moved to a foreign country with no modern forms of communication. Whenever I brought her up, they would literally—literally—avert their eyes and fall silent until I gave up. After a while, I did.

So did Hanna. Her text message responses fell from every day to every other day, then every week, and so on. This is how disownment happens. It's not like some final sentence declared during some family tribunal. Disownment is a gradual kind of neglect. Since Mom-n-Dad gave up on Hanna, Hanna decided to give up as well. I get that.

But I never gave up on her. I still haven't.

It's a scary thing to watch someone you love vanish from sight.

I talk a lot about Hanna with Q. Q is what I call my top chap, and I am his.

I'm forever grateful for Q's patience with me, because I can't imagine it makes Q feel all that good to hear how Mom-n-Dad rejected a boy with the same skin color as his.

Q's full name is Q Lee. He Lee and me Li. Like two brothers from Korean and African-American mothers. His parents, Mr. and Ms. Lee, are normal people who seem forever astonished that they gave birth to such a meganerd of a son. Q has a twin sister named Evon who is so smoking hot I can barely look at her. You say Evon Lee like *heavenly*.

Q's *Q* doesn't stand for anything; it's just Q. Q decided to rename himself a couple months ago on his eighteenth birthday. He was originally born as Will. Will Lee.

Show us your willy, Will Lee, they would say.

Good choice on the name change, Q.

Like most nerds, Q and I spend our time watching obscure movies, playing video games, deconstructing the various absurdities of reality, and so on. We hardly ever talk about girls, for lack of material. Neither of us has dated anyone. The farthest I have ventured out into girl waters is when I accidentally kissed Gina Iforget during a game of spin-the-ballpoint-pen in junior high. It was supposed to be on the cheek, and both Gina and I missed and touched each other's lips instead. Ooo-ooo-ooo.

The only time and place we even obliquely approach the subject of girl is when we happen to find ourselves sitting on the shore of Lake Girlfriend.

Lake Girlfriend is at Westchester Mall. Westchester Mall is the biggest mall in Orange County. For some reason, they leave all their doors open well past midnight, long after the stores have all shut. The mall becomes a beautifully empty, serenely apocalyptic space that no one in all of Southern California seems to know about.

Only two security guards patrol all seventy gleaming acres of the deserted mall. Their names are Camille and Oscar. They know me and Q and understand that no, we are not dating; we are just two guys with strange ideas of how to pass the time.

Lake Girlfriend is a fountain in Westchester Mall's Crystal Atrium by the Nordstrom anchor store. It is a low polished structure formed from simple modernist angles. It bears a fancy brass plaque that says DO NOT DRINK—RECLAIMED WATER. Above, nameless jazz infuses the cavernous faceted space with echoey arpeggios.

I call it Lake Girlfriend because maybe if I give it enough confessions and offerings, a girl will rise from its shimmering surface and offer me her hand.

Q and I sit tailor-style on a stone ledge the color of chocolate by this fountain. We watch the water bubble up from an octagonal top pool, push through a stone comb, and descend staggered steps to a pool floor sequined throughout with glimmering coins.

I reach into my army-surplus rucksack and take out my Tascam, a sweet little device no bigger than a TV remote, and record the sound: low, rich syrup layered with pink noise and the occasional pwip of large bubbles. Practically a complete riff unto itself. I click the recorder off and stash it away so that Q and I can begin.

"Ideal traits in a woman," I say. "You go first."

Q rests his chin atop his fists. "Speaks at least two other languages."

"And?" I say.

"Can play the oboe at a professional level," says Q.

"Q," I say.

"Ivy League professor by day, ballet renegade by night."

"I'm assuming this list isn't based in reality," I say.

"A guy can dream, right?" says Q.

It's a little hard to hear him over the white noise of Lake Girlfriend, and I think that's the thing about this place that makes it easy to talk about things like ideal girls. It's like talking out loud to ourselves, but in front of each other.

"Your turn," says Q.

I think. A hundred faces scroll through my mind, all pretty in their own way. A thousand combinations of possibilities. Everyone has loveliness inside if you look carefully. Lots of the world is like this. One time I halved an onion and discovered its rings had squashed one by one to form a perfect heart shape at the core. One time—

"Frank?" says Q. "You gotta move your mouth to speak."

"Wull," I say. "I mean."

Q looks at me, waiting.

"Basically I guess she has to be kind, is most important."

Q raises his eyebrows. "So no meanies. Got it."

"And she should make me laugh," I say.

"Any other vital criteria?" says Q.

I think. Anything else—hobbies, musical tastes, fashion sense—doesn't seem to matter that much. So I just shake my head no.

Q gives the fountain a shrug. "That's super romantic, like in the most basic sense."

"Basically," I say.

We both stare at the fountain for a moment. Then I mark the end of our visit to Lake Girlfriend with the ritual digging into my front jeans pocket for sacred coins, one for me, one for Q. Q tosses his in with a fart sound. I give mine a squeeze and flip it into the water, ploop. The coins are added to the submerged pile of random wishes: good grades, job promotions, lottery dreams, and, above all, love.

No one comes rising out of the shimmering water.

Q doesn't know it, but I've secretly left out one criterion for my ideal woman. It's one I'd rather not say aloud, even though it's the one I worry about the most.

My ideal woman should probably be Korean-American.

It's not strictly necessary. I could care less. But it would make things easier.

I've toed the dating waters only twice before, and each time something has held me back from diving in. A paralysis. I think it comes from not knowing which would be worse:

9

dating a girl my parents hated or dating a girl my parents loved. Being ostracized or being micromanaged.

Then I consider how Korean-Americans make up only 1 percent of everyone in the Republic of California, out of which 12 percent are girls my age, which would result in a dating pool with only one girl every three square miles. Filter out the ones who are taken, the ones I wouldn't get along with, and—worse—add in the Ideal Woman criteria, and the pool gets even smaller. Lake Girlfriend shrinks down to a thimble.

So I shelve the notion of an ideal girl for now. I realize I've been shelving the idea for years.

"A guy can dream," says Q.

"A guy can dream," I say.

chapter 2

metaphor incoming

Mom-n-Dad's store also has two names, like me and Hanna.

Its official name is Fiesta Hoy Market, which I won't even bother to translate because goddamn, what a stupid name. Its second name is simply The Store. The Store is its name-name.

Mom-n-Dad work at The Store every day, from morning to evening, on weekends, holidays, New Year's Day, 365 days out of every year without a single vacation for as long as me and Hanna have been alive.

Mom-n-Dad inherited The Store from an older Korean couple of that first wave who came over in the sixties. No written contracts or anything. Just an introduction from a good friend, then tea, then dinners, and finally many deep bows, culminating in warm, two-handed handshakes. They wanted to make sure The Store was kept in good hands. Good, Korean hands.

The Store is an hour-long drive from the dystopian

perfection of my suburban home of Playa Mesa. It's in a poor, sun-crumbled part of Southern California largely populated by Mexican- and African-Americans. A world away.

The poor customers give Mom-n-Dad food stamps, which become money, which becomes college tuition for me.

It's the latest version of the American dream.

I hope the next version of the American dream doesn't involve gouging people for food stamps.

I'm at The Store now. I'm leaning against the counter. Its varnish is worn in the middle like a tree ring, showing the history of every transaction that's ever been slid across its surface: candy and beer and diapers and milk and beer and ice cream and beer and beer.

"At the airport," I once explained to Q, "they hand out title deeds by ethnicity. So the Greeks get diners, the Chinese get laundromats, and the Koreans get liquor stores."

"So *that's* how America works," said Q, taking a deeply ironic bite of his burrito.

It's hot in The Store. I'm wearing a Hardfloor tee shirt perforated with moth holes in cool black, to match my cool-black utility shorts. Not all blacks are the same. There is warm black and brown black and purple black. My wristbands are a rainbow of blacks. All garments above the ankles must be black. Shoes can be anything, however. Like my caution-yellow sneakers.

Dad refuses to turn on the air-conditioning, because the only things affected by the heat are the chocolate-based candies, and he's already stashed those in the walk-in cooler.

Meanwhile, I'm sweating. I watch a trio of flies trace an

12

endless series of right angles in midair with a nonstop zimzim sound. I snap a photo and post it with the caption: *Flies are the only creature named after their main mode of mobility.*

It makes no sense that I'm helping Mom-n-Dad at The Store. My whole life they've never let me have a job.

"Study hard, become doctor maybe," Dad would say.

"Or a famous newscaster," Mom would say.

I still don't get that last one.

Anyway: I'm at The Store only one day a week, on Sundays, and only to work the register—no lifting, sorting, cleaning, tagging, or dealing with vendors. Mom's home resting from her morning shift, leaving me and Dad alone for his turn. I suspect all this is Mom's ploy to get me to bond with Dad in my last year before I head off to college. Spend father-n-son time. Engage in deep conversation.

Dad straps on a weight belt and muscles a hand truck loaded with boxes of malt liquor. He looks a bit like a Hobbit, stocky and strong and thick legged, with a box cutter on his belt instead of a velvet sachet of precious coins. He has all his hair still, even in his late forties. To think, he earned a bachelor's degree in Seoul and wound up here. I wonder how many immigrants there are like him, working a blue-collar job while secretly owning a white-collar degree.

He slams his way out of the dark howling maw of the walk-in cooler.

"You eat," he says.

"Okay, Dad," I say.

"You go taco. Next door. Money, here."

He hands me a twenty.

"Okay, Dad."

I say *Okay, Dad* a lot to Dad. It doesn't get much deeper than that for the most part. For the most part, it can't. Dad's English isn't great, and my Korean is almost nonexistent. I grew up on video games and indie films, and Dad grew up on I-don't-know-what.

I used to ask him about his childhood. Or about basic things, like how he was able to afford a luxury like college. He grew up poor, after all, poorer than poor. Both my parents did, before Korea's economic supernova in the late eighties. Dad said he would go fishing for river crabs when food ran low. Lots of people in the sticks did.

"Tiny crabby, they all crawling inside my net," he told me. "All crawling crawling crawling over each other, they stepping on each other face, try to get on top."

"Okay," I said.

"That's Korea," he said.

When I asked him what that meant, he just closed the conversation with:

"Anyway America better. Better you going college here, learn English. More opportunity."

That's his checkmate move for most conversations, even ones that start out innocently enough like, *How come we never kept up with speaking Korean in the house?* or *Why do old Korean dudes worship Chivas Regal?*

So for the most part, he and I have made a habit of leaving things at *Okay, Dad.*

"Okay, Dad," I say.

I grab my phone and step into the even hotter heat outside. Corrido music is bombarding the empty parking lot from the carnicería next door. The music is meant to convey festivity, to entice customers inside. It's not working.

¡Party Today!

Buzz-buzz. It's Q.

Pip pip, old chap, let's go up to LA. It's free museum night. Bunch of us are going.

Deepest regrets, old bean, I say. *Got a Gathering.*

I shall miss your companionship, fine sir, says Q.

And I yours, my good man.

Q knows what I mean when I say *Gathering.*

I'm talking about a gathering of five families, which sounds like a mafia thing but really is just Mom-n-Dad's friends getting together for a rotating house dinner.

It's an event that's simultaneously ordinary and extraordinary: ordinary in that hey, it's just dinner, but extraordinary in that all five couples met at university in Seoul, became friends, moved to Southern California together to start new lives, and have managed to see each other and their families every month literally for decades.

The day ends. Dad changes shirts, trading his shop owner persona for a more Gathering-appropriate one: a new heather-gray polo that exudes success and prosperity. We lock up, turn out the lights. Then we drive forty minutes to the Kims'.

It's the Kim family's turn to host the Gathering this time, and they've gone all out: a Brazilian barbecue carving station manned by real Brazilians drilling everyone on the word of the night (*chu•rra•sca•ri•a*), plus a wine-tasting station, plus a seventy-inch television in the great room with brand-new VR headsets for the little kids to play ocean explorer with.

It all screams: *We're doing great in America. How about you?*

Included among these totems of success are the children themselves, especially us older kids. We were all born pretty much at the same time. We're all in the same year in school. We are talked and talked about, like minor celebrities. *So-and-so made academic pentathlon team captain. So-and-so got valedictorian.*

Being a totem is a tiresome role, and so we hide away in the game room or wherever while outside, the littler kids run amok and the adults get drunk and sing twenty-year-old Korean pop songs that none of us understand. In this way we have gradually formed the strangest of friendships:

- We only sit together like this for four hours once a month.
- We never leave the room during this time, except for food.
- We never hang out outside the Gatherings.

The Gatherings are a world unto themselves. Each one is a version of Korea forever trapped in a bubble of amber—the early-nineties Korea that Mom-n-Dad and the rest of their friends brought over to the States years ago after the bubble burst. Meanwhile, the Koreans in Korea have moved on, become more affluent, more savvy. Meanwhile, just outside the Kims' front door, American kids are dance-gaming to K-pop on their big-screens.

But inside the Gathering, time freezes for a few hours. We children are here only because of our parents, after all. Would we normally hang out otherwise? Probably not. But we can't exactly sit around ignoring each other, because that would be boring. So we jibber-jabber and philosophize until it's time to leave. Then we are released back into the reality awaiting us outside the Gathering, where time unfreezes and resumes.

I call us the Limbos.

Every month I dread going to these awkward reunions with the Limbos, to wait out time in between worlds. But every month I'm also reminded that most of the Limbos are actually pretty cool.

Like John Lim (character count: seven), who made his own game that's selling pretty well on the app store.

Or Ella Chang (nine), who shreds at the cello.

Or Andrew Kim (nine), who cowrote a pretty popular book with his YouTube partner.

I used to think the character count in our names was a weird Korean thing.

But it wasn't a weird Korean thing. It was just weird.

I think the type of person who is willing to live in a totally different country is also willing to make up their own weird traditions. Weird makes weird.

Weird also makes for incredibly lucky lives for us kids, and for that I'm always grateful. For real.

At tonight's Gathering the Limbos are holed up in Andrew's room, playing a multiplayer brawler game.

"Hey," I say.

"Hey," they say.

There's John Lim steering his controller in the air, as if that will help anything. There's Andrew Kim, hissing with effort. There's Ella Chang, calmly kicking everyone's ass from behind her horn rims.

"Wanna play?" drawls Ella.

"In a sec."

One of the Limbos is missing. I wander around the house until I find her: Joy Song, sitting alone among big Lego bricks in the pastel room of Andrew Kim's little sister.

Joy Song (character count: seven), second name Yu-Jin Song (nine).

When we were five, six, seven, Joy and I used to sneak the crispy bits off the barbecue table before it was time to eat. We used to stand on our chairs, hold noodles as high as we could, and lower them into each other's open mouths below. We used to put blades of grass down each other's pants, until one day I caught a glimpse of her front and understood that it was now time to be afraid of girls. I've been afraid ever since.

Now Joy Song sits in the corner smelling her upper lip. She glances up at me—*oh, it's just Frank*—and keeps her upper lip curled. It adds an edge of defiance to a face otherwise made up of simple ovalettes. She returns to what she was doing: arranging the Lego bricks in a line.

She's also listening to music through her tiny phone speakers. It sounds like bugs shouting.

"Isn't that just the best way to listen to music?" I say. "Really respects the artistic intent of the musicians."

"Hi, Frank," says Joy, joylessly.

"How you been?"

"Oh, not much," she says, answering some other question in her head.

I sit at the pile of Lego and feel like I'm ten. "You wanna build something?"

"It's just that the solid ones are ABS plastic, and the clear pieces are polycarbonate."

"Oh-kay." I notice that Joy has changed her hair. On the outside it's the usual ink-brown shell, but the inside layer has been dyed a lime green that's visible only in flashes.

She runs her hand through her hair—green flash—and stops, holding her head sideways. Lost in thought. "You can't 3D-print ABS or polycarbonate. At least I can't. I don't have the requisite tech."

She releases her hair, and the green layer becomes hidden again.

Me and Joy both go to Palomino High. Our classes never intersect. No one outside the Limbos knows we're Gathering friends. When we pass in the hallways, we just kind of look at each other and move along.

Now that I think about it, why *don't* we Limbos hang out outside Gatherings?

"Let's make a tower," she says.

We fall into an old habit: building a four-by-four tower with the colors ascending in spectral ROYGBIV order. Chk, chk, brick by brick. We do this for a long time, in silence.

The noise of the party phase-shifts, and I look up to see my mom peering in from the doorway. She doesn't have to say anything. All she has to do is look at me, then at Joy, and smile this corny tilted smile.

After Mom vanishes, Joy rolls her eyes hard and groans to the heavens.

"Joy, will you marry me so that House Li and House Song may finally be joined as one?" I say.

"Shut the fuck up," she says, and throws a Lego at me.

She's got a bizarre laugh, kind of like a herd of squirrels.

"God, I'm so screwed," she says finally.

"What's going on?"

"Wu—you know Wu."

Of course I know Wu. Wu is Chinese-American, third gen. Wu is six two, 190 pounds of fighting muscle; a hawk-eyed warrior prince somehow lost in the American high school wilderness. A single glance from him frequently makes girls walk face-first into their lockers.

Wu is 99 percent likely to go to the University of Southern California, which is in Los Angeles. His dad went to USC. His mom went to USC. They have USC license-plate frames on their cars. They still go to the football games.

I once saw Wu and Joy making out between a pair of columns, and the sight of her ovalette jaw moving with his angular one produced that paralyzing mixture of revulsion and fascination you get when you're seeing something you know must surely exist but never thought you'd see with your own eyes.

20

Q thinks Joy is gorgeous. As a non-Gathering friend, Q is allowed to think that.

Wu's full name is Wu Tang.

Yep.

Joy continues. "Wu's all, *I want to meet your parents.* I'm all, *no,* but he keeps insisting. We had this big fight."

To understand why this is an issue, it's helpful to know that basically every country in Asia has historically hated on every other country in Asia. Koreans hated Chinese, and Chinese hated Koreans, and have forever. Also Chinese hated Japanese hated Koreans hated Thais hated Vietnamese and so on. They all have histories of invading and being invaded by one another. You know how European countries talk shit all the time about each other? Same thing.

"That's stressful," I say with a frown.

Joy and I are up to green bricks now. I hold one up and notice it's the same color as the green hiding in her hair.

"I don't just have boy problems," says Joy. "I have Chinese boy problems."

Koreans hating Chinese hating Koreans hating blablabla.

"Racists," I say.

Joy just nods. She knows I'm talking about her mom-n-dad.

I know this is the point where one of us should say some-damn-thing about Hanna. But what is there to say?

There's plenty to say. But I've said it over and over and over, so many times that I don't have to even actually say it anymore. Now I'm just super tired of saying it.

Our parents are racist. I wish things were different. I miss

Hanna. I wish things were different. Our parents are racist. I miss Hanna.

Chk, chk. We build until we reach the violet bricks. There's a bunch of white and black and brown bricks left over.

"What should we do with these?" I say. "They don't fit into the rainbow spectrum."

This is a ridiculous and obvious metaphor, and Joy smacks my forehead to point it out.

"Metaphor incoming, doosh," she says.

Then we just kind of stare at each other.

"Fuckin' parents, man," I say.

chapter 3

more better

Mom's driving me and Dad back home from the party. It's a long way from Diamond Ranch back to Playa Mesa. The neighborhoods start all Korean, then go Mexican, then Chinese, then black, then back to Mexican, then finally white.

Playa Mesa is in white.

We're only at the first Mexican when Dad quietly throws up into an empty to-go cup.

"Eigh," says Mom. "You drink too much, Daddy."

"I'm okay," says Dad.

"Eigh," says Mom, and rolls down all the windows.

Dad seals the lid on the soda cup and leans back with his eyes closed. The straw is still sticking out of the top. It's like Satan created a drink daring all to take a sip.

The fresh air helps with the smell.

"You don't drink like Daddy, okay?" Mom says to me through the rearview mirror.

"Okay, Mom," I say.

"One time, one man, he drink all night, drink too too much? He sleep, he throw up, he choking in his sleep? He die."

I've heard this story before. "That sucks."

"Really don't drink, okay?"

"You got nothing to worry about, Mom."

And she really doesn't. I've had about two drinks my entire life, and I didn't bother finishing them. Same thing with top chap Q, Q's sister, Evon, or any of my other friends. We're all sober kids, all in the same Advanced Placement (AP) classes, and therefore do not get invited to parties and their concomitant opportunities to imbibe. We wouldn't drink even if we did.

We are APs, or Apeys for short. We do not go to *keggers* or *ragers*. Instead of parties, we find empty parking structures and hold midnight table reads of *Rosencrantz and Guildenstern Are Dead*. We pile into my car, a teenaged front-wheel-drive Consta with manual windows, and drive halfway to Las Vegas just to see a meteor shower and get a good look at Orion's scabbard in the flawless black desert sky. To be clear, we never actually continue on to Vegas. Whatever happens in Vegas, whatevers in Vegas, who cares. We turn the car around and head home and wonder about life outside Earth, and whether we'll ever encounter aliens or they're just ignoring us because we're still so embarrassingly primitive, or if the Fermi paradox is true and we really are the only intelligent beings in the entire universe.

Traffic is super light—just a stream of lights rocketing along at eighty-five miles per hour—and already we're up to Chinese. Dad points it out.

"This all Chinese now," he says. "Used to be Mexican, now totally Chinese. They take over whole this area. Look, signs say HONG FU XIAN blablabla, ha ha ha."

"Chang-chong-ching-chong?" says Mom, laughing too.

"You guys," I say.

"They eating everything," says Dad. "Piggy ear, piggy tail, chicken feet, everything they eating."

I facepalm, but with my knee. Koreans eat quote-weird-end-quote stuff too: sea cucumbers, live octopus, acorn jelly, all of it delicious. White people, black people, Indian, Jamaican, Mexican, *people*-people eat weird, delicious stuff.

I want to say all of this, but I find I can't. It'll just get me nowhere. My parents are just stuck on thinking Koreans are special.

"Ching-chong-chang-chang?" says Mom again.

Dad laughs, steadying his to-go drink from hell, and for a second I can imagine them before they had me and Hanna. It's a paradoxically sweet vignette. Mom-n-Dad warmly muttering to each other in Korean, most of which I can't understand, except for the startling appearance of the word *jjangkkae*, which means *chink*.

If I were like any other normal teenager, I would lose myself in my fartphone (that's what Q says instead of *smartphone*, because all we're doing is farting around on social media anyway), giving out crappy likes on the crappy feeds, maybe crafting beats if I felt like being creative. But then I would only get carsick. So all I can do is be present and in the racist moment.

"You guys are so racist," I say instead.

I'm so used to them being racist that I can't even bother arguing with them anymore. It's like commanding the wind to alter direction. *You are aware that non-Koreans populated the United States of America before you came here, right?* I used to say. *You're aware that Korea is this tiny country, and the world is full of people you know little about, right?*

Arguing with Mom-n-Dad is pointless, because the wind will blow wherever it wants according to its own infuriating wind-logic. Only the insane would keep trying to change them. Especially when they end things with their *just-joking* defense. Like now:

"No racist," says Mom, wounded. "We just joking."

"Joy Song has a boyfriend and he's third-gen Chinese," I say.

I of course say no such thing. Saying that would instantly make Joy's life hell once her mom got the call from my mom, and my mom is always making calls. Then Joy would build a drone in her garage and order it to dice me up with lasers in my sleep.

But part of me itches to do it anyway. Because this is America, and because I want to force the issue. *Did you know,* I would say, *that Korean-Americans make up only 0.5 percent of the entire population? Did you think about that before you came here? Did you think you could avoid the other 99.5 percent of the country for very long?*

I don't say any of this. Instead, I talk about Q.

"What if Q was Chinese? Would you be all *ching-chong* in front of him?"

"No," says Mom. She looks almost insulted.

"So just behind his back."

"No, Frank."

"Do you call Q geomdungi behind his back?"

"Frank, aigu!" Mom's glaring at me through the rearview mirror's slash of light.

Geomdungi means the n-word.

"Q is okay," says Dad. His eyes are still closed. It looks like he's talking and sleeping at the same time. He sounds reasonable and soothing, even when he's drunk. "Q like family. I like Q."

Dad says this despite the fact that Q has only ever hung out at my house a handful of times in all the years we've known each other. There is a secret to why this is.

The secret is in the smiles. Mom-n-Dad, all smiles, and Q, too. Everyone smiling, pretending the specter of Hanna is not right there before us. By Mom-n-Dad's internal wind-logic, Q is fine—Q is a friend, Q is a boy. There is no family name at stake here.

But still, I'm afraid Mom-n-Dad would possibly say or do something carelessly hurtful to my most top chap. So the few times Q's been over, I've kept things simple and quick: say hi to Mom-n-Dad, smile-smile-smile right up the staircase, and head straight into my room for shitty old video games on my shitty old system. Eventually I just found myself hanging out at his house all the time. It's easier than all those smiles.

Q first pointed out the smiles a long time ago. He was

angry. I was angry too. Who wouldn't be? We sat all night with our anger, discussing it, shaping it, until it became a kind of energy shield defending us. I vowed to protect Q from any harm my parents could potentially dish out. I ranted out a fiery apology, going on and on until Q finally stopped me with an arm hug to say *You didn't pick your parents, and neither did I.*

That's what Q tells me whenever my parents say something ludicrous: *I didn't pick your parents to be my best friend in the whole world.*

The car is quiet but for the whistling wind. For a second I think the issue has been successfully forced, copious science has been dropped, minds have been quietly blown, we are all one human race, this is the United States of America, I have a dream that one day every valley shall be exalted.

But then Dad keeps going.

Dad keeps dream-talking.

"Q is so-called *honorary white*. You know *honorary white*?"

"No he's not," I say, but Dad just keeps on going.

"Daddy, sleep," says Mom.

But Dad does not sleep. "Black people always no money they having. Always doing crime, gang, whatever. Make too many baby. That's black people."

"Dad, jesus, that's not true," I say. All I can do is shake my head. This sort of drunken rambling is familiar territory for me. I find a painted line on the highway and follow it as it dips and rises and splits into two. We change lanes and the tires do two fast, sharp drumrolls.

But then Mom sits up. "It is," she says. "I wondering, why

black people behaving like that? Our customers? So many, they behaving like that. Ninety-eight percent."

Mom likes to make up fake statistics. So does Dad. It's annoying as hell.

I snarl at the window. "So, slavery, decades of systemic racist policy, and the poverty it created don't have anything to do with anything."

"1992," says Mom, "we coming to United States, only we have three hundred dollar. That's it. We stay friends' house almost two year. Dr. and Mrs. Choi. Only we eating ramyun and kimchi rice two year."

That's not the same thing, I think. I don't bother listening to the rest.

Mom-n-Dad are like this big ice wall of ignorance, and I'm just a lone soldier with a sword. I just kind of give up. I find myself missing Hanna big-time. She used to argue all righteous with Mom-n-Dad all the time, like the lawyer she eventually became. She wouldn't back down a single millimeter, not for shit. She would take the argument all the way to the limit, and then just hold it there. Like:

Where does Korean-ness begin and end?

What about kids born from Chinese or Japanese occupiers? What about those comfort women? Should their Korean cards be canceled?

Don't you think you should have to live in Korea to be fully Korean?

Don't you think you should have to be fluent in Korean to be fully Korean?

Why'd you come to this country if you're so Korean?

29

And what about me and Frank?

She was brave—braver than me—but now I wonder if being brave is worth it. The brave go first into battle. But that makes them the first to go down, too.

I wait for the car to get quiet again before saying:

"What if I dated someone black?" I want to add *like Hanna*, but don't.

"Frank, stop it," says Mom, and gets a grave look, like *That's not funny.* She glances at Dad. Dad is asleep. His to-go cup is tipping. She puts it in the center cup holder, which somehow makes it even more disgusting.

"What about white?" I say.

"No," says Mom.

"So only Korean."

Mom sighs. "Why, you have white girlfriend?"

"No."

"Don't do it, okay?" says Mom. "Anyway. Big eyes is better. Nice eyes."

Mom is obsessed with girls having big eyes. Joy's mom is obsessed with girls having big eyes. Same with the parents of the other Limbos. We tried figuring out why once at a Gathering. Someone said it must have something to do with a bunch of round-eye American soldiers saving them from civil war, which led to a close examination of the size of General MacArthur's eyes, which pivoted to theories about big-eyed characters in Japanese anime, which devolved into a big Lego-throwing debate about which was better, Japanese manga or Korean manhwa.

"You marry Korean girl," says Mom. "Make everything easier."

I dig the heels of my hands into my eyes. "Easier for you." I want to add, *I could care less if she were Korean,* but we've beat this horse before and it's an incredibly durable creature.

"Not just us," says Mom. She's indignant. "Easier for everybody. Korean girl, we gathering with her parents, we speak Korean together. More comfortable, more better. We eating Korean food all together, going to Korean church together, more better."

"So, more better for you."

"No," says Mom, louder. "You will understand when you have baby. Okay: pretend you have mix baby, okay? People say, 'Oh, what nationality this baby?' Too headache for baby. For you too! Where baby belong? You think about baby."

So I think about baby. Not my baby, but specifically the future baby of Hanna and Miles. I've seen *mixed* babies before, and like all babies ever born, they're adorable. Who could be so cruel as to reject a *mixed* baby?

What the hell am I talking about? I hate that word, *mixed.* Just a couple generations ago people called French-Russian babies *mixed.* Now those babies are just called *white.* This word *mixed* is just brainlock messing with my head.

I give up. "Okay, Mom."

"Anyway," says Mom, calm again. "I know lot of nice girls."

I massage my temples. I've reached the end of the discussion, where there's nothing left to do but say *Okay, Mom.*

"Okay, Mom," I say.

chapter 4

just bad enough

I don't really like calculus.

But Calculus class? That's a different story.

Calculus class takes place at the ungodly hour of seven o'clock, before the rest of humanity is even conscious. It's unreasonable. Mr. Soft knows this. That's why he has a box of coffee ready, and a dozen donuts, two for each of us.

Mr. Soft has the lights dimmed. He has quiet jazz playing on a sweet vintage boombox. Mr. Soft is one of the gentlest human beings I know.

Mr. Soft's full name is Berry Soft.

"You want a little something special this morning, Frank?" says Mr. Berry Soft, very softly. "I brought my espresso machine today. More than happy to make you a cappuccino."

Our desks are arranged in a rough circle, with Mr. Soft tailor-sitting atop a stool, his glowing face underlit by an antique overhead projector literally from the year 1969 that he likes to draw on with wet-erase pens. No laptops, no phones. Just concepts and principles and longhand problem solving.

"Just look for the stuff in common between the nominators and denominators," says Mr. Soft, drawing by hand. "See what cancels out. Chop chop, flip these guys here, chop, and we're left with the answer."

"What is the answer?" says Brit Means, who sits next to me.

"I mean, it's thirteen over five," says Mr. Soft. "But that doesn't really matter. What matters is the process."

Brit Means glows in the light of his wisdom. "The process," she says. Then I realize she is nodding at me through narrowed eyes. I nod back without quite knowing what we're nodding about.

Like most of the other Apey boys, I find Brit Means a little weird and a little intense, and can't help but be fascinated by her. She walks the halls like a time traveler noticing small differences created by minute shifts in quantum chaos. She can sometimes seem like a beautiful foreign exchange student from a country no one's ever seen.

Once, I found myself sharing the shade of a tree with her on a hot day just after school. I was waiting for Q; she was waiting for her ride home.

"Most human structures are made out of wood," she said to the tree. "Wood is trees is plants. Human clothes are cotton: plants again. We live in nature every day without realizing it. We live *inside* plants."

"Huh," I said, secretly marveling at a sudden acute impulse to kiss her.

Back in Calculus, Q passes the box of donuts around. Brit leans over to choose one, drawing close enough for me to smell the shampoo in her wet hair.

Next to her sit Amelie Shim, Naima Gupta, and Paul Olmo, always in that order.

"So I'm supposed to give you turkeys a test for the suits," says Mr. Soft. "What questions do you want on it?"

We all think. It's so early.

"Just email me, okay?" says Mr. Soft. He's so soothing. "You're all getting As anyway. I hate this grading bullshit." Even his swears are soothing.

"Thanks, Mr. Soft," says Q.

"We all know we're doing the work here, right?"

We have an assignment to calculate the volume of solids formed by rotating area formulas around axes. Nothing too crazy. But Mr. Soft wants to make things interesting by having us sketch the resulting volumes on paper, in charcoal, by hand.

"To really get a sense of how the volumes feel," he says.

It's a pair assignment. Paul Olmo leans over to Q and whispers something. Q nods.

"Me and Paul are gonna do our volumes in clay," Q announces.

"Nerds," I say.

Q just looks at me like *So?*

It's Paul's turn with Q, since I got to partner with him for the last assignment. We rotate among us three to ensure equal friend time. Before I can wonder who I should pair up with, Brit Means speaks.

"Frank, will you be my partner?"

"Thanks you," I find myself saying.

Thanks you?

The bell rings. I see Q looking perhaps as astonished as me—Brit always partners with Amelie—and he offers me a covert fist bump. I naturally mistake the fist bump for a high five, and the whole thing becomes this strange gearshift pantomime: the awkward greeting ritual of male nerds everywhere.

• • •

Playa Mesa is a giant pyramid-shaped peninsula set at the edge of the Pacific; Brit Means's house is on the side opposite from mine on that pyramid.

We sit at her hulking dining table and start our assignment. Brit's mom designed the table; Brit's dad built it. Atop the table sit garlic pita chips in a wooden bowl, which Brit's dad carved himself. The table sits in the bulb of a large, curvaceous kitchen, which Brit's mom designed and Brit's dad built. Brit's parents are architects. They habitually design and build stuff—big, ornate, well-constructed stuff—like no big deal.

In walk her mom-n-dad, in matching hoodie sweats, matching lambskin slippers, holding matching mugs of tea. They are of identical small stature and seem to have come from the same lat and long within Europe many stout generations ago, and remind me of kindly druids from a video game I used to play.

"We'll be upstairs," says Brit's mom, and then she smiles

this tilted corny smile. It's the same tilted corny smile my mom gave to me and Joy at the last Gathering.

What is happening?

"Nice to meet you, Frank," says Brit's dad.

They vanish upstairs in unison.

Brit and I sit alone.

Brit regards me for a moment, like you would a favorite painting in a museum, and speaks suddenly: "You take the odd ones, I'll take the evens."

She means the assignment. She tucks her hair behind her ear and flicks her Zeichner Profi 5.0 mm mechanical pencil, effortlessly performing Around-the-Worlds, Weaves, See-Saws, regular Sassys, and Ultra Sassys.

More like Ultra Sexys.

I try to eat my lower lip. Then I remember the first Rule of Being a Person: no auto-cannibalism. I eat a garlic pita chip instead. So does Brit. We compulsively reach for more, munching and munching, and of course our hands touch in the bowl. We both draw back as if the chips are electrified.

"Sorry," she says.

"Me too," I say.

"Huh?" says Brit.

"I don't know," I say.

For some reason, this makes Brit smile this smile that says: *But I do.*

"Wanna get through this stuff?" she says.

"Right," I say.

Solving the problems is the easy part. It's the sketching

that takes time. Brit plays some music on her phone, but then switches to a proper wireless speaker.

"I hate listening on tiny speakers," she says, seconds before I can, and my heart does a triple jump.

Once I recover, I get started on the work. I sketch small—less surface area to cover—and finish fast. Brit picks up on my tactic and sketches small, too. Our pencil leads scritch and scratch. She elbows me.

"You're such a cheater."

"I'm still doing the assignment," I say. "I'm just being efficient about it."

"Done," she says.

We retract our leads and set our pencils down.

"Yours look good," I say.

"Yours look good too," she says, gazing at me.

Dear lord Flying Spaghetti Monster in Pastafarian heaven. I think Brit Means is flirting with me.

"What do you wanna do now?" I say.

"I don't know, what do you want to do?"

She sits closer. Now is the moment in the teen movie where I sweep the homework to the floor and kiss her. But like I said, my kissing track record is exactly one item long, and was an accident.

I'm pretty sure Brit's kissing track record is as short as mine. But she must be ready. Right? Why else would she be sitting so close? Is that how this works?

I have no idea how anything works. I have no idea what is happening. I stare back into her eternal ancient gray eyes

37

looking all ancient and gray and eternal into mine and find that they are also inscrutable. I could be totally wrong. It could be that Brit's just the strange type of girl who likes to sit close and stare and say nothing.

"Forgot my glasses," says a voice, and we look up just in time to see Brit's dad's hoodie vanishing around a corner.

"Let's go outside," says Brit, suddenly standing. "There's something I want to show you."

• • •

We step out into a night full of crickets on loop. Like most of Playa Vista, there is only one streetlamp for miles. Outside that single icy cone of light is the pure impenetrable darkness of the new moon sky, with only the stars and the glint of many parked cars visible.

"What's with all the cars?" I say.

"Someone's having a big house party. I'm pretty sure it's Armenian independence day." Brit hops and crouches, inspecting the cars. She moves like a long-haired imp.

"Look," she says, and cracks open one of the cars.

"Brit," I say, laughing.

"They're never locked," she says, opening it farther. "I find it so revealing about people's biases. People just assume certain things about certain neighborhoods. They wouldn't leave their doors unlocked like this over in Delgado Beach."

"Well, Playa Mesa is freakishly safe, after all."

"If we did a study, we would find a correlation between unlocked cars and neighborhood income levels, I bet you a million bucks."

"Ha ha," I say, but stop short. Because to my horror, Brit has ducked her head inside the car and is now emerging with a tin of mints. She pops one in her mouth. She tosses me a mint, too.

"Have one," she says.

"You're insane," I say, and laugh, and look around.

But I eat the mint.

Brit carefully closes the door, then latches it shut with a bump of her hip. "People keep the artifacts of their lives in their cars. Makes me feel like an archaeologist. A car-chaeologist."

"We're gonna get busted."

"Frankly, Frank Li, you're being paranoid," says Brit, with mock sass. "Anyway, even if we do get busted all I have to do is be all, *Oh-em-gee, I'm so drunk, anyway you should really lock your car, bye!*"

Brit has switched to California Valley Girl Patois with no effort, and it makes me twitch a little.

In Language class Ms. Chit would called this *code switching*. It's like switching accents, but at a more micro level.

The idea is that you don't speak the same way with your friends (California English Casual) that you do with a teacher (California English Formal), or a girl (California English Sing-song), or your immigrant parents (California English Exasperated). You change how you talk to best adapt to whoever you're talking to. But it's not just about adaptation, as Ms. Chit explained. People can code switch to confuse others, express dominance or submission, or disguise themselves.

I've always thought I'm pretty good at code switching. But

the way Brit does it is true mastery. It's like watching her become a different person entirely. It makes me wonder what other codes she can speak.

"This one . . . No, there's a blinking light on the dash," she says. "This one, maybe."

She pops the door open: "Aha."

"I am jacking cars with Brit Means," I say.

"Tell me, though: is it jacking if they're unlocked?" she says.

"How long has this been a hobby of yours?"

"Only a couple months. I've found alcohol, cash, just cash lying out in the open. An old instant camera. It's crazy."

"Wait, are you keeping this stuff?"

Brit unearths something. "Look. High-fidelity compact discs. Who listens to CDs?"

She flings one at me and I fumble to catch it like a Frisbee. It's all in Armenian.

"Dude, put this back," I say. I wipe the disc clean of my fingerprints, just in case the FBI gets called to investigate, and start to fling it back to her when she quickly hits the car's lock button and slams the door shut.

"Too late," she says, giggling. "You're stuck with that."

"I already said you're insane, right?" I say, and slip the disc into my back pocket.

"And to answer your question, no, I don't take the stuff. I just redistribute it to other cars."

"That's hilarious. It's like a metaphor for something."

"For what?"

I think for a moment. Metaphor not incoming.

Is this bad? Sure. It's just a little bad. To be sure, it's nothing compared with what other kids are doing, like failing out or getting pregnant or arrested or, in the case of Deckland Ayers, drunk-racing his brand-new Q2S sport coupe into a pole and failing out in the most permanent and tragic way.

But for Apeys, it's just bad enough.

And I love it.

"Hey, a minivan," I say. "A trove of treasures."

The minivan is the same as Q's mom's, so I know it has sliding doors on both sides. I guide Brit to the minivan's shadow, quell her sputtering giggles by squashing her cheeks with both hands, and then try the handle with practiced familiarity.

Click, whoosh.

Inside the van are toddler seats and stuffed animals and spilled puffed crackers and so on. I guide her in and can feel every sinew of the small of her back with my open hand. And together, we slowly slide the door shut behind us. The silence is absolute and ringing. I can hear her every breath. I can hear the brush of her fingertips on my shorts.

"It smells kinda good in here," she says.

And it does, because here we are, crushing toasted Os beneath our knees. Releasing their stale aroma. The space we are in is small and new and secret, and no one else in the world knows about it because no one else in the world is here but us two.

Brit is waiting. Brit is *nervous*. As nervous as me.

I find our mutual nervousness strangely comforting. It makes something in my heart loosen its grip and let go.

I pull her in and our mouths fit perfectly.

This is really happening to me. I am kissing Brit Means.

And, I realize, this is really happening to Brit Means, too.

Has she been planning this? How long has she liked me? To think, we've been friends all through high school, and this—this kiss—has been waiting in plain sight the whole time.

"Hi," I say, breathing.

"Hi," she says.

Her gray eyes are dilated wide to see in the night. We kiss deeper this time, and I don't care that she can now taste the garlic pita in my mouth because I can now taste it in hers, too. The silence focuses in. Every shift in our bodies crushing another piece of toasted cereal. The fierce breathing through nostrils flared wide. It takes me forever to realize the dome light has come on.

The light is on inside the van.

Someone has clicked a key fob remote. Someone close by, getting closer by the second.

We spring apart and duck.

"Oh shit," says Brit. Her eyes have tightened.

I'm still gasping for air. "Okay. Uh. I think we should probably go."

In the far distance, voices.

"I think you're probably right," she says, and snorts.

Brit Means snorts!

I pull the door handle and slowly slide it open. We slink out into the street. As quietly as I can, I slide the door shut, but it needs one good shove to latch closed. Usually I can get

Q's mom's van to shut with barely a sound. But I guess it must be my heart dropping beats or the fact that my arms feel like they're in zero-g, because the best I can manage is a crisp, clearly audible *chunk*.

"Ei," says a voice. "Inch dzhokhk yek anum?"

"Go go go," I hiss.

"Sorry, can't understand you," yells Brit.

We sprint into the darkness, leaving a trail of giggles behind us.

Just bad enough.

But so good.

chapter 5

plane crash

I'm in class the next morning, struggling to keep my eyes forward. I know Brit is too. I can feel it. We are like two horse statues facing the same direction.

Horse statues?

Q's eyes rally between Brit and me. I smile back with derp teeth. He knows something is up.

What the hell is up with your stupid face? say his eyebrows.

"Frank and Brit, nice work with the volumes," says Mr. Soft. "Could you draw a little tinier next time?"

I am barely listening. I like hearing him say *Frank and Brit* like that. Like we're officially *Frank-n-Brit. Frankenbrit.*

Brit smiles. She glances at me and bites her thumb, breaking the first Rule of Being a Person.

"Q and Paul, you turkeys ready?" says Mr. Soft.

Q gives me a parting eyeroll, gets into character, and stands. "Yes."

He and Paul approach a lumpy cloth spread on a table and lift it to reveal six grapefruit-sized geometric forms done in KlayKreate.

"Behold," says Q. "The new Platonics."

For the first time in my short life, I want Calculus to never end. But it does, and after we leave the classroom I find myself doing something I never normally do: walk and text.

Meet me behind the greenhouse at lunch?

My phone buzzes back.

Okay, says Brit, with a little purple heart.

The day passes. AP Bio, AP English Lit, and finally my favorite, CompSci Music, where I get some serious time hammering out live beats on the flashing Dotpad made up of the samples I recorded at Lake Girlfriend. I think about the coins in the water there.

Thank you, Lake Girlfriend.

Physical performance is the future of electronic dance music, I believe. As good as my timing is, I am still human and therefore prone to being off by a few milliseconds here and there, which is why performed music will always have a warmth and intuition that perfectly sequencing computers can't match. Next I want to try making electronic dance music with acoustic instruments, in a band with other people, no amplification. Call it *chamber step*, maybe.

I've got the room nodding their heads. I've got Ms. Nobuyuki nodding her head.

But I feel phantom buzzes in my back pocket the whole time. It takes all my effort to stay focused until the final measure of the song.

Class ends and finallyfinallyfinally it's lunch. Just gotta check in with Q before going off on my own.

I find Q waiting for me by the elephant tree: this big melted biomass of spiny leaves and branches oozing its way out of a rectangle in the concrete. Apparently it's not a tree, but a giant yucca evolving along its own isolated vector.

Q's already got his miniature hero figurines—a tiny wizard, elf, and paladin—standing in delta formation on a lunch table. His dice are lined up and waiting: a four-sided pyramid, a cube, an octahedron, dodecahedron, and finally the twenty-sided icosahedron. Paul Olmo's sitting next to Q with his graph paper, ready to start mapping dungeons and marking the locations of dragons.

"Hey," I say. "Just wanted to let you know I gotta go meet someone, so."

Q dims his eyes. "Oh my god."

"What?" says Paul. Paul Olmo looks exactly like his elven archer figurine.

"We'll pick up the campaign tomorrow," I say. I mean the Dungeons & Dragons game. "Sorry."

"My god," says Q.

I just nod. Yes, Q. Yes.

Q rises and hugs me like a father sending his son off to college.

"I'll see you guys later," I say.

"Oh my god," shouts Q.

"What happened?" shouts Paul.

I leave.

I walk the glossy hallways like an adventurer discovering a

cave full of crystals. Past the teachers' lounge exuding coffee and microwave food. Through a seldom-used back door leading into the seldom-seen teachers' section of the parking lot, at the end of which stands the almost-never-visited greenhouse.

I'm halfway across the parking lot when I realize I've left my lunch in my locker.

Whatever.

Because behind the greenhouse, among the hoes and wheelbarrows and bags of soil, there she sits. On a large up-turned pot, like a magical creature. Just smiling now at my arrival. Hair blowing in the wind like a ribbon in water.

I glance behind me. No one there. I take a sidestep and put the greenhouse between me and the rest of the world.

"Hey," I say.

"Hey," says Brit Means.

"Hey."

"Hey."

She stands. She takes a step toward me.

And we just kiss.

Everything falls silent. The birds stop singing. The wind stops. Blades of grass release their bend and straighten in the motionless air. A flap of corrugated metal pauses its squeaking as a courtesy.

I long to feel those little muscles in the small of her back—and so I do, and I can't believe I am allowed to do this. Even more unbelievable: *she* feels *mine*, too. As if she's been longing, too.

When we stop for air, the wind around us resumes. The grass relaxes.

"Are you sure we won't get caught back here?" she whispers.

"If we did, I guess that would make things official."

"Last night didn't make things official?"

"I guess it did, huh," I say.

"Pretty sure we're official."

"You said *we*."

"That's right."

And we kiss some more. The sun, ignored, sprints around the earth and hurries back to its original position, just to see if it can sneak in a whole revolution without us noticing.

We don't notice a thing.

I'm torn between wanting to kiss and wanting to stare at her face, so I decide to stare at her face for a minute. I can see myself actually reflected in her eyes, tiny bulbous Frank Li twins, and my gaze bounces back and forth between them. In the even tinier reflections of the eyes of those two reflected Frank Lis are in turn reflected two tiny Brit Means, and so on and so on infinity plus one.

"Whoa," says a girl's voice.

We freeze, as if freezing will make us somehow invisible.

Brit dares a glance to the side. "Oh, Joy."

I turn, and there's Joy Song standing there with a face like a lemur. She is tethered to a powerfully tracksuited Wu Tang, who gives me a chiseled smile like *Nice, bro.*

We should spring apart, but I'm thrilled to find that Brit doesn't move an inch; we stand there with both hands clasped, like defiant dancers interrupted.

"Hey," I say to Joy.

"Awkward," sings Joy after a moment, and finally we can all laugh a little.

"Is this like your guys' spot or something?" I say.

"It's all good," says Wu Tang. Everything he says he turns into a little dance move. "We got other spots. Like the roof." He does this little pointing maneuver.

"Oh, word?" I say.

"Wurd." Point.

"But Joy didn't want to get her new skirt dirty." He says it all stupid like *durr-tay*.

Wu Tang is so stupid that he loops it all the way around until stupid starts to seem kinda cool.

"Aha," I say.

"Okay, well," says Joy, and turns to leave.

Brit's hands are getting sweaty in mine. I can feel my body cooling. I can feel the wind moving in the gap between us. The moment's been cut short.

Joy mutters to herself. "Guess I'm not the only one with a problem." She winces at her own words.

"Okay, bye," I say loudly. I need Joy to go away, even though I know she's right.

Brit Means is white.

"Problem?" says Brit. She's irked, and she has every right to be. But how am I supposed to explain what the word *problem* means here? Where do I even begin? *Chinese boy problems?* Me and Joy's conversation at the last Gathering—hell, every conversation I've ever had at Gatherings—seems so divorced

49

from reality that it's like we speak a different kind of English there, one that doesn't translate to this dimensional plane. So I just say:

"It's nothing, I'll tell you later."

"Big eyes, though," mumbles Joy, and again winces at herself.

"Huh?" says Brit.

"Oh my god, shut up," I tell Joy. I say it in my five-, six-, seven-year-old voice.

"I'll shut up," says Joy.

The air has changed. No doubt about it. It no longer feels quite like I'm here with Brit and Joy's here with Wu. Right now it's feeling strangely like *I'm* here with *Joy*, and we've each brought our respective *problems* along.

Right now it feels like planes of reality crashing together. I have my reality, which Joy has never been a part of. Joy has hers, and I've never seen it either, aside from little glimpses of her closed room when it's the Songs' turn to host a Gathering. And there is the entirely separate reality of the Gatherings themselves, plowing right through the middle of everything like an armada of icebreaker ships.

Joy gives me a sad look: *You know I'm right, Frank.*

My eyes drop to her shoes: *You are, Joy.*

A buzzer bell razzes the silence. It's like a signal for all of us to stop holding hands. So we do, and the two couples now become four people standing apart.

chapter 6

dying

It's Friday. Brit's absent today to go on a trip with her parents. They're designing some kickass private residence in wine country, so they're making a little family vacation out of it. They'll even let Brit taste a fine wine or two, like a 1984 Cabernet Merlot Pinot Somethingsomething.

When I try to picture sipping fine wine with Mom-n-Dad, I snort so hard that Q looks up from his game thing.

"What?" says Q.

"Nothing."

"Is Brit Means a funny girl?"

"Huh? No. I mean yes."

We're sitting in front of the school, waiting for Q's mom to pick us up. Q is tapping away, building some kind of sprawling miniature factory full of conveyor belts and automatons on an alien planet.

"Mom says Italian for dinner, by the way," says Q.

"I love Italian."

"Then why don't you marry Italian?" says Q.

My phone buzzes. I always keep it on vibrate—Q and I find ringtones depressing and believe they are forlorn cries for validation in a noisy, jaded world. "I'll laugh in a sec," I say, and look at the screen.

At a rest stop now, says Brit. *Already missing you super bad*

Me too, I say. *The missing you part, not the rest stop part*

lol my funny boy

Please say that one more time

My funny boy

I miss you too, I say.

I miss you more

No I miss you more

No I miss you more

Ha we stoopid

"So this is how it ends," says Q.

I look up from my fartphone. "What?"

Q gestures sadly at the screen. "Our friendship."

"Shut up," I say, and laugh, and Q laughs too.

But just to make doubly sure, I turn the phone off and make an unmistakable show of stuffing it deep into my backpack.

• • •

"To the left," says Q. He passes a dish of olive oil.

"To the right," I say, and pass the basket of bread.

"Now dip, baby, dip," we say.

Q's mom snaps her fingers in time to the music: a clean KidzRock! version of a racy booty-house classic that legend

52

says was once banned from the radio. Q's mom looks forever pleasantly surprised, even when her face is at rest. Q's dad gets up to bring waters, and performs the most perfect dad-dance along the way. Q's house is always filled with music and dad-dances. Q's mom-n-dad even *kiss* sometimes.

Dinner at my house is a goddamn wake by comparison.

Q's sister, Evon, wanders in like a doe appearing in a wood, rose-gold headphones and all. She glances down with mild astonishment: *Dinner is happening? Oh my.*

The Lees pray before dinner. But they do it quickly, with eyes open. They don't even bother to turn the music down. They go to church on Sunday, but not if there's a big game on. They're *postseason Christ fans*, Q likes to say.

"Good Lord in heaven bless this food and bless this family and bless Frank for blessing this table and our house with his blessed presence," says Q's dad so quickly it sounds like he's muttering to a sink yet again full of dirty dishes.

"Amen," says Q.

"Amen," say Q's parents.

Evon is too hot for *amen*s, and says nothing.

"Amen," I say. Being Korean-American, I'm technically Presbyterian by default. But I couldn't even tell you what a Presbyt is or what it tastes like, to be honest.

Another KidzRock! song comes on, scrubbed of any bad words. It's cute how Q's parents still play this music for us even though we're technically adults at this point.

"Q says you have a girlfriend now," says Q's mom.

"Jesus christ almighty hang gliding up in heaven," I say to Q.

"Do you deny it?" says Q.

"No, I supply it," I sigh.

"Then what's there to hide?"

"I'm happy for you," says Q's dad, chewing with alarming speed. His glasses slip, and he pushes them up, and chews and chews, making his glasses slip again. "Is she very dope?"

Q and I laugh so hard that a noodle comes poking out of one of Q's nostrils.

"You're so funny, Mr. Lee," I say.

"Frank, come on," he says. "Call me David."

"Okay, Mr. David."

"Oh, so, Dad," says Q, "I need you to write to the teachers about next week."

Next week is this geek trip Q is taking up north to Stanford—also known as The Harvard of the West—where his geek uncle is doing a PhD. Q's plan is to get into Stanford and shoot lasers into live monkey brains to see how they react. This is called *optogenetics*.

"I bet you're crunk for the trip," says Q's dad.

"Yes, Dad, I am extremely crunk," says Q.

"Should be tight," says Q's dad.

"So tight," says Q.

I cough into my noodles.

"Okay," says Q's mom. "Now you've got me laughing."

Q's dad simply sits and chews and feigns obliviousness. He excels at being king of the dorks; he is proudly aware of this particular genius of his.

"So do your parents like this Brit girl?" he says.

"Honey," says Q's mom.

"We haven't set a date for the wedding yet," I say.

That gets a nice laugh. Except for Evon, who's still lost in her own private musical world. Q's mom waves a hand in front of her face.

Evon takes off the headphones and takes a small bite. Meanwhile, Q scrambles to finish his food.

"Yesssss," he says. "I win."

"Win what?" says Evon.

"Yeah, I didn't know this was a race," I say. I share a quick look with Evon.

"Q is a baby," she says.

"We're literally the same age," says Q.

"Body of a teen, mind of a baby," says Evon.

"Although technically," says Q, "I'm older since I emerged from the vagina three seconds before you did."

"Lord, I beg you have mercy on me," says Q's mom.

"Come on," says Q. "Let me show you my game."

"Okay," I say.

We bolt up from our seats and dash off, but a mighty *ahem* stops us.

It's Q's dad, eyeing our dirty plates. "Ten years and I still have to remind you, Frank?"

"Holy cow, is it really ten?" I say.

"It is really ten," says Q's dad. He's looking at us with gooey eyes, and I know he still sees us as little kids flinging our bikes down onto the front lawn.

Q and I look at each other and say, "Huh!" at the same time.

On the way into the kitchen I spot a photo of me and Q and

my parents from three years ago, at our junior high school graduation.

I point at the photo with my chin. "You still have that thing?"

"Yep," says Q, putting our plates into the sink. "Do you?"

"Yep," I say. But that's not true. I have no idea where our copy of the photo is. There are no matching photos of Q in my house. The last time Q was at my house was months ago, when he came to drop off something I'd left at his house. I can't actually remember the last time he stepped foot past the foyer.

"Game on," says Q.

• • •

I'm watching a little homunculus run around a 2D landscape from a God-view perspective. Q clicks and pans with the speed of a card magician. It's fast, but not incomprehensible. He's mining resources and building an elaborate system of factories to bring his homunculus hero through the Stone Age, Iron Age, and beyond.

We're in Q's room. Q's room is pretty small, with just a small desk, two narrow bookshelves, and a sofa (Q prefers sleeping on sofas, because they are dual-use). What Q's room is is mostly screen. A tiny projector sits on a faux-marble cornice and throws the giant view of the game onto a blank wall that Q has painted with some kind of special projector screen paint for maximum image quality.

"The story is," says Q, "you've crash-landed on this alien planet, and you have to build up an escape rocket from scratch using whatever's on hand."

"Cool."

My pocket buzzes, and I sneak a peek. There's a picture of Brit looking with one big eye through a wine goblet like it's a magnifying glass.

I single-thumb three hearts back and put it away.

"But the aliens don't like me," says Q. "Because I'm cutting down their forests and polluting their environment. So you also have to build weapons to kill them off."

"Wow, that's super amoral."

"I know, it's a bummer aspect of the game's design. It's called *Craft Exploit*."

"Also, since you're the interloper here, shouldn't *you* be considered the alien, not them?"

"It's conflicting, right? Definitely a dude made this game."

Q spots six warships approaching, and decimates them with a flurry of tiny missiles.

"Probably a white dude," I say.

"Would explain the colonialist impulse," says Q.

Another buzz, another photo from Brit, this time of a package of paper napkins named Napkins à la Maison de Beaujolais. Brit's added her comment beneath: *J'adore French-for-no-reason branding.*

I stifle a chuckle and stash the fartphone before Q can notice.

"Still, the game looks fun," I say.

"It is," says Q. "Open source, too. I coded these lift-sorters, right here."

"Badass," I say.

Yet another buzz. I want another peek. I want another hit of Brit.

But Q pauses the game. "Your phone's really blowing up, huh."

Q stares at me.

"Fine," he says finally with an eyeroll. "Answer it."

"Just one last one, I promise," I say.

"The last one? Or the last-last one?"

We're coming back Sunday night! says Brit. *Frank Li, I frankly need to see you.*

I feel my stomach wave hello. My ears grow warm. Gravity eases enough to loosen all the joints and nails and screws holding the world together until all its pieces are slowly tumbling free in a soft huge space lit only by the white rectangle beneath my thumbs. My *girlfriend* is texting me.

I Frank Li need to see you too.

Can I come to your house?

Impossible, I think. Just forming the words would be impossible: *Mom-n-Dad, this is Brit, and we're going to lock ourselves in my room for hours like they do in teen movies.*

I'm racking my brain for alternate venues optimized for romance, but then I do a mental facepalm. I'm not free Sunday night.

I type carefully. *Shit, Sunday night I gotta help Dad out at work,* I say, and add a sad face for extra sincerity. She must not think for a second that I'm blowing her off.

Q has paused the game. He's making eyebrows: at me, at my fartphone, at me again.

"Almost done," I say.

"Sure."

"Really, almost done."

58

"Like our friendship."

Q turns back to his game. He's up against a huge sudden wave of attacking aliens (I mean indigenous peoples) and frantically clicks to defend himself (I mean commit genocide).

I'll see you Monday, I say finally.

I don't know if I can wait that long, says Brit.

"I'm dying," says Q.

I stash my phone. I could text all night, but: enough.

"I'm dead," says Q.

"Let me try."

"That's the guilt talking, right there."

"If I exterminate the aboriginals, will you be a happy exploiting camper again?"

"It's a game. I don't make the rules."

"I know," I say. "I know."

chapter 7

planet frank

I'm back at The Store. The three flies buzz above me. It's not as hot today, so the chocolate can sit outside the walk-in cooler.

It's quiet. I look around, examining things. There's a security camera system, aimed right at the counter and cash register. Beneath the counter is a little white button—press it, and the cops show up in minutes, at least in theory. Beneath that is a drawer, and within that is a loaded .38 Special revolver Dad has fired only twice: once at the firing range, and once into the sky during New Year's Eve.

I snap a pic of scrolls of lottery scratchers encased in Plexiglas and post it with the caption *Stupid tax?*

My dad is mopping the floor when I see him stop, thump his aching arched back with a fist three times, and then resume.

"Dad," I say. "Let me do that."

"You know how to doing?"

"It's mopping."

He makes a point of showing me anyway. He holds the mop handle lightly, with just his fingers, and works it to one side like a gondolier would. He rinses the mop in a wheeled bucket, squeezes it in the vise, and continues on with an almost-easy stroll. It's a weird way of mopping, to be sure, and when he finally lets me do it I can feel the strain in my back after just a few long sweeps.

Dad works the cash register from his tall stool. An antique alarm clock radio from 1982 plays Korean AM church music and preaching. I understand none of it.

It's relaxing, this mopping.

Bing-bong. A crazy-haired white man enters, dressed all in black, with plastic bags attached to his every limb. Mom-n-Dad have mentioned him before: The Store's one and only white customer. Without a single word Dad grabs two six-packs of beer—Porky, the cheapest brand—and bags them: plastic, then paper, then plastic again. He's got everything ready by the time the man even reaches the counter.

"Hey, Frankie," says the man. I've always wondered if he's homeless. He looks—and smells—homeless.

My dad's English name is Frank, too. Frank Sr.

"Charles," says Dad.

Charles casts a wild eye at me and holds it.

"My son," says Dad.

"I've seen you," says this crazy Charles dude. "You going to college?"

"Gonna try," I say as normally as I can, to offset the crazy.

"They teach you how to mop in college?"

"Uh," I say.

61

Charles turns to Dad. "Only got a hundred, sorry."

"No problem," says Dad, and makes change.

Charles aims his blue-white eyes at me again. "I bet your folks keep you real clean," he says, and makes to leave. But before he does, he gives me a tiny scroll of paper with icy hands.

"That's for you, if you're so smart," says the man, and leaves, bing-bong.

Dad scoots me back behind the cash register. It's like he's worried I'll fall prey to more Charleses if I'm exposed out among the aisles.

"He very unique person," says Dad. "Million dollar, he having. He own house, too."

"Wait, really?" I say. I want to examine the scroll, I want to hear more from Dad, but bing-bong, now here comes a young man with his wife, holding a small baby.

"Paco," hollers the young man, and salutes Dad.

Paco is short for *Francisco*, which is Spanish for *Frank*.

"Luis," says Dad. "You out today? When you afuera?"

"Yesterday, patron. I'm officially on probation."

"Congratulation," says Dad. "Beautiful baby, eh? Hey, consentida. ¿Qué es nombre?"

"Veronica," says the wife.

"Anyway felicitaciones," says Dad. He tickles the little baby, and the wife holds her higher for him.

The young man, Luis, slides beer and diapers across the counter. "Gimme a loosy too, holmes."

"You got it," I say. I tap a cigarette from an open box under the counter and slide it over all sneaky-style. Luis feigns an

62

itch and discreetly tucks it behind his ear. On his shoulder is a homemade tattoo: F People, the local gang.

"This your son?" says Luis.

"Frank, you saying hi," says Dad.

"Hey," I say. "Nice to meet you."

"Your dad's a crazy dude, but he family," says Luis. The words are kind, but he says them flat. He's examining me: the quality of my skin, my hair, the quality of my clothes, my watch. We come from different worlds. I feel it. His wife is clutching a damp wad of bills and food stamps. That money, I think. There are invisible trails of money everywhere. I can feel those too.

It's not a good feeling.

I start to ring him up, but Dad stops me. He bags the stuff in a flurry and shoves it all into Luis's arms.

"Congratulation," says Dad.

"Thanks, Paco. You know I'm gonna pay you back."

"Whatever you want," says Dad with a smile.

They leave, bing-bong. And The Store is quiet again. I touch the phone in my pocket, like a reflex: Brit should be back from her trip by now. I want send her a quick *When can I see you tomorrow?* But where? Our budding relationship can't just be a clandestine series of greenhouses and minivans.

"Luis get out yesterday, eleven months sentence," says Dad.

"For what?"

Dad wipes his face with a rag. "Oh, he carjacking, involuntary manslaughter."

"Jesus."

63

"He pulling white lady from driver side, he throwing her away, car hit her. She die."

"No way."

"Luis used to be very cute little boy."

"Oh yeah? Like when?"

"Maybe six, seven years old. His daddy run away, maybe Arizona, they speculating. Anyway, no daddy, no money. He going gang. Mexican boy, all they going gang."

"Dad, not every Mexican kid joins a gang."

But Dad is already dream-talking in his own world. "All they going. Gang."

Talking to Dad can be like this. You wonder if you're actually talking to someone or just sitting in on an inner monologue that happens to be spoken aloud. In these moments I do a mental shrug, stop talking, and just try to let the jeong do its thing.

Jeong is kinda hard to pin down. I mean, I'm not exactly expert on all things Korean, but I guess the closest meaning would be something like *bonding* or *affection*. I mostly understand it as *shutting the hell up and just being together*.

Jeong is nowhere near as satisfying as all the hugs and kisses and *I love you*s other kids get from their parents, but hey, it's what I got. So I'll take what I can get.

We stare at the open doorway for a moment. Is the jeong building? I think so. Outside it's getting to be dusk, and the world is just black silhouettes against a sky of fire.

I think about how Mom-n-Dad know the names of all their customers and their kids. They know who's dating, who's getting married, who's pregnant. They know who's been shot, who's been arrested, who's gone to jail. They know all these things sometimes even before the families themselves.

They are the keepers of all the news and gossip and drama that passes over the tree-ringed counter, and that makes them the only oral historians for a tiny world that might otherwise go unremembered.

"You study hard, okay?" says Dad. He begins mopping again, even though the floor is already clean. I've never seen him truly idle at The Store. "You bringing book here, you reading. Right now it's quiet time, everybody they eating dinner."

I think about how determined Mom was to have me here at The Store on Sundays to hang out with Dad. I can't bring a book and ignore the guy.

"I'm okay," I say.

"You reading some poetry. You know John Donne? So-called metaphysics."

We covered those guys in AP English. "Come live with me and be my love" and all that. Most of it sounds like dudes trying to get laid, to be honest.

"Yeah, I know," I say. "We studied John Donne."

I don't know why I say this. Here's a conversational opening, and all I want to do is cut it off: *yeah, been there, done that, nuff said.* I can see Dad's face fall a millimeter. My ears get hot, like they always do when I realize I'm being stupid. Me and Dad bonding is like trying to spot-glue two jagged rocks together. There are only so many points of connection. Plus I had no idea Dad even read poetry.

So I say, "What about John Donne?" and Dad instantly brightens.

"He write poem, so-called 'Flea.' He say, 'Mark but this flea, and mark in this, How little that which thou deniest me is.'"

I like this poem, actually. It's a weird one. The guy is trying to use a bloodsucking flea as a metaphor for getting some chick to have sex with him. He's got game—a weird, sixteenth-century kind of game.

"'It sucked me first, and now sucks thee,'" I say.

"'And in this flea our two bloods mingled be,'" says Dad.

He repeats the last part to a phalanx of glass Guadalupe candles. "'Two bloods mingled be.'"

Bing-bong. Another customer. But something's wrong. I see Dad freeze up and stare.

A white girl has entered The Store.

It's Brit Means.

"Hi," says Brit, and scoots behind the counter—*behind the counter*—to give me a hug. All I can do is stand frozen and watch as Dad's eyes go big, then shrink, and then harden.

"Heyyyyyyy," I say.

"Aha," says Brit. "There are those lottery tickets."

She saw my photo, duh. And my exact location.

She touches a small ice-cream fridge and raises an eyebrow. "And you have Chocolate Bobaccinos."

Normally, this would be cause for celebration. A cry for attention on social media, answered in person with a hug by a beautiful girl.

Normally.

Brit finally notices Dad leaning against his mop handle,

66

and I can see her take a moment to code switch. She stands a bit more erect. She clasps her hands together.

"Hello," she says. "I'm Brit."

Dad looks at her, then at me. "You friend?"

Your turn to speak, Frank. "Yeah, well, we're in Calculus, we had, um, have, an assignment together, so."

"You same classmate?"

"Yes," says Brit Means slowly. "We're in class together. It's the same class. It's Calculus."

My feet leave the ground. Just an inch. My soles can't find any purchase.

Brit is talking like you do with an exchange student, or someone hard of hearing.

I try to stomp my feet back to earth, because this code switching shouldn't bother me. Everyone talks different with parents. Even if it's the same language.

It's a tiny shameful wish that keeps me suspended in the air, a white-noise whisper: *I wish Dad could speak English right.*

Dad seems satisfied with Brit's credentials. "Nice meet you," he says.

"It is very nice to meet you too, Mr. Li," says Brit.

I give Brit a little helpless look, and she clues in. Brit's not stupid. She can tell I haven't told my parents about her yet. She can tell Dad's not as open about all this boyfriend-girlfriend stuff as, say, her druidic dad is.

So Brit plays along. She seems to recognize that hugs don't happen around here. So she crosses her feet and hugs herself tight instead.

Dad finally lowers his gaze and pretends to mop the floor. He turns his back. He busies himself away.

Brit leans in an inch. "Hey," she says.

"He understands English fine, you know, he just sucks at speaking it," I say quietly. "You don't have to talk slow or anything."

Brit looks slightly horrified. "Did I? Oh god, I didn't even notice."

"You're good," I say.

"I'm that person."

"You're good, really," I say. Out of the corner of my eye I see Dad mop his way farther toward the back of the store. I find her eyes, smile into them. "Hey, I'm really happy to see you."

She brightens. I'm itching to touch her. I can tell she's itching to touch me, too. It's ridiculous. "Can you take a break or something?" she says. "We could go for a walk."

I shake my head, probably a nanosecond too quickly. "I don't know if we should. I mean, not around this neighborhood."

Does that sound terrible? Fuck, it sounds terrible.

But it's true. One lap around the block for her would be a fool's parade. Same for me, too, but everyone knows I'm Frank Sr.'s kid, even if I don't remember who they all are, because I'm here so infrequently, which somehow makes me feel kind of like a dick.

"Oh," says Brit Means with quiet surprise, as if remembering the existence of a world outside Playa Mesa.

"Hey," I say.

"It's okay," she says. "You're busy, and I'm keeping them waiting anyway."

She glances outside. Them? She means her parents. Waiting, in a car parked just outside. They must have stopped by on their way back from their trip. Of course. Why else would they be out here, an hour away from Playa Mesa?

There's a *chunk*. Dad's vanished into the walk-in cooler. I sneak a kiss on Brit's cheek.

"I'll see you tomorrow at school, okay?" I say. "Okay?"

"Okay," says Brit, and trails those fingertips of hers along the back of my pinky before leaving.

Bing-bong, and she's gone. My floating feet touch ground again.

There are too many worlds in my head—Palomino High School, The Store, the Gathering—all with their own confusing laws of nature, gravitational strengths, and speeds of light, and really all I want to do is reach escape velocity, bust out into space, and form my own planet tweaked just how I want it.

Planet Frank. Invitation only.

I take out my phone. *Miss you already.*

Brit begins to write something back. She takes a long, long time. But in the end, all she says is:

Me too.

chapter 8

i propose to joy

A week goes by, and it's time for another monthly Gathering. Dad drives, as a kind of up-front compensation for the likely fact that Mom will have to drive his drunk ass home from the Gathering tonight. In the back seat I feel something in my front pocket: the tiny paper scroll, the one crazy-man Charles handed me at The Store on Sunday.

I unscroll it. It is a photocopy of many handwritten words, all traveling in a spiral toward a central drawing of a naked man, woman, and fetus inscribed in a triangle, circle, square, and finally a pentagon. It feels vaguely astrological. Vaguely satanic. The words don't help, either:

The Sept of Man inscribes the Septs of Wo-Man
and Child in a tri-planar Möbius tetramid resting
upon the Present plane. The fourth plane is Fear,
the fifth plane is Hope, the sixth plane is Absolute

Solitude. The seventh plane encompasses all planes and is therefor Known as the Infinite Realm of the Vaginal Ouroboros.

And on and on.

My mind is blown, but not in any kind of good way.

"Mom," I say. "Have you ever read these things?"

Mom glances up from her phone. "I never read. Charles, he crazy."

"You keeping paper," says Dad. "Maybe true things he writing."

"Sure," I say.

Then Mom-n-Dad fall silent again, thinking their thoughts.

I want to take a picture of the scroll and send it to Brit, but then I'd have to use the flash, and then there would be questions, and then I just kinda give up on the whole idea.

I roll the scroll back up and pocket it. I make a mental note to show it to Brit later.

If this were a movie, now is when I would say my piece, tell them about me and Brit, and there would be arguing and bickering but then the whole thing would end in group hugs and tears, and Mom-n-Dad would realize the melting pot that is the American dream.

This is why I prefer horror movies. There are no group hugs in horror movies.

We get to the Songs' house: a sleek bunker straight out of *Architecture Porn*, overlooking a quiet cove by the sea. Not one, but two gleaming QL7s are parked on the hexagonal concrete driveway. Joy's dad has done well for himself since coming here. Better than my dad, even though they all started off equal. At least I assume they did.

We enter, take off shoes, bow, all that. Mom-n-Dad force me to say hi in Korean, and when I do everyone makes a big deal out of it. Then Mrs. Song, a watchful osprey of a woman, makes Joy do it.

"Insa jyeom hyae," she says, and prods Joy's shoulder blade.

"Annyong haseyo," says Joy, barely audible.

Everyone makes a big deal out of it.

"Okay, you have fun," says Mom finally, smiling all stupid.

Everyone—Dad, Mr. Song, Mrs. Song—is smiling at us, all stupid.

"Eyyyy," I say with jazz hands.

The parents finally vanish to admire the spread—it looks like Mrs. Song has been experimenting with French roasts and sauces—and Joy and I now stand alone.

"Hey," I say.

"Hey."

"Where's all the other Limbos?"

"There are no other Limbos."

I stare at her. "Are you serious?"

"Dude," says Joy. "We never have Gatherings on week-nights. That didn't raise a red flag for you?"

"Huh," I say.

"They sent my little brother to a slumber party. A slumber party, Frank. This whole thing is a setup," she says.

"Huh."

Joy looks up at me with a mock-serious face, like we're in a sci-fi epic. "They're mating us like a couple of goddamn zoo pandas, Frank."

I do a spit take, but dry. That was funny. This whole thing is funny, if funny suddenly became exasperating. I know they've always thought the idea of me and Joy falling in love was cute. But now they've gotten serious about it. They're executing some kind of thought-out plan. And now I realize why.

Because Brit came to The Store.

Because Dad told Mom, and Mom told the families.

This is some kind of roundabout, twisty-turny, circuitous intervention.

If only Brit were aware of the drama she inadvertently caused. If only she knew tonight's Gathering was, in a way, all about her.

"I guess we should go upstairs and consummate," I say.

Joy Song literally slaps my head.

"Fuck," I say.

But it's a good slap. Strong and dry like three rigid fingers on a batá drum.

"Ugh, let's just play video games or something," says Joy, and begins climbing the stairs. "Your parents are stupid."

"*Your* parents are stupid."

"Good comeback."

"*Your* parents are stupid."

We laugh because it's funny but then stop because the funny doesn't last.

We climb the rest of the stairs, and I notice she has a tiny tattoo on her ankle. I never knew she had a tattoo.

We reach Joy's room, and it's not at all what I expected. Actually, I had no idea what to expect. But it definitely wasn't this technological garage lab. An entire wall is pegboard, holding coils of cable and solder and wire and tools. Six computer monitors dominate a vast desk made from what looks like a door resting on heavy-duty pipe parts. There is a 3D printer steadily extruding something into existence. There are bins of robotics parts and mini computer breadboards.

This isn't Apey-level. This is something else.

"Damn," I say.

"You've seen my room before, right?" Joy searches her memory. "I guess it's been a while, huh."

There's a lot of hard science stuff here, but also a NEVERTHELESS SHE PERSISTED poster done in luscious calligraphic swashes. The rug is bright orange and canary and lime, all clean and fluffy and fresh. The scent of sandalwood fills the air.

There's a crystal chandelier, and below it a bed full of childhood stuffed animals, plus a single stray bra that I just kinda stare at.

Joy shoves the bra under a pillow.

I sit on the floor, and Joy's eyes go big. "Frank Li, have you started smoking?"

"Huh?" I see where she's looking: the little paper scroll, about the length and diameter of a cigarette, has fallen out of my pocket.

"Oh," I say. I unscroll the paper. "This dude gave it to me at The Store."

In a flash Joy is on the floor sitting close to me, looking at the paper with eager eyes.

"Go ahead, check it out," I say helplessly. So much for showing this to Brit first.

"Oh my god," says Joy, reading. "Vaginal Ouroboros? And look at the guy's little pee-pee."

"There's a teeny-weeny vajayjay, too."

"It's like an insane version of that NASA Pioneer 10 plaque drawing."

"Ha, it kinda is."

"You need to frame this. No, wait—you should totally etch this into metal and sneak it into space like a message from humanity."

"Like, troll the aliens."

We laugh and wiggle our be-socked toes.

"Did you show this to Hanna?" says Joy. "She'd crack the hell up."

"Not yet." Joy has always liked Hanna. I suspect she wants to be like her, not with patent law but industrial design. I know *I* want to be like her.

"How is Hanna?"

"She's good, still in Boston, stacking it up. Still with Miles." My voice cuts in half. There's an anger in my heart the color of dark red ready to paint the walls with curse words, but there's no point in getting into all that. I could rage to the sky, but Mom-n-Dad would stay as silent and unmoving as those big stone heads on Easter Island. Joy knows all this without me having to explain it.

So I just say, "You know she married Miles?"

Joy gets quiet. She looks at me with big eyes.

"They went to city hall," I say. "Took ten minutes and cost twenty-five bucks."

Now we both get quiet.

"So," I say.

"So," says Joy. "Tell me more about Brit."

"Welp," I say, hooking my thumbs in my armpits like some kind of proud corn farmer, "she's super great. You and Wu doing good?"

"You didn't get all excited and tell your parents about her, did you?"

"You're funny. You and Wu doing good?"

Joy flops up onto the bed. All the animals bounce. "Eh, we fought again."

I find a tiny stray bolt in the sherbet-colored carpet. There are tiny nuts, too. I start trying to find one that fits. "What did you fight about this time?"

"The same shit. He wants to take things to the next level, but he doesn't understand."

"So, like, anal?"

Joy laughs. A stuffed animal hits me hard in the temple.

"I mean he doesn't understand how I can't just keep coming up with infinity number of excuses for my parents as fast as he wants. He wants to meet up almost every single night. It's impossible. I can't keep up with that kind of demand."

"I feel you," I say. "I'm in the same boat now."

"Hop aboard," says Joy to the ceiling.

I try another nut, and another. No match yet. There are more, hidden deep in the carpet's pile. Something wells up in me, and I jam my fingers into the carpet and grip hard.

"The whole thing is just so absurd," I say.

Joy goes "Mmm" in agreement.

I pull up the carpet and release it. "Think about what they're trying to do with us."

"Mate us like a couple of goddamn zoo pandas."

"I mean beyond that. Once upon a time they left Korea. They came here. They had kids."

"Mmm."

"They cherry-picked what they wanted from American culture, but for the most part they built this little Korean bubble to live in. They watch nothing but Korean shows, do business with nothing but Korean people, hang out with nothing but Korean friends."

"Build Korea Towns."

"And that's fine. I get that. If I moved to, like, Nepal, you bet I'd go crazy without my American movies and Double-Double cheeseburgers and English-speaking friends."

"I think there's an In-N-Out in Nepal."

I laugh. "But you know what they're doing right now? With us? They want us to stay inside their bubble."

Joy sits up and looks at me with her head tilted.

"Their little dream," I say, "is that we get married and have kids, and that those kids will marry nothing but Koreans and have more kids, and that their bubble will stay intact after they're gone. They want us to take care of it forever."

Joy closes her eyes tight. She looks like how I feel: stuck. We're both stuck. But we're also both tired of being stuck. She keeps her voice even. "As if we had this huge blind spot for the ninety-eight percent of our school that's *not* Korean. That's like trying to fool ourselves that we're not really here in America. That's impossible."

"Mmm."

Joy sighs. "Is it wrong that I sometimes wonder if Wu's even worth the hassle?"

"Damn," I say. "Poor Wu."

"No, shit, I take it back. I love Wu. I really do."

"Tell me what you love about him."

"Well, first, he's totally hot."

"Blah, blah, blah," I say.

"But also, he's really kind, and he loves his family, like, you should see him with his mom and dad and sister and other sister who's a bitch but whatever. He's so sweet."

"That's actually really cool."

"Right? And he's secretly smart about business. Not what *kind* of business to run, but *how* to run it. You know?"

"Sure."

"You think corporate operational management is boring."

"No, not at all."

"You do."

"No way, no," I say. "I just don't really know what it entails. Or care. Because it's so totally and completely boring."

"Dick!" But she says it in a kindhearted way.

"Okay, your turn: what's so great about Brit Means?"

I find a nut, screw it onto the bolt. Perfect fit.

This means something. Brit Means something.

I sigh with contentment and begin. "First of all, she's totally hot."

"Blah, blah, blah," says Joy.

"And she's smart, and passionate about the environment and biology and stuff. But at a deeper level?"

"Like anal?"

I snort, then recover. "She just really likes me. And I just really like her. I'm sounding basic, huh."

"But you can't tell your parents about her."

"Doosh, way to bring shit down."

"Sorry. I'm just so sick of what they want versus what I want."

"Eh, it's okay."

Joy sits up to look at me. "Really, I'm sorry."

We look at each other, she with her Chinese boy problem, me with my new white girl problem.

I think about Hanna. Was Miles worth it? Does she cry every night in his arms over Mom-n-Dad's stonewalling? Maybe she's hardened her heart to it. Maybe she left the bubble, and then burst it with a sharp kick before walking away.

I fast-forward into Hanna's future. When she buys her first home, do Mom-n-Dad visit? When she has her first child, do they come to the hospital? And Miles, the poor guy—what will he feel like as the years pile on?

There are no good answers for Hanna. Not ever. Just living in between worlds forever, in a limbo much deeper than I yet know. I find tears swelling my eyes with their warmth. I blink and blink and blink. I want to float off the ground, so I clutch the carpet again to anchor me.

What kind of answers could Hanna possibly have about Mom-n-Dad, who love her—and whom she can't help but love back—but also never want to see her again? They made a choice, and ultimately they chose the amber bubble over all else.

Oh my god, Hanna, did you make the right choice?

And am I destined to eventually face the same choice?

The mere existence of such a choice makes me want to punch the world flat.

It's just me and Hanna. The Book of Li ends with us two.

I take a breath. Joy hasn't noticed my wet eyes. When she is looking elsewhere, I squeegee them dry with my thumbs.

It occurs to me that the brainlock is not with us Limbos. It's with *them*.

Our parents are fooling themselves that they're not really in this world, here in America.

And I get an idea.

"Huh," is all I can say. "Huh."

"What?"

"Listen." I take a breath. "I just thought of a big what-if."

"How big?" says Joy.

"This is going to sound weird."

"I'm totally okay with weird."

"My big what-if," I say, and look into Joy's eyes. "It's more of a proposal."

"Uh," says Joy.

I drum my fingers on my knees. "You have a Chinese boy problem. I have this white girl problem. Our parents have these big, huge blind spots—racist blind spots—in their brains. What if we used those blind spots to our advantage?"

Joy raises an eyebrow. "What do you mean." She says it like a statement, not a question.

"What I propose we do is this." I take a breath and hold it. "I propose we pretend to date each other."

Joy stares at me.

I gallop a little in my seat. "We pretend to date each other, because you know the parents are just gonna let us date and date and date as much as we want, right? School nights. Holidays. Whenever. But on every date—"

Joy's eyes go big. "On every date, we meet up with our date-dates."

I point my fingers, Wu-style. "Wurd."

Joy's frozen with this incredulous smile that grows and grows until she explodes with her weird rapid-fire squirrel army laugh. She laughs and laughs and laughs.

When she stops, I notice that the party downstairs has gone silent. They're trying to *listen*.

"You're crazy," says Joy.

I fold my arms and smirk the righteous smirk.

"But you're a fucking genius," says Joy.

chapter 9

total perfect mind control

Joy and I huddle in close over our phones.

"So I just text you when Wu wants to go out?" she says.

"Yeah. And then I make sure to set up a date with Brit for the same day and time."

"But they can't know."

"You mean Wu and Brit."

"'Oh hey there, Brit Means,'" says Joy in dumb-boyfriend voice. "'I'm just pretending to date Joy as my rent-an-alibi so we can see each other without any questions from my super-racist parents who hate ninety-eight percent of the country.'"

"You put it like that, I guess it wouldn't go over so well," I say.

"But just logistically it makes life so much easier," says Joy.

I smile at her. *Right?*

"So then you just text me back when our dates are in sync, and vice versa?" says Joy.

"That's a lot of texting," I say. "Oh, I know: we should make a shared calendar."

"Nerd," says Joy.

I just look at her like *So?*

"Actually, a shared calendar might make sense," says Joy finally.

I send her an invite. She accepts. I create a test calendar event for tonight on my phone, titled FRANK AND JOY OFFICIALLY START DATING.

Joy's phone buzzes; she sees the calendar event, laughs.

"Okay, then."

"Okay, then."

"Frank!" yells Mom from downstairs. "Dinner ready!"

I nod at Joy. "You ready for this?"

Joy nods back, and for a second we feel like two rangers getting ready to jump out of a plane.

The way we do it is this: we hold hands and walk down the stairs together. I've held her hand plenty of times in the past: during thumb wrestling, ersatz seances with the other kids during Halloween, or interminable prayer circles before holiday feasts. That's always been with other people present, though—this time, it's just me and Joy.

"Your hand is all sweaty," says Joy as we descend.

"That's all you."

"You."

"You-you."

Once we reach the bottom of the stairs, we execute the final part of the maneuver: turn, make sure to fall into the parents' line of sight, hold hands for a half second longer, and then let go quick. The point is to appear as if we forgot to stow our PDA until it was *just* too late, because that's how into each other we have miraculously become over the last ninety minutes up in Joy's room.

It works.

"Ahhhh," say the parents.

"What?" I say, all innocent.

"Eat," says Mom.

"Eat, eat," says Joy's mom, fussing with Sternos under ornate silver pans.

"You want wine?" says Dad.

This is when I know they're falling for the plan. Wine?

We grab some food. Dinner's French food done all Korean-style, meaning in the form of a buffet and in quantities that are way, way too much. I pile my plate. Joy piles hers. When we get to the last buffet pan, I see that Dad is waiting for us.

He *escorts* us over to the kids' table and hustles out chairs for us, like a swarthy maître d' from Middle Earth, and we sit. The kids' table is usually larger than this. There are usually more Limbos. This table is meant for only two. We sit facing the adults; the adults sit facing us. It's like a sweetheart table at a goddamn wedding.

It's silent for a moment. Then someone—Mrs. Song, fiddling with her giant Korea-only phone/tablet thing—abruptly puts on an adult contemporary rock song: some insipid string of croony cliches.

Meanwhile Dad pours the wine all the way to the rim of our glasses as if it were orange juice and we were six.

I never knew I could feel this way / The clouds are breaking it's a brand-new day

Joy is vibrating, like she's itching to flip the table. "Oh man oh man, I can't do this."

"Stay strong," I whisper.

We both crack up.

The parents freeze and gaze at us with these big, dumb happy-donkey smiles. Then they all catch themselves and clumsily resume their adult conversation, like drunks trying to be sly.

It's excruciating, but it's *working*. So it's a sweet pain.

"Let's toast," I say. "I hear booze can help."

We can't lift our glasses—they're too full—so we duck our heads and sip and immediately regret it, because damn, who seriously drinks wine straight up like that without at least mixing it with Sprite or something? Alcohol, I don't get you.

"Hey," whispers Joy. "Watch this."

"What?"

"Just look at me for a three-count."

I look into her eyes for three seconds, and out of my right ear I can hear the grown-ups' table fall dead silent.

"Now look at the grown-ups' table."

I do, and so does she, and the drunks pretend to chatter again.

"Look back at me," says Joy.

And I do. I always assumed her eyes were black for some reason. But they're not. They're a deep hazel. I find myself wondering if they would be big enough to meet Mom's ludicrous size requirements. Her upper eyelids have that little double fold to them: that ssangkkeopul so coveted by Koreans they'll risk cosmetic surgery to get it.

I don't have ssangkkeopul. Does that mean I should be envious?

Eh, whatever. I like my eyes. They're black, by the way, like the soul of an ultra-rare level twelve chaotic evil anti-paladin.

"Huh," I say. "I never noticed you have ssangkkeopul."

Joy attempts to look at her own eyelids, which is funny. "They went like this after puberty for some reason. Mom says they make me look tired." She blinks, tugs her eyelids flat.

"Stop doing that, dude. It's like Chinese-Japanese-look-at-these-dirty-knees."

"Jesus, that shit."

"Sorry to remind you."

Chinese-Japanese-look-at-these-dirty-knees was a racist song white kids used to sing to kids like us when we were little. It was always accompanied by the pulling of the eyelids, to make things extra ching-chong.

"Anyway," I say. "Your eyes look nice just the way they are."

Joy just starts laughing her full-on Joy laugh, eekeekeek-honk-eekeekeek, because two things are happening right now: the grown-ups' table is as dead silent as fascinated meerkats, and the music playing is actually singing the words:

You're beautiful just the way you are / Girl, you know you're a shining star

"Ah, fuck," I say, and laugh too.

"Look back on three," says Joy. "One, two, three."

We do, and the parents start talking again.

I feel the potential of immense power. Total perfect mind control will be mine.

Dad approaches and knocks his heels together to stand at attention, and I swear he considers a curt bow but decides against it. He sees my still-full glass. "You no drinking wine?"

"Dad, I'm so full, I'm gonna barf."

"Eigh," says Mom.

"You wanna go visit the vomitorium so we can keep eating?" I say to Joy.

"That's disgusting," says Joy, and giggles, and nudges my shoulder.

And the parents fall silent again. Really, it's like a light switch.

Finally it's time to leave. Me and Joy execute the fatal finishing move of tonight's smashing inaugural test run.

"I'll get the car warmed up," I say. It's chilly for Southern California, meaning an arctic 60 degrees, and Mom likes a warm car even if it increases the likelihood of Dad throwing up in a to-go cup.

I go outside. Joy follows me.

I do just like we planned: start the car, crank the heat, and leave the vehicle.

Then, in full view of the Songs' open front door, I lean in to Joy and make like I'm kissing her cheek.

"We're a couple of goddamn zoo pandas," I whisper into her ear.

She laughs.

Let me tell you something. I live to make people laugh. Parents, siblings, friends, lovers, doesn't matter. I just have to. If you for some reason don't know how to make someone laugh, then learn. Study that shit like it's the SAT. If you are so unfortunate as to have no one in your life who can make you laugh, drop everything and find someone. Cross the desert if you must. Because laughter isn't just about the funny. Laughter is the music of the deep cosmos connecting all human beings that says all the things mere words cannot.

Joy laughs and we separate, and the orange rectangle of the Songs' front door has become crowded with silhouettes.

This is gonna work gangbusters.

frank li

in

love

chapter 10

old new loves

Joy and I spend the next couple of days working out the kinks in our system. First, I set a calendar event titled OLD NEW LOVES MOVIE WITH BRIT. Joy immediately deletes it.

Dumbass, don't use any names, she writes.

Aha, I write back.

So I make a new event titled simply SATURDAY: F—OLD NEW LOVES MOVIE. The *F* very cleverly stands for *Frank.*

A day later I'm in Calculus, and we're going over test answers together. Q got a perfect 100, for he is Q. Q also scored a perfect 1520 on the PSAT, forever ago.

I got a 97. So did Brit. She reached over and drew a fat heart around my number, which is totally middle school, but I do not care one single bit.

I feel a buzz and dare to take a peek at the screen:

SATURDAY: —TITANFIST *3 RESUSCITATION* MOVIE

Titanfist 3 is one long bro-yell of a movie, and I can so clearly picture Wu fist-pumping at the screen while Joy buries herself in her seat that I have to stifle a laugh.

"Mr. Frank, are you seriously looking at a phone in our sanctuary of learning?" says Mr. Berry Soft.

"I'm so sorry," I say, and put it away. I give Brit a quick grin and her nose crinkles happily: *What are you up to?* A wave passes through me. A wave of something. Mischief? Thrill? Daring?

Mr. Soft holds his gaze, not mad or anything, just patiently waiting. "Anything you'd like to share?"

I do want to share. I want to stand on my desk and declare, *I have my first real date with Brit* to the class. But I just offer a contrite smile and shake my head no.

"Next week our SAT boot camp starts," says Mr. Soft, "so let your brains rest. No homework this weekend."

"Aw," says Q with genuine disappointment.

"I am blessed to have you as a student, Mr. Q," says Mr. Soft. "Pound sign blessed."

• • •

Later, I gather things from my locker for the weekend. I look at my warped reflection in my cheap stick-on mirror. I've never thought of myself as good-looking. But Brit must think so. Wouldn't that make me officially good-looking? I slam the locker door shut to reveal Q's face inches from mine.

"Jesus," I say. "You scared the poop out of my butthole."

"We're hitting the Blood Keep bonus level tomorrow," says

Q. "Me, Olmo, you, and the Patel brothers on webcam. Bring your headset, because it's us versus a friggin' demigod."

"Q, Q, Q," I say. "Listen."

Q's face falls. "No."

"I have a date."

"Urghhh," says Q.

"Pull yourself together, old chap," I say in my best posh lockjaw.

Q closes his eyes. "Deep breath, soft focus." He opens them again. "Right, then. My boy Frank, I am quite delighted for you. And this date is . . . ?"

"Dinner and that *Old New Loves* movie."

"Brilliant."

Q eyes me, like my face suddenly got different. Maybe it has.

"And your parents are cool with her?" he says.

I inhale sharply and yank my backpack straps. "Mhm," is all I say. I don't want to tell him just yet about my covert dating strategy, which probably seems ludicrous if you look at it up close. But ludicrous times, they say, call for ludicrous measures.

"Wow, that was easy," says Q. "How did things turn around with them? Did something good happen with Hanna?"

"Why?"

"Huh?"

We both stare at each other for a moment, confused. My phone buzzes.

"That's her, gotta run," I say.

By *her*, I mean Joy, saying, *Pick me up in 30.* But Q doesn't need to know that right now.

"I'll just be at the Blood Keep, then," says Q.

• • •

I drive home in my unenthusiastic Consta as fast as I can and pound up the stairs to my room to get ready. I have just enough time for a five-minute shower, hair gel touch-up, and a fresh shirt: my favorite one with the dog sipping tea in hell saying *This is fine.*

I'm tipping my head back to clip my nose hairs in the mirror when a voice sings softly at me.

"Where you going tonight?"

It's Mom, leaning against the doorjamb.

"Dinner," I say. "Then a movie."

"Good, good," says Mom with obvious relish. "What movie?" she asks, as if the film choice will augur my future.

"It's called *Old New Loves.*"

"What it's about?"

"Mommy, you don't bothering Frank, okay?" calls Dad from the other room. "He must be get ready."

"Sound like love story," says Mom. "Joy like it, I bet. Girl like love story."

"Mom," I say. "I gotta go."

Dad appears in the doorway next to Mom, holding keys. "You take my car."

I look at him. I've never driven Dad's car before. He holds his keys out like a chef would a big pinch of salt.

"Thanks, Dad."

"Mmm," says Dad.

Mom-n-Dad stand all smiles in the doorway, blocking me.

"Can I . . . ?" I say.

Finally they clear the way. "Okay, go," says Mom.

I hammer downstairs and jump into Dad's QL5, and by the time I'm backing out, Mom-n-Dad are already in position to wave me off like I'm going out to sea.

• • •

I get to the Songs' insane beach cliff house and text Joy from the car.

Standing by

Roger, says Joy.

Joy comes exploding from the giant designer cherry front door, and as she whirls once to wave bye to her parents, I see her hair flash green in the blue light of dusk. She slams into the car.

"My dad used to have one of these," says Joy, glancing around at the faded interior. She smells like rose, like an actual rose.

My heart is pounding. I can tell from a single pulsing sinew in her neck that hers is, too.

"Let's do this," I say with a grin.

As we drive away, I can see Joy's parents waving and waving until we are out of sight.

"Do you know what my parents actually said just now?" says Joy.

"What?" I say, taking a turn a little too fast. The thrill of the caper is slowly ebbing to make way for another thrill waiting in the wings: Brit and I sitting close, dreaming together of love on a big screen.

"They said, 'Don't wake us up when you get home.' Can you believe that? They basically just said I could stay out as late as I want."

I nod and nod at her in happy disbelief. "My dad gave me his friggin' car."

"I bet we could go out every single night and they wouldn't care," says Joy with wonder.

"Dude," I say, and high-five her.

"Whoa whoa whoa," says Joy. "Got a visual on the package."

We're approaching her movie theater. In the distance stands Wu, the aforementioned package, before a *Titanfist 3* poster, trying to imitate the crouched fighting stance of the twenty-story-tall robot depicted there. But he's not satisfied with his pose, so he shakes it off and tries again.

"Go, go," I say.

Joy releases her seat belt. "So don't worry about getting me home, okay? Wu'll give me a ride. He'll insist."

I imagine Wu pulling up to Joy's doorstep, to the confusion of her parents. "But—"

Joy preempts my concern. "I always have him drop me off at the wrong house a couple doors down. It's worked out so far."

"Damn," I say. "Poor Wu."

"You mean poor Wu if he ever met my parents," she says,

and slams the door. She calls through the glass: "Go do you."

"You too."

And I'm off again.

Alone in the car, I take a deep breath, hold it for a second, and feel a calm silence seep into my mind. The handoff is complete; all that's left to do is get Brit and enjoy the evening.

I let myself sink into the cracked leather seat. I roll down all the windows. I dangle an arm to catch scoops of dewy air outside, and my hand becomes the rudder of a boat cutting through a perfect sheet of water.

Brit's house looks different during the day. There are jewel-colored succulents dotting a gravel yard like little sculptures; didn't notice those the night of our calculus assignment. There is a mermaid carved from driftwood hanging over the front door. It looks historical and beloved. And the door itself, painted red—it looked brown that other night—has a small silver knocker the shape of a dog's butt.

I can't help but compare it with my house: a low-snouted cookie-cutter ranch house with a blank green lawn in front, all practical. My parents work too much to carve mermaids for the threshold. But they must be working toward that kind of stuff, right? Toward that time in life when the hustle eases up, the body relaxes, and the mind begins to contemplate the ideal door knocker.

Otherwise what is the point?

The dog butt jiggles. The door opens to reveal Brit.

"Dog butt," I say, pointing.

"You like that, huh," says Brit.

She's changed clothes too, and now wears a tank top with a battleship bearing a bar code on its hull, with the caption LET'S SCANDINAVIAN.

"I love that shirt so hard," I say.

She draws a hand down my chest to examine my shirt and says, "I love yours, too."

Then something occurs to her. "I forgot my sweater. The movies are always so freezing. Come in and say hi."

She runs upstairs and suddenly I'm in her house again, alone for the moment. I scan in all the details I can: a bouquet of old blueprints rolled up in a tall vintage milk can, a framed French movie poster the size of a bedsheet, a photo of Brit when she was little, tumbling around with her parents in a colorful ball pit. Everything in the room holds intent and emotion and significance.

I think again how different things are in my house. Mom collects chicken-shaped ceramics for no real reason, the cheaper the better. Dad likes souvenir hooks. Any kind of hook from anywhere, the cheaper the better: Hermosa Beach, Los Angeles Airport, Scotty's Castle.

My parents' house feels like it's constantly on the way toward something. Brit's parents' house feels like it arrived there a while ago.

"We meet again," says a voice, and it's Brit's dad, approaching in a gray hoodie.

"Hey," I say.

And with that, he gives me a hug. "I had a feeling about you, buddy. You want a beer?"

"Uh," I say. "I'm eighteen?"

"Ah, right. How about some weed, then?" He hugs himself and laughs. "Just kidding."

"Good to see you again, Frank," croons a voice, and it's Brit's mom, also in a gray hoodie. Brit appears behind her, holding a thin sweater.

I regard the four of us, parents in matching hoodies, kids in matching novelty shirts, and want to giggle at the cuteness of it all. A moment passes through the room like a warm up-draft in a night vale.

"We should get going," says Brit.

"Don't want to miss the previews," I say.

"I was just going to say that," says Brit, quietly impressed, and gives me a tilted smile.

"Before you go," says Brit's dad, "I wanted to give you something. Brit says you're into found audio assemblage."

The words *found audio assemblage* ping-pong around in my mind. So there's a phrase for it. And Brit's dad knows it. An incredible feeling pricks my skin, like when your name is called over the loudspeaker at an awards assembly and every-one looks at you.

Brit's dad hands me a small round tin. "When Brit's mom and I were still just courting back in Brooklyn, I had this hobby of recording subway sounds. You might dig it."

"Whoa," I say, accepting the tin. "Are you sure?"

"See what it inspires," he says, and gives Brit a wink.

Brit does not eyeroll or sigh or do any of the teenagery things teenagers are supposed to do. She holds her gaze upon me, like she's sure I'll do something great with this small old tin. And indeed her look makes me want to do something great.

• • •

The best part of *Old New Loves* isn't the movie itself—although it's great, a perfect blend of rom and com, two of my favorite things in the world—but the part before the movie where Brit and I are in line waiting to get snacks. In line, among the other couples young and old, boys with girls holding their thin sweaters and men with women holding their thin sweaters, plus the occasional boy with boy or girl with girl also holding their respective thin sweaters.

I feel like I've joined a club. A club of couples.

"Can we get extra jalapeños for the nachos?" says Brit to the cashier.

"I was just going to say that," I say, drunk with wonder.

We give the previews our full attention and whispered critique, because it turns out we're both like that. We give the movie our full attention, too. By the end a single hot tear is shining down my cheek, and Brit wipes her own eyes before wiping mine.

We save our kissing for the end credits. I can taste pepper and cheese and she can too, because we both get the urge to wash our mouths out with soda before trying again.

"Much better," I say.

A short drive away there's a dumb little cafe over in Crescent Beach, the kind of place with oars and license plates on the walls and old music and older patrons. There's no reason to ever go to a cafe like this, really. I mean: it's even called Scudders.

Except now with me and Brit sitting side by side in a booth with cups of cocoa, it's the perfect place to be.

"I love Scudders," I say. I take out my Tascam and record a length of ambient audio—all soft clinks and murmurs and long chair scrapes sounding like whalesong—then put it away.

"It's beautiful in its own way," says Brit, examining a cluster of glass floats. "Not kitschy, though. I hate kitsch. Kitsch is not seeing something for what it is, but what you think it should be."

"It's like making fun of someone else's taste."

"It's so mean," says Brit.

I think about Mom's chickens and Dad's hooks. Are they kitsch? Am I mean about them?

I realize I kind of am. It makes me wonder if chickens and souvenir hooks were big in Korea in the eighties.

"It really is mean," I say, vowing to be better from now on. There's a glass clock on the wall filled with bubbling amber liquid and shaped like a beer mug. It must be fifty years old. "See, that's not kitsch right there. That's beautiful."

"Are you okay for time, by the way?" says Brit.

"I'm good," I say. "We have tons of time."

"Yesss," says Brit like a kid.

We have tons of time because I now have a special arrangement with Joy, I think. But Brit turns to face me and her hair dips into her cocoa, banishing the thought from my mind as I rush to push her mug aside.

"Your hair got in your drink," I say.

She sticks the wet lock in my face. "Taste it," she says.

"Gah," I say. But I do.

"You're crazy, Frank Li," says Brit.

We both get serious for a moment. In this particular moment, right here. Sucking cocoa from a girl's hair is weird. Who does this sort of thing? And who lets them? But Brit is letting me. She *wants* me to.

I am extremely proud to be the only person who has ever sucked Brit Means's hair.

We order more cocoa, and then a plate of fries. We don't look at our phones once. I know there's at least an hour before Return to Base, which is the time Joy and I have agreed to each return home just in case we need to keep our timelines straight. Eventually the waitstaff begin upending chairs. On the drive home we both scoop the air with our hands sticking out either side of the car like wings.

"Angle your hands just right for liftoff," I say.

"I'm trying," says Brit, laughing this far-off laugh that sounds a little like crying.

"Liftoff, liftoff," I shout.

At the red door, which I now clearly see as red and not brown, we kiss one last time before the silver dog butt. I dance down her steps and do not fall or falter once.

I drive home and park outside to keep the garage door rattle from waking everyone. I slip off my shoes and align them perfectly with Mom-n-Dad's in the glossy brown tiled entranceway.

When I get to my bedroom, someone has left my desk lamp on to help me see in the dark, and my bed is perfectly made.

I flop onto it and begin slipping into sleep when I remember to send one quick message.

Confirming, back at base now.

Me too, back at base and in bed, says Joy.

How did it go?

Really great, says Joy. *I felt like Cinderella liberated past curfew.*

And you didn't turn into a pumpkin.

Ha! How was B?

Gangbusters, I say. *A perfect night.*

Well highfive then

Highfive indeed.

And Joy sends me an animated picture of two soccer players attempting a high five, failing, and smacking each other in the face simultaneously.

"Good night, Joy," I say, before falling into a clear, deep sleep.

chapter 11

gem swapping

At The Store the next day I am useless. I forget to bag things, I give out the wrong change, I stare right past customers' eyes.

"You terrible," says Dad, laughing with glee. "Right now you in so-called state of perpetual distraction."

But he's not mad or anything. He just laughs and laughs, because he thinks I'm dating Joy Song.

Brit and I text for a bit later that night, but not as much as you'd think. It's like we both want to save it up for Monday when we see each other again at school. So I bid her good night, retrieve Brit's dad's gift—the small round tin—and open it to reveal a small spool of old audiotape. I carefully mount it onto an old portable Sony reel-to-reel from my collection of audio equipment. I begin digitizing my favorite clips. At one point, I hear Brit's mom's voice amid the screeching din of the subway car.

Look at those two, she says.

Get yourselves a room, says another male voice. Brit's dad.

Are we like that? she says.

Well, I sure as hell hope so, he says.

They sound a little like me and Brit. I wonder: what did Mom-n-Dad sound like when they were *courting,* as Brit's dad put it? There's no recording; even if there were, it'd all be in Korean. Which I guess could get translated. But would it still feel the same?

Monday rolls around. In Calculus, Brit drops her eraser and I pick it up for her.

"Thank you," she says, eyes ablaze.

"You're welcome," I say.

"Well, you two are cordial," says Mr. Soft, with a perplexed look like someone may have just farted roses. "Okay, turkeys, brief history of the farce that is the modern SAT."

Class ends. I give Brit a long parting look, and she holds it until she vanishes around a corner.

"Amore," says Q. He claps his hands. "So. Blood Keep ended badly. Paul Olmo's mage is dead."

I shoot Q a look. A character dying is a big deal, and unlike in video games it's permanent. "No shit. What happened?"

Q shrugs. "Got greedy. He's been running this scam where he ripped off our party's gems and swapped in fake ones so no one noticed. But oh, they did."

"Paul did this?" Paul turned in loose wallets to the lost and found. Paul didn't steal.

"The party offered him an ultimatum: battle them or preserve some of his dignity through suicide."

"Jesus."

"You think you know people," says Q, breathing mist onto his glasses.

I can see two dozen gem-shaped metaphors incoming, and I just have to laugh.

Just then Joy Song emerges from the crowd, eating from a bag of gigantic grapes. I know these grapes. They're called wang-podo. *Wang* is Korean for *king size*, and *podo* just means *grapes*. Anyway, I think Koreans have a thing for really super-big grapes.

Joy sticks her tongue out and sidearms a wang grape—*thwack*—onto my neck.

"Fuck," I say, laughing.

"Hahahahaahehehehahahaha," says Joy.

I pick up the grape and fling it at her.

"Aaaaaaa," says Joy, and runs away. But she looks back to share a grin with me.

Q just gives me a sober look. "Oooookay?"

"Well," I say, struggling for words. "We're family friends, right? But we got to talk with each other at a Gathering, like really talk, and it turns out she's super cool."

"Uh-huh," says Q, still with that look.

"Don't think with your mouth open," I say.

Later, I'm driving us to Q's house. Tonight is chicken tetrazzini, but with Louisiana hot sauce because only someone with the taste buds of a baby would eat that shit plain.

"So, you like Brit," says Q slowly.

I swim the car side to side. "I like Brit, yes."

"Then what was that whole Joy thing?"

"Joy and I are good friends," I say. "Just up until now I didn't know how good of friends we could be."

"So you're just really good, really brand-new friends."

"Basically."

Q's phone buzzes, but he ignores it. "Why didn't you just say that, then?"

I feel Q's words pinging around in my brain.

Why didn't you just say that?

Why didn't you just say?

Why didn't you?

Why?

I should tell Q everything. I don't want to deceive him about my . . . deception.

That sounds weird.

"So listen," I say. "There's something you should know about me and Joy. Let's just say we have a special relationship. With special benefits."

Q's eyes widen.

I put up jazz hands. "Whoa whoa whoa. Not *special benefits* special benefits."

Q's fartphone buzzes again. It's his mom, who Q puts on speaker.

"Will?" says Q's mom. She still calls him that. "Please do not put me on speaker."

"Too late, Mom."

"Can you pick up your sister from the dojo on the way home, please?"

107

"I'm in the middle of a very important conversation, Mom."

"We're happy to do it, Mrs. Lee," I say. Q punches me and I barely feel it.

"Thank you, Frankie."

Q hangs up and aims a finger at my eye. "Continue."

"More like to be continued," I say back. "Let's get your sister first."

• • •

We shovel our way through dinner, sweating heroically from the spice. Evon is apparently too smoking hot to perspire the slightest bit, even after seconds.

She offers me a napkin. "So. Brit."

I look at her, but her beauty is too painful and I must avert my eyes.

"I think that's sweet," says Evon. "Although isn't she a little young?"

"She's literally three months younger than me."

"Anyway, it's cute."

"Wait," I say. "You know I'm like a month older than you, right?"

"And I'm three seconds older, because—" says Q.

"Stop," says Q's mom.

We forget to clear our dishes, are reminded to, go back to clear our dishes, and run upstairs to Q's room to start cramming for the SAT. I can tell Q is dying to ask me questions about Joy, and I too am dying to tell Q everything, but we get the work out of the way first because we are those kids and the test is only a couple days away.

The SAT is a ridiculous exam, written as if it were geared toward aliens visiting Earth for the first time.

Valentine's Day is an important celebration of love and deep friendship where people send each other traditional "valentines." If there are 110 valentines to be sent within a group, and each member of that group must send one valentine to everyone else in that group, how many people are in the group?

"It's eleven," I say. "Each person sends ten valentines, because you don't send a valentine to yourself, and eleven times ten is 110."

"Yay, your logic is mind-altering," says Q. We close our books. "Now: about your special relationship with Joy. Are you or are you not playing two girls at once?"

"That's awful, no!"

"Are you one of these so-called players, plotting to use Brit to make Joy jealous enough to leave Wu and get together with you?"

"No, but that is impressively complicated."

"Give me the straight dope. Don't make me wrassle you."

"Listen."

"I'll take you down."

"We're dating, but it's all fake."

Q stops. He makes a stank-face. "Hah?"

I take a breath and continue. "We made our parents think we're dating, so that way I can go out as much as I want with Brit, and Joy with Wu."

"Because Brit is—"

"Mmm."

"And Wu is—"

"Right."

"And your parents don't—"

"Exactly."

"Ahhhh." Q nods and nods, appreciating the cleverness of the setup. But his face contracts. "You're swapping gems."

I think about Paul Olmo, waiting to unload his sachet of glass baubles while the rest of the party was asleep.

"I am not swapping gems."

"A gem swap this is."

"Did you steal my charger?" says a voice. It's Evon, dressed in a shiny outfit that could be meant for either sleep, exercise, or a night out.

"You're rudely interrupting a prolonged dialogue of great intensity," shouts Q.

I toss her a Loco-Lime™ green charger from my bag. "Use mine."

Evon snatches the charger out of the air without looking—impressive—and points it at me. "At least some boys are gentlemen." She shuts the door behind her.

"Shut the door," says Q, too late.

"Anyway," I say, returning to Q. "It's a win-win setup."

I can see Q consider me and Joy's scheme as if considering the integrity of an algorithm, and his eyes dart brightly back and forth until he hits a snag.

"But for how long?" he says finally.

"As long as we can," I say with a shrug. "Summer? Graduation?"

"And then what?" says Q.

"Then we're in college, and we can *really* do what we want."

Q levels his brow at me. "And then?"

"No *and then*," I say, quoting a favorite movie of ours.

"I just think you'd be better off coming clean to your parents, even if you take months to do it."

"I'm not pulling a Hanna."

"Hanna did it too abrupt and without warning," says Q. "You should ease them into it. Ease." He carves a gentle path with both hands.

I don't want to go down this path of his. "Do I seriously have to formulate a long-term parental diplomatic strategy just to date a girl? I mean, you wouldn't have to."

Q concedes this point. "In theory. In reality the whole thing is moot, unless—"

Q cuts himself off. Is he thinking of someone?

I pounce. "Unless what? Unless *who*?"

I study Q's face. It's fascinating: Q is suddenly *shy*.

"Come on," I say. "Who is it you like?"

Like I mentioned, Q and I normally never talk about romantic interests. But he must have them. Sure, he's a huge socially awkward nerd—but he's a boy just like any other boy. It just feels weird to talk about romance with a friend you've had forever. He liked a girl one time in middle school—Kara Tram—and we barely talked about it. She moved away, and that was that.

Q thinks with his mouth open for a long moment before speaking. "That bit of information is only for the queen herself, old chap."

"Amelie Shim."

Q's lips go tight. He shakes his head. "Mmm."

"Naima Gupta."

Q sighs. "No, and it doesn't matter anyway. The *objet* of my affection is already going out with someone else."

"That sucks."

"It positively fellates."

"What can you even do?"

"Just pine away," says Q. "I can pine like a tree."

I lean in and whisper. "Who is it?"

"So we get to college, and then what?" says Q, ignoring me. "Your parents will still call and visit. And what about after college? Are you still swapping gems? One day, college ends. And then?"

This is exactly what I didn't want to talk about. I just wanted to talk about how sweet me and Joy's setup is, and how freaking magical my night with Brit was. Not this future crap.

"Hanna is *and then*," I blurt. "You know how she married Miles at city hall? Because she knew Mom-n-Dad would never show up to a real wedding? That's *and then*. She and Miles'll have kids, and they'll grow up, and Mom-n-Dad will get super old, and that's *and* fucking *then*."

"Hey, hey," says Q.

"She married a black dude. You of all people know how basic this bullshit gets. Come on, man."

Q puts an arm around me and squeezes my shoulder. "I feel you. I really do."

"I don't know *and then*. No one does. I just—I had a really great night with Brit. One of the best ever. That's all I really want to talk about right at this moment. This moment in time is about all my brain can handle."

"Okay, okay, okay," says Q, calming me. "I feel you."

"Sorry."

"You're good," says Q.

"Got a little worked up."

"It'd be weird if you didn't, old boy."

I smile at him. "You're so great, you make that wall in China feel like a chain-link fence."

Q smiles back. "You're so cool, global warming's scared of you."

"You're so bomb, they had to evacuate the building."

And so on. This is our version of the Dozens, except instead of insulting each other's moms, we hurl compliments back and forth. We call it the Baker's Dozens. In a round of the Baker's Dozens, no one ever loses and everyone wins.

"I'm happy you're happy, and to hell with everything and everyone," says Q, squinting at me through his invisible monocle and raising an invisible gimlet. "To this moment in time."

"To this moment."

We invisible-toast.

chapter 12

illuminating

"Frankie-ya, you want beer, something?" says Dad. "Joy, hi, nice see you."

Dad sets a six-pack of beer—nice stuff, supposedly, IPA something-or-other—onto the floor as if feeding a cage of strange animals, and steps out again. It's the Kims' turn to host tonight's Gathering.

"Daddy," says Mom's voice. "Don't give alcohol."

"They take SAT, should be relaxing now," says Dad.

Yes: I took the SAT this morning. Although it feels a little like the SAT took me.

First, I sneezed on my test booklet, a prodigious specimen, and had nothing to wipe my nose with except the test booklet itself.

Then a girl's cell phone went off, and she was almost disqualified but for an impassioned three-minute speech about her dreams of becoming a pediatrician. That bit of theater was entertaining, sure, but it also destroyed my concentration.

When we Apeys gathered by the flagpoles, I could tell by the way everyone was kicking at the balding grass that they hadn't done so well, either.

"It's not over by a long shot, guys," said Paul Olmo. "Let's grind our butts off for test two."

"Grind our butts off?" said Naima Gupta.

"You know what I mean," Paul said. "Come on, isang bagsak."

Isang bagsak is this Filipino thing where we all applaud in unison, going faster and faster until we end the whole thing in one big clap. Paul calls it a *unity clap*.

Our unity clap didn't go so well either, and just wound up sounding like sarcastic praise.

Looking around at the Limbos now, I can tell we're all thinking the same thing: *I could've done better.*

I glance at the beer. "I don't really drink, Dad."

"Thank you, though," says Joy, and gives Dad a sweet look. Man, she's good.

Dad holds the look for a moment before gazing back at me. Then he seems to remember there are other people in the room. "Everybody doing good job today," he says. "When is next SAT?" he adds.

With that, the room sags. Dad just acknowledged out loud that we fell short.

Mom-n-Dad vanish downstairs to the game of yut nori being played by all the parents on a big fuzzy mink blanket, named *mink* not because it's actually sewn from murdered minks but because it's as soft and thick as a mink coat. Yut nori is this dice game from a million years ago but instead of dice you throw fat dowels carved from solid birch wood. Then you move little tokens around on a board. I think it might be one of the first board games ever invented. I don't know. I should look that up.

I can hear the sticks from down below, plinking with a clear, ancient sound that feels out of place here in modern-day suburbia. Each throw of the sticks elicits oohs and aahs, or groans, or roars of laughter. I want to take my Tascam down there to record that beautiful, almost crystalline birch tone, but I'm afraid that if I do, everyone will look at me weird and start asking questions.

So I stay and stare at the ceiling. Joy stares with me.

"Stupid SATs," says Joy. "I can't wait for kindergarten to be over." That's what she calls high school: *kindergarten*.

Joy's plan is to get into Carnegie Mellon University, in faraway Pittsburgh, so she can learn how to make the AI-powered robots that will eventually decimate humankind.

Ella Chang is here, crocheting some kind of amigurumi demon rabbit with fine needles. John Lim is here, playing *Craft Exploit* on a tablet. Andrew Kim is here too—it's his room, after all—idly doing arm curls and staring and staring at the beer until he can take no more.

"Fuck it, I'm having one," he says, and twists it open with thespian gusto. Andrew has been on a low-carb regimen to lose ten *camera pounds*, as he calls them. Andrew's plan is to become the first Asian-American actor to, quote, *bang a white chick in a major feature film full-nude no merkin*, end quote.

I had to look up *merkin*.

116

"You guys want?" says Andrew, holding out bottles. "Booze cures anxiety."

"I'm good," I say.

"I better not," says Joy Song.

"Dulls the mind," says John Lim.

"Gimme one of those," says Ella Chang, and stares at John with bemused defiance. She and Andrew toast. They take a long pull. I knew Andrew partied, but I had no idea about Ella. Between school and cello practice, where did she find the time?

Joy said *I better not*, as in *I better not drink*. So I ask her, "Wait, what happens when you drink?"

Before Joy can answer, Andrew belches.

"She talks," says Andrew. "A lot. I was at a party Wu was at that one time."

"Andrew at a party, surprise," says John, eyes on his screen.

"Joy was all blah-dee-blah-dee-blah," says Andrew.

"Shut up," says Joy, laughing.

"So wait, are you still with Wu?" says Ella. She's already on to her second beer. It's been like forty seconds.

Joy freezes. "Uh, mhm, yeah, yes. Why?"

Ella blinks. "Oh," she says. "Oh. Nothing. Never mind."

Then I freeze, too. Me and Joy thought all about keeping up our charade for the parents, but we hadn't thought about the Limbos. Do we fool them too? Or are they down? Telling them would be a risk—a potential leak in our boat.

But the fact is: we all go to the same school. We nod at each other in the hallways. It would only be a matter of time before they began to suspect things. Trusting the Limbos with our secret might be the only path of action.

"I gotta pee," I say, and pad down the hall in my socks to find a dark, empty bedroom. I text Joy right away.

Master bedroom

After thirty long seconds, Joy's silhouette appears in the doorway.

"Dude," I say.

"What?"

"I think we have to tell them."

The birch yut nori sticks clink, and the parents all shout with glee.

"I can't hear you." Joy comes over and sits next to me on the bed.

"I said, we have to tell them," I hiss in her ear.

"What? Why?" says Joy. But then she gives me a look: *You're right.*

"If they knew, they'd think we're crazy," I say. "But I bet they would keep our secret if we asked them. I bet they would be cool like that. Except maybe John."

"That fucker just wants to see the world burn," says Joy.

"I know, right?"

"But you know John's secretly in love with Ella, don't you?"

"No."

"Dummy, John likes every single thing Ella puts up. He pontificates forever in her comments, too. Every. Single. Post. Haven't you noticed how at Gatherings he spends the whole time ignoring her?" Joy waggles her eyebrows.

I laugh as quietly as I can. "Ella would cut his heart out and sun-dry slices for her pasta salad."

"Oh my god, Frank, that's so gruesome."

We grin at each other in the dark for just a second, then remember the task at hand.

"What I'm saying," says Joy, "is that maybe John can be trusted with a secret since the boy has a little secret of his own, capiche?"

I imagine a mobster Joy blackmailing John into silence, and snort. "I think he's cool," I say. "I think they're all cool. If anyone's going to understand why we're doing something this crazy, it'll be other Limbos."

"Good point." Joy heaves a single breath in and out. "Okay. Let's tell them."

I stand, take Joy's hand, and slingshot her off the bed.

When we return to Andrew's room, I see John holding court before a rapt audience.

"And then I saw him vanish with her," says John.

"That Brit Means girl," says Ella.

"I can explain that," I say, startling the room.

The Limbos stare at me, waiting.

"So here's the thing," I say.

"You and Joy have an open polyamorous relationship," says Andrew.

"That's exactly right, how did you know," says Joy flatly.

"Let him talk," says Ella.

"So," I say. "Me and Joy have come to this agreement, whereupon the arising of certain occasions for socializing of a romantic nature between, say, myself and a certain member of the female population who might cause tension within a certain traditionally minded population of our shared ethnicity, uh."

"We're fake-dating," says Joy.

"Ohhhh," say the Limbos.

"So you can go out with Wu and as a bonus avoid confronting deeper issues of identity and family," says Ella.

"Dang, Ella," says Joy.

"And you're with Brit Means," says John.

I nod. I look at Joy. We shrug. We make shy little jazz hands.

"So can you keep a secret?" I say in a small voice.

Ella claps her hands to her temples and squeezes with joyful disbelief, breaking the silence. "I love it. You guys are pulling some crazy shit."

Andrew punches the air. "Craziest! Shit! Ever!"

Ella gives me a sappy smile. "You look handsome in love, Frank."

John bolts to attention at this. He tries to speak, but can only move his mouth like a speared fish gasping for water.

It's too pathetic to watch. So I facepalm, but with the door frame. "I'm gonna pee."

"Like, really pee?" says Ella, still holding her head. "Or just fake-pee?"

• • •

I pee for real. I slam the soap plunger, wash my hands, and dry them using the floral towel set out special for tonight's Gathering. I notice my hands are shaking. Me and Joy just took a big risk and blew cover. Can the Limbos be trusted?

Even with their promise of silence, they could still let something slip purely by accident.

Why does everything have to be so complicated?

For a brief flash, I think to myself, *Fuck everything.* I consider ending things with Brit. Spending senior year as a monk. Saving all my dating for college. The logistics will be easier then. Why bother with all this workaround life-hackery?

I step out into the hallway and my phone buzzes with Brit's custom pattern—dot-dot-dot, dash-dash-dash, dot-dot-dot, Morse code for SOS—and that bitter flash of *fuck everything* vanishes in a little green poof of shame. I could never simply forget Brit. She's a book I just started reading, and I need to know where the story goes.

"Hey, you," I say.

"Hi, Frankly," says Brit. She's in a quiet room somewhere, with the mic close to her mouth so that her voice sounds like it's right in my head.

"That's my nickname for you: *Frankly,*" she says. "Isn't it convenient that your nickname is also your full name?"

"I'm calling you *Britmeans*, then," I say. "Breans. Beans? Hey, Beans."

She clicks with quiet laughter. "We can work on that one."

The sounds of the party bark and babble around me, and I have to cup my phone to protect our conversation.

"Where are you?" says Brit.

"I'm at this Gathering thing," I say. "It's loud. Can I call you later?"

"What's a Gathering?" says Brit with genuine curiosity.

A warm feeling comes over me. My forehead, which I've

121

been holding tense this whole time, goes slack. Because I realize that for Brit, I am the book she just started reading, too.

"So," I say, "my parents and their friends promised to keep in touch when they came to America, and every month we have these get-togethers. We've had them ever since I was a baby. Before, too."

"That sounds incredible."

"It kinda is," I say, because Brit is right. It *is* incredible. Suddenly that game of yut nori downstairs clicks into place in the cosmic timeline: it's not just a board game, but an ongoing celebration of sorts that says, *We came all the way here. Look at us now. Look what we brought with us.*

The roomful of Limbos suddenly becomes the most precious of life's achievements: children who will never want for anything, who speak native English, who will go to the best schools in the world and never have to run an office furniture rental service (like Joy's parents), a dry cleaner (Ella's), a beauty supply (Andrew's), a tourist gift shop (John's), or a grocery store (mine).

These amazing children, the living proof of so much hard work and sacrifice in an alien land, now come blundering like idiot clowns out of Andrew's room and spot me standing there with my phone cupped in my hands like a boy clearly talking to his girl.

"Who you talking to?" says Andrew. "Is that Brit?"

"Behold," says John, as if witnessing a mystery revealed. "Frank Li in love."

Ella rushes up to me, reads my phone screen, and turns her face to meet the mic. "Hi, Brit."

122

"Hi, Brit," say Andrew and Ella and John.

"Buzz, buzz, leave him alone," says Joy. But then she, too, hoots cross-eyed into the mic. "Brit means it, mothafucka."

Andrew's mom screeches from downstairs: "Dinner ready!"

The Limbos go tumbling down, making faces at me the whole way. Joy gives me a stage wink before turning, hitting her elbow on a doorknob, and muttering, "Fuck." I guess she had that beer all right.

"Who was that?" says Brit, laughing.

"Friends," I say. "All us kids of the parents. They get buzzed off of one beer."

"They sound so crazy. I wish I could see."

"Eh, it's boring," I say. "I mean not boring, but not like fun-fun."

"It's family stuff."

"Yeah."

"I get it," says Brit. "Still, I would love to see it. I would love to see you out of your usual context."

Her words *love* and *see you* gently topple me so that I must lean on the wall.

"Like it would be so endearing to see what Frankly is like around his mom and dad and sister. How does he move? How does he talk?"

The mention of Hanna makes my heart clench.

I know I can't both date Brit and prevent her from meeting my parents. Meeting family is not only inevitable, it's *normal*: *normal* people date, things get serious, and then they start meeting the people most important to them. It's just what *happens*. I've already met Brit's parents, twice, and I liked it. I liked seeing her with them. I get what she's saying about different contexts.

The idea of keeping worlds separate—the world of Frank-n-Brit and the world of Mom-n-Dad—sounds about as impossible as, oh, I don't know, keeping the worlds of Korea and America apart here in Playa Mesa.

You can't keep them separate for long.

I can hear what Brit is going to say next before she even says it.

"Maybe I could come over to your context this weekend?" she says. "See Frank Li in his natural habitat?"

"Oh yeah, totally, that would be sweet, sure," I say, which translates to *Think, dammit, think.* My toes start to float off the ground. No way I could've said no to her. That would've been tremendously weird. But how do I deal with an actual visit?

"That would be amazing," says Brit. "Sorry."

"Why sorry?"

"I made a promise to myself to stop saying *amazing* so much. It's a dead word."

"That's an amazing goal," I say, to buy my brain more time to scramble up a plan.

"Stupid," she says, with a smile in her voice.

Finally an idea hits me: safety in numbers.

"I could get my mom to cook up some Korean barbecue," I say. "We could invite a bunch of Apeys and have a gathering of our own."

"Oh," says Brit.

I wince, because I know what she'd been picturing, and I know a big loud barbecue party was not it. I know she had an image of an intimate dinner with Mom-n-Dad, like how white kids do it in the movies. She wanted to be *introduced*.

There's a pause, and I can feel Brit let that image dissolve away.

She brightens. "Yeah, that sounds amazing. Not amazing, um."

"How about *illuminating*?" I say.

She can say *amazing* in every sentence for all I care. I exhale with relief. This way, in this party-type situation, Brit gets to meet Mom-n-Dad—like normal couples do—and I get to keep my ruse with Joy intact. I can kill two birds with one stone, to use an unnecessarily violent expression.

"Illuminating," she says, and I can hear her smile again.

I realize I'm gripping the doorjamb, hanging on to her voice.

Mom screeches from below. "Frankie-ya! Dinner ready!"

"I gotta go."

"I'll miss you."

"I'll miss you more."

"Oh my god," says Brit. "We're becoming those people."

We hang up. I stare at the small chandelier glowing above the staircase landing.

"Illuminating," I say to the chandelier.

• • •

Dinner is a little bit of everything: Chinese-American beef with broccoli and fried rice, Japanese sashimi and miso, Korean chapchae and eun daegu jorim, and finally Italian-American lasagna.

Dad passes out more beer to us at the kids' table, again to Mom's protests. But everyone's well into the party spirit, and she lets it go.

"It's nice one," says Dad. "So-called Belgian Trappist ale."

"So you get these at a wholesale discount?" says Joy's dad. His accent is there, but his English flow is light-years ahead of Dad's.

"It's most expensive one we selling," says Dad.

"Then I'll take three, Mr. Li," says Joy's dad, and pulls a hundred from his wallet. I want to roll my eyes and say, *You're rich, we get it. You're the richest, smartest, most hard-working immigrant in American history, ever.*

"Aigu, you put away money right now," says Dad.

They laugh, and finally Joy's dad accepts a bottle with both hands and says, "Well, thank you very much, my sunbae."

"You welcome, hoobae."

Sunbae—as in senior, mentor—is what Joy's dad calls Dad, since Dad got to America first. Dad calls Joy's dad *hoobae*—as in junior, understudy, noob. They've been calling each other this for decades, and now it's become this little comedy routine they like to perform. I guess it's funny because they're both the same age?

I guess it's funny because Joy's dad has so clearly outgrown his mentor in every way?

Joy pours a glass. I eye her: *You sure you should have another?*

Something changes in Joy. She becomes almost coquettish. She hoists the bottle with both hands, aims it at my empty glass, and says loud and clear:

"Let me pour you a glass, yubs."

The entire room dips for a second, then comes roaring back up with an *Aaaaah*.

Yubs is a Konglish (Korean-English American Casual) abbreviation of *yeobo*, which means *honey*. Not honey like beespit, but honey like what couples say to each other.

Impressive. I tilt my head to concede her brilliance, and slide my glass toward her like a player relinquishing his stack at poker. I lift the glass, then take a sip. It's absolutely terrible. I can't understand why anyone would drink water that has had hops and twigs and shit rotting in it for weeks.

The adults lose themselves in their own conversation, and we Limbos lean in close around the table.

"Dang, Joy," howls Andrew. "You need to get into acting."

Joy bats her lashes. Her face is getting nice and red from the booze.

"Not if it means doing this China doll crap all the time," she says. She lets her face fall, and it becomes regular Joy again, complete with wry smile.

"So it really works," says John. "I mean, why wouldn't it work—it makes perfect sense."

"Maybe we should all fake-date," says Ella. "John, be my fake-date buddy."

"Why, is it because, who do you like?" says John.

"You first," says Ella.

"Nice try."

Joy and I exchange eyebrows. Are they flirting?

I frame the air with my hands to grab the Limbos' attention.

"You guys. Just to reiterate, just so we're absolutely clear, I need you to promise us that—"

Mom appears at the kids' table. "Everybody have a fun?"

She of course gives me and Joy little back-and-forth glances, cha-cha-cha.

I need her to leave. Just for this next part. So I say, "Word."

"What word?" says Mom.

Joy flashes me a look: she's clued in. She says, "We have an all-in type conversating happening right here."

"What?" says Mom, and leans back an inch.

The slang is working. Hanna and I used to do this, and I know the other Limbos can, too. If you ever need to hide sensitive conversations from your particular mom-n-dad, one of the easiest ways to do it is to start going heavy with the California Teen Tribal. Hides words right in plain sight.

Hanna and I used to do lots of things. Now she's gone, and now check me out: master of my parental universe. I am behaving like Ideal Son in Mom-n-Dad's eyes. I have cheated my way into their favor. Hanna, meanwhile, lives in exile.

What's that called?

Survivor's guilt?

I turn to the Limbos. "Before we get all ratchet up in this bitch, I need formal verbal confirmation from the entire squad to keep a certain setup on the DL. Don't go posting on main. You feel me?"

Mom looks around and around, her brains nicely scrambled.

"I feel you hard, bro," says Andrew.

"Hard AF," says Ella.

"Spank you, guys, I mean it," says Joy. "Hashtag Spanx."

"Why spanking?" Mom furrows her brow and retreats, and our table of Limbos is left alone once more.

"Hashtag keep it one hundred YOLO swipe right," says John, who is terrible with slang.

We all look at him for a moment until he settles down.

Andrew reaches out with both hands to clasp Joy's shoulder and mine. "You have our word. You crazy kids."

"Are they so crazy, though?" says Ella. "We all just want to love who we want to love."

And with that, Ella has brought the table to a profound place. I can feel it. I know the others can, too, for whatever secret reasons they have in their hearts. It doesn't so much matter what our specific secrets are. What matters more is the fact that we have to keep space for so many of them, all the time. We all sit and nod for a moment, letting Ella's words float before us.

We all just want to love who we want to love.

chapter 13

thank you booleet

The next day I call Mom at The Store to ask if she wants to oh, you know, host a little barbecue party on Saturday, and without even saying yes she goes into Mom Mode: she'll have to leave The Store early to get the meat, stay up a little later the night before preparing and marinating, get Dad to clean the grill, and so on. She's so busy muttering her to-do list to herself that she literally hangs up on me.

She acts like it's going to be this huge pain. But the truth is: Mom loves the chance to host my friends. Because she knows (a) they aren't judgmental, (b) they're American kids who will gush over every bite, and (c) she can be openly proud of her cooking without having to fake humility for once like she does with a Korean audience.

I pause, then tap away at my phone.

Heads up, I say. *I'm throwing a barbecue party, but I am intentionally not inviting you because the package will be present.*

Aha, says Joy. *The package*

I just didn't want you to hear about it from someone else.

Keep our stories straight, roger that, says Joy. *Over and out*

Then Saturday comes. I wake up later than usual, just before noon. I pad downstairs to hunt for milk and cereal in the kitchen. In the fridge sits a hulking silver bowl of marinating meat waiting to be grilled.

Brit begins peppering me with messages.

5pm, right? Ish?

What should I wear?

Sure I shouldn't bring a dessert or anything?

Each message strikes my thick, stupid skull like a pebble slung by a shitty little magical imp that I can't shake. My nerves jangle anew. *Frankly, this feels dangerous. Too risky, frankly.*

"Shut up with the *franklys*," I shout to no one.

Mom gets home early from her a.m. shift at The Store. Dad stays at The Store, because—you guessed it—Dad has never missed a day of work at The Store for almost as long as me and Hanna have been alive. Mom puts on an apron, this freebie she got from the beer distributor with the mentally incongruous image of a bikini girl wearing a fuzzy hat and hugging a giant beer bottle, along with the words GRIZZLY BEER GRAB A COLD ONE.

"I beg you to not wear that," I say.

Mom looks down at the bikini girl. "Why? It's brand-new one. Miguel give me free."

"Does it go inside out?"

Mom unties it, flips it over, and ties it again. "What's the matter with you?"

"Nothing."

"Your teacher coming tonight?"

"No."

"Just friends?"

"Just friends," I say. The words taste terrible.

Just friends just friends justfriendsjustfriendsjustfriends

"Help me," says Mom, and when I slide the heavy cold hemisphere of meat out of the fridge, I realize that whatever happens next, I am responsible for.

I help set out the bowls and bowls of banchan: kimchi, lotus root, cucumber kimchi, acorn jelly, spinach, bean sprouts, potato salad, roasted anchovies, all that good stuff. A kaleidoscope of dishes, a feast in wait. While Mom chops stuff up, I carefully cover each banchan bowl with plastic wrap. Then I look up: it's almost three o'clock.

How is it almost three o'clock?

"I haven't showered yet," I say to no one.

"Aigu, stink boy," says Mom. "You so stink."

Mom is trying to be funny, so I give her a little laugh just to be a good son. But panic is rising in me. People will be arriving soon. Brit will be arriving soon.

"I'll be right back," I say, and leap up the stairs.

I let the steam fill the shower. I don't really wash. I just let the hot water run over my back for a long time. I start writing at the top of the glass shower door.

B-R-I-T

B-R-I-T

When I rinse the letters away with the showerhead, I realize that some finger oil has stuck to the glass so that when it fogs, her name is still slightly visible.

This means something. Brit Means something. This means that when I step out of this white fog, things will be different. Mom will see Brit—really *see* her—and Brit will be great, and they'll make each other laugh. Later that night in bed, Mom will report her astonishing findings to Dad: *Brit so nice, she having so big eyes, same like Joy. More better than Joy.* Dad will grumble at first, but when he sees the light of realization in Mom's eyes, he will relent.

American girl, they okay.

When Mom-n-Dad say *American*, they mean *white*. When they refer to themselves—or me—they say *hanguksaram*, or *Korean*. I never call myself just *Korean*. I call myself *Korean-American*, always leading first with *Korean* or *Asian*, then the silent hyphen, then ending with *American*. Never just *American*.

White people can describe themselves with just *American*. Only when pressed do they go into their ethnic heritage. Doesn't seem fair that I have to forever explain my origin story with that silent hyphen, whereas *white* people don't.

It's complicated. But simple. Simplicated.

Brit Means refuses to call herself *white*, and uses *European-American* instead. Because Brit is wise and aware.

B-R-I-T

I turn the water off and hear voices.

Voices!

I scramble to dry off, run a hand through my hair, and get dressed. I hop downstairs. I'm still sweating from the hot shower. I can hear Mom has switched to Polite Guest English, the dialect she saves for non-Gathering visitors.

"No, why you bringing so expensive one? You don't have to doing."

"It's for everybody."

"What it is?"

"It's a French fruit tart with a, um, crème pâtissière filling."

"Oh, you French?"

"Haha, no, um."

"Anyway, very very pretty. Thank you, okay?"

"You're so welcome, and thank you for—"

"Should be put in refrigerator."

I rush in. "I'll do it."

Mom nods at Brit. "Booleet? Bleet? I'm sorry."

"Brit, that's right," says Brit.

"Hard to pronouncing," says Mom as she heads out into the backyard with a tray.

"Hey," I say to Brit.

"Hey," says Brit to me.

And we execute a Standard Friend Hug. It's the worst hug ever. I can feel Brit's restraint. I can feel her being careful in front of Mom, who can still peer at us through the sliding glass.

Only then does my mind calm down enough to notice what Brit's wearing. Not her usual jeans, or ironic tee shirt, but:

A dress.

An honest-to-god dress. A simple cotton thing, nothing fancy, but to me she looks beautiful enough to send a fleet of seamen off to their doom. It's a dress for a grown-up dinner.

"You look amazing," I say.

"Aa-aa," says Brit, wagging a finger at the word *amazing*.

This is impossible, this urge to kiss her. I take a mental step back: here is Brit Means, standing in my kitchen, infusing it with her exotic scent.

"You look . . . *beguiling*," I say.

Brit smiles at a nearby bronze figurine of a bronco bucking an astonished infant cowboy. "Your parents have super-weird taste."

"I don't even see it anymore."

"Humanity's greatest strength—and also the reason for its ultimate downfall—is its ability to normalize even the bizarre."

"Brit Means, everybody."

Brit takes a breath for courage. "Where's your dad?"

"He's at The Store. He's always there. But you get to meet Mom, so that's a start."

I touch her shoulder, then feel Mom's eyes through the glass, and lean back to fake a more platonic posture. *Just friends.*

Brit shakes off some thought and powers up a bright smile. "I'm just happy to be here. With you. And Cowboy Baby. Really just Cowboy Baby."

I want to hold her badly, like a boy who believes a hug can convince the world.

Brit keeps on smiling. "I'm dying to try this barbecue."

The doorbell rings, and all the Apeys come wandering in: Q, Paul Olmo, Amelie Shim, Naima Gupta. Even Q's smoking-hot sister, Evon, is here, wordlessly noting her surroundings like a trained assassin.

Q looks around, too, perhaps spotting what's changed since he was last here. It feels strange having him over. I wish it didn't. I wish it felt more like when I'm at Q's house.

"Hi, Brit, hi, Frank," shouts Naima Gupta.

Amelie Shim points at a four-foot-tall bronze statue of a giraffe wearing a pith helmet and says, "This is like he's dressed up for safari but what's he gonna see like humans right because that would be ridiculous to have a giraffe go on safari to see other giraffes."

"I think this is a genuine Wyatt Thomas original," says Q.

"No," I say.

"Shut up," drawls Q, his eyes still on Amelie.

The glass door slides open and Mom pokes her head in. "Dinner not ready. You playing meanwhile."

"We playing meanwhile," whispers Amelie with a giggle. It's okay because her parents have even worse accents than Mom-n-Dad.

We migrate to the backyard—all of us except Evon, who borrows my Grape-Escape™ purple charger so she can ignore the world with her phone on a couch—and Q unrolls a small duffel on the grass to reveal a serious badminton set.

Badminton, the sport of nerds.

It takes a while to set up; it takes a while to start playing. I toss glances at Brit every now and then; she catches them, then tosses them back underhand. We bring out a gentleness in each other. It's a gentleness that glows unwavering even as the Apeys roll and holler around us and Mom barks for help over the sizzling grill cover, shaped like a hubcap to let the excess grease drain away.

"I'll go help," says Brit.

"I don't want your dress getting splattered," I counter.

"I don't mind."

"Polite fight," shouts Naima Gupta. Naima shouts a lot.

"Brit," says Q. "Get a racquet and get on my team."

Brit gives me a look, *Are you gonna be okay?* and I respond with a nod: *Go play.* I stand next to Mom and help keep the meat moving.

"She should be wearing tee shirt, not dress," murmurs Mom.

"She probably just wanted to be a little fancy for her first KBBQ," I murmur back. The *K* in *KBBQ* stands for *Korean.* As does the *K* in K-pop, K-fashion, or K-dramas. There's of course no such thing as ABBQ, A-pop, A-fashion, or A-dramas.

"Anyway," says Mom. "Dress is pretty."

I glance up at Brit. *Mom thinks your dress is pretty,* I want to yell.

Doesn't that count for something? It must count for something.

Q serves, smashing the shuttlecock into a white laser blur. Brit catches a tricky return from Amelie, and Q flicks his racquet and sends it rocketing down. Paul dives for the save setup; Amelie smashes it to the ground.

"That one's for Totec," shouts Paul Olmo, high-fiving Amelie but missing. Totec was the name of his doomed mage.

In the end Paul and Amelie win. Q ducks the net to give Paul a crushing hug. "Good game, man," says Q.

"I was wrong to swap out those gems," says Paul Olmo into Q's shoulder. "I understand that now."

"You're all right," says Q.

"Dinner ready!" yells Mom. Then, quietly: "Why she not here yet?"

I shoot Mom a look: *Who?*

But I know she means Joy. "Oh, she can't make it. It's her turn to teach a rotating seminar webcast about 3D printing techniques using nonrigid biomorphic materials."

I read somewhere that ultra-specific lies make the best lies, and it turns out to be true.

"Oh," says Mom, frowning. She examines me for a moment, perhaps wondering if me and Joy are having a spat. She shrugs it off, puts on a smile, and yells again.

"Dinner ready!"

In an instant we're all devouring food. To my horror, Mom offers forks only to Paul Olmo, Naima Gupta, and finally Brit Means. They all smile politely and demonstrate that yes, as hard as it may be to believe, they can use chopsticks just fine. I know this sort of well-intentioned ignorance is no biggie to Paul Olmo and Naima Gupta, who have awkward immigrant stories of their own. And Mom already knows Q and Evon—who has emerged to feed—can use chopsticks, despite their wacky African-Americanness.

But I feel bad for Brit, whose immigrant stories have most likely been washed away like surf erasing sandwriting. She may call herself European-American, but to most of the world she's just white. As a member of the majority, she belongs everywhere. As the product of a long, mixed-up heritage, she belongs nowhere.

Right now I can feel her wanting to fit in. She picks up rice from her bowl like *See? I can do it,* but then drops it, perhaps from nerves. A little crestfallen look twitches her brow. So I pick up some rice, then drop it too.

"Crap," I say, cleaning up my mess.

I find Q giving me a look like *What a gentleman.*

Brit stands up. "Anyone want more to drink?"

"I get it," says Mom.

"No, please, you relax," says Brit. "You've made this amaz—this *stupendous* feast."

Brit winks at me and I'm a little starstruck.

"Hear hear," says Paul Olmo.

"Thank you, Mrs. Li," says Evon with uncharacteristic charm.

Brit fills everyone's glasses from a pitcher of cold barley tea.

"Thank you, Booleet," says Mom.

"You're welcome, Mrs. Li," says Brit. "What's your first name, if you don't mind me asking?"

I freeze. This is all Brit's family talking right here. Most kids, never mind Korean kids, never ask about the first name of the adults in their lives.

"Eun-hee," says Mom. "English name is Diane."

"Your names are so pretty," says Brit, and holy shit does Mom actually blush a shade. This is pristine territory Brit has discovered. And I was there to see it happen.

The doorbell rings, and I feel a squirt of bile in my gut. I know who it is even before she opens the door.

"Hello?" says Joy Song.

"Aigu," says Mom, scooting away to the entryway. "You late."

"I know, I'm so sorry, Mrs. Li," says Joy.

"Shoes off," says Mom.

Joy realizes she's rushed halfway into the house in her boots, and now must backtrack. "Shit."

"Frankie-ya, Joy here," yells Mom. Then, to Joy: "You sit next to Frank."

I can hear it. Everyone can hear it. Mom has switched from Polite Guest English to Family Casual, just for Joy. Brit glances at the door, then at me, oblivious. What in God's hipster beard is Joy Song doing here? I close my eyes and will a hole to open up and swallow me.

Before any hole can appear, Joy takes a breathless seat next to me. Everyone scoots their chairs to make room.

"Hey, everybody," says Joy. She quivers like a beetle has just snuck up her sleeve.

"Do you guys know Joy?" I say to the crystal salt and pepper shakers, which are purely decorative and never actually used. The shakers say nothing.

"I know Joy," says Q. I shoot him a look. He looks back at me with naked fear.

"I know Joy," says Brit.

I can feel the world tilting—tables and chairs sliding to one side of the room, trees outside groaning with the increasing angle. When Brit showed up to The Store, it felt like two worlds colliding. Now she's here in my house, meeting Joy, and it feels like a third planet has joined in.

Mom slams the world level again by plonking a plate before Joy. "You eating."

I dare a quick glance: *What the fuck, dude?*

Joy looks back with helpless eyes. *It's not my fault.*

Are the Apeys staring at us? No—they're all back to happily

devouring their food. Evon finishes, excuses herself, and disappears behind a high-backed lounge chair.

"Oh," says Brit to Joy, realizing something. "Are you one of the Gathering friends?"

"Yeah," says Joy. "I've known this bozo since we were little."

"*Brit means it, mothafucka,*" says Brit with a quiet smile.

Joy smirks. "That was me, ha."

"That's incredible that you've been such good friends for so long," says Brit.

"We're not like friends-friends, though," says Joy, and it's the wrong thing to say, but she can't close her stupid mouth fast enough to trap the words. So she keeps going, especially now that Mom is examining her performance. "We're like family friends, like family-family. Anyway, I guess you could say we're really close."

This seems to satisfy Mom, who smiles and waddles out of the room with two kitchen trash bags.

Joy has just misted the room with bullfart, and I'm so convinced Brit can smell it that I want to facepalm the table to see how high I can send the plates. Instead, I stomp on her foot.

"Wow," cries Joy to no one. She tries to stomp me back but only hits bare hardwood. "Wow, this tastes amazing," she shouts.

This is getting stupid quick. I have to break up this table. I point at Q. "Is it time?"

Q springs to attention. He digs in his bag and produces a small game console.

"Time for *Let's Heart Dancing*?" he says.

Everyone groans, but once Q has it set up and is dancing in his strange—but infectious—blind shaman style, people can't help but join in. Brit grabs a controller and begins punching the air with her elbows. She glances at me, and I want nothing more than to be her dancing partner in a vectorized video game world of our own. But a jab in my ribs jolts me out of my dreaming.

"Your fuckin' mom called my fuckin' mom," hisses Joy. "She's all, *Frankie invite you too, right?* What the fuck was I fuckin' supposed to do?"

"Fuckin' pretend you were sick or some shit!" I hiss back.

"Fuck you, like I had a fuckin' choice!"

"Go Brit, go Brit," shouts Naima Gupta over the thudding music.

"You need to evac in five," I whisper. "I'm fuckin' trying to do something here."

"What the fuck do I say?" says Joy. "I can't just eat and run."

"SAT study. Go."

I get up, grab a controller, and dance with Brit. We face the screen and move in sync. Out of the corner of my eye I can see Joy bowing to Mom with both hands on her thighs, the picture of meek apology. She's doing it: expressing regret for having to leave early, adamantly refusing leftovers, impressing upon Mom the urgency and importance of not keeping her fictional SAT study buddy waiting, gracefully berating her own lack of planning and rudeness.

She's good.

"Frankie-ya," says Mom. "Say bye to Joy."

"Bye, Joy," I say, not missing a beat.

"Aigu, Frankie, stop playing and say bye."

"It's okay," says Joy. "Isn't he so silly?"

Joy holds a finger-phone up to her ear—*Brief me later*—and leaves.

We've reached the part of the song where Brit and I must actually dance touching each other, and we do—just both palms joined, practically puritanical in its innocence, but to me it feels like getting married. Me and Brit, making asses out of ourselves with everyone as our witness. Including Mom, who just shakes her head with bemusement.

The dance ends. Brit and I heave our chests and watch the score rack up.

"Frank ninety-two, Brit one hundred," shouts Naima Gupta. "Purr-fect."

I'm so happy for Brit that I thrust my hands in the air to cheer, and immediately punch a solid wooden ledge by the fireplace.

Brit snatches up my hand. "Ouch. Are you okay?"

"I'm purr-fect," I say, laughing. I've skinned my middle knuckle, but who cares.

I feel like I've dodged the swing of a huge razor-sharp pendulum. Tonight was a close one. But it was worth it. Brit and I sit jammed tight next to each other on the couch with the others, and she rests her sweaty arm on top of mine, and for a long moment I can picture things how I'd like them to be. Not how others think they should be, but how I want them: my terms, me, me, me.

One day, I'll sit on this couch and kiss Brit Means like it's nothing.

Suddenly Brit springs up. "I'll help," she says to someone. To Mom.

For Brit has spotted Mom clearing the table. When she tries to help, Mom holds her at bay with gentle refusal. But Brit leans in, armed with powerful manners of her own. A spectacular polite fight ensues that culminates with Mom awarding Brit an apron and a place at the sink. Brit's good. Really good.

I try to help, but Mom shoos me away. "Go play," she says.

"Yeah, go play," says Brit, and draws a long line of soap-suds down my forearm. She gives me a look like *Can you believe I'm washing dishes with your mom?*

The fake dating, this fake barbecue, all of it on paper equals me lying to Brit. All of it equals me treating my gentle, smart, kind girl bad. I know this, but I find it easy to pretend other-wise for now—because look at them, washing dishes like this. This must count for something in the long run. Right?

● ● ●

Everyone leaves at the same time. I walk them outside; Mom stands in her apron, waving from the porch.

"Thank you, Mrs. Li," says Q.

"You welcome, Q," says Mom.

"That was so amazing just the way the barbecue was mari-nated so perfectly and all those dishes must have taken you for-ever to make but they were totally worth it," says Amelie Shin as she vanishes into Q's car along with the rest of the Apeys.

"잘 먹었습니다," says Brit out of nowhere. *Chal mogosumnida* is the proper way to thank a host after a meal: *I ate well, thank you.*

"Holy shit," I say.

"Oh," cries Mom. "You speaking Korean?"

"Well," says Brit. Now it's her turn to blush. "The Internet does."

"천만에요," says Mom. *Cheonmanaeyo. You're welcome.*

Brit gives me a sly smirk. I frown and arch an eyebrow, impressed. Who studies vocab the night before a date?

A nerd. A beautiful nerd.

Q toots a farewell toot. As he backs out of the driveway, there's Dad, pulling into the driveway. Dad gets out in time to wave hi-bye at Q's car full of Apeys. Then he turns toward the house and sees me, sees Brit.

"Hey, Dad," I say. "How was The Store?"

"Oh, same-o same," says Dad, which is his version of *same-old, same-old.* He smiles at Brit. "Nice see you again." And he heads into the house.

Brit and I look at each other like *That went better this time.*

"I'm gonna walk Brit to her car," I say.

"Very be careful," says Mom.

"It's fifty feet," I say.

When Brit and I walk the ten paces to her car, the urge to throw my arm around her waist almost sends me into shouting floor spasms. She smiles. But she's quiet. I dare a glance at the front doorway: Mom is gone, leaving only an empty orange rectangle of light. So I hook an index finger and tip Brit's chin up to face me.

"Hey," I say. "You're my favorite, did you know that?"

Brit takes my hand in hers. I check to make sure it's not visible from the front door.

"I know what I'm up against," says Brit, because Brit Means is not stupid.

But I pretend anyway. "What do you mean?"

"I know your mom wishes you were with Joy."

"Did she say something to you?"

"She didn't have to," says Brit, playing with the thick part between my thumb and forefinger. "But man, she really, really wishes it. She knows Joy's with Wu, right?"

"She doesn't, because I'm pretending to date Joy to hide you from Mom-n-Dad."

I of course say no such thing. Part of me wants to just do it. But I think about how much those words would hurt Brit, so I leave them unsaid. Instead I say:

"I'm sorry about Mom. It's such bullshit."

"It's okay," says Brit. "It's just—you've seen how my family is. I'm not used to being held at a safe distance. And look at me. I'm as safe as safe bets get."

"You're way better than safe," I say. "I so want to kiss you."

"Me too, frankly."

"Here we are, wanting to kiss, and we can't. I'm sorry."

We stare at each other for five otherworldly seconds. Five seconds on Venus.

"Can you bear with the bullshit?" I say. "I promise you it'll be worth it."

I'm saying it to myself, too. *I promise all this gem swapping, all this deceit upon deceit, will be worth it.*

"As long as we're honest about what we're dealing with," she says, all trust and smiles, and gets into her car to drive away.

Her word *honest* slithers up my pant leg like a vine of shame. Her car slides around the corner and fades away. I stand there as the night increases its volume around me.

My phone buzzes. It's Joy.

Everything okay?

I survived, I say.

I'm sorry

Not your fault! Can't avoid the physics of parental forces.

Joy types for a while, then says: *Everything would be so much easier if only we just actually liked each other lol*

"If only," I say.

chapter 14

more true

5PM   J+F: DEBRIEFING

6PM   J: DINNER (LOCATION TBD)

       F: WE ALL SCREAM FOR ICE CREAM EXHIBIT @ THE HENRY GALLERY

8PM   J: SKEEBALL TOURNAMENT @ GAMEDOME

       F: BEACH

11PM RETURN TO BASE

Making the drop is kind of a pain this time around—apparently Wu's decided on a Cheese Barrel Grille right behind the very place I'm taking Brit, this pop-up art event thing called *We All Scream for Ice Cream*. I let Joy out of the car.

"Go do you," I call through the window, quoting Joy back to her.

"You too," she says, strutting backward.

Then I drive over to Brit's. I climb the steps to her house and knock on her red door and she appears immediately, as if she'd been waiting just on the other side.

We stand there for a moment, just admiring each other. Her tee shirt reads WHAT HAS FOUR LETTERS, which takes me a second to get. Brit immediately kisses me. She hangs on to my neck. And when Brit's dad appears, she doesn't let go. Again, I'm amazed at how comfortable her family is with open affection.

"Hey, Frankie," says Brit's dad, dressed in a gray tracksuit, cradling a beaker of tea.

"Hey, Mr. Means."

"I read in the paper about this ice-cream exhibit thing. They're calling it *art for the Snapstory generation*."

Snapstory is an app where you can share photos. Everyone uses it, everyone loves it, everyone hates it. It's basically this horrible corporate surveillance machine that cranks out non-stop soul-crushing envy as a side bonus.

"Eh, I'm taking a break from Snapstory these days," I say. It's true. I feel so much happier not having to obsess over getting or giving likes.

"Really?" says Mr. Means. "I was just thinking I should get up to speed on Snapstory."

"It's a super-self-conscious, super-judgy place. You can't just be yourself."

"So everyone there is faking it." He sips his beaker.

I nod with a knowing eyebrow: *Pathetic, right?*

I shake Brit's dad's hand and dance away with his daughter down the steps, and when we get into the QL5 to drive away, Brit puts her hand atop mine atop the drive shifter knob and we sit in silence like a young king and queen sharing a scepter.

The pop-up museum is in what once was Playa Mesa's old factory district. There's a bunch of hipster restaurants and bars in converted warehouses; people my age go there to pretend we're adults already. Hanna used to take me here before.

Before she got disowned.

I park and snap a pic of the outside of the museum: it looks like a corrugated hangar that's been attacked by giant multi-colored scoops of ice cream. But I don't Snapstory it—I text it to Hanna.

Guess where I am.

Look at you, hipster, writes Hanna in a rare quick response. I wonder where she is. Is she at home, curled up next to Miles? On the train going home from work?

I miss you, I want to write. Also, *I'm dating Brit by fake-dating Joy.* But me and Hanna don't really talk like that. Instead we use the world as our backboard, like squash players.

I'm growing a beard and a man bun after this just to piss you off, I say. This means *I wish you were here.*

You do and I'll come back and cut that shit off myself, says Hanna. This means *I miss you too, little brother.*

And when I say *I dare you,* I really mean: *I wish you could come home and everything could be simple like it used to be.*

I wait and wait for a response, then give up. When Hanna goes silent, it could be ten minutes or ten days before she writes again.

"Who's that?" says Brit.

"Hanna."

Brit knows I have a sister Hanna. She knows I love her. She knows she's cool. Brit knows because I've told her so. But she doesn't know about the Miles situation.

"Tell her I say hi," says Brit.

"I will," I say, but I don't.

Inside the museum we find ourselves surrounded by a forest of towering sugar cones and Popsicles the size of felled trees.

Brit cranes her neck in amazement. "Guh, I feel like Brit and the Brownie Factory."

"I feel like Frank and the Frozen Yogurt Factory."

There's a swing made of licorice; there's a climbable wall of gumdrops the size of watermelons. In the distance, I can see people swimming in a pool full of rainbow-colored jimmy sprinkles. Everyone is doing the Snapstory dance: swing the phone up, pose for the photo, then chimp around the screen hunting for the perfect emoji, stickers, and filters to post with.

"This place is manipulating my brain at the ganglion cellular level," says Brit. "Must. Take out. Phone."

"Stay strong, dammit," I say, shaking her shoulders. They're awesome shoulders.

"Must. Snapstory."

She takes her phone out of her back pocket, raises it, and tucks her face close in beside mine.

"Come on, one selfie," she says, laughing. "Let's brag about us. Let's make everyone feel like shit compared with us."

For a full second, panic racks my body like a fever. I imagine our selfie going up, then one of the Limbos seeing it, then one of their parents perhaps catching a glimpse over their shoulder, then phone calls to Joy's mom and my mom, and then the slow rumble of suspicion and its impending questions looming dark in the sky.

But no way in Pastafarian hell can I deny Brit a selfie. To do so would be incredibly awkward. Like ruin-the-night awkward.

So we take the selfie. At the last second, Brit kisses my

cheek. The kiss is captured. She tags it, stickers it, face-filters it, the whole nine, until it becomes a perfect mess of a social media garbage plate. Then she hits Share. It's undeniably a boyfriend-girlfriend selfie. There is nothing at all friend-friend or study-buddy about it. She writes a caption:

Love demands you do stupid things like post goofy selfies, but if that's what love takes, then I can be stupid all day. At #WeAllScreamForIceCreamExhibit with @frankofhouseli

Wait. Is Brit saying she loves me?

I look at the photo, then at Brit. I want to know how it would feel to say the word *love*. But I'm scared of where that would lead. I'm scared of the stakes it would raise. I find myself standing paralyzed before a whole entire next level to our relationship.

"There's a whole entire next level to this exhibit," says Brit, and leads me up a flight of vanilla wafer stairs. At the top they're handing out samples of ice cream with bizarre flavors, like jasmine and bacon caramel.

"I'll try the jalapeño pistachio," says Brit.

"Getting crazy," I say, kissing her cheek. "I'll try the cinnamon churro."

"Frankenbrit!" says a voice in strong California Surfer Local.

It's Wu.

"I saw your post, so I figured—" says Wu with a little pop-n-lock move "—we'd come check it out to kill some time."

Joy appears from behind a gummy bear the size of a real bear. "The wait for Cheese Barrel Grille is like ninety minutes."

I have to stifle a laugh. Joy absolutely despises Cheese

Barrel Grille, whose presence fatally undermines any hipster cred the warehouse district might've had. She hates it down to its spelling of *Grille* with that extra French-for-no-reason *e*.

French-for-no-reason is originally Brit's joke. Brit is here, Joy is here, Wu is here. We're all here standing close together, and it makes me feel like my deception is hidden only by the thinnest of curtains, ready to be revealed by the slightest accidental breeze. My head starts to spin and my heels leave the floor just a millimeter.

Wu starts performing for a selfie video, and he hook-arms Joy into the frame, where they make goofy faces and stick out their tongues and laugh. But as soon as he stops recording, he's all business, tagging and captioning and whatever. Brit leans in to help Wu spell tags correctly. While they screen-chimp, I whisper to Joy.

"Seeing all of us together is kinda freaking me out."

But Joy seems lost in her own thoughts. "We're fighting."

Fighting? A moment ago they were having fun for the camera. Then I remind myself that social media is all a lie. "Why?" I say.

"Same shit," says Joy. "He feels like I'm holding him at a distance. Because I am."

"Wait, so it's hashtag?" says Wu to Brit. "Not circle-A?"

"Hashtag," says Brit. "And then hit Share."

"Nice, thanks," says Wu with a moonwalk step. Then he notices Brit's tee shirt.

WHAT HAS FOUR LETTERS

Wu thinks. "I don't know. What has four letters?"

"That's the joke," says Brit. "What has four letters."

Wu stares and stares.

"*W-H-A-T*," says Brit, counting on her fingers. "Four letters."

"It's the word *what*!" cries Wu. He claps his big hands once. "Which has *four letters*! Fuck, Brit Means, that's funny—but like mind-blowing also?"

He looks around at the room as if to say, *Have you seen this fucking tee shirt?* Many, many girls stare back at him. He elevates his elbow, runs a hand through his hair, and stuns every single one of them with his eyes: zap-zap-zap. Their boyfriends lead them away like orderlies.

"I just wish we could be ourselves, out in the open like everyone else," says Joy. I can see a weariness in her eyes. She looks tired.

"I wish the same wish," I say.

Joy's left buttock starts vibrating. She reaches into the pocket and holds up a restaurant pager flashing angry red.

"Baby, our table's ready," says Joy.

"Fuck yeah," says Wu. "See you, Brit. See you, my Asian stud brotha!"

He gives me a devastating body slam of a hug. Like many things Wu Tang, *Asian stud brotha* somehow makes sense coming only from him and no one else. When he says it, I start to think, *I am Asian; I am a stud; I am a brotha.* Even though by the next minute I'll have no idea what any of that meant.

I watch them leave. I watch and watch. I realize what I'm watching for: a lookback from Joy.

Joy looks back with a smile and a shrug. *Wish me luck, Frank.*

"Wu is so . . ." says Brit, searching for the word.

"Dumb?"

Brit looks shocked. "No!"

"It's okay, you can call him dumb. He's dumb. I still like him."

"It's just that Joy's so . . ."

"Smart?" I say, with a little pride. For Joy is my very good friend, maybe better than I fully realize. I'm proud to know her.

Brit nuzzles my neck. "You're smart."

"I'm not so smart," I say. "I'm kind of a dum-dum."

Brit giggles. But it's true. Only a dummy would keep a girl like Brit a secret. Only a dummy would think that made any kind of sense. Or that it was in any way fair.

• • •

"Should be peak sparkles right about now," says Brit. "Wanna see?"

I have no idea what she's talking about, and I don't care. I hold her hand. We zip into jackets and stumble out onto an empty beach. The moon watches over a sandscape gone blue and ice cold. There is no one there. The world is ours.

I cinch Brit's hoodie down tight around her face and she does the same to mine, and we both look like cartoon characters waddling toward the pounding surf. Just for fun we attempt a kiss. It's as awkward as flipping a light switch with your nose. I love it.

"I've never been to this beach," I say.

"Technically it doesn't exist," says Brit. She points. "This city doesn't want it, and neither does that one. Oh, there's the sparkles."

At first I think it's just the white foam catching the meager light. But when my eyes adjust, I see it: an alien blue glow blooming and dissipating wherever the ocean churns. Peak sparkles.

"My brother studies marine biology," says Brit. "The way he explains it, the sparkles are caused by tiny dinoflagellates that glow as a defensive response when they get tossed around. So their beauty isn't what it seems, because really they're undergoing trauma."

Metaphor incoming. "Sorry, dinoflagellates," I say.

I sneak my hand up her jacket and feel the small of her back; she tucks her fingers under my belt. We stand strapped snugly together like this. It feels like we've known each other forever already. Maybe this is why people get married? For this cozy feeling? Because I could savor this cozy feeling for a long time.

It's a ridiculous scene. The moon hangs low and full like a lamp. The sea, a shining sheet of mercury.

I reach up into my jacket pocket—into our warm little world—and extract earbuds for me, earbuds for her. I hit Play on my phone. And I get to simply behold her face transforming as she listens to what I've titled "Song for Brit." She doesn't have to say anything. I can see the memories flickering silver and gold in her eyes like a music video.

It's a song cut and pasted together, using sounds from every time me and Brit have been together so far. There are the plinks and scrapes from Scudders, a tweaked *Purr-fect!*

sample from *Let's Heart Dancing*, a layer of ambient room tone from our first partner project at her house. On top of it all I added water sounds from Lake Girlfriend. It's our brief but brilliant history, in a single track.

As we stand here in this perfect-perfect setting, listening to the movie soundtrack of us, Brit and I become familiar A-list stars in a classic romantic film everyone knows and cherishes. I know what will happen next. Everyone knows.

We kiss, drawing circles upon circles over and over again. Then she says it:

"I love you."

She says it like it's something that urgently needs to be said. Like something she really needed me to know. And as soon as she says it, concern shadows her eyes. I sense that she was assuming I loved her too. That I would say "I love you" back. But now she might be wondering: what if I didn't? What would she do with all the white sand on this beach? All these blue sparkles? That damn moon out there?

What would Brit do?

She says it again. "I love you, Frank Li."

Our movie is shot day-for-night in monochrome. The song ends. We let the earbuds fall away, leaving no soundtrack but the ocean and air.

Do I love Brit? I do. I think I do. But there's a gap that keeps my love from seating properly. It wiggles. It is imperfect. Is it something I can fix? I don't know. If not, is it something I can get used to? Is it something I can live with?

I realize this gap is my problem. Brit does not have this gap. It is easier for her to love—simpler, less complicated.

My love is slightly misshapen. My love is nonstandard. It requires workarounds.

Is it the same love, then? Does it matter? I have no idea. I've never been in love.

My ignorance leaves me with two ways to go: either say fuck it, I don't know anything about love, so I'm going to wait and conduct more research—or fuck it, I don't know anything about love, so I'm the perfect lab rat, and dive on in.

The fact is I *want* to love Brit. That has to count for something. Sure: there is a gap, it wiggles, it's imperfect. So I'll press gum into the gap and hope it stays. It's a workaround.

I say it: "I love you too."

Brit's face breaks with joy. She didn't need to be concerned after all. We are here, on this cold shore, safe and warm in our jackets like an old couple gazing at the horizon of time. Brit is an old soul. I can feel that. She has this strange patience that belies her age. For most kids this would be the moment where we tear each other's clothes off and do it right on the beach. But Brit's not most kids.

We both sense it's time to kiss, so we kiss again. She smells like set sun and musk and ice cream. I zip open my jacket; she zips open hers. The zippers are mirrored, so we connect the two jackets together into one single cocoon of warmth. She pulls her hands into the cocoon and wraps them around my body to feel my torso with her thawing fingertips, rib by rib.

"I love you," she murmurs, like she's falling asleep. "It feels so good just to be able to say it finally. I love you."

I feel a buzz. Return to Base.

"I love you too," I say. Saying it makes it feel more true. I get the feeling that the more I say it, the truer it will feel over time. And eventually this truth I've created will weave itself into every fiber of my reality, until it moves naturally with my every gesture like a favorite shirt I can't help but wear always.

chapter 15

alone together

We drive back. I gaze out at the illuminated triangle formed by the lines of the road stretching ahead of us in the dark, mirroring our own forms as we lean against each other to meet in the center of the car as I hold the wheel steady.

Something official has happened to me and Brit. We said three words few ever say to each other. It's hard for me to pin down exactly what the precious words signify. They are a pact, a declaration. Also a kind of relinquishing. Saying *I love you* is the cry of the helpless. All you can do is confess it and hope it shows you mercy.

IloveyouBritIloveyouBrit

"Get closer," I say, so she snuggles in harder. It's not safe driving this way—I can't see my mirrors, I've got only one hand on the wheel—but I don't care because all I have to do is keep the car straight, and that seems easy enough.

When we get to Brit's house, she whispers in through the open car window:

"I love you. I love saying *I love you*. It's like I learned a new word today."

I lean over. She leans in, cantilevering her body on the sill, and gives me a single kiss like a drinking bird toy. I watch her climb her staircase. When she gets to her red door, my phone buzzes again. Stupid calendar alerts. I pull it out to Snooze—until I notice the screen.

"Everything okay?" calls Brit from above. She can see my face glowing in the car.

"Just spam," I say.

Brit blows me a kiss and vanishes into her house. I check my screen again.

Hey, I'm still here in the warehouse district . . . Need a lift if you're around
Bad night
Too much fucking drama
Hello?

It's Joy. Why is Joy still at the warehouse district? Where's Wu? Why does she need a ride?

On my way, I say.

I slam the car into Drive and whip it around.

• • •

When I get there, Joy's sitting on an ice-cream sandwich bench, smoking a cigarette. Like a real-life, burning-tobacco, smoke-in-the-lungs cigarette. I march up to her and flick it out of her mouth and into a puddle.

"What the fuck are you doing smoking?"

"Now I have to go bum another one," she says.

Behind us is a floodlit alley crawling with hipsters packing away giant ice-cream cones and waffles the size of mattresses. At least Joy wasn't sitting totally alone in the dark.

"Come on," I say. "It's super late. We gotta go home before people start to worry."

Joy just grabs my hand, forcing me to sit next to her, and digs for her phone. She raises it for a couple selfie.

"What are you doing?" I say.

"Just act happy and shit."

The best I can manage is a dour smile, which Joy makes up for with an expert head tilt, peace sign, and duckling pout. Then she texts it away—to her mom.

"Mom will see it, then your mom will see it, they'll squeal like piggies, and now we have a few more hours to burn," says Joy, flinging her phone back into her purse with weary disgust.

I'm still stunned from her little pose for the camera just now. She just went from misery to ecstasy and back in seconds.

"You have serious mental problems," I say.

"No, you do," says Joy.

"Good comeback."

Joy smacks her lips with distaste. "Do you have any mints? My mouth tastes terrible."

"Smoking is like sucking on Satan's big toe after his morning jog around the ninth circle," I say.

"No such thing as Satan."

"Are we just gonna sit here and do—*this*—all night?"

Joy thinks, comes up with nothing. She suddenly looks so sad. Just so, so sad.

I lean over. "Hey. What happened?"

Joy blinks and blinks and blinks until two perfect clear droplets escape from her eyes, and when she blinks again the droplets break into glossy streaks down her cheeks. The tears are making her mad. Or maybe she's mad at herself for letting me see them? Whatever the reason, she grips my shoulders and buries her face in my chest.

"I think Wu's gonna dump me," she mumbles. Big sniff, then another. "I think I deserve it."

I can feel her hot face. I have a good view of her scalp; I can see bits of green in her hair. She smells exhausted. There's an empty piercing in the top part of her left ear—three of them, in fact. Tiny holes, evidence of a fashion lark.

"He's not gonna dump you," I say. "You guys have been together forever."

She presses her face into my chest harder. "He hates me. I made him hate me. I suck, Frank."

I push her off me and look at her. "What the hell happened?"

"You know what he said?"

I watch her as she does this nervous thing with her fingertips, like she's knitting invisible thread.

"We're eating our stupid shitty food at that stupid shitty restaurant," says Joy. "And he's all, *Frankenbrit's only been together for like a couple weeks, and they're already borderline married-slash-OTP.*" She says it in California Boyfriend Informal.

"He's just exaggerating," I say as gently as I can.

"He's all, *Brit's already met Frank's parents at a family barbecue and everything, and I know Frank's met Brit's parents.*"

"Yeah, but—"

"He's all, *How come we're not like Frankenbrit? We've been together forever, dur dur dur, how come we're not like Frankenbrit?*"

She's blinking again, and this time she presses her face to my chest in time to hide the tears.

"And the thing is, he's right," cries Joy. "Because I'm a bad person."

I shake her. "Stop it. You're not a bad person."

Joy's eyes are poofy and pink now, as if she were tired of it all.

She pounds her palm with a fist. "I just felt like, we shouldn't have to sneak around and fake-date and whatever. We should be able to just fucking get everything out in the open and be honest with each other."

I bobblehead. "Stop, whoa, whoa."

She pounds her palm again. "All this time, Wu's had no idea my parents were racist against him. So—"

"Joy, what did you do?"

"So I straight-up told him."

Now I freeze. Even the hipsters behind us have gone quiet. A floodlight switches off. Joy shrinks a centimeter.

"You did not."

"We've been together for almost two years, and this whole time I figured I wouldn't tell him to protect him, right? Because who wants to hear that shit, right?"

"Waitwaitwait," I say, stunned. "What exactly did you say?"

164

"He was all, *You lied to me* and *Are you ashamed of me* and I said no. No way. But that reeks bad, because what kind of girlfriend hides her boyfriend from her parents for *almost two years*?" She punches out that last part into her palm, too.

Then she boxes her own temples. "I am the worst."

"Joy," I say carefully. "Did you tell Wu about our arrangement?"

Joy shoots me a look. "Hell no, dummy."

"Oh dear sweet baby jesus," I say.

"I just told him I've been hiding him from my parents for almost two years," she says with resignation. "Lying, basically."

We both stare at an object in the dark road before us. It's a blueberry the size of a kickball.

"You and me both," I say. "So I guess we can be the worst together?"

"That frankly doesn't make me feel any better, Frank Li."

"Just saying you're not alone." I grip the edge of the ice-cream sandwich bench and bounce my legs.

"That makes us alone together," says Joy. "There is no possible world in which we can just be ourselves on our own terms. This is it."

"Come on," I say. But she might be right. But then again, why stop being optimistic? But then again-again, would only a fool be optimistic, knowing what I know? That no matter how old I get, or how far I travel, I will never simply get to love who I want?

Will I have to wait for Mom-n-Dad to die first?

Getting dark in here, Frank.

"So Wu just bailed on you," I say.

"No, I left him," says Joy, wincing at the memory. "I really am the worst."

"Huh?"

"I told him it wasn't easy living with racist-ass parents, that he needed to be a little more sympathetic to my situation, and then *I* got up and left *him* at the table."

I'm impressed by her colossal stupidity. "Wow."

"The worst. It me."

"It really is."

"Shut up."

I search my memory. "Yeah, I can't think of anyone worse than you."

"Shut up," she sings with a smile. But in the next instant she grows sheepish with sorrow again. "He's not texting me back. I made the boy I care about feel like shit. It's not funny."

"Of course it's not funny," I say. "Hey. You're not the worst."

I pull her in for a side-hug. Her head fits nicely in the crook of my neck, like it belongs there. I feel the compact sinew of her shoulder—not as soft as Brit—and wonder if Joy's secretly athletic: running and jumping and capering on strong arched feet.

It's easy to rest my cheek atop her head and simply inhale the scent of her scalp. She smells like an afternoon nap in the sun. I press my mouth and nose closer.

Huh, I think. *Just the slightest pucker and this could be a kind of kiss.*

I mumble into her hair. "Maybe it's for the better? That you guys had a fight?"

"You mean to cut him loose gradually."

"This is getting super heavy," I say. "Never mind. You love Wu. Wu loves you."

And I do give her hair a little imperceptible kiss. Because I don't want her to be sad. Surely one tiny kiss can stem such a tide.

Joy sings quietly. "I love Wu, Wu loves me, we're a happy family." She ducks out from under my arm to face me. "Do I love Wu?"

My phone buzzes. It's Mom. I auto-text her back: *Be home soon.*

"I'm assuming you've said the words *I love you* to each other?" I say.

"Lots of times," says Joy with a single nod.

"And you felt it? Each time?"

"I think so. I don't know. I don't know anything."

"Wait, what are you telling me right now? That maybe you don't love Wu after all?"

"No," cries Joy. She makes a quick desperate search for words and finds none. "It's just that, tonight, I realized how I've been keeping him like this"—she stiff-arms me—"for our whole relationship, and I'm wondering: can you truly, truly say you love someone who's always been held at arm's length?"

I hold her arm with both hands, mostly to admire its fine lithe structure. She hooks her fingertips to my hand and lets them cling there. Her question is rhetorical, and I realize that the answer—if we're already being brutally honest here—is no.

My phone buzzes again, and again it's Mom calling. *Leaving right now, be home really soon, I promise,* I say.

I'm still stuck on *I love you.* "When you say *I love you,* what exactly do you mean by those words?"

Joy lets her arm fall. "I don't know, Frank. I'm beginning to think it was just a thing to say. Like a ritual or a habit that couples are supposed to engage in to signify *Hey, we are a real couple-couple over here.*"

This rings true. The gum holding my love for Brit is still there, but I don't know for how long. "Shit," I say.

"Why, did something happen with Brit tonight?" says Joy.

"No. Yes. Maybe." I offer a brittle smile.

Joy sits up, as if she's eager to stop being sad. "Tell me."

I see me and Brit on the beach, with the moon, and the sand, and everything. My heart does a lazy flop. I am thrilling inside—or is it quaking? Am I in love? Or am I in fear? Are they two sides of the same coin?

"So," I begin. "We're at the beach tonight, just us, alone."

Joy leans in. "Uh-huh."

"And we walk out to the sand."

"Did you do it?" she says, like a little devil.

"No, we did not do it."

"I'm rooting for you guys. Even if Wu and I break up, I'll sit in a cafe or something and wait out the night while you guys are together."

"We don't know if it'll come to that yet."

"You guys are perfect for each other." Joy does a funny thing: she holds my earlobe between her thumb and forefinger and rubs it three times, like a lucky charm.

Joy retracts her hand and blinks with attention. "So what happened next?"

I work hard to articulate this next part. "We're just standing there. I know what she's about to say. I can feel it. It's like the chorus to a song you kind of already know how to sing even though it's the first time you're hearing it."

Joy keeps her eyes locked on mine. "I don't get you music people, but I trust you."

"It's like she had the whole thing planned. So when she says it, I'm just floored, but I also expected it in a weird way?"

"Goddammit, man, what did she say?"

"She said the words *I love you.*"

"*I love you,*" says Joy, impressed.

I nod. "*I love you.*"

My phone buzzes again. Mom. "Jesus," I sigh. I auto-text: *Be home soon.*

As soon as it sends, it buzzes again. And again, and again.

"Gee-zuss." I answer the phone.

"Frankie-ya," says Mom. "Frankie-ya, where are you? You coming, right now."

"Mom, I'm in the car right now as we speak."

"You coming right now, please," says Mom. Something's wrong. Her voice feels dented. And she never says *please.*

"Hey," I say. "Is everything okay?"

"Daddy," says Mom. "We in hospital right now. They shooting."

Joy's hand is upon mine all of a sudden. She's looking at me. She knows something's wrong, too.

"One man with gun," cries Mom. "He shooting Daddy. He shooting Daddy!"

shake the world

upside down

and see what sticks

chapter 16

wait-and-see mode

The hospital is sage green. I sign a form and slip it through the window.

"Are you two together?" says the woman behind the thick glass.

I can't seem to understand English at the moment, so Joy cuts in: "No, we're just"—she glances around—"we're just friends."

"I wasn't asking if you were married," says the woman.

We sit on the hard seats.

We're here, I tell Mom.

Doctor is here one moment ok i come out soon bye

Is dad okay?

Daddy okay he stable don't worry

What do you mean by stable?

Mom doesn't write back. She must be busy talking with the doctor.

Everyone occasionally harbors the secret wish to be free from their parents' rules and constraints. Everyone fantasizes now and then of living untethered from the burden of family. But fuck, I just felt the string connecting me to Dad yanked hard by forces beyond my control, and all I can feel is relief that it did not snap.

I don't know what sort of bond me and Dad have. But I know I need it, whether I even want it or not.

One time when we were little, I whispered to Hanna: *Do you love Mom-n-Dad?*

She whispered back: *Don't we have to?*

Me and Joy wait. She wraps an arm tight around my shoulders and pulls me in for an urgent whisper.

"Your dad's gonna be okay," she says, and wipes a tear I hadn't noticed was there. Then she rests my head on her shoulder, just as she rested hers on mine not too long ago. It's like my heart has turned to lead and is now too heavy to carry alone, so Joy is helping me. She drove us here. She checked us in.

I look up to see a little boy across from us, smiling at us from behind a chair. He's probably waiting for me to kiss her, I think. He thinks we're together.

Buzz-buzz. It's Q. I unlock my phone and hand it to Joy.

"Just read it to me," I say. I don't know if I can even formulate a sentence right now.

"You want *me* to read *your* phone."

"I am a man with nothing to hide, Joy Song."

"Metaphor incoming," mutters Joy. She reads. "*I trust*

tonight's romantic masquerade proceeded most excellently, old bean?"

Joy lowers the phone. "Is this how you guys really talk?"

I rake my face with a limp hand, like a weary king. "Just tell him what's going on."

Joy tells Q. Q drops the Old Boy routine and declares he's coming over as soon as he can, over and out.

"Shit," I say. "Tell him it's too far. Tell him it's too late at night."

"He's already in the car," says Joy. "True friends can be such a pain, right?"

I smile at her. She smiles at me. Across the way, the little boy giggles aloud and stares at both of us.

Buzz-buzz.

"It's Brit," says Joy, offering me the phone.

"Just read it to me," I say.

Joy eyes me—*really?*—and reads. "*I love you I love you I love you,* heart eyes emoji, heart eyes emoji, blowing kiss emoji, two pink hearts emoji."

I sit up and look at my phone screen.

"You were serious about the *I love yous,*" says Joy.

"Tell her *I love you* back, no emojis."

Joy squints at me. "You should let her know what's going on with your dad."

"No way," I say, and instantly hate myself for saying it. "I couldn't stop her from coming over, and then—"

"And then nuh-duh-duh-dee-duh, got it," says Joy, nodding. She types *I love you too!* and turns off the phone. I like

175

that she understands my trepidation without me even having to explain it. I like that she knows the last thing anyone needs is all the drama of Brit showing up, me having to act like we're not together, and all the rest of it.

Q sends updates on his ETA, and each time, Joy holds out my phone for my thumbprint before giving me her reports.

I like that Joy Song is taking care of me.

"Li?" calls a voice.

We look back, and a trim Korean-American nurse finds our eyes. When we approach, he tweaks his mouth into a frowny face.

"I'm so sorry, our security protocol is family members only," he says.

I lean in. "Come on, holmes, my dad's just been shot."

The nurse taps his fluorescent clipboard three times—*let-me-think*—and says, "All right. This way."

We get to the room—an actual room with a door, not one of those curtained-off deals—and the nurse announces us with some Korean I don't quite grasp, and then I see Dad lying in bed peering back at me through an oxygen mask the color of ocean glass. I see Mom leaning over him, watching his every breath.

I thank the nurse and take a step closer. I see little tubes coming out from under the blanket, connected to a big syringe, an IV drip, something else.

Mom looks up. "Aigu, Joy, you don't have to coming."

"Mom, is Dad okay?" I say.

Mom starts fussing to clear a chair for Joy to sit in. "Too far. You driving?"

Dad is shot, I just got here, and now Mom's playing host? The whole thing makes me snap.

"Mom, what the hell happened?" I bark.

"Why you shouting, Frank?"

"I'm sorry," I bark.

"Frank, Frank, how about you sit?" says Joy.

"I've been sitting forever."

Then Joy gently encircles my wrist with her cool fingers, and I relax.

"They shooting three times," says Mom. "One hit the lung, cracked one rib. Make a hole. Doctor already put the Band-Aid. Doctor so good. He like you, Korean, but no speaking Korean."

Sorry I grew up in the wrong country, I want to snap. I'm in a bad mood. I just want answers.

"Mom," I say, as evenly as I can. "*Who* shot Dad? *When? How bad* is it?"

"American man, Caucasian man, he coming in," says Mom with disgust. "I never seeing him before. Only white customer is Charlie, right? That man come in, he asking Daddy how much is the lottery ticket, he so stupid."

"The sign says the price right there," I say. Because it does.

"Then he take out kind of antique gun, and he shooting."

"Bmfmfmfbm," says Dad through his mask.

"What?" I say.

"Small bullet, only twenty-two caliber. White man, he run away." Out of nowhere, Mom laughs. "At first Daddy feeling okay, not that much pain. He calling police. But then, oh boy. Hard to breathing. Because tiny-tiny hole in lung."

"Ai-oh-gey," says Dad. *I okay.*

"Wait, so the guy didn't take any money?" says Joy.

"No money," says Mom. "He going to three other store, smog check store, water store, dambae-jip, he shooting them too, every time he take no money."

Dambae-jip means *smoke shop.*

"Anyway police catching him. He so crazy white man."

"Wait, so they caught the guy?" I say.

"They catching. He shooting three more people. Nobody die. Everybody okay. Daddy gonna be okay, doctor say."

I fall into the chair. Joy catches me halfway down to make sure I don't miss the seat with my ass.

"That's so crazy," says Joy.

"I buy big bag of Nachitos," says Mom. "You want Nachitos? Too spicy. Daddy love Nachitos."

"I'm okay, Mrs. Li," says Joy. "I can't eat food that's too maewo."

"You don't like maewo stuff?" says Mom. *Maewo* means *spicy.* Mom smiles, because Mom can't deal with spicy food either. She's been known to eat Nachito chips on top of rice to cut the heat, which is almost as weird as my habit of eating Nachitos with chopsticks to keep my fingertips from turning fiery orange.

While they go on and on about spicy food, I basically just let myself slip into a complete space-out.

Dad just got shot.

The bullet was small, and hit him in a safe enough spot.

But what if the bullet had been just a little bigger?

What if it had hit his left side, not his right, and gone through his heart?

I feel like this moment should be more . . . momentous. But instead, there is Mom, talking about spicy foods, and there is Joy, sitting for all the world like the perfect Korean daughter. She's even got her knees lined up neatly together and her hands folded in her lap.

I see Dad, staring at me through his mask. He looks frail. I've never seen him frail before, and a vision of him convalescing in old age flashes in my mind. But: he's smiling.

Dad is *happy*.

And I understand why. Mom is taking care of him. Joy is taking care of me. We are all here together. His son has chosen a proper girl. All four of us are keenly aware of the specter of death, and remain defiantly alive. Cozy, even. Here in this small emerald room.

I glance at my phone for no reason. Q is twenty minutes away. Nothing from Brit. Why would there be anything from Brit? It's late and she's off prancing about in dreamland in her sleep, where me and her are a genuine, authentic Dating Couple.

"Are you okay?" says Joy.

I'm breathing faster and faster. "Can we . . . go . . . outside?"

"Sure, yeah," says Joy, urging me up. She stares and stares into my increasingly vacant eyes. "Go go go. We'll be back, Mrs. Li."

Joy hustles me through the maze of corridors like a Secret Service agent scrambling the president, and we make it outside into the freezing night air to stand under a cube of brilliant blue-green light. I hunch over my knees and breathe and breathe and breathe.

"Slow it down, you're having a panic attack," says Joy. "Deep breath in through the nose, slow breath out through the mouth. That's it. Make a long *shh* sound."

"Shh," I say. "Shh-h-h-hit fuck piss."

Joy stifles a laugh and puts on her serious face. "In through the nose, shh-h-h-hit fuck piss through the mouth."

"Oh man," I say. "I think I almost just lost Dad. Oh wow."

My eyes are dancing. Something inside my chest is clenching tight. I stop speaking.

"What do you need?" says Joy. "What do you need? A hug?"

I nod.

So Joy hugs me, and my thoughts evaporate into cloud form, then fall again to crystallize into something different. My arms spring up to embrace Joy's back. I've hugged her plenty but never like this, never with the whole length of my body, and I feel like I'm clinging to a raft.

"What if all three shots hit?" I say. "What if he bled out? What if it was a bigger gun? He could've died so easily to-night, but for some random reason he's going to be okay, and now we get to pass around a bag of Nachitos like we're just hanging out."

I'm babbling. "Shh," says Joy.

"Seriously, what if he died? He would just get erased, and the world would just go on, and he knows so little about me and I know so little about him, and fuck, if he died, then that

180

would've been it, just like oh, come to America, have this kid named Frank, work at a store, die. You know Dad never talks about his childhood? Almost never? He's already a huge question mark, and if he fucking died, I wouldn't even know who I was missing."

"You still have plenty of time to get to know him," says Joy. "You'll get sick of him. I promise."

"He could've died, Joy."

"He's gonna be okay."

"And then that would've been *it*."

"He's gonna be okay."

When Joy releases me to examine my face, she wipes my tears with her sleeves one by one, left, right, then left again, then right again.

I lift her hair, find the green there, and smile at it. All at once my tears stop. My face feels hot and swollen, like someone just kicked a soccer ball at me.

"Thanks," I say.

"Your eyes are brown," says Joy.

"They're black," I say.

"No, they're brown," says Joy. She turns my head in the light and peers closer. "Mhm, brown."

My whole life, I think, *I have been wrong about my own eyes.*

"Whoa," says a voice.

It's Q.

Joy and I separate. "Hey," I say.

Q examines my face. "You've been crying."

"I have indeed, old chum."

181

"Cry away, I say. Let it all out. How's your dad doing?"

"He's gonna be fine. We just got the medical intel."

"My fingers should help with your swollen face, due to my perennially poor circulation," says Q, and places a palm over my left cheek.

"Hey, I have bad circulation too," cries Joy. She offers her hand for Q to feel, and he's impressed. She places it on my right cheek.

We're a strange trio, under the cube of light like this.

I take out my phone and begin texting.

"That's not Brit, is it?" says Q.

"No, because then she would want to come here—" says Joy.

"And then nuh-duh-duh-dee-duh," says Q, nodding.

Hey, Dad got shot at The Store. We're at the hospital now. Perforated lung, but he should be okay. Doctors are in wait-and-see mode.

I wait and wait. Two long minutes go by. No one responds slower than Hanna. It's not just the time difference.

So the official word is he'll be okay? she says finally.

Yep, he'll be okay for sure. Mom's not even worried.

That's rare lol

I just figured you should know.

Actually . . . mom already emailed me (!) But thanks Franks

This is a first. Mom hasn't written Hanna in forever. *So all it took was Dad getting shot, huh,* I say.

You're positive Dad's gonna be okay

Positive.

Absolutely sure

Yes, Big Sister Hanna.

Then tell him I've completed my conversion to full black, says Hanna.

I laugh so hard, Joy and Q struggle to keep my cheeks cool. Then they read Hanna's message and start laughing, too.

Racist, I say.

Just turning my tears into funny hunny

My thumbs hesitate. I've never said this part before.

I love you, big sis, I say.

And instantly, fastest she's ever responded, Hanna says back: *I love you too boo*

Hopefully I'll get to see you soon, she adds.

You're coming home?

I wait and wait, but Hanna doesn't respond.

"Aw," says Joy, and gives my cheek a squeeze.

The meaning of the words *I love you* could not be clearer in my mind. Much clearer than earlier tonight with Brit, and shaped differently. I say the words because I know—we both know—that one day Mom-n-Dad will be no more, and neither will House Li as the world knows it. It will become something else.

It'll be just me and Hanna, piecing together our memories of our crazy parents to see how complete a picture we can manage. It will of course never be complete. It will of course be mostly inaccurate. We will of course screw the whole thing up.

And once we eventually grow old and go, that'll be that.

chapter 17

maybe it's different

I open my eyes.

All my joints feel frozen. My left foot is completely asleep. I feel someone touching my face, then realize it's my own hand, which has also gone completely asleep. I look down to see my body curled like a pretzel into one of the hard seats in the waiting area.

Outside, dawn is breaking.

My mouth tastes like stale Nachitos. "What time is it?"

Q and Joy duck into my field of vision. Their mouths are quivering with barely contained laughter.

Finally they can no longer hold it. "Bahahahahahahahah," they say.

I sit up and my body lights up with sharp tingles. "What?"

Now it's the staff's turn to laugh.

"Good morning, Sleeping Beauty," says the nurse from before. It looks like his shift is over. "Your dad's being discharged now."

I stand and almost immediately fall. "How long was I asleep?"

Joy and Q are still laughing. "Long enough."

Then Joy aims a sheepish finger at a nearby mirror. When I go to look at it, I see my face has been covered in multicolored scribbles.

Not scribbles. Signatures.

"I had the whole ER staff sign your face," said Joy. "You snored for four hours straight through the whole thing."

"We love you, Frank," says the reception woman behind the glass.

"Your dad's gonna be just fine," says someone else.

"It's on, the story's on," says the reception woman. She tap-tap-taps a remote to increase the volume on a nearby TV.

"We begin *Wake Up! LA* today with a night of terror last night in Hancock," says the TV, "where police say a man in his midthirties went on a shooting rampage at four separate establishments, injuring five."

"Huh," I say. A shot of Fiesta Hoy Market briefly appears, then a photo of a white guy with eyes gone dead.

"The suspect is undergoing questioning by detectives as well as forensic psychologists," says the TV.

"If that suspect had been black, he'd be too shot-dead to question," says Q.

"Right?" I scoff, and shake my head.

"Typical," spits Q.

"I'm gonna wash my face."

"Wait," cries Joy. "Let me take a picture of it first."

As she does, I say, "Just please don't—"

185

"I won't," she says, meaning *I won't Snapstory this.* She tucks her phone into her back pocket for no one else to see.

• • •

When Mom appears pushing Dad in a wheelchair, I hurry to hug them both.

"Okay, okay, okay," says Dad, as if warding off a slobbering puppy.

"Okay, okay, okay," says Mom, same.

We don't hug much in House Li. For Mom-n-Dad, hugging must feel like *When Animals Attack.*

"They writing whole your face," says Mom, covering her laugh. "I signing for Daddy."

"Mom!"

"Joy start it," says Mom. "She so funny. Especially for girl."

"Oh, for a girl," says Joy, laughing. She and I share an eyeroll—but a happy one.

"Girl normally should be smart and quiet and calm," says Mom. "But Joy so crazy."

That's what makes her so badass, I think. And fuck it, it's true. So I say it:

"That's what makes her so badass."

Dad's take-home bag drops to the floor, and Q swoops to retrieve it.

"Thanks, Q," says Dad.

"But of course, Mr. Li."

"Q is funny name," says Dad. "Thank you, thank-q, thank-kew, ha."

"Glad you're enjoying it as much as I do, Mr. Li."

We wheel Dad out into the early morning sun. Mom holds my hand like when I was a little kid. I can feel Joy next to me. Q's got one hand on my shoulder.

Weirdly, I feel like today is one of the best days of my life. It's a wonderful feeling. We survived something together, we five.

Then my pocket buzzes.

Where are you?

Is Q with you?

It's Brit. It's early Monday morning. Time for Calculus.

"Right," I say. "Today is school."

"And tomorrow's SAT round two," says Joy. "I'm taking the day off to catch up on sleep. You should, too. Sleep is just as important as study when it comes to taking tests."

My score for SAT round one, by the way, wound up being 1310, which is good but not The-Harvard-good. Joy got a disappointing 1280. Freakin' Q got 1590—ten points away from perfection, to Q's endless irritation.

"You can't just take the day off from school to study for the test," says Q.

"Pretty sure I just did," says Joy.

"She *is* crazy," says Q.

We laugh, but I stop short. Because I can picture Brit in class staring at my empty seat, without a clue about what kind of night I've just been through. Because of me. Because I didn't let her in.

But really, isn't it my parents who aren't letting her in?

I look at the five of us again, walking free in the fresh

dewy air. We seem so happy and light and open to all the possibilities the world has to offer. How can it be, then, that Mom-n-Dad see Brit as white and nothing else? How can that possibly be, now that the world has just shown us we are all human, and mortal, and fragile?

They see Joy as some ideal girl, when in fact she isn't. They see Q as a school buddy, when in fact he is my brother. How do they see me?

And who are Mom-n-Dad, really? What I see—the little I'm able to see—can't be the whole picture. There are depths to them I can't fathom yet. I probably never will.

I realize there's only a tiny handful of people I really, really know who really, really know me back. Q is one. After tonight, Joy is officially another. I know Brit, but Brit doesn't know the me of last night. And that's my fault.

The morning suddenly turns and becomes dry and hot and blinding.

"I think I'm gonna go in to school," I say. "Right after I drop Mom-n-Dad home."

"No, we go to Store," says Dad.

"You're insane."

"Customer waiting," says Mom. "And police coming today. They taking picture and testimony for report."

"You could take one day off, you know," I say. "Just a couple stupid days would be okay after freaking getting shot in the chest."

Q puts a hand on my arm. "Hey. Just let them go be them. Let you go do you."

"I say that," cries Joy.

Joy gives Q a high five so robust he must nurse his palm afterward.

• • •

Mom drives Dad to The Store, to my unending flabbergast. Q drives Dad's QL5, first dropping Joy off at her house and then taking us to Palomino High School, home of the Conquistadores.

It's lunch when we get there. I'm not even hungry—I barely know what time it is—but I head to the cafeteria anyway.

"We should split up," I say.

Q thinks about that for a moment, then says, "Good thinking," because he gets it. He knows if Brit saw us together, she'd know something happened last night. And I don't want her to find out that way. The reason I wanted to come to school was not to maintain my flawless attendance record, but to fill her in myself. Honorably. In person.

But it's too late. Because there she is.

"Where were you guys?" says Brit.

"Uh," I say.

"I think I should pee," says Q, and vanishes like the world's clumsiest ninja.

"You look like you barely slept," says Brit, scanning my face. "Did you fix a car or something? Is that grease?"

I thought I'd washed all the writing off, but I guess a few stray marks remain around the edges. There's no good way to explain my face. It's all a you-had-to-be-there joke. So I just find myself laughing.

"It's signatures."

"Signatures," says Brit. "On your face."

"I had the craziest night. Let's go to the greenhouse."

"Okay," says Brit, confused. "I guess we'll just go to the greenhouse."

As we walk, I squeeze her close so I can feel her hips move with mine with each stride. I smile. I yawn, then yawn again, then remember that yawning is something I do when I'm nervous. I can feel Brit's eyes watching me.

"What happened?" she whispers.

"I'll tell you in a sec."

We turn a corner into a deserted hallway, head outside, and duck behind the greenhouse like usual. Brit slides a hand under my shirt and kisses me.

"Your breath smells terrible," she says.

"I ate a bunch of chips," I say. "Sorry."

"No, I don't care." She kisses me again.

"Hi," I say.

"Tell me what happened last night before I start to worry," she says.

I wind up with a deep breath. "Okay. So. Dad got shot—no no no, listen, he's okay. I spent all night at the hospital."

Brit backs up an inch and simply looks at me with incredulity.

I plow ahead. "The staff were so great. They all signed my face while I was sleeping." I leave out that the signatures were Joy's idea. I leave out Q. I feel sick doing this.

Brit sits silently, letting this information trickle through her mind.

I swallow spit gone all sour. "I'm so, so sorry I didn't call you. It was just such a crazy night. It was late. I was freaking out."

She rotates one degree away from me on the rickety bench. My ears begin to throb. She doesn't have to say anything. I can see it in her eyes, which become flat with a growing melancholy. *You didn't call me.*

"I love you," she says to the tiny flowers before her. "Do you love me?"

I jump at this. "Of course I do."

"Could you please say it, maybe?"

"I love you, Brit Means."

As soon as the words leave my lips, she clutches my arm. "Help me understand. Me, I share everything with my parents. They share everything with me. My dad will text me during class about a new sandwich he's discovered."

She laughs at the memory.

"Maybe it's just different with your family," she says.

You're goddamn right it's different, I want to say. *We barely speak the same language. Literally. You have any idea at all how lucky you are your whole family is fluent in the same freaking language?*

Instead, I say: "I'm sorry. I should've called you."

Brit doesn't seem to hear me. "When you love someone, you want to share everything with them."

Brit is fluent in the language of Openness, and I realize now that I am not.

I should explain this to her, but it's all so tiresome and

complicated, and my brain feels staticky with fatigue. So I say "I love you" again and again as a kind of stopgap, because it's so much simpler just to be in love with Brit behind the greenhouse where no one in the world can see us.

chapter 18

black black sheep

"If you bake cookies in either square, triangle, or circle shapes, and have six different colors of icing, how many different combinations of shape and—"

"Eighteen," says Q.

"Jesus, at least let me finish the question."

It's after school. We're in his room.

Q yawns. "I think we're fine for tomorrow." He means our second official try at the SAT. There is no school the rest of the day. So we'll either celebrate, or hide in our beds dreading the two weeks it takes to receive our scores.

"Hey, Internet, dim the lights," says Q to the room.

"Dimming the lights," says Q's smart speaker. The ceiling lights soften.

Q picks up a game controller. He yawns again and again.

"I can't even muster the energy to play anything," he moans, and drops the controller to lie back with an arm over his eyes.

"Life is pain," I say.

He ignores my ribbing. "So how did your talk with Brit go?"

"Good," I say.

"But."

"There is no *but.*"

"There's always a big *but.*"

I sigh—that's a timeworn joke of ours—and lie back with an arm over my eyes, too. There we lie, both with our arms over our eyes. "She was definitely hurt, and I definitely apologized and promised her I would be more open with things."

"Wait. How?"

"I don't know. I'll figure it out."

"By making her Korean?"

"That feels racist. Are you being racist?"

"Your parents are the ones who are racist. They're not gonna change anytime soon."

I already know all this. There's nothing to say, so I just let my arm press into my eyes until the green-and-black checkerboards begin to swirl.

"Listen," says Q, softer now. "Don't get mad. But you need to prepare yourself for the imminent possibility of telling Brit the whole awful truth of what you've wrought."

"Thanks for having my back."

"I have your back. Your back I have."

"Doesn't feel like it right now."

"Listen—" Q tries to lift my arm up but I hold it firm, and when he releases it I just wind up hitting myself in the face. He does it again and again.

194

"Why do you like hitting yourself?" he says.

"Gyahguahghghah," I say, finally bolting up to slap-fight the air. "Why can't I just date Brit and have fun like a normal teenager? Why can't everyone just leave me alone?"

Q carves out a perfect cube of air with his hands. "Because, listen: the longer you date Brit, the more you will eventually hurt her. You are amassing a debt of emotional pain that you will eventually have to pay for. You need to tell her sooner than later."

I grip my knees. He is right. Fuck you, Q, for being so damn right. I don't know how to tell Brit she's on a collision course with the hard wall that is Mom-n-Dad. The thought terrifies me. The thought of what could happen afterward terrifies me.

"But I like her," I say.

"Then you have to decide how hard you want to fight your parents for her."

"But I'm scared to fight."

Q opens his hands. *There is the conundrum.*

I don't have to mention Hanna. Q already knows.

"Do your parents want you to date only black girls?" I say.

"Ha, to keep me pure black?"

I laugh. We've laughed before about the notion of a pure black. There are so many kinds of black. Nerd black, artistic black, old-skool black, super-black (see also: super-Koreans). *Black* can mean a million things. "It's funny to hear you call yourself black."

"But I am," says Q plainly. "I'm black."

"I thought you hated all that black-versus-white crap."

"It's a false dichotomy. White is an artificial construct."

195

"Amen," I say.

"Black is an artificial construct."

"Preach."

"But the fact is, as long as white motherfuckers keep being the way they're being, we're stuck with these words. They're gonna call me *black*. And they're gonna call you *Asian*. And to them it means we're all the same. But we know the truth."

We're entering strange, sensitive territory. Q and I have talked about race a million times, but mostly to make fun of it as an abstract, intellectual concept. We've never really gotten that personal about it, until now.

"So you *don't* hate having to call yourself black," I say carefully.

"I'm proud to be black. Black can be whatever you want it to be. That's what my parents always said from when I was little."

I imagine Q having heartfelt conversations about race with his parents as a kid. Conversations I never have with Mom-n-Dad.

"So I'm guessing they don't care who you date, then."

"You mean like your racist-ass parents?"

"Yes, like my racist-ass parents."

"Nope."

"So it's not Amelie."

"Nice try," says Q.

"Not Naima."

"I've already told you," says Q, not bothering to open his eyes. "She's in love with someone else. The whole thing is moot."

196

"But I could help Cyrano de Bergerac you one fling before summer."

Q lifts his arm and peers at me. "I think we should focus on solving your problem first before we move on to mine."

This shuts me up. I realize what I'm doing. I just want to be carefree, like in those teen movies where all the kids (meaning all the white kids) get to play their guessing games and act out their love dramas and lie tête-à-tête on moonlit lawns to gaze up at the stars. To wonder about all those higher things: the universe, fate, other philosophica. Not mucky-muck bullshit like the racism of their parents.

"I wish Korean could be whatever I wanted it to be," I say. "Korean's like the opposite. Korean's just the one thing, and nothing else."

"Super-Korean," says Q.

"Bingo," I say. "You know there are these Koreans out there who actually believe Korean is its own separate race, with its own single origin? Forget rich versus poor or strong versus weak; for these fools it's like Koreans versus Earthlings."

Q settles in to the end of the sofa opposite me and wiggles his toes into my armpit. "Korea is one of the most homogeneous countries in the world, old bean. Sorry that was the hand you were dealt."

"I could start my own successful billion-dollar music service, but to these fools I'd still be just some Korean guy."

"A man can be president of the United States, but to similar fools he'd just be some black stereotype. Everything else is trumped for these fools."

"Kinda wishing I could be white right now. Without the actually being white part."

"White can be anything it wants and be white last, not first."

"Although, eh, too many war crimes."

"True," says Q.

"I just know I'll never be able to do Korean right. You know what I mean?"

"Me and my family," mumbles Q, "we get shit all the time just for the crime of being ourselves. None of our DC relatives think we're black enough. We got shit when we moved from black Baldwin Hills to white Playa Mesa for Dad's job. At the last gathering, my uncle made fun of my *bougie* accent and said he'd have to *take away my black card*." Q lifts his arms to make air quotes each time, but with just his middle fingers facing out. He calls them his *fuck-off quotes*.

Q has Gatherings of his own? And they're just as annoying as mine?

Huh.

"We West Coast Lees have always been the black sheep of the family," says Q. "The black black sheep. So yes, I know what you mean."

"Hey, Internet, what are black people?" I call to the room.

"Ha ha," says Q.

I feel something squeeze my toes, one by one.

"Are you squeezing my toes?" I say.

"Mhm," says Q.

One, two, three, four, five, six, seven, eight, nine, ten.

With that accomplished, Q speaks. "You're a Korean black

198

sheep. So are your mom-n-dad. They left Korea for here, after all. We're all Limbos to some degree."

"Probably," I say. "Except Kyung Hee."

"Who's Kyung Hee?"

"Ella Chang's sister. She's getting married this weekend."

"Wait," says Q. "Your dad isn't gonna try to go to a wedding in his condition, is he?"

I sigh. "He is, even though he really shouldn't. It's this whole stupid pride thing."

"That sounds super Korean."

"You want super Korean, you should see the groom-to-be. He's this Korean dude, like Korean-Korean. Kyung Hee's basically Korean-Korean too. She's fluent, lives in K-town. She doesn't even use her English name anymore."

Q gives a sleepy gasp. "So she chose the tribe."

"Yup, she chose the tribe."

"Good for Kyung Hee. Hey, Internet, what are Korean people?"

"It must be so simple for her. She's chosen to be Korean. None of this hyphenated bullshit. Oh hey, Kyung Hee, where you from? *I'm Korean, Frank.* Full stop. I understand that. I just am unable to make that choice for some reason. You know?"

Q just breathes up into the room.

"Did you just fall asleep on me?"

"No," says Q, but it's a sleepy cry, like he's dreaming of being leg-humped by sewer pipe monsters.

"Don't you fall asleep on me, William Lee," I say.

Q does not respond. His breathing fills the room like a

white noise machine. Pretty soon, my eyes close too. So little rest last night at the hospital. We sleep like two boys in a canoe set adrift.

I have a vivid, insane dream where I am walking in a pulsating forest of moist black trees all strung up with red pinlights. Brit walks with me. She's in a futuristic yellow glow-in-the-dark dress I'm afraid will get stained from the trees. I know the trees are the insides of Dad's lungs; I know the spongy ground we walk upon is the slowly rising tissue of his diaphragm.

The whole thing could be creepy. But it's beautiful in a gross way. Brit is just as wonderstruck as me. Her hand in mine can read my mind well enough to hear me think, *Get a load of that up there,* and we both marvel at the light of the full lemon-lit moon. It's not really the moon. It's a round perforation 0.22 inches in diameter letting in sunlight from the outside world.

When the moon blots out, I know it is because a great eye has moved in to peer at us through the hole. I let go of Brit and wave at it with both arms amid the constellation of blood-red stars adorning every dark limb. The eye belongs to Joy—I know this—and I bet she can see me way down here.

I wave and wave and yell and yell.

"Joy! Joy!"

chapter 19

hey internet what are

"Hey, Internet, what are black people?"

Here's what I found: The definition of black varies by country. In the US, people classified as black are defined as having roots in sub-Saharan Africa, and black is generally associated with those having darker skin tones. The term black has many meanings and connotations, many of them controversial and still a subject of debate today. The full article is 13,881 words. Would you like me to continue?

"Hey, Internet, what are white people?"

Here's what I found: The definition of white varies by country. In the US, the term white is ever-changing. The category that once only included English and Scandinavians expanded to include those once considered to be nonwhite, such as Germans, Greeks, Iranians, Irish,

Italians, Jews, and white Hispanics. The full article is
13,752 words. Would you like me to continue?

"Hey, Internet, what are Asian people?"

Here's what I found: The definition of Asian varies by
country. In the US, Asian people are defined as origi-
nating from Southeast Asian countries like Cambodia,
China, Japan, Korea, Malaysia, Thailand, Vietnam, et
cetera. Until 1980, India and Pakistan were not con-
sidered Asian. Although technically in the Asian con-
tinent, countries like Armenia, Georgia, Chechnya, and
Turkey are not considered Asian. The full article is
6,390 words. Would you like me to continue?

"Hey, Internet, what are Korean people?"

Here's what I found: Koreans originate from North or
South Korea, with 7.4 million expatriates living mostly
in the United States, Vietnam, China, Japan, the Phil-
ippines, Russia, Uzbekistan, Australia, and Canada.
Ancient Koreans were craniometrically more similar
to Kazakhs and Mongols than Chinese or Japanese. Al-
though most Koreans believe they share a single com-
mon ancestor, recent research suggests that belief to be
a myth crafted by the widespread customary doctoring
of genealogical records. The full article is 7,016 words.
Would you like me to continue?

chapter 20

born stuck

9. Every generation has challenges it must face on its own terms. Therefore humanity is _____ to repeat its mistakes even as it slowly evolves forward.

    A) *blessed*

    B) *wont*

    C) *loathe*

    D) *deigned*

    E) *doomed*

20. Evolution is less a _____ than it is a _____.

    A) *line—squiggle*

    B) *contest—struggle*

    C) *statement—question*

    D) *march—scramble*

    E) *decision—reaction*

When I leave the testing room (née the chem lab) to meet up with the Apeys at the elephant tree, I see they all feel the same way as I do: all smiles.

"High fives?" I yell.

"High fives," yells Q.

We all high-five in a great, slapping melee that devolves into mutual facepalms. Not surprising, for nerds like us.

"SATs can suck it," I say.

"Fucking bitch-ass piece of cake, motherfucker," says Q.

We all blink at his outburst of profanity.

Q caresses his elbows. "I mean, it was pretty easy this time."

"Easy-peasy," says a voice. It's Brit, bounding into the group. She's wearing a shirt that says BUT WHO WASHES THE WASHCLOTH?, another one of my favorites. I catch her in my arms. In the spirit of Openness, I kiss her in front of everyone.

"Get a room," says Naima.

"Yeah, find lodging," says Paul.

Brit dangles from my shoulder. She's squeezing it. Sweet 1993 Keanu Reeves Buddha, Brit Means likes my shoulder muscles. "I'm still weirded out by that one about evolution," she says. "*Evolution is less a line than it is a squiggle.*"

"I chose *march* and *scramble*," says Q.

"I chose *decision* and *reaction*," says Amelie.

"I think it was a trick question," I say.

"What did you choose?" says Brit.

Brit blinks dramatically. She's high on rocking the SAT. We all are high on rocking the SAT. We all feel we scored at least 1400, which is 95th percentile. We all feel like we more than made up for our mediocre first-round attempt.

"I chose *contest* and *struggle*," I say. "Because a *contest* implies a level playing field. Evolution isn't level. Creatures are stuck with whatever they're born with. Some creatures

204

are big and strong and fast. Others, though, are too small, or too slow, or mutated. There's nothing they can do to overcome the bad hands they were dealt at birth. The herd leaves them behind. They're the first to get eaten. Evolution is not some contest. It's an arbitrary roulette wheel of murder."

The Apeys stare at me, agape.

I clap my hands to clear away the heaviness I've just spewed forth. "So! How are you gonna celebrate the day, you guys? Paul, you go first, then go clockwise."

Paul: "Play *Pax Eterna*!"

Q: "*Pax Eterna*, baby. See you there!" (High-five. *Pax Eterna* is this new online game where, eh, whatever.)

Amelie: "Maybe I'll go to Boba Castle?"

Paul: "Sweet. We can all go in my car."

Naima: "Can I come? I don't know how to drive! Ha ha!"

Brit: "I'm gonna hang out with my baby."

Me: "Where?"

"Anywhere, don't care," sings Brit.

"The SAT hit us bad for round one," says Paul Olmo. "But we hit back for round two. Let's knock it out with a unity clap."

We all begin clapping, at first slow like fat rain that then accelerates into a pounding tropical typhoon.

"Isang bagsak!" says Paul Olmo, and we all strike a single clap of thunder in unison to end the storm.

• • •

So? I say. *Test? Gut check?*

Crushed it, I think, says Joy. *I cheat death. You?*

Flattened it. Feeling psyched. Today the test dies so that we may continue to live.

Let's college! says Joy.

I laugh and put my phone away, because now here's Brit approaching. She hops up onto the low wall I'm sitting on and rivets three little kisses along the length of my neck.

"What's so funny?" says Brit.

"Tickles," I say. But really I'm still laughing because of Joy.

Me and Brit wait for her dad to come pick her up. She tried telling him not to bother, that she and I were going to spend the rest of the day out together, but by then he was already in the car, and he's apparently the only one on the planet who is disciplined enough to not even look at their phone while driving.

I realize I'm hungry. I reach into my bag and unwrap a little circular pastry from a square of wax paper. I offer Brit one.

"What is it?" she says.

"Homemade marzipan. Someone brought a bunch to The Store yesterday for Dad."

When I take a bite, Brit peers in close to examine the result.

"What's in it?" she says.

"No idea," I say. "Just eat, don't think."

I unwrap one for her, and she takes a bite, then another, then another, and it's gone.

After a beat, Brit says, "So how's your dad?"

I feel a twinge—short and sharp, but with long sustain that takes time to ebb from my chest. Brit senses it, of course. She touches her thigh to mine to let me know: *I forgave you a while ago now. We're okay.* And I relax. Body language is a real thing.

"Dad's good," I say, reaching for another piece of marzipan. I have a dozen. "He's frickin' back at work at The Store. He got himself a padded stool to sit on, though—woo-hoo."

"Really pampering himself," says Brit.

We laugh for a few seconds and dangle our legs off the wall. I find myself smiling sadly. I keep thinking, *Shouldn't Dad be doing what he loves? Not working his life away at The Store all the time?* But then I think, *What is it exactly that he loves most? He has no hobbies. No friends. What if The Store is it?*

"He's a weird guy," is all I can say.

"He just speaks a different language than you," says Brit. She unwraps another piece of marzipan. Brit Means likes marzipan: noted. "And I don't mean Korean versus English."

"Do you feel like you speak a different language from your parents?"

"I feel like everyone speaks a different language from everyone else." Brit smiles. "Except us."

"We finish each other's—"

"Sandwiches," says Brit.

"Come here." And I kiss her.

"Wait, I'm still eating." Brit gulps down her pastry to continue kissing me. Our legs stop moving. Everything goes still. This stillness is something to live for.

When I open my eyes, I see someone watching us from around a corner. It's Joy. She crosses her eyes and tongue-kisses the air, then vanishes. I snort.

"What?" says Brit.

"Nothing," I say. "Your shirt is funny."

"I love you," whispers Brit.

"Love you too," I say. I realize I left out the *I* part of that sentence—*I love you too*—but correcting myself would be strange, so I just leave it.

"I could feel you wanted to say more about that evolution question on the SAT," she says. She says it in that whispery, intimate Brit Means voice of hers. "But you stopped yourself. Why? I want to hear what's on your mind."

Okay.

"It's just," I say. "Being me? My whole Korean-American situation?"

Brit squeezes my arm and waits.

At first, I can't tell why this is so hard for me. But really I'm lying to myself. I know exactly why it's hard for me. Because down this conversational road is the acknowledgment of a fundamental difference between me and Brit—a fundamental difference of *being*—and I can't bear to admit that such a difference exists. Brit—wise, awakened, aware Brit—belongs to a white majority whether she wants to or not, and is entitled to all its privileges—also *whether she wants them or not*.

"I feel like I don't belong anywhere and every day it's like I live on this weird little planet of my own in exile," I say all in one breath. This is impossible to talk about. But I force myself to. "I'm not Korean enough. I'm not white enough to be fully American."

As I think of what else to say, Brit speaks. "My dad called you an *honest-to-goodness, red-blooded, all-American kid*. He said it was obvious from the moment he met you. He really likes you."

Obvious? Really? Because for most people *all-American* means—

"For most people, *all-American* means *white*," says Brit.

I lock eyes with her and see infinite recursive reflections of the two of us. Suddenly I feel like we've stepped into a new land. Brit and I are starting to talk about the hard stuff. It's a step toward giving her the hardest truth of all: *my parents are racist.*

"I love my dad," she says. "But he can be a lefty bullshitter sometimes. I don't doubt he sees you as this *all-American* boy. But I also know that if it weren't for me, seeing you as you-you and nothing else, it probably wouldn't occur to him to call you *all-American*. Just like it wouldn't occur to him to think of himself as anything but white."

Her *nothing else* makes me wonder what exactly I am, but I shake off the thought. Because Brit sees me. As in really sees me. That's a rare thing.

There's a car approaching.

"And here he is," says Brit.

"With your mom," I say, squinting.

The car looks like it once used to be some kind of military vehicle but has been painted sky blue with white clouds all over it. Brit's mom-n-dad sit in the front, dressed in clothes that could easily be mistaken for safari gear.

"Hop in," says Brit's mom.

"Actually," says Brit, "Frank and I were gonna—"

"This is what's known as being spontaneous," says Brit's dad. "Also, we're buying you two lunch to celebrate."

"Can't argue with free food," I say.

We yank open the hatchlike door, and Brit shoves me in by my butt.

• • •

The spontaneous plan is to go to the Mocha-Dick at The Shops & Restaurants at Playa Embarcadero Beach Pier, but when we get there, the Mocha-Dick is no more.

"Mocha-Dick used to stand right here," says Brit's dad with wonder.

The Mocha-Dick, named after the article that inspired Melville's seminal novel *Moby-Dick*, had long been an institution ever since Playa Embarcadero Beach Pier was erected. But its sign—crafted in the shape of a whale breaching high between two ocean swells—now bears the name YOUNG DONG SEAFOOD & KOREAN BBQ.

"I guess let's go grab us some Young Dong," says Brit's mom without a hint of awareness of the breathtaking joke she has inadvertently just let fly. She even growls out the word *grab* and everything.

"Oh my god," says Brit, unable to breathe.

"In through the nose, and shh, out through the mouth," I say, and suddenly I wish Joy were here to see this magnificent sign. I snap a photo to send later.

Inside we're greeted with a robust *Eoseo osipsio*, which means *welcome* but really loud. We score a killer table next to a floor-to-ceiling glass window overlooking a dock laden with sunbathing seals, a harbor bristling with boats, and the open sea.

"How's your dad?" says Brit's mom.

"He's busy working at The Store like always," I say with a laugh. "I guess he's recovering pretty well."

"I find their work ethic tremendously honorable," says Brit's dad.

I can only shrug. Mom-n-Dad's work ethic doesn't feel all that special to me. That probably makes me a spoiled second-gen brat who doesn't know how good he has it.

But isn't that what Mom-n-Dad wanted?

"The weird thing," I say to no one, "is he seems *happier* since being shot."

Brit's mom gives an eager nod. "I feel that makes a strange kind of sense. When your world gets shaken upside down, maybe you're just grateful for what sticks. Your father's trauma might be unexpectedly clarifying."

I'm guessing Brit's mom is a hobbyist psychologist—both Brit's mom-n-dad are smart enough to be hobbyist anything—and I wish I could have her work on my dad in an interrogation room. Maybe Brit's mom could solve the riddle of him.

Brit's dad opens the menu, flips through it, puts it down. He turns to me. And here it comes: "Maybe it'd be easier if you just ordered for us, Frank?"

I smile, but inside I'm irked. Brit's dad, despite his very Anglo last name of Means, would never be able to explain everything about, say, Irish cuisine. More importantly, he would never be expected to. Brit's dad is only ever expected to be one thing, and that's plain old generic American.

I'm not knocking Brit's dad or anything. I'm just saying it must be nice.

Because I'm still expected to be the Korean expert, whether

211

I know anything or not. In other words, I'm still expected to be Korean *first*, *then* plain old generic American second. That damn hyphen in *Korean-American* just won't go away.

I can't say any of this out loud, because I'm at lunch with Brit's parents and I want to keep things nice and light. So:

Hi, I'm Frank, and I'll be your Korean Food Tour Guide for the duration of today's meal.

Our waiter brings us tiny glasses of not water, but cold barley tea.

Brit's dad fishes out his reading glasses. "Now what's this we're drinking here?"

"Uh," I begin. "It's cold tea. It's called, uh, boricha."

"Boricha," say Brit's parents, impressed.

"Oh, this tea has a wonderful roasted body to it," says Brit's mom.

I hand the heavy menus to the waiter. "We'll just get three kalbis, a mul naengmyeon for me, maybe one of those small squid pajuns to start."

The waiter hollers out, "Kalbi segeh mul naengmyeon hana haemul pajun hana!"

"Yeh!" the kitchen crew hollers back.

The food comes at us with blinding speed. First, all the banchan: tiny dishes of spinach and roasted baby anchovies and potato salad and spiced jelly and so on.

"Oh my goodness," says Brit's mom. "You're going to have to explain all of these, Frank. I'm afraid we're a little bit—"

"We're terribly white," says Brit's dad.

"Dad," says Brit, in the same voice I use for Mom-n-Dad. In my mind I can hear her say: *It's European-American.*

I vow to keep things nice and light.

"So, uh, okay," I say. "This is spinach. This is kimchi. You guys know kimchi. This is kimchi too, but with cucumber. Same here, but with radish."

"Can I ask what this is right here?" says Brit's mom, pointing to the jelly.

"Mom," says Brit. "Let's just eat, okay?"

I stare at the jelly for answers. I love this jelly. But I have no idea what it's made of.

"Uh," I say. "Some kind of nut?"

"Oh, here comes a bowl of something interesting," says Brit's mom.

It's the mul naengmyeon, a steel bowl of ice-cold noodle soup accompanied by side bottles of vinegar and mustard. It even has crushed ice floating in it, just how I like it. The waiter jabs into my bowl with the scissors, cutting the long noodles down to size.

"That is just wild," says Brit's dad. "What kind of noodles are those?"

I rack my brain. Finally I find the answer: "Buckwheat!"

"And the broth, what is that?" says Brit's mom.

I rack my brain again. "I don't know." I laugh, but I feel like I'm failing as Tour Guide.

I glance at Brit. She's staring at her mom-n-dad with a firm smile.

"Fewer questions, more eating, please," she says.

Brit's dad freezes, suddenly terrified that he might have been offending me. "It's just that this is all so new for us, and we're so curious," he says.

"Maybe a little too curious," says Brit's mom with a laugh. "I'm sorry if we put you on the spot."

All of this is totally fair. What's new to them is familiar to me. But I can't help wondering: if I were with Paul Olmo eating Filipino food—which I know nothing about—would I pepper him with questions too?

Would I?

"Dad, you love cheese, right?" says Brit.

"I do," says Brit's dad.

"And you're a quarter French, right?" says Brit.

"So they tell me."

"Do you know every last detail about what goes into making a good chèvre?"

"You're saying so why should Frank know every last detail about all this," says Brit's dad. "Point taken. Excellent, excellent point." He gives Brit's hand a squeeze. And then, surprisingly, he squeezes mine too. He nods with this wistful sort of look that says, *I learned something new today.*

People who let themselves learn new things are the best kind of people.

"Brit's right," says Brit's mom. "Her dad doesn't know anything about cheese other than how to stick it in his mouth and chew." She brightens the room with a chirpy laugh.

I join in. "Hey, I have no idea what buckwheat even looks like, let alone how to turn it into noodles. I just know they taste good."

As soon as I say these words, I realize I've discovered the point. The point is not about playing Food Tour Guide. It's not about peppering Paul Olmo with questions. The point is being able to say *I have no idea.* Without apology. With confidence, even. The same confidence Brit's dad would have before a marble slab of unlabeled cheeses.

I have no idea, I realize, is a big part of who I am.

We eat too much, eat some more, and lean back in our chairs. Brit's dad takes care of the check.

"Here's to high SAT scores and fat college acceptance packets," he says.

On the way out of the restaurant I feel the eyes of the kitchen on me. Were they listening to our table conversation? Did they expect me to have all the answers, too?

Whatever, I think, and smile.

Outside, me and Brit find a place to sit by ourselves while her mom-n-dad shop for antique glass floats and carved light-houses and lobster mittens and so on.

"Sorry about all those questions," says Brit. "My parents can be so ignorant sometimes. I had to save you."

I touch her chin. "It's all good. I've gotten questions before. You don't have to save me."

"You're telling me I don't have to save the boy I love. You would do it for me."

This stops me. "I would. It's true." Say she were stuck in some conversation with an ignorant sexist bro. You bet I would stand up for her.

So why have I never stood up for Q?

I frown at this. Every time my parents have spouted their racist theories against black people, supported by their bull-shit fake statistics, why haven't I called them out?

Because my parents are the hand I was dealt, the hand

I'm stuck with. I wish I could say something. For Q's sake and mine. Mom-n-Dad will never really see the actual me if I keep my thoughts hidden away like this. But I'm scared to call them out, if I'm being totally honest. Because a child has to belong somewhere. What if you call out your parents, and all they do is slam a door in your face in response?

"The older I get," says Brit, "the more my tolerance for dumb bullshit gets paper-thin."

"Makes sense," I say. But it doesn't, not fully. There's a tidbit I want to say, but it doesn't feel like the right moment. I wonder if it ever will.

Here's the tidbit I want to say but can't find space for: if Brit's tolerance for bullshit is paper-thin, mine is mantle-thick. Because unlike her, my parents' bullshit is a core part of my life. My parents' bullshit has the power to decide every hour of every day, on and on into the future.

Brit's bullshit, on the other hand, washes off easily. She'll always be free to date whom she wants, study what she wants, do whatever she wants just how she likes. Her bullshit will only ever amount to life lessons during meals, and not much more.

I'm not knocking Brit or anything. I'm just saying it must be nice.

"Can I tell you a secret?" says Brit.

I wait. Brit rests her cheek on my shoulder.

"I'm embarrassed by my parents," she says.

"That's not really a secret," I say. "The real secret would be someone who thinks their parents are insanely cool. My parents embarrass me like it's their job. But, you know. I'll always love them."

We watch a huge pelican cruise just above the water, hunting.

"You know all these unarmed teens getting shot by cops?" says Brit out of nowhere.

I look at her. "Okay?"

"I started seeing all these articles about how to have The Talk with your kids. Meaning black parents, with black kids, who have no choice but to have The Talk."

"Q's dad gave him The Talk when he was seven."

"My parents don't even know that a thing like The Talk exists. Whenever yet another kid gets shot, all they do is shake their heads, yell about *systemic racist policies* and the *prison industrial complex*, and get all fired up about equal rights—but then it always ends with *You should feel lucky you don't have to ever worry about this.*"

I don't tell her what Mom-n-Dad would say about a police shooting. Usually it's *If making trouble, police shooting, that's it.* I once watched as Hanna tried to argue with Dad—this was pre-Miles—to no avail. It was like debating a giant baby. I want to tell Brit she *should feel lucky* that her parents even recognize injustice toward black kids. That's way more than I'll ever get from Mom-n-Dad.

"They can't even see their own privilege, and I hate that," says Brit. She puts her cheek back on my shoulder. "I read somewhere that you need to hate your parents in order to leave them."

"Because if you loved them, then you'd never be able to leave?"

I feel her nod. "Something like that, I guess."

The pelican soars, then dive-bombs the ocean like an anchor falling from the sky.

"I love you," says Brit.

"I love you," I say immediately, making sure to remember the *I* this time.

chapter 21

lime-green nebula

The rest of the week flies by. I look at Brit a little differently now. Like there are more rooms than I realized in the house of her heart, and not necessarily neat-and-tidy ones.

The next "Song for Brit" will be in a minor key, that's for sure.

Mom drives Dad to The Store, to keep him from straining his chest bandage, and they'll work a full day together instead of in shifts. Other than that, nothing changes about those two. Dad's been shot, but he just keeps on keeping on. Still not sure how to feel about that. But it's not like my feelings can change what they choose to do.

Our calculus teacher, Mr. Soft, cancels all homework to reward us for completing SAT round two and lets us play *Bird Slingshot* for the duration of class. He tells us to say *It's parabolas* if anyone asks.

In secret, I send Joy the photo of the phallic YOUNG DONG SEAFOOD sign.

You're my first dick pic, says Joy. *Thank you.*

You already know why I send it in secret: so that Brit doesn't think I like Joy or anything.

Joy sends me a photo of a huge painting of a black iris flower by Georgia O'Keeffe from her Art History elective, accompanied with an intrigued-face emoji. The black iris looks like a close-up of a monumental vagina.

You're my first slot shot, I say. *Thank you.*

All day I think about our little photo exchange and burp out little laughs at random times, like a crazy person.

There's no possibility of going out with Brit this weekend, because the whole thing is being swallowed up by Kyung Hee Chang's wedding. To review: Kyung Hee is Ella Chang's older sister, and the same age as Hanna. Kyung Hee was supposed to be an only child; Ella Chang's appearance was something of an accident. Ella Chang always tells us she feels like the collateral fallout of her parents' bottomless lust for each other.

They fucked too hard for the condom, she says, and we Limbos all reliably reply with a big *Ew.*

The most I'll see of Brit this weekend is for a trip to the suit rental shop to get me fitted for the wedding. So after school I take Brit in the obstreperous Consta over to Just a Formality, where we wander through aisles of seemingly identical attire.

Mom's armed me with a blank check. And now Mom texts me:

Pick suit whatever but NO MORE BLACK please Frank ok and also make sure you necktie matching Joy dress.

She appends a photo: a sleek indigo cocktail dress laid

out on a bed with matching silk shoes and a big amethyst necklace.

The parents are playing dress-up with us now? Are we dolls?

I would roll my eyes, but they're busy staring at the photo. It's gonna be so funny seeing Joy all dressed up. Not funny. Weird. Not weird. New. I don't know.

I put away the photo lest Brit get the wrong idea.

"I wish I could go to this fancy party with you," says Brit.

"Eh, too much ethnic homogeneity," I say.

"It could be interesting," she says. "Being the odd one out for once."

Inside I wince. *Try being the odd one out for twice. Or thrice. Or forever. Be glad you have the luxury of going back to being the even one in whenever you want.* But I shut up about that. I'm with Brit in a suit shop. I'm going to have fun.

I make Brit try on a men's vest—sexy—and a men's fedora—also sexy—and a men's velvet smoking jacket—maybe not so sexy. I find a trim-fitting charcoal suit, brown leather shoes and a brown leather belt, and an indigo-ish tie. I give Brit my phone to hold while I change. The necktie part takes forever. I close my eyes and visualize an instructional video from the Internet.

I step out of the fitting room transformed. Brit drops my phone at the sight.

"Marry me," she blurts, then claps a hand over her mouth for her outburst.

Then she body-slams me back into the fitting room, where

221

suddenly her mouth and hands and legs are all over me. An *ahem* from the distant cashier counter forces us to spring apart.

I straighten up, pose like a goofy pirate atop a mountain of treasure, and have Brit snap a photo. I take my phone and send it to Mom.

Ok looks good, says Mom. *You renting.*

I close the door to change. And in the privacy of the fitting room, I silently send the photo to Joy, too.

I'd hit it, says Joy. *Then quit it only to re-hit it*

I laugh once through my nose.

I notice the scab on my once-bloody knuckle has fallen off. The skin underneath is perfect and healed. It's like nothing ever happened.

Knock-knock. "Are you jerking it?" says Brit from the other side of the door.

"How'd you know?" I say, write back *hahahaha* to Joy, and then delete our entire conversation.

• • •

The wedding is on a big boat that goes nowhere.

It's an old steam cruise ship made for an old rich white guy, from back when there was no such thing as income tax or HR departments.

He was a self-made, self-educated millionaire who got to keep every cent he earned, said the tour brochure.

I fold it into my pocket and remind myself to bring it out later for my regular discussions about American mythology with Q. Lately we've been covering the trope of *One Day When I'm Rich.*

The ceremony takes place on the expansive open front part of the ship (the Internet calls it the *bow*), which looks like it's been TP'd with satin ribbons and lace and bursts of white hyacinth that fill the air with honey and vanilla. We sit in the halogen sun amid a vast layered arena of sound: the iron creak of ship parts, the plash of seawater, the distant ostinato—krr! krr!—of hundreds of dumb seagulls.

The sounds are beautiful and rich and unexpected. I raise my Tascam to grab good lengths of it all. I'm not the only one hoisting a device. All three hundred attendees are taking pictures of everything. Kyung Hee's wedding will be the most documented event in this ship's history.

Mom looks down her reading glasses at her phone to take a photo of Dad, who takes a photo of me. The only evidence of Dad's injury is a bulge where his chest bandage is. Otherwise, he looks neat and trim and suited up like everyone else.

There are other moms-n-dads, super-old halmeoni (grand-mas) and harabeoji (grandpas) in traditional hanbok. Tiny sleeping babies. Small dogs in luxury dog strollers. Little boys and girls, kicking their sparkling patent leather shoes. Big boys like me, big girls like Joy, if she's here yet.

Every word of the ceremony is in Korean, so I only catch about 5 percent of what's being said. I lean in close to Dad, and he whispers his insane translations.

"He saying, 'Woman body like church cathedral. Man is head, woman body. Cathedral womb make baby, so-called immaculate conception, jesus christ almighty. He born, he die, blood coming out, everybody contaminated with sin.'"

"Thanks, Dad," I whisper, and lean back again.

Blood? Die? Sin?

This is a wedding?

Suddenly a string quartet breaks into song—good old Pachelbel's canon—and the wedding party assembles. When Ella Chang steps forward in a silver dress, I whip around to find John Lim. There he is, recording her with his hand over his heart like a lovestruck Victorian.

The rest of Team Wedding assembles. There is the groom, a chiseled K-drama star lookalike leapfrogging the ranks at Samsung North America. He winks at his buddies and mutters something in Korean, and they all chant something back, and the whole party chuckles in response. I lean in to Dad for answers.

"Groom, he eating too many baby octopus, but he say don't worry, soju killing them in stomach. His friends saying, 'Drink, drink, drink,' ha ha."

Hilarious!

The string quartet changes tack— Wagner's Bridal Chorus, no surprises here—and Kyung Hee appears. More invocations in Korean: "Marriage is work" and "Joining of the families" and blablabla according to Dad's whispers. We sit. We stand. We sit. We stand.

Kyung Hee and the groom kiss a single dry kiss, and then it's ding-dong done: the quartet busts into an upbeat Mendelssohn march, and we all get up to herd ourselves into the cool indoor reception area of the ship.

"What'd you think of the wedding?" I say to Mom-n-Dad.

"They doing good," says Mom.

"It's nice one," says Dad.

"Pretty soon you," says Mom.

"Mom," I say.

Mom tugs my jacket straight, then glances with astonishment past my shoulder. "Omona. So pretty."

Omona means *Oh my god*.

And Mom's right: there's Joy, peering at me with plum lipstick and crushed onyx eyeliner, luxe goth. Just standing there in that dress.

Not just standing. Joy is _____.

   A) *shimmering*

   B) *coruscating*

   C) *scintillating*

   D) *effervescing*

   E) *freaking gorgeous*

My IQ drops to ten. "What the fuck," I whisper.

Mom nudges me forward. "Go."

"Have a fun," says Dad.

Dad is smiling. Mom is smiling.

I ignore them. The reception hall is a gallery of silhouettes surrounding a single shaft of violet luminescence, and in that light awaits the maiden of—

"Frank," says Joy.

"Yo," I say.

Joy folds her arms and examines me, then admits, "All right, you look hot."

"You look"— I fish for the right word but come up short, so fuck it—"you look amazing."

"I don't feel amazing," says Joy, casting sidelong glances with her elaborate, glistening eyes. "I feel exposed. This dress is all like, *boobs*!"

"Ha ha ha ha ha," I say. "Hahaha ha ha haha ha."

The forest around us turns into a constellation of eyes, all watching. Cheshire-cat smiles flicker on and off. People are *watching*. I catch a glimpse of Joy's parents. Their clothes look like they cost ten times as much as Mom-n-Dad's.

"This is a live-fire situation—we should get into character," I say. For some reason I add, "Hold my hand."

"Copy that," says Joy.

We clasp hands. Hers is ice cold, like when it was on my cheek at the hospital. It would be ice cold running up my bare arm for sure.

There's a flowery table with a guest book. There's a pyramid of champagne glasses. A futuristic DJ rig manned by a huge guy in a tracksuit. There's a parade of sumptuous flower wreaths on tall stands, gifts from families and local businesses, all flanking a sliding pile of impeccable gift envelopes—probably tens of thousands in cash, just sitting there. There's an eight-foot-tall ice sculpture of a—

"Of a," I say, squinting hard at it.

"It's a tiger," says Joy.

"Getting attacked by this eagle up here."

"So goddamn random," says Joy.

"I love it," I say.

"I hate it," says Joy. "But so much that I love it?"

"I feel you."

Her hand has gone hot and moist in mine, so I switch to warm up the other one.

There's another table I can't quite understand, made of bare steel and full of gray pinwheels and tubes and what look like dead flowers. It stands in front of plain sealed blackout doors. Maybe it's some weird Korean thing I don't know about?

"Torture table," says Joy.

"Blood carnival game," I say.

"Traditional Korean meat bingo," says Joy.

"Self-serve acupuncture," I say.

And so on. We do this until our faces hurt from giggling.

Eventually we go sit at the kids' table. Andrew Kim, John Lim, and Ella Chang are already there. Our table must be too big, because there's a couple free chairs. We sprawl out and claim it in the name of the Limbos.

"Dude, there are like no non-Koreans here," says Andrew Kim. He's wearing a maroon prom tux, because every wedding has that guy. He throws an arm over one of the empty chairs and scans the room. "She's hot. She's hot."

"Please explain this whole thing you're doing," says Joy.

Andrew leans forward to explain. "Right now I'm *inhabiting my character*. I'm helping out with an indie thing up in LA. I play this super-shallow bro type, but who is secretly a kickass spy?"

"*But*?" says Joy.

"Yeah, how is that a *but*?" I say.

Andrew just looks at us.

Joy explains. "You're implying that a bro is diametrically opposed to a kickass spy."

"What she said," I say.

Andrew thinks, then comes up with his checkmate move. "I got eight hundred on the Writing section."

It's moronic banter, the kind Hanna would love, and suddenly I miss my big sister. I take a selfie in my suit and send it along with *Miss you*. Hanna of course probably won't write back until tomorrow or next week or whenever.

"You look like a princess," blurts John Lim to Ella Chang.

Ella Chang smiles, then sweetens it with a nose wrinkle. "You look like a magician."

"Wanna dance?"

"There's no music right now, John."

"When the music starts, that's what I meant," says John Lim.

I can't take any more, so I lean in to Joy. "Wanna ditch and pretend to smoke cigarettes?"

"Heck yeah," says Joy. "Just one rule: no talking about him."

She must mean Wu. "Oh no."

"Don't make me cry. My makeup." Joy dabs at her eyes with the tip of a napkin.

I'm about to ask what happened when a booming voice destroys the air around us.

"Okay, everyone, are you ready to shaking loose and party?" says the voice.

It's the DJ. He's got an accent. If he has an accent, and everyone here is Korean, why not just speak Korean?

My question is cut in half by a jet of white hissing from a hidden smoke machine. Beats rattle the century-old rivets in the ship's hull. Beams of rainbow light slice across the tables.

"Ladies and gentlemen of Kang-Chang wedding 2019, aboard such a beautiful Landworth classic steam cruise ship from days of yore, your new Mr. and Mrs. Kang!"

The music dips, only to drop a ten-megaton four-beat onto the trembling chinaware. A spotlight burns away at a tall heart-shaped sheet of glitter that rips open to reveal Kyung Hee and her new husband bursting through. Comets of tinsel eject everywhere. She's wearing a black flapper dress; he's wearing a canary zoot suit.

"Some kind of Gatsby thing?" I scream.

"What?" screams Joy.

"Everybody in the place / clap your hands and see

"what a heart full of joy / make it easy to be

"full of love and the things / that important to me

"feel so good deep inside / perfect time wed-ding," raps the DJ.

With that, the music lowers to a merciful level to allow the newlyweds to be led by a squirrelly coordinator in a headset from table to table, where they bow and thank the guests. Meanwhile, rivers of stone-faced waitstaff bring out plates of food. Exactly fifteen minutes later, they take the empty plates away.

The newlyweds arrive at our table.

"Heyyyy," say we Limbos.

"It's so cute seeing you guys all dressed up," says Kyung Hee. "Look at my little sis!"

Ella Chang wrinkles her nose—"Yay!"—then goes neutral again.

The groom says a bunch of stuff in Korean.

"Uh, we suck at Korean," says Andrew.

"I said there's booze over there and no one's carding," says the groom. His jawline could sharpen swords. He points right at me and Joy like a machine inspector and says a bunch more stuff in Korean to Kyung Hee. She says a bunch of Korean stuff back to him, and together they giggle and give us love-eyes. I don't need to ask what they said.

The newlyweds move on to the next table: another kids' table, with three boys and two girls sitting in mirror-image arrangement to ours like doppelgangers from an alternate dimension.

The super-Koreans.

They rise from their languor to greet the bride and groom. They bow in this hip, fluid manner that demonstrates how much they really own bowing. They toss perfect bangs and mumble in perfect Korean. And their perfectly disheveled clothes, I realize, are matching white outfits with matching black lapel carnations.

They look so put-together. I could be put-together too if I had *chosen the tribe*, to quote Q. Suddenly I feel a little shabby. Far from put-together. More like left-apart.

"Why are all the super-Koreans in Asian Death White?" I whisper to Joy.

"Maybe they're a K-pop group," Joy whispers back.

"Why not."

White is the color of oblivion in lots of Asia, not black like it is in America. Movies there fade to white. People think all-white cars look badass. I have a vintage Japan-only Asian Death White mini-disc player in my collection, and I think it looks badass.

The newlyweds vanish. The robotic waitstaff bring in another course of food. A timpani drumroll rumbles forth out of nowhere.

"And now, ladies and gentlemen, it's greetings from under the sea," says the DJ.

Kyung Hee appears in the spotlight in a tight green sequined dress and a wig of bright red hair. The groom looks like a pirate prince. The room applauds. I raise a hand and Joy claps it, like giving me a high five over and over again.

"So it's *Mermaid Romance*," I say.

"Why not," says Joy.

"And give a warm welcome to a very special presentation by friends of the groom," says the DJ.

The lights cut out. The super-Koreans spring to attention. I notice they're wearing Asian Death White headset mics—when did they get those?—and one of the girls emotes an impassioned speech in a spotlight while a soulful electric piano plays.

"What's she saying?" says Joy.

"Something about the sea being really deep—I can't catch it all," I say. My Korean is only barely better than hers, which isn't saying much.

A beat drops—this museum-quality late-nineties hip-hop jam—and the super-Koreans skip in time up to the dance floor, where they begin to perform a goddamn song.

"I was fucking joking when I said K-pop group," says Joy.

The super-Koreans begin to clap, and now everyone's clapping with them, and I start to get that classic Limbo feeling that I get whenever I'm surrounded by this much Korean-ness: that I am a failure at being Korean, and not doing so great at being American, so the only thing left to do is run away and hide in my own little private Planet Frank.

The super-Koreans now clap at us: *Come on, clap!*

"I did not sign up for this shit," I say.

"Fuck's sake," moans Joy. "For the sake of Saint Fuck."

"Let's go," I say.

We sneak away in the dark and leave the Limbos, who now clap along in a daze, and escape into the dusky air where the only sound is the muffled music coming from behind the windows and the pink noise panorama of the ocean's surround. The seagulls have gone quiet for the day. The sun hangs low and fat and orange.

We find a spot where no one can see us, lean on the rail, and watch the sunset. I pass Joy an invisible cigarette. She inhales, exhales, and passes it back to me.

"I needed this, I think," says Joy. "I needed to get out of my own head."

"Everything okay?"

Joy bumps my shoulder. "I'm chilly."

"It did get cold, didn't it," I say.

"That means give me your jacket, stupid."

Right, duh. I drape it over her shiny shoulders. It's a shame to cover up shoulders that shiny. She snuggles in, looks back at me with twin eyes ablaze, and says:

"Thanks, yubs."

I can only gaze at her. Behind us, the music thuds on. A word pops into my head:

if

if if if if

ifififififififififififif, until the word ceases to be a word and becomes a nonsense sound you make while thinking hard.

As in *if there were no Brit.*

What am I saying? There is Brit. We are together. I say it slow: *I. Love. Brit.*

But if there were no Brit, says a voice, *I would probably go after Joy.* It's true. I would.

This is news to me. I fold it up and put it away.

"So," says Joy, gearing up to tell me something. "About me and Wu."

"I thought we weren't supposed to talk about Wu."

"We officially broke up."

Joy tilts her head back to catch tears in her eyes like raindrops. "Here come the tears for real," she says. But there's no stopping it. A gray streak leaks from her mascara and extends down her temple.

"Listen. Wu? He's sweet. He's kind. But he never made me laugh. Not really. Not in that way where you're laughing but you have no idea why. Or where you laugh for so long you have to take a break just to rest. You wouldn't know because you're so stupid. Who makes me laugh, Frank? Tell me."

I swallow. My feet are leaving the ground. "You're gonna say *me*."

"Of course I'm gonna say *you*."

I look down and see her feet have left the ground, too.

That's never happened before.

It's always been my feet only, and no one else's.

"Well, I'm gonna say *you*, too," I say.

"Me too what?"

"You make me laugh," I say. "No one makes me laugh like you do."

"I know, Frank, that's the thing." Joy thumbs the corners of her eyes dry.

"And you're crazy," I say. "It's crazy how crazy you are."

"Because you make me crazy."

"I make you crazy?" I say.

"You make me insane," cries Joy. Then her voice shrinks. "Do I make you crazy?"

She's staring at me hard now, and I'm locked into her gaze. There are two tiny sunsets burning in those eyes of hers.

"Do I make you crazy?" she says again.

"Yes," I say finally. "You do."

Joy cradles my pinky in her palm. "Oh, Frank. Just listen to me and don't laugh. I got all dressed up today. I was so nervous. I was scared out of my mind. Because all I could think was, what if I got all dressed up, and what if it was all just for you, and it turned out you didn't love me back?"

The world zooms away to become a speck. We drift and drift until we find a lime-green nebula full of fragrant breathable air. The stars here are light as Christmas tree ornaments—the slightest touch and they sway slowly in this new atmosphere.

I try out the words. They are easy to say.

I love you, Joy.

I don't forget the *I*. I don't have to practice. I don't have to anything.

The words are there right on the tip of my tongue. They were always there.

I love you, Joy.

Joy Song, seven letters long.

"Don't be scared," I whisper. "Don't cry."

I wipe a tear on her face very carefully. I follow the gray streak of mascara and blend it with my thumb. I have to get in close to do this. I've never been this close before.

Our kiss stretches the nebula into a thin green laserline that spans whole systems. I hold her tight against me so our bodies almost fuse, crushed so hard that I pause out of worry—she lifts her ovalette face and breathes at me, *I'm fine, Frank, I am more than fine*—before kissing her again. I inhale all the scents of her secret world: the soap of her shower, the vanillin of lotion, the burnt perfume of the hot iron that ran through her hair just before tonight. She tastes like wedding food and lipstick wax and salty tears.

She tastes just like Joy.

We don't even notice that the wall we are standing behind is not a wall, but two plain blackout doors that have at some point opened to flood the air with pop music. We don't notice the DJ, who now says, "Ladies and gentlemen, in honor of

Kang-Chang wedding 2019, I am pleased to present sparkle lights!"

We don't see the table—the Korean meat bingo table—full of gray steel rods and other implements. They ignite and whirl. They're fireworks, and they're all going off at the same time in a blinding, buzzing fire hazard of a display.

Only once we are engulfed in gunsmoke do we notice what's just happened. The whole wedding party can see us in the brilliant shower of magnesium white. They were already clapping. Now they clap even harder. The super-Koreans see us, too. They're panting from having just finished their routine. They clap in our direction with arms weirdly stretched sideways.

They've willed the big moon of the spotlight to shine right on us, and now we stand in its crystalline light.

chapter 22

fire day

Monday comes.

Monday comes from the Old English *monandæg* and means *moon day*.

By the end of this moon day, I will have a black eye.

But let's back up first.

The wedding.

Oh, the wedding.

We danced. We sat at the table and ate. The bride and groom had two more costume changes: traditional Korean formal, then Celebrity Dance-Off.

The Limbos all took turns punching us. *You were faking that you were faking?* said Ella Chang. *You guys are so next-level,* said Andrew Kim.

I guess things change, said me and Joy.

John Lim had a drink too many, liquid courage gone wrong, and wound up crying with his head in Ella Chang's lap while she sat erect and stoic and unmoved.

Amore.

Ella heaved John's head upright and slapped him into composure. They're doing it right, Ella and John. They're keeping their thing a secret from the parents, who would only get all up in their business and start planning the next Chang wedding.

We hung out with the super-Koreans. They were really cool and friendly. They're no different from us Limbos, except that they're 100 percent fluent in both languages and can electric-slide effortlessly between cultures while being perfectly confident in identifying as Korean first, American second, and are basically better at everything than I could ever be, so fuck them.

Joy and I snuck away a few more times during the night like smokers needing one more hit. Her hands did indeed feel cold against my bare arm, and my bare chest, and around my bare waist. I knew what was happening was wrong. In the great ledger of love, it no doubt counted as cheating.

There was one song during the night, a fist-pumper of a dance track that had me and Joy and everyone hopping up and down right until the words *This could be the night / Wrong feels so right*. Me and Joy landed on our heels and just stared at each other: a quiet island of guilt at the center of a raging ocean.

For the late-night part of the wedding all the Olds got up to sing noraebang for the exhausted audience. Mom-n-Dad crooned out an old duet ballad—something about a baby in a boat and a snowy tree—and just for a second I could see them as a couple and not my parents. During their long final note I worried that Dad's injured lung would burst from the strain.

But it didn't. Everyone thundered with applause at his vocal heroism. Dad wasn't just okay—he sounded great. I clapped hard, too, and Joy kissed my cheek.

I had this weird feeling. Like I was a boy who had everything. Dad was okay. I was in love—unequivocally, uncontrollably in love. Cleaved to Joy for all the world to see. The super-Koreans nodded at us with hipster approval.

But.

As the party began to dissolve, I found my jacket abandoned on a chair and checked my phone. I knew what I would find there.

How's the party going?

Send pix if you can, dying to see you in action in that suit

Can't wait to hear all about it tomorrow

I love you, good night zzz

Brit.

Brit alone in her room on a silent Saturday night, checking her fartphone for messages from me. Not bored, for Brit finds the world too fascinating to ever truly get bored. Not upset, for Brit knows how weddings can be.

But she has no idea how this particular wedding was.

The reception party ended. Mom-n-Dad and Joy's mom-n-dad bowed and bowed in farewell. I gave Joy's hand one last squeeze, as if to say, *Goodbye, upside-down world. Time to bring it right side up again.*

While I drove my tipsy parents home—Mom nodding off, Dad again with his to-go cup from hell—I gritted my teeth and accepted the hard fact that in order to remain a good human being, I would have to tell Brit at school. Monday.

Moon day.

At Calculus, Brit mouths *I love you* over her desk. I don't have the black eye at this point. I smile a brittle smile, then pretend to get caught up in something Mr. Soft is saying. She doesn't notice a thing. Neither does Q or any of the other Apeys. I feel like I've traded one huge secret for another one the same size, different shape.

Me and Brit—me-n-Brit, Frankenbrit, oh god—split up for classes with a quick hug, and then it's back to AP Bio, AP English Lit, and CompSci Music. It all goes well. Everything goes well, as usual. Except for this bomb in my heart. I jump when the bell rings. I jump again when my phone buzzes.

Greenhouse, says Brit. *Now!*

And I walk the empty corridor with dread.

Outside, the light is orange and strange and tinged with a sour burning scent. I heard somewhere there's a wildfire happening close by. I can't possibly worry about wildfires right now.

When I round the corner, Brit ambushes me.

"Finally," she says, and kisses me so long and hard I have to brace myself against the side of the greenhouse.

"Did you miss me?" she says.

She feels different. She feels like I'm about to leave her. And I feel different. Like a liar. I've been a liar for some time now, and the only way out of this razor-blade briar patch I've created is to plow straight through.

"Yeah, so, listen," I say.

"Tell me all about this crazy Korean wedding," she says with an eager wiggle.

The green nebula. The kiss. The fireworks. Joy's cool fingertips.

"The wedding was . . . eventful," I mumble.

"Did anyone fall down on the dance floor?"

"No."

"Did anyone make any crazy last-minute speeches?"

"No."

Brit looks perplexed. "No strange wedding crashers?"

"It was on a boat, so no."

Brit holds my face as if checking for fever. "Are you okay?"

There's no fever, because I find I've somehow turned to stone.

Just say it, Frank.

"So, listen, Brit," I say. "I need to tell you something."

Brit continues to hold me for a moment as her face tightens. A gray flake of ash falls onto her eyelash; she blinks it away. She recoils in confused horror, as if my face has suddenly vanished. Her arms release. She hugs herself amid the gathering ash storm.

She must see something on my face, because all at once she looks ill. "Oh god."

"I'm sorry," I say, then cut short. Every word I can think to say sounds terrible.

Brit takes a step back and holds her fists at the ready. She breathes hard. The air sharpens like a blackened edge. Some invisible voice whispers into Brit's ear, and she looks at me like she has just learned the horrible solution to a long-ignored puzzle.

"It's Joy, isn't it," she says.

Wise, aware Brit, with her beautiful power to see things others can't—whether she wants to or not. My insides hang unmoored. I had been hoping to ease into this. No idea how, but still. Now there's no way but straight through. "Brit," I say. "Listen."

"We were just at the ice-cream museum," says Brit, recalling the evidence of past events. "She and Wu were together. We saw them. *We* were together."

I force myself to talk. "I can't explain it. I think I've liked her for longer than I realize." I'm not explaining things to her. I'm explaining them to myself.

Brit begins to plead. "But that's not fair. You love me. You love *me*."

"I'm so sorry." I'm about to vomit from nerves right now. I need to find words that make sense to Brit. "I have to be honest about what's in my heart. For better or worse. I can't help what's happening to me. And I'm sorry it has to hurt you."

Now Brit is tilting her head at me. "Is this because it's easier to be with someone Korean? Is this why you, why you, why you're dumping me right now?" Brit's eyes go full and glossy with tears.

"It is not any Korean thing," I say. "No."

"And I got your mom to like me," she says sadly. "I worked hard for that."

The sky is getting more and more orange, to the point where it is almost brown. We probably should go inside.

"She didn't know," I say, and instantly regret it. It's a slip. I'm wanting to explain to Brit that none of this is her fault, that I did in fact like her a lot, that she is an extraordinary person. But my tiny three-word slip threatens to turn into an avalanche.

"Wait—what?" says Brit.

"Nothing," I say. *Nothing?* Come on, Frank.

"What do you mean, she didn't know?"

Brit changes. She grows red. She smells different, like someone I don't know. She's clenching her fists.

"Frank, what do you mean, she didn't know?" She raises her voice. "Look at me, look at my eyes, and say it slowly and clearly."

I can't look at her. The words just dribble off my lips:

"I pretended to date Joy so I could go out with you in secret."

Brit barks a horrified laugh. She rips the long skinny flowers from the earth and clutches them.

"You hid me from your parents?" says Brit. "Like something to be ashamed of?"

"Brit, you don't know what it's like, being stuck between—"

"You two are like con artists," says Brit. The tears wash down her cheeks, and she examines me with a hard mixture of disgust and disappointment. Disaggustment. "I have no idea who you are. You two deserve each other."

She clutches her fist again and rends the poor flowers in two and flings them at my face. She doesn't punch me. This isn't where I get my black eye, not yet. She just sprints away and leaves a trail of sobs behind her.

In the distance I can see a jagged red fire line just cresting the hills.

• • •

Due to poor air quality, students are advised to go home early and stay indoors, say the announcement speakers. *The fire is 50 percent contained, and rain is expected tonight. We'll be sending out an email.*

The bell rings, and students disgorge into the hallway. Q finds me.

"Fire day!" he says, and holds up a high five. "*Pax Eterna* at my house, baby!"

I just look at him.

Q lowers his hand. "You okay?"

"No."

"What happened?"

"I just hurt someone real bad."

"What? Who?"

"Can I tell you in the car?"

Q checks my arms and head as if looking for damage. "Can you tell me now?"

"Q," I say. "We live in Southern California. It is our custom to hold all important conversations inside automobiles."

Q puts an arm around me and we walk slow, slower than we usually walk, like hospital patients doing a turn about the ward. Eventually we reach the school entrance.

From behind a column a tall, muscular prince with the eyes of a hawk sidesteps into our path.

Wu.

"This is for Joy," says Wu Tang, and punches my head.

That makes no sense, I want to say, but the crack of the ground on the back of my head stops me. I go down with even timing, like the crisp pop-krak of an electro backbeat. A speck of ash falls into my eye from above. Saying *This is for Joy* might not make sense, but the punch does. The punch makes perfect sense.

I just have to laugh.

"What the fuck," shouts Q. "Help!"

I turn to see Wu holding Q at bay. "You gotta let me do this, bro," says Wu, before turning back to me.

"Fuckin' steal my girl?" says Wu.

"No," I say, shielding my face. "Yes. I don't know."

"Fuckin' steal my girl?" says Wu.

"She stole me. We stole each other. I'm sorry, okay?"

"What the fuck is going on?" says Q.

"I thought we were buds, Frank Li," says Wu. "Then Brit comes up to me."

When I look up, I see that I'm the one who's hurt Wu, not the other way around.

Shit.

"I'm sorry," I say. "I'm really, truly sorry. I mean it."

Wu dismisses some dark thought with a flick of his cowlick hair. He straightens. Then he offers me his hand. He offers it like he's remembering protocol from some *Rulebook for Gentlemen*: *When a man is down, offer him a hand up.*

I take his hand and rise. My eye is already throbbing.

Wu takes a step back and examines me. "You disappoint me so bad, bro."

"I'm sorry."

"Nurse's office is down that way," says Wu to Q. "Take him there right now, get some ice on it."

"Uh," says Q.

"I can't tell you how sorry I am," I say.

"Just go," cries Wu, and turns his back to leave.

Wu walks with his fist cocked and raised, and one by one slams seven locker doors shut on his way out.

chapter 23

you eating melon

Traffic is hell—most of the roads heading into the hills are closed because of the brush fire—but Q and I hardly notice. We roll up the windows of the grumbling Consta, close the vents, and enjoy the AC. Three fire trucks go screaming by, whee-whee-whee.

We hardly notice because I'm busy telling Q everything, as instructed. I tell him:

- How the words *I love you* never quite traveled the air right toward Brit
- How I often found myself thinking of Joy first thing in the morning
- How such signs are now obvious in hindsight
- How the stupid touristy Landworth ship will forever mark the most romantic night of my short life so far

- How this black eye is really a passport stamp on
  my face, finally letting me out of the purgatory
  of Love Customs and into the welcoming area of
  Gate J Arrivals (the *J* stands for *Joy*)

"Your metaphors are giving me the pre-puke drools," says
Q. "Please don't ever try to become a writer."

"I think I've been through a lot."

Q smiles at me. "Now that I know the whole story, you
clearly deserve that eye. But Joy feels right. I'm happy for you."

Q puts the car into Park to give me a side-hug. Someone
honks at us from behind.

"Eat my butt cheek," shouts Q to the rearview mirror.

We get to Q's, crunch the white gravel path to his Byzan-
tine double front doors, and are greeted with howls of worry
and concern from his mom.

"It was a tetherball accident," I say.

"You need to stop taking tetherball so seriously," says Q's
mom.

"Tetherball is not a sport," says Q's dad, with a pair of
glasses atop his head, another pair on his face, and another
around his neck. "But that does not mean it's harmless."

We eat—this incredible osso buco—forget to clear our
dishes, and run upstairs so Q can show me this *Pax Eterna*
game everyone's talking about.

"Poor Brit's gotta be heartbroken," says Q while the game
loads. "But the heart wants what it wants."

"I hate myself for hurting Brit," I say. "But I had to be honest with myself."

"I'm really, terribly, awfully happy for you, old bean," says Q.

"It would've been worse to string Brit along, right?"

The game is ready. But Q can't seem to shake a nagging thought. "You didn't choose the tribe, did you?"

"That's a valid question. But no way." I switch hands to hold my ice bag. But now I find myself wondering:

Did I fall in love with Joy because we have more in common?

A favorite book of mine, the sci-fi comedy classic *Hitchhiker's Guide to the Galaxy*, says the secret to flying is simply to fall toward the ground without actually hitting it. The way you do this to forget the fact that you're falling, even as you're falling.

I love Joy because she is smart. Because she is ambitious, and a huge nerd endlessly fascinated by the built world around her. I love Joy because we go way back to when we were kids, and that counts for more than I realize. I love Joy because she is gorgeous.

But that's the obvious stuff. At the core, I love Joy because she makes me laugh. A girl who can make you laugh is worth laughing with forever. And you know what? I love Joy because I make her laugh, too. When I'm with her, I become totally unself-conscious. I no longer think about who I am, or where I am, or when. I am simply present with Joy. I forget about the ground, and miss.

"I chose Joy," I say. "Fuck the tribe."

Q nods, impressed.

"Joy is my tribe," I say.

Q nods.

"And so are you," I say.

It's like Q was waiting for me to say that, and he breaks into a big shy smile. We smile together for a long moment like this. Senior year is almost halfway over. Then it's graduation. After that, college. In the meantime, I will see Joy as much as I can. But I will not neglect Q, either.

Twin sister Evon comes in, scans my face with a sexy cyborg gaze. "Tetherball, huh."

I shrug.

"Do you have a phone charger I could borrow?" says Evon.

"Don't you already have like seven of my chargers?" I say.

Evon snatches a Citrus-Spin™ orange charger from my bag and darts away into the magical deer forest where she dwells.

"Look how incredible this is," Q says, turning my attention toward his huge screen. He scrolls through lists and lists of little maps, all marked with red Xs and the word FAILED.

"No one has won a game of *Pax Eterna*, not me and Paul Olmo, no one."

I lean forward. "Huh?"

"So, in *Pax Eterna* each time you start a new game, you get this pristine tropical island with everything you could possibly need, all there and ready," says Q. He moves his God-hand cursor to give me a rapid-fire tour. "Ore, water, fertile lands, blablabla."

I squint at dozens of tiny black skull icons. "Are these dead bodies?"

Q strokes a pretend beard. "My god, it's happening all over again."

"How do you win?" I say.

"The way to win *Pax Eterna* is to build—and hold—a successful, stable society for a full month. There's a twenty-thousand-dollar jackpot prize. No one's done it yet."

I examine data in a sidebar. "So they've made a game out of the biggest human challenge ever. World peace."

"Here's the thing," says Q. "Anyone can join any *Pax Eterna* game in progress. So in me and Paul's island here, there's only two factions, but already they've started killing each other. And it's only been a couple hours."

"Jesus," I say. "No one's ever gonna win that jackpot. Just like no one's figured out world peace."

"It's the mystery of the ages," says Q, lost in the screen.

"The only winning move is not to play," I say, quoting one of my favorite movies ever. I have no idea how this applies, but I toss it out there just to see how Q will react.

Q clutches his head as if it's gonna burst. "Not to play," he says. "I gotta call Paul. Thank you, Frank Li!"

• • •

When I get home, I give Mom the same excuse—tetherball gone wild—and beg off her insistent offers to boil up some Chinese herbal medicine (hanyak, pronounced hawn-yawk) to speed the healing. That stuff is a blood-brown suicide drink of pickle juice and coffee and silt and pure fear.

Mercifully my phone buzzes—a video call from Joy—and I make my escape.

"Hey," I say.

"Oh my god what the fuck did Wu do I'm gonna run him

251

over with my car three times to make sure he's dead," shouts Joy.

Video call. Joy can see my face. Aha.

"Don't," I say over the screaming. "Don't run Wu over."

"I'm gonna re-kill him," says Joy, "after I kill him."

"Just—just—" I say, and an idea comes to me. "Just come over."

This stops Joy.

I see her face change. She gets it.

Just come over.

Because now she can finally go to the house of her official, certified boyfriend as an official, certified girlfriend.

And when she does come over, my god, when Joy Song does indeed show up at my doorstep in her sweatpants and her too-big Carnegie Mellon University sweatshirt and her hair done up in a spiky, sloppy bun, my heart beats two beats faster.

She bows to Mom and says *annyong haseyo* in her shitty Korean.

She holds my head. She kisses my eye. In front of Mom and everything.

"Ow," I say, but with wonder, like a boy who's just hit his head on the ornate ceiling of heaven.

"Aigu," says Mom at the sight of the kiss. "Make germs."

But Mom's smiling, too.

And then—and *then*—we go *upstairs*. To my *room*.

Alone.

Just like they do in the movies.

"I cutting melon," says Mom, and vanishes. *I cutting*

252

melon means *I'll give you a few minutes alone together, but because I'm your mother and this is my damn house, I will bring you a snack as a pretense to make sure you're not up there having sex.*

When we get up there, we of course don't shut the door—so not quite like the movies, but close—and find a spot out of sight to attack each other with kisses.

"Get in as many as you can," Joy breathes into my ear.

"Stolen moments," I breathe back.

Joy has a tiny brown mole on the back of her perfect neck, and I love it to death.

"Melon," says Mom.

When Mom enters, all she sees is me and Joy sitting quiet and neat as can be on separate chairs, like we were waiting this whole time.

She sets the tray of melon wedges before us, first apologizing that they're not that sweet, melons weren't on sale, etc. That's just host humility talking. But I see she's used the nice cocktail forks, the ones with the tiny peach birthing two microscopic doves and the word JUST. I hold one up to let Mom know I appreciate her enthusiasm and approval.

Joy bunches her shoulders and says, "Jal meokgesseumnida," which translates dorkily to *I'm gonna eat well* but really just means *thank you* as a form of mealtime grace. Anyway, Mom eats it up. I want to jab Joy in the ribs and tell her, *We don't have to pretend anymore.*

But then I realize Joy's not pretending. She's just being nice.

She's just being.

Mom leaves us again. She'll of course be back soon to pick up the tray. But until then, Joy and I are alone. I eat melon. Joy eats melon. We stare at each other.

"Do you think Brit's doing okay?" says Joy.

I hang my head a centimeter. "Probably not."

"Are you doing okay?"

"Better," I say, "now that everything's out in the open. You think Wu's okay?"

"Ask your face," says Joy.

We stare at each other some more.

"Life is funny," I say.

Joy scoots an inch closer. "What is?"

"I think I probably liked you for longer than I realize," I say. "But I unconsciously nixed you as a possibility from the start, because I was paranoid about our parents trying to micromanage us. Because that's what old-skool Korean parents do when families, you know, merge."

"You think we would've started dating sooner, if it wasn't for them?"

"Maybe," I say, and scoot closer. "But whatever. We're here now."

Joy smiles. "I feel like we made it through some weird test."

"We did," I say. And indeed, I can feel it: a relief, a lightness slowly dawning among the dark clouds of guilt.

I run my hand through her hair and examine the green hiding there. I've always wanted to do this. And now I can.

"You know," says Joy, "I've always thought you were cute from when we were little."

This blows my mind. "I think you're hot," I say.

"Shut up," says Joy. She scoots in close. She pins my arm down with one hand and feels my biceps with the other. "Make a muscle," she says.

So I do. Joy's hand dives into my shirt and begins roaming around my chest, my back. Her hand is cold and thrilling. It reaches up to cool the back of my neck.

"Keep making a muscle," says Joy, and kisses me with her melon-sweet tongue.

No way can I keep making a muscle. I dive into her shirt as well. My hand is hot and stutters along her skin. This sweatshirt is much too big for her. I discover the clasp of her bra.

But then I hear the front door scrape open downstairs. We both freeze.

"Frankie-ya!" calls Mom. "Daddy home!"

Dad's home? It's only seven. Dad doesn't get home for another two hours.

Joy and I creep to the top of the stairs, where we greet Dad with a loud "Hi."

"Oh," says Dad, bewildered. He looks tired. He looks like he just survived a long hike. "Joy here? Hi, Joy."

"Hi, Mr. Li," says Joy.

"You're home early," I say.

"Few customer today," says Dad. "Fire making whole of sky smoky. Everybody staying home."

I'm puzzled. Mom-n-Dad work at The Store every day, from morning to evening, on weekends, holidays, New Year's Day, 365 days out of every year without a single vacation for as long as me and Hanna have been alive, even on slow days.

Dad manages a smile. "Nice see you, Joy."

"Nice to see you too," says Joy. She's quietly bursting. Am I, too?

Because here we are.

It wasn't pretty along the way, but here we are.

"You eating melon," says Dad, and laughs brightly through his fatigue. His eyes linger on us for a moment—his son and his girlfriend, both of the tribe—just long enough to feel like pride. And say what you will, but things are already easier this way. It feels like a guilty pleasure. It feels like a cheat code.

My girlfriend of the tribe.

Mom-n-Dad walk away. If I remain still, I can manage to hear them. At first the Korean is simple enough for me to understand.

> MOM: *Did it take a long time?*
>
> DAD: *No.*
>
> MOM: *Did it hurt?*
>
> DAD: *A little. I'm okay.*

Then the Korean gets too advanced and is cut short with a latch of a door.

"Did what hurt?" I whisper.

"Probably his chest wound," says Joy.

"Man, it keeps hitting me that Dad got shot," I say. "That actually happened."

"Everything's okay now," says Joy.

Joy holds me. I hold her back. We are both carrying and being carried at the same time, in a hug that defies gravity.

chapter 24

the same school

The next few weeks before winter break are an ontological free-for-all. It's like someone accidentally bumped the settings of reality, fumbled to fix them, and wound up only making things worse. Up becomes down, light becomes dark, the water in the toilet bowl starts spinning the other way from usual. Counterclockwise? Clockwise?

I forget.

Calculus becomes boss-level awkward as Brit stonewalls me. Mr. Soft chops away at his nominators and denominators. But the Apeys can feel that me and Brit are no longer together. Worse, they can sense I was the one who did the leaving.

For a few days, Brit wears long baggy clothes, then tight clothes, all black, all white. She shockingly cuts her hair almost entirely into a bob that, it turns out, looks pretty damn good on her. It's like she's trying on different Brits to see which one is real. I want to hug her. I want to tell her she's beautiful and she will find the right boy, that it just wasn't me. She's right there, after all. But I can't reach out to her. I would never dare intrude.

Meanwhile, me and Joy keep our own relationship on the down low. Neither of us want to hurt Brit or Wu. Or deal with questions from friends. They know me and Joy are now Frankenjoy, but we keep ourselves out of sight and hopefully also out of mind.

We can't bear to hide on the roof or behind the greenhouse— too many associations—but we do manage to discover a beautifully awkward bit of space formed between the old brick school, its newer concrete wing, and a cluster of tall AC units grinding away in the heat, loud enough to mask any sound. It is a literal slice of heaven.

On weekends we see movies, hit the taco trucks (*Cheese Barrel Grille never again,* said Joy), or hang out at Joy's house and snuggle up by the quartz fire table glittering poolside as the sun sets on the Playa Mesa peninsula.

Openly. With her parents around.

Her parents like me. I think. They're too formal to really tell.

No one wins a game of *Pax Eterna.* The jackpot remains untouched.

Q remains single. His object of affection still a mystery.

I see Brit in the hallway, and papers spill out of her binder as I pass.

I catch eyes with Wu, and he misses an easy free throw on the yard.

I feel a little like a poltergeist leaving chaos in my wake.

The college applications either already have flown off or are gassed up and on deck. Already I'm dreading the months of March and April. That is supposedly when the bulk of responses will come in. I've heard stories of soul-crushing displays of elation on the feeds by friends, and friends of friends, and people you don't even know. So-and-so got into your dream school, but you didn't! Give their post a big smiley, why don't you?

To hell with that kind of trauma. I've already tried brokering a protocol for Social Media Silence for the spring months among the Apeys and the Limbos, but people looked at me like I was a time traveler from the 1800s. So I instead did the next best thing: brokered a protocol with the two most important people in my world, Joy and Q.

We opted for snail mail notifications.

We instructed our parents to hide any and all mail from our eyes.

As a final precaution, we set up email filters to quarantine any errant messages from schools. We did that part together at Cafe Adagio, our laptops arranged in triangle formation, a sort of nerdy blood pact: we do this whole college thing together.

We have the same agreement for test-related emails. Emails like this one, just now:

Dear Test-Taker,
Thank you for taking the SAT on December 1, 2019!
We are pleased to inform you your test scores are

I don't read the rest. I take out my fartphone.

Don't click the link yet, I say to both Joy and Q.

Wat link, says Joy.

OMC THAT link, says Joy. The *C* stands for *Cthulhu.*

Rendezvous at the Consta asap, I say. *We shall click together!*

But it's only third period, says Q.

I guess we should wait then, I say.

Shut up, says Q.

As soon as the bell rings, we all speed-walk from our re-spective classes straight to the Consta in the parking lot. Once we hit the streets, I let the engine zoom.

Q closes his eyes and chants, "Sixteen, sixteen, sixteen." He means a perfect score of 1600.

Cafe Adagio is near Peninsula College. Cafe Adagio feels cool. The baristas move slow and don't care if you sit there all day. Flyers and posters cover every inch of the walls. It's full of students hunched over stickered laptops, no doubt doing beautiful things: writing poetry, modeling physics, composing symphonies. I look at them, and it hits me: I'm going to be one of these college students soon, forging my own path beyond the boundaries of the textbook. Some are intense with focus, others frustrated, others lost in their own creative dreams. They're putting in time for the long game, because they know it'll be worth it in the end, and I admire them for it.

The Cafe Adagio password today is *straightUpGrindin.*

I buy drinks from the alarmingly hip and beautiful male barista. Tea for me and Q, coffee for Joy. Coffee is disgusting, no matter how much milk and sugar you cut it with. Before I can even sit, Joy grabs my hand and forces me to fingerprint in to my laptop.

"Ready?" says Q. "Click on the count of three."

"One," I say.

"Fifteen sixty," cries Joy. "Oh my god I got fifteen sixty."

I rush to kiss her, then see my screen has updated, too. "Fifteen forty," I yell.

We both look at Q, who has become an amazed zombie. I turn his laptop.

"Sixteen," I say. "You got sixteen, old bean."

I stand. "People of the college! This fine fellow right here just achieved a perfect score on the SAT!"

The students applaud—*pat-a-cake, pat-a-cake, baker's man*—then put their headphones back on and resume their work.

"I did it," says Q, very quietly.

"We did it," I say, and high-five both Joy and Q. Q high-fives me and Joy, and Joy high-fives Q and me, and after a while we have to use both hands to keep up.

"We can go anywhere," says Q, still staring at his screen.

"I bet I could even get into Stanford," I wonder aloud. I look at Q. "We could go to the same school."

"Pittsburgh, I'm coming at ya," says Joy.

This stops me. Joy and I, Frankenjoy, are finite.

"Does CMU have a computer music program?" I say. I place my hand atop hers.

261

"Frank," says Joy. She places a hand atop mine atop hers.

"I'm just wondering," I say, and complete the double-decker hand sandwich.

"You need to go where you need to go," says Joy. "We all do."

"It's just kinda dawning on me," I say. "I'm having a hard time imagining it."

"Everything looks different already," says Q. "Goodbye, cup. Farewell, napkins."

"Until it's time to go, we have each other," says Joy. She fondles my earlobe.

The barista appears at our table and sets a slice of pound cake in front of Q. "On the house, Mr. Perfect Score," he says, and leaves with a flip of his long black bangs.

My phone buzzes with a calendar alert. "Oh, hey, it's free museum night up in LA. This exhibit called *The Edible Wunderkammer: Snack Food Curiosities from Thirty Countries.* Let's go."

Joy slams her laptop shut and bolts up. "We leave now, we can beat the traffic."

I get up too, but Q remains. "You guys go ahead," he says.

"You're not coming?" I say.

"Go and have a *date*, you know?" says Q. "Have the best date you possibly can."

I hug his head. "What are you gonna do?"

"Eat my free cake," says Q. "But first I might just want to sit with it for a while."

"Just sit," I say, nodding.

"I did it, Frank," says Q. "I did it."

We get in the car. The messages are rolling in. Paul Olmo scored 1480. Amelie Shim got the exact same. Naima Gupta scored a decent 1390, but there's one final round, and I'm sure she'll break 1400 like she wanted to. As for the Limbos, John Lim, Ella Chang, and Andrew Kim all scored in the high fourteens or low fifteens. Excellent all around. The world feels like it's accelerating on its axis.

I hear Brit Means scored 1540, same as me. Should I text her congratulations? I want to. But I probably shouldn't. I probably have no right.

Whatever. *1540, same as me, major congrats!* I say.

After a long pause, Brit replies. *Congrats to you too, amazing*

I want to point out that she used *amazing*, but don't.

I guide the lugubrious Consta on to the freeway, where it propels us northward. Joy takes care of the parental management protocols on both our phones while I drive: *Headed to LA* and *Might be home late* and blablabla. Mom-n-Dad write back, *Have a fun.* Joy's more fluent, better-educated parents write *Have a great time.*

It's funny. To the parents, nothing has changed. My drama with Brit and Joy's drama with Wu have been invisible to them. To the parents, Joy and I started dating one night at a Gathering and have been together without a hitch ever since. We swapped the gems out, then swapped them right back. And no one was the wiser.

"Can I just say again how nice it is not having to fake-date anymore?" I say.

Joy leans over to kiss my cheek, my ear, my neck, and it is hands-down-at-ten-and-two the most erotic thing that has ever happened to me in the Consta or anywhere else.

We reach downtown Los Angeles in record time. But there's a road closure, then another, then another. When Joy checks the map, it's full of angry red lines.

"Crap," she says. "There's some kind of festival going on. It says another hour just to get around it."

I refuse to let this bring me down—I'm in too good a mood. "Let's roll with it, then," I say. "To the festival?"

"To the festival," says Joy, like *Why not?*

We get out of the car, skip like idiots on the sidewalk for a quarter mile, and reach the packed festival entrance thumping with music.

46TH ANNUAL
LOS ANGELES KOREAN WINTER STREET FESTIVAL
PRESENTED BY
AJU ELECTRONICS NORTH AMERICA

We stare agog at the throngs of people. K-pop pounds from towering black steles of speakers. Streamers crisscross the venue. On a rainbow-lit stage, little kids in white doboks warm up for an ultra-cute hapkido demonstration. Dancers in traditional dress float among the crowd, twirling ribbons affixed to their hats in long flowing swirls.

And the food. There's barbecue, sure, kimchi, sure, but then there's all the other stuff that most people never get to see— fiery red tteokbokki rice cakes, perfect pyramids of kimbap seaweed rice, patbingsu shaved ice with sweet rice bean, even mountains of freshly roasted beondegi.

Joy points at the beondegi stall. "You eat it," she says.

"You eat it," I say.

Beondegi are silkworm pupae. The stall owner beckons me in Korean, and I ask for a sample in English. It's not bad— nutty, mushroomy, and with a fantastic crunch—and I imme- diately kiss Joy to let her taste it, too.

"Ew," she says, licks her teeth in contemplation, then orders a paper-coneful.

We stroll along, and we stroll along, and there's a samul- nori percussion quartet banging out a frenzied brass whirl- wind of beats, with one crazy old man dancing along and twin toddler girls holding their ears shut. I record it with my Tascam—these rhythms remade with electronic instruments would be a sick kind of mash-up.

We hop up and down. Joy's hair flashes green and black, green and black. Above us garlands of cafe lights sparkle to life against a cool velvet sky. I guess the sun set without telling us.

Farther along is another little stage, fancier than the first, with an ensemble of samgo-mu dancers performing in ornate individual stalls lined with traditional barrel drums. They're all women, all impeccably dressed in shimmering hanbok, all with deadly perfect timing as they strike drums to the left, right, and before them in unison with their sticks. At one point they bend way, way back and whack out a crescendo of unrelenting eighth notes on the booming drum skin, then the cracking rim, then back.

"Abs of steel," yells Joy.

She kisses me as the drums thunder louder and louder to completion. Applause erupts. There is something happening here inside me. I look at Joy and can tell she can feel it too. The lights, the music, this great celebration of a culture that we supposedly belong to. Everyone here, looking like we do. The food, the drums, the kids in their white doboks. One of them looks like me when I was little.

Me and Joy grew up exposed to this world. We know all of its elements, even if we don't always know their names in Korean. They're not weird or exotic to us. They have the feeling of home.

If not for the skyline of Los Angeles in the background, I can fool myself into thinking I'm in Korea. Even better: I can fool myself into thinking that *I am Korean*.

Me and Joy move forth, skipping like idiots.

Joy stops in her tracks. She slowly points to a delicately fluttering pink-and-white booth decorated with hundreds of tiny soft pillows, each the size of a baby's cheek.

"It's those sweet rice cake thingies," moans Joy.

Some of the cakes are plain; some are filled with sweet red bean paste, some with powdered sesame. The more exotic ones here have mango frosting and even chocolate.

I rack my brain for the word. *Chalttok*. Pretty sure these cakes are called chalttok.

Behind the booth smiles a gentle old woman in a simple country hanbok looking like she just stepped out of a fragile scroll painting.

"I want that sesame one," says Joy, transfixed like a child with desire.

I begin working up an ember of courage. Because suddenly I find myself having this urge to order in Korean for my girl.

The food, the drums, the little kids in their white doboks.

I point and say, "I chalttok dugae jeom juseyo." Two of these cakes, please.

The old woman's smile fades to a flat line, then darkens to a scowl. She starts barking at me with the black crescent of her mouth. I can catch most of her words.

"Chalttok?" says the old woman. "I don't know what this chalttok is. Maybe you should learn to speak Korean right."

The food vanishes, the drums go mute, the white doboks collapse, suddenly empty of their children.

I got *chalttok* wrong. It's *chaltteok*. The difference is small, like *cheese* versus *jeez*. But a person would never ask for extra *jeez* on their pizza.

A native person.

"You fucking kyopos are all stupid," says the old woman. It's like she's deliberately using basic Korean to make sure I understand every word.

Kyopo is what they call a Korean person living abroad. I don't know who *they* is. I don't seem to know anything right at this moment. Except for the fact that my feet are leaving the ground again. You already know how they do that at moments like these. It is an alarming feeling, but also comforting, and I know that makes no sense.

"What is going on?" says Joy. "What did she just say?"

I look around. The K-pop pounding out of those speakers? Indecipherable. All this signage? Gibberish. The people? They look like me, but I know it is all some kind of elaborate visual trick. I could pass a hand right through them as though they were phantoms.

I fooled myself into believing I belonged. My brainlock is the best brainlock.

"Let's go," I say.

I pull her toward the festival exit and the gray, drab world beyond. I want to vanish like a ghost and pretend me and Joy never stumbled upon this place.

"Hey," shouts a male voice. "Wait up."

A hand touches my shoulder, and I turn. A young man, just a little older than me. He looks like me, knits his brows like me, frowns like me. Unlike me he wears a blue LA hat and a tank shirt and has muscular arms inscribed with fine geometric tattoos.

He offers me a fancy clear sealed bag containing four sesame rice cakes. I can't bring myself to call them *chaltteok* right now. *Rice cakes* they will be.

"Dude, I'm so fucking goddamn sorry my grandma was such a dick to you just now," he says. "Bitch can be such a bitch-ass, salty-ass bitch sometimes."

This outpouring of heartfelt profanity fills my soul with warm orange light. It also cracks me up. I look at Joy: she's covered her mouth to hold the chuckles in.

"That was your grandma?" says Joy.

"She calls me stupid all the time because my Korean fuckin' sucks."

I blink. My parents have their problems, but at least they've never called me stupid for not knowing Korean.

The guy jiggles the bag. "Take 'em. My way of saying sorry."

He's earnest, this guy. He really wants me to take the bag. So I take the bag.

"We'll save these for dessert, I guess," I say with a shrug. "Thanks."

The guy gets an eager look in his eye. "Wait, you haven't had dinner yet?"

"Uh," says Joy.

"Follow me," says the guy. When he sees our hesitation, he stomps his foot and waves hard like he's performing a *party-people-get-down* move on stage. "Come on, babo saekkidul," he says with a happy twinkle.

"He just called us stupid fuckers," says Joy.

"I like this guy," I say. "Let's go."

He skates through the stalls and people, and me and Joy tap-dance single file to keep up with his nimble fat white sneakers. We pass the samulnori quartet, then a stage thundering with K-pop dancers, until we reach the far end of the festival grounds.

It's not as fancy here. Just a ring of parked food trucks and folding tables filled with diners. This crazy corrido-cum-trap-beat mash-up vibrates the air with the steady tempo of a gangster stroll, overlaid with mouthy rap in both Korean and English. I've never heard shit like I'm hearing right now. It is sublime. I capture it all with my Tascam.

In doing so, I capture the guy's name, too.

"I'm Roy Chang," says Roy Chang, "and this is my whip right here."

He gestures toward a red food truck emblazoned with the words ALL DAE EVERY DAY. The *dae* means *big*, and there's a five-foot-tall 大 character in case you don't get the pun.

Roy spots my Tascam. "You a musician?"

I nod sheepishly.

"Enrique's a music nerd too," says Roy. "I'll introduce you."

Roy pounds the truck. "Hey, yo, two express VIP orders, kimchi quesadilla hana, jidori gochujang chicken and waffles hana, tres cervezas, por favor!"

"Al gesseo," says Enrique, as in *roger that*.

Roy seats us at a table, and the food follows in a flash.

"What's in this?" I say, intrigued.

"Just eat, don't think," says Roy.

So we do. And once I start eating, I simply cannot stop. It is a perfect mix of all the comforts of my life: the kimchi of home, with the cheese and tortillas and pickled cactus I love from being a Californian, and finally waffles, because waffles.

"Gnughngh," say me and Joy.

"They like it," says Roy to Enrique, who's come over to watch us gorge ourselves.

Enrique jabs a thumb at Roy. "They call this guy the future of American cuisine, ha."

"How the fuck can I be the future if I'm already here and I'm already a grown-ass American?" says Roy.

Enrique asks to have a listen to my music—including "Song for Brit"—and he likes it so much that he gives me his email address so we can keep in touch. I give both him and Roy my email address too, without hesitation. Because I have this strange feeling that we've already somehow met, and it's like we all graduated from the same school.

We finish up our food, drink our beers. We get up.

"Can we grab your seat if you're leaving?" says a voice.

I turn. It's me again, another guy who looks like me, except now way older: crow's-feet at the eyes, receding hairline. He's with his wife, who is black. Standing between them is their daughter, who looks about seven. She's dressed like an elf.

"Absolutely," I say.

"Your daughter's so freaking beautiful," says Joy.

"Say thank you, baby," says the wife. They all seem used to such compliments.

"Thank you baby," sings the daughter.

I want to give the family my email address, too. But that would be weird, and so me and Joy bid farewell to Roy and Enrique and stroll away slow.

I take out my phone and start typing.

"Who are you texting?" says Joy.

I show her: *I miss you, big sister Hanna.*

Joy smiles and touches Send. And right away, Hanna's reply appears on the screen.

Miss you too Frankie

chapter 25

the best fart

It's late. The freeway is a blank ribbon for us to travel upon. Orange streetlamps zip overhead like the sun rising and setting in looping time lapse.

We're both quiet. Just processing the evening.

When we near Playa Mesa, Joy touches my hand.

"I don't want to go home yet," she says.

"Okay," I instantly say. It's eleven thirty. I want to watch the sun rise with Joy. Then I want to watch the sun set with Joy. Over and over.

She takes my phone and engages the parental management protocols, and once we receive the *Have a fun* confirmation, I guide the recalcitrant Consta to the one place I know we can be alone and free and private.

Westchester Mall, the biggest mall in Orange County, Southern California.

The parking lot is dead as a lava flow. I drive straight across acres of painted white herringbone and park right up front. We walk up the grand entrance ramp and enter.

It's empty inside. All the luxury stores, shuttered. The notes of the world's tiniest sonata drift down like dust from the top of the track-lit cavern. I love coming here because it makes me feel like I'm the last person on the planet, and ever since I was little, I've had a fantasy of being the last person on the planet.

I murmur this quietly to Joy, because this space around us feels holy and deserving of a soft voice.

Joy holds my hand and matches my step. "That sounds like it would be terrifying."

"Oh, it would only be for like a year," I say. "Like a temporary pause."

"And then what?"

"And then one morning I would wake up and unpause, and everything would pick up right where it left off."

"I guess that might be fun for a year," says Joy, biting a dry spot on her lip. "A planet-pause. Although I'd be afraid of going insane."

We pass by a great funnel carved from wood with two slots to accept coins, with the sign DONATE FOR SCHOOL SUPPLIES IN OUR DISTRICT: WATCH YOUR COINS SPIN AND SPIN!

"I think tonight I realized why I've always had that fantasy," I say.

Joy does this move I like, where she releases my hand, slides her hand up my arm, squeezes once, then drops her hand back into mine again: catch.

"Okay, little boy Frankie, why?" says Joy.

I think about that mean old grandma, and Roy, and the food trucks.

"Because then I could just be whoever I wanted, and no one would be around to judge me."

Joy smiles to our strolling feet. "That old woman was psycho, wasn't she."

We pass the food court. There's Pretzel Wrestle, still wafting yeast and butter. There's the shitty Italian place, shitty Asian fusion place, shitty Tex-Mex place, then three hamburger joints. A one-stop microcosm of mainstream white American cuisine.

"I feel really myself when I'm with you," I say. "I think that's why I wanted to come here."

"To see us totally out of context?" says Joy.

I smile. Joy gets it. She gets all of it. "Come here."

We kiss. To my surprise, she grabs my ass with both hands.

"I can't believe I get to do this with you out in the open," she says. "Great idea to come here, Frank Li."

In the distance I hear a short radio squawk. Joy's head bolts up.

"What was that?" she says.

"Probably Camille or Oscar," I say, meaning the security guards.

"Should we go?" says Joy.

"No, they walk super slow and chitchat nonstop. Let's stay as long as we can—come on."

I lead Joy around a corner and head down a long dogleg

toward the Nordstrom anchor store. Once we're out of any possible line of sight, I slow down to our usual stroll.

We kiss and kiss. We kiss each other *while walking*. There's no one around but us. We're on planet-pause in our little abandoned paradise.

I lead Joy to a fountain in the Crystal Atrium. It is a low polished structure formed from simple modernist angles, surrounded by a stone ledge the color of chocolate.

"So much for Lake Girlfriend," I mutter.

"What's Lake Girlfriend?" says Joy.

FOUNTAIN CLOSED FOR MAINTENANCE:
DO NOT CLIMB

The fountain is drained of water, revealing a dusty calcified lake bed full of mesh and hoses and stained light fixtures.

It's also full of coins.

Joy's eyes are still twinkling. "Dude, there's like a hundred bucks in there."

"Dude," I say.

Then I get an idea.

I jump into the fountain and begin collecting coins, using the front of my tee shirt like a basket as I squat.

"Come help me," I say.

"You're insane," says Joy.

But she jumps into the fountain, too, and begins collecting coins alongside me. I bump her, almost spilling her take. She bumps me back. In a few minutes, we stand with our tee shirt bellies full of hundreds of coins, like grinning mutant marsupials.

There's a radio squawk in the distance, followed by a shout.

"Hey!" says a voice.

"This way," I say. Me and Joy step out of the fountain and run like hobbits with legs akimbo back up the length of the dogleg.

As we scamper along, Joy looks at me with realization. "I know what we're doing!" she cries.

And she does, because she's the first one to reach the great donation funnel carved out of wood. It must be six feet in diameter. We kneel at opposite ends, dump our tee shirt payloads onto the floor, and each hold our first coin in the slide slot.

"On three," I say.

"One," says Joy.

"Two," I say.

"Three."

We release. The two coins dance around in perfect graceful arcs until they reach the funnel bottom, where they accelerate in gravity-defying horizontal circles of perfect centripetal force. Finally they plink-plink into the treasure abyss below.

"Those two are me and you," I say.

"You're so cheesy," says Joy. But I can tell she loves it.

"More coins," says Joy.

"Faster," I say.

We slot in coin after coin, and soon the wooden funnel thunders with a metallic wind. I pause to record a good length of it with my Tascam. It sounds like an endless flock of fighter jets soaring just overhead.

WATCH YOUR COINS SPIN AND SPIN!

It only takes us about ten minutes to get through all the coins. Sometimes the coins reach the bottom without collision; sometimes they clash and cause a big sloppy avalanche. It's both exhilarating and meditative. We don't try to engineer either conflict or harmony by fine-tuning a precise rhythm or using matching denominations or anything like that. All we do is keep slotting the coins in as fast as we can.

This is the real metaphor, right here.

Finally the last coins plink-plink away into the void, leaving a philosophically significant silence of remarkable size.

"How cool was that," says a female voice.

Me and Joy look up. Twenty feet away stand Camille and Oscar, in their ill-fitting security uniforms.

"Never have I witnessed such beauty emerge from everyday objects," says Oscar.

"How long have you been standing there?" I say.

"For most of it!" says Camille. Camille has a way of talking that sounds like constant whining, even if she's agreeing with you or wishing you well. "Frank, you know officially those coins were property of Westchester Mall!"

I stand and tap the sign by the funnel.

DONATE FOR SCHOOL SUPPLIES IN OUR DISTRICT

"Think of the children," I say.

"The Westchester Group thanks you for your generous donation on their behalf," says Oscar.

"Aren't you going to introduce us, Frank?!" says Camille.

"Uh, this is Joy," I say.

Joy shakes hands with Camille and Oscar, who then share a look of approval.

"Frank," says Oscar. "Please be aware that all sectors are ours to patrol this evening except parking structure Europa top level, northeast corner, and we will attempt no patrol there. That area remains in perpetual penumbra because of a malfunctioning lamp."

I smile.

Oscar holsters the walkie. "Go, young lovers."

• • •

We drive in silence. It takes a while to even find parking structure Europa, given the size of the mall. While I drive, I notice a strange nervousness has fallen between me and Joy. I catch her staring at me. She catches me glancing at her.

We are driving to the top of an empty parking structure.

Why?

I don't even know. I just feel compelled to go. Joy, too: there she sits, with her fingertips tented upon her knees in eager anticipation.

Oscar was wrong about the malfunctioning lamp. *All* the lamps up here are off, leaving nothing but pristine moonlight. I park at the farthest, highest corner. The night is sapphire clear, and we can see lights stretching beyond the curved back bay of Playa Mesa all the way to San Marco, Paloma,

Karston, and beyond. To our right is the pitch black void of the Pacific dotted by the lazy pinpoint strobes of oil platforms at rest.

"How late is it?" I wonder.

"Pretty late," says Joy.

"Should we head home soon?"

Joy replies by cracking her window open an inch. So I crack mine, too.

"I feel shy," says Joy, and laughs.

"You know, humans laugh to each other to break emotional tension," I say, and laugh too.

Then we fall silent again. The leather seats creak every time I move a millimeter.

"Your shirt's all stained and shit," I say.

"So's yours," says Joy. She reaches to touch my abdomen.

I lead her in for a kiss that turns into two that turns into a dozen, easy. Joy suddenly hates the passenger seat she's in. She kicks against the insides of the car and twists her body around to clamber over the idiotically located center console with its infernal parking brake and hindering drive shifter.

Finally she settles, straddling my lap, and straightens her hair: *Here I am. Hi.*

It's just a pause, long enough for us to gaze at each other in the moonlit dark. The windows are already fogging right on cue, despite being cracked. She and I are lead stars in a classic romantic film everyone knows and cherishes. We can feel the next part coming up.

We kiss long and slow. We stop for a breath.

"I want you," says Joy. "Okay?"

She is scared to death saying this. I can see it in her eyes. I can smell it on her skin. Because love is more terrifying than anything. Love is a mighty blue hand coming straight for you out of the sky. All you can do is surrender yourself and pray you don't fall to your death.

I try to reply, but my throat sticks. I clear it.

"Okay," I say.

We kiss again. The mighty blue hand is taking us somewhere—we don't know where, it's terrifying, but here we go. My hand discovers the skin just beneath her shirt—a place I have touched before, but now that there is only bare skin, it feels totally new. She accepts my touch as a kind of permission to touch me back. Suddenly her hands are gripping every part of my torso with an urgent but delicate probing.

I suddenly hate Joy's shirt. She hates mine, too. Off they go. I already know where the clasp of her bra is, and undo that. Joy elbows the horn once—toot—and we giggle.

"Does this thing go back?" she says, meaning the seat.

"It does," I say, and reach down to press a button.

The leather seat inches back slowly, oh my god for an eternity does it recline, and makes a long fart sound along the way. It is the best fart for the moment. We crack up and cover our mouths with wonder: are we really going to do this?

We are.

We do.

chapter 26

the bad joke

Bing-bong.

Bing-bong.

It's just Dad, working the floor near the entrance with a mop.

Bing-bong.

The trio of flies square-dance above me.

It's hot. Southern California always skips spring for summer. The chocolate is in the walk-in cooler.

I'm wearing an outfit of warm blacks: orange-black pants, brown-black Kraftwerk tee. I pick at my wristbands, also all warm black.

On the surface, it looks like nothing has changed. I am Frank, The Store is still hot, Dad is mopping as usual.

But in reality, everything has changed. It's hot because the world wants to remind me: one day soon it will be summer, school will end, and we'll all go to college. Me. Q.

Joy.

I don't want to think about that just yet.

And Dad: hidden beneath Dad's usual work tee shirt is a small round scar as smooth and shiny as a drop of tan paint. You couldn't guess the guy recently survived a gunshot.

And me?

I once read some graphic novel where the hero lost his virginity and was disappointed to find that he felt the same the next day. Boys, he figured, weren't like girls. They didn't have hymens to break. There was no physical evidence of the event. The next day the hero felt nothing but anticlimax.

What a stupid graphic novel that was. It got everything wrong.

Because if you cut and pry me open right now, you will discover my insides sparkling like a geode across every spectrum imaginable. Look closer and you will see whole cities of crystal teeming with tiny minions of living light all pulsing in chromatic order—ROYGBIV—as they deliver their novae along my limbs.

Novae, nova, Latin for *new*, newly born stars.

I lean on the counter and grin like an idiot.

Inside me, everything has changed.

I take out my fartphone and message Q.

I lost it, old bean.

Your mind? says Q.

Last night, I say.

There's a pause, then a hailstorm of openmouthed surprise faces.

How do you feel? says Q. *Can you fly?*

Let me see, I say. *Nope, not yet.*

"Aigu," says Dad, thumping his back with a fist.

"You need to let me do that," I say.

"I am okay," says Dad.

I glance down at the cash register. The paper ticker tape is streaked with pink, which means it's running out.

"Dad, can you change the register tape?" I say. "I don't know how."

"Okay," says Dad. "I doing."

While he fiddles with the register and a new roll of tape, I grab his mop on the sly. When Dad finally looks up, the whole floor is gleaming.

"Frankie-ya," says Dad with a chuckle. "Don't mopping!"

It's too late—I'm already wringing out the mop in the bucket and taking it out back to dump the gray water. Dad peers at the floor tiles, the corners, the edges, then at me.

"Anyway you doing good job," he says.

This is Dad's way of saying *thank you*, so I say, "You're welcome."

There's a flurry of customers—waves, they always come in waves—including Charles, who gives me yet another tiny scroll to study. I unroll it. There is a penis, a sperm, an egg, and then an embryo in a sac. It says

FROM WATER INTO WATER INTO WATER

BACK TO WATER AGAIN

First of all, what's with dudes drawing penises? Stop drawing penises so much, dudes. Otherwise, I'm surprised to find myself understanding this scroll. I think. Maybe. Humans are mostly water. Water of different kinds: blood, bile, saliva, blablabla. Those waters mix with other waters, and out of that comes life. It's a miracle and a mystery.

Water is life; lack of water is lack of life. It makes me think of the windward and leeward slopes of a mountain. The windward side will trap precious moisture, and the leeward side will be forever deprived of it, creating a lush green slope on one side and a barren gray one on the other, separated only by a thin, sharp ridge. Bugs born on the leeward side know only struggle. Bugs born on the windward side, only bounty.

Immigrant metaphor incoming. Say you're born into a war-torn country. You cross a border—which could even be invisible, not even a thin sharp ridge to define it—and suddenly you may find yourself on the windward side: a safe, clean, modern society.

How is that?

I don't know. The first hard part is crossing that ridge. It's also the simplest.

The other hard part—learning how to actually live life on the green windward side, well. That's more complicated.

Pretty good scroll this time, Charles.

"Dad," I say. "Were you scared when you first came to the States?"

"Me?" says Dad. "No."

"Really?"

"Mom scared. Me, maybe little bit scared. Anyway, scary."

"Wait. So you *were* scared."

"Yeah, I'm scare long time. We first coming, no nothing. English? Only so-so. Only menial job we can getting. Money?

Aigu. Three hundred dollars only we having. Almost two years we staying—"

"Then you stayed at Dr. and Mrs. Choi's house for two years eating nothing but ramyun and kimchi rice, mhm."

Dad smiles at the ground. He knows I've heard this a million times.

"I'm just curious, Dad. What were you scared about when you first got here? What was your single greatest fear?"

Dad smiles, thinking. He's not necessarily happy, though. He just tends to smile when put on the spot. It's more wincing than smiling.

"We scare," says Dad, "maybe we coming all the way to United States, no nothing we having, maybe we borrowing money from friend, maybe we borrowing money from family. Maybe no success business, kids going bad school, maybe no house having. Waste time. Go back to Korea, aigu. They trouble making. Whole family becoming financial burden to everybody. Everybody say you failure making, better stay Korea first place."

"So, shame."

Dad nods gravely. "Paek family—you never meet them—car wash business they trying. Total money they losing. Finally? Go back Korea. Oh boy. Whole their family they prisoner, so-called financial bondage. Mr. Paek have heart attack. He die."

Dad slices the air with the back of his hand. "Not me. No way."

"Are you not scared of anything anymore?"

Dad laughs. "No."

"You're all set?"

"We doing okay, Frankie. You going college? Nice girl meeting? Make beautiful baby? That's it. I die, oh, Frankie-ya, you doing good, I smiling smiling. Final breath I taking before *shuffle off this mortal coil*." Dad laughs his cuckoo laugh.

I laugh too. "Dang, Dad, why you gotta go straight to death?"

I have the urge to ask him straight up about Hanna. This feels like a chance to do that. Or maybe not—because he stops laughing on a dime. He gets this weird lost look. Scared, almost. Is he thinking about her right now too? Is he wondering if he'll never see Hanna again before he dies?

Dad can't seem to figure out where to set his eyes, so he looks at the clock.

"Hey, you organizing walk-in cooler yet?" he says.

"Uh, no."

"Ya, you go doing right now. We going Gathering soon."

"All right, all right, I'm going."

"Hurry up," he barks.

"Okay, Dad, jeez."

I grab my jacket and shut myself into the howling cold of the giant fridge. Things with Dad always go like this. We're talking, everything's great, and then suddenly he'll get all psycho about something and shove me away. It makes me feel like a lunar lander on approach that only winds up sling-shotting away instead of making contact.

I slam cases of beer and juice around. I marry loose cans to form complete six-packs; I rotate in new milk and set aside expired cartons. I'm so annoyed that I'm working at double speed, so fast that when I emerge out into the heat, I catch Dad doing something with a guilty look.

He's got a skinny plastic orange container. It's pills.

"What are those?" I say.

"Just vitamin," says Dad. He's already in his Gathering-appropriate polo shirt. "Medicine bottle I reusing. B12, calcium, fiber. You better taking vitamin too."

"Teenagers don't need vitamins, Dad."

"Anyway we going now. Pali kaja." *Hurry up, let's go.*

"Let me see those vitamins."

"Pali kaja," says Dad, pocketing the bottle. "You driving, okay?"

We get in Dad's old QL5. I notice the front edge of the driver's seat has frayed and split open.

"Fine, let me take some of your vitamins, then," I say. I say it too loud, like I'm insisting on picking a fight. But I know those are not vitamins.

"This one only old people special taking," says Dad. "I buying regular multivitamin tomorrow, for you taking."

And then Dad's quiet the whole drive. Normally he'd be pointing out the fluctuating ethnicities of the passing neighborhoods, or how all small businesses everywhere are struggling except ours thanks to Mom-n-Dad's hard work and sheer guile, but not this time. I want to figure out what the hell's going on with him. I want to ask:

- What are those pills really?
- Are you mad I came home so late last night?
- Are you feeling guilty about Hanna?

- Are you feeling weird about me leaving soon for college?

I even want to ask:

- Can you tell I lost my virginity last night, and does it make you feel awkward?

I teeter on the edge of asking these questions but never do, because I know I won't get any real answers anyway. Makes for a terrific thirty-minute drive.

We get to the Songs' house. I step out into the air made briny and sweet by the nearby ocean and six plumeria trees, each individually underlit. Who has the time and money to install a special light for each tree like that?

Rich people.

I reflexively look at Dad, who's busy snapping a loose thread from the front edge of his passenger seat. So that one's tearing, too. Again I wonder if Dad is happy. I wonder if he's envious of how Joy's dad managed to race so much farther ahead of him despite starting from the same line. I wonder if he's envious, having saved for so long to buy his prized QL5 only to watch his junior mentee go on to buy a QL6, and then a pair of QL7s.

I hope not. I hope he had a fixed finish line that he one day crossed and stopped running because that's just his kind of happiness.

Here's what I imagine rich people like Joy's dad to be like:

forever chasing a finish line that's actually the horizon, never to be reached. Is that a kind of happiness too?

Joy's dad's face appears on a security screen before we can even touch the doorbell.

"Ri-sunbae osyeotseumnida!" he cries. *Mentor Li is here!*

Inside smells all warm and garlicky and sagey. I mumble my *annyong haseyo* and bow, give Mom a hug—she's already here, having called a Ryde on her fartphone for the first time ever, very exciting—and climb the stairs to Joy's room, where the Limbos are.

"Hey, guys," I say.

"Hey, Frank," say the Limbos. I notice John Lim and Ella Chang are sitting next to each other, but not touching. That's some discipline, right there.

Andrew Kim's on his back gazing up at his phone, using it for what he calls *mirror training*, which is where actors study and perfect their own facial expressions.

Joy appears all in black. When she takes my hand, I can see our blacks match: cool on cool. "There you are," she says. "Can you help me with something real quick?"

"Huh?"

"In this room."

She leads me quickly to the vast shimmering darkness of her parents' master bedroom and spins around to give me the longest kiss in the history of people ever.

"I missed you," she breathes.

"Me too," I breathe back.

"Expect regular breaks like this all night."

"Roger that."

"Ooo," say two small voices.

Me and Joy shoot our gaze to a corner of the dark room, where little people crouch by a potted plant.

"Ben, you guys go somewhere else," barks Joy.

Ben, Joy's little brother, darts giggling out of the room. He's followed by Anna Kim, Andrew Kim's little sister.

We roll our eyes in sync, get back into character, and reenter the Limbo room.

"You just flip the circuit breaker if it trips," I say. "Just turn stuff off first."

"Good to know," says Joy. "Thanks."

The three Limbos look at us, unimpressed with our charade. No one has ever been interested in circuit breakers, ever.

"Why bother pretending?" says Ella. "Just tell us you're going on a make-out break."

"Make-out break," says John Lim, in a way that sounds like *Good idea, Ella.*

"Everybody!" shouts a voice from below. "Dinner!"

We turn to head down. John Lim and Ella Chang dawdle.

I look at Joy: *Aw, let them dawdle.*

Dinner is Joy's mom-n-dad's version of gastropub food: craft beers, whiskeys, hearty roasted chicken and beef sliders and sweet potato fries and so on. It's great. They even give us kids those little flights of beer, where you get four tiny glasses of different beers—ales, IPAs, lagers, I have no idea—on a slat of wood with the words BAR SONG burned into it. Pretty extravagant.

The grown-ups sit at the grown-ups' table. The big kids sit at the big kids' table. The two little kids—Ben Song and Anna Kim—bury themselves on a far couch with a tablet and play *Karate Fruit Chop*.

I take a sip of something called a Scotch ale, immediately start to feel shit-faced drunk, and push it away. Andrew Kim pounds his like it's an energy drink.

"My old friends," says Andrew Kim. "The sky changes, and will ever change again, and still again."

"Huh?" I say. The guy is talking like fake Shakespeare. Fakespeare.

John Lim sips his tiny beer. "I think he's trying to be philosophical."

Andrew nods slowly, like he's at church.

"Anyway, I think what Andrew wants to talk about is the winds of change, as in graduation, and then summer," says Ella. "And whatever happens to us after."

"I mean, I guess we find out where we got in soon enough," says Joy. "School's basically over. Only thing left to do is have fun in the meantime, right?"

"That's the only thing to do," says Ella. "We have to just be open to whatever may happen in college, so that we can grow as individual people."

Joy glances at me, I glance back, and we squeeze hands under the table. There will come a day—super, super soon—when I will give Joy one last dip before she twirls away to the other side of the country.

"I've been trying not to think about it, to be honest," says Joy.

"Me and Ella will be at UCLA together," says John, all bright and clueless. John and Ella's first choice is nearby UCLA, and no doubt they'll both get in.

"John," says Ella, and throws a chastising look.

John opens his mouth to speak, but there's a weird outcry from the grown-ups' table nearby. It's Dad.

"I never taking single loan," shouts Dad. "Not even dollar, not even penny."

Joy squeezes my hand and whispers. "Is he drunk?"

"Probably," I say. I look closer. "Actually, no, he hasn't touched his beer."

The whole room falls silent.

"Mr. Li," says Joy's dad gently in his excellent English, "you have to understand, my businesses rely on leverage because of high up-front costs. That's just life in the professional services industry."

"I'm not be caring what is leverage or whatever," says Dad, still loud. "Only thing you making is debt. You not making real money. This house not real. Bank owning."

"What the fuck is going on?" I whisper to Joy.

"I have no idea," says Joy.

I see Mom grasp Dad's upper arm. "Daddy, stop it."

But Dad shakes her off. He aims a finger at Joy's dad. "Don't criticizing me. I'm totally pay off my house. No debt, nothing. I'm working hard every day. You say my business not safe, somebody shooting me, I'm stupid?"

"I didn't mean it like that, Mr. Li," says Joy's dad. "It was a bad joke."

"씨발 이거 완전히 병신같은 새끼네," says Dad, his voice rising. "Somebody sue you, you go bankrupt. Nobody suing me. I making all the time cash only. Nobody suing me. I am okay."

I can see Joy's dad's face twist darkly. Dad's just called him a stupid fucker. In front of guests. In his own house.

"오~ 그렇게 다 아는 사람이 사는게 겨우 그 정도야?" says Joy's dad. I'm not sure what that means. "No one will sue you because you have nothing to win. No one wants your tiny old house. No one wants your dirty broken car. That car is one month of my mortgage. That's it, 이 새끼야."

Both men stand. I can't catch any of this next part. My head's spinning too fast to even really hear any of it.

"너는 지금 선배한테 그딴 식으로 말해?" says Dad. "그것도 내 마누라랑 식구들 앞에서?"

"여긴 내 집이야. 내 가족이고. 내가 당신을 여기 초대한거야. 당신이 예의에 맞게 굴어야지," says Joy's dad.

"내가 니 선배야. 나한테 예의를 지켜야 하는건 너야."

"그냥 실없는 농담이었고 아차 싶어서 사과했잖아. 그런데 당신 열등감때문에 그걸 가지고 계속 물고 늘어지는 거잖아. 그건 당신 문제지 내 문제가 아니야."

"제발 그만," says Mom.

"상종할 가치도 없어," says Joy's mom.

"그게 무슨 뜻이에요?" says my mom, incredulous.

"알지 모르겠는데, 씨발 지금 여기는 미국이야," says Joy's dad. "당신이 말하는 선배니 후배니 하는거 여기서는 상관없다고."

"니가 나보다 잘난거 같냐?"

"암 당연히 내가 낫지. 너보다 집도 좋아. 차도 좋아. 심지어 차도 두대야!"

"우리 딸은 대학다녀. 그거 한두푼 드는거 아니다. 우리 아들도 곧 스탠포드 대학에 갈꺼야. 나는 중요한데다 내 돈 쓰지 누구처럼 집이니 차니 쓸데 없는데 안써," says Dad.

"학비 못대줘서 당신 아들 스탠포드 못갈꺼잖아. 뭐 어차피 갈 실력도 안되지만," says Joy's dad.

Something in Dad suddenly hardens and dies.

"그래 당신이 나보다 미국엔 먼저 왔어," says Joy's dad. "그래서 뭐. 한국에서도 가난했고 여기서도 깜둥이나 멕시칸 같은 못사는 애들 상대로 술이나 팔잖아. 아들도 당신이랑 똑같이 끝날꺼야. 우리 딸은 안 그럴 꺼지만."

"Dad?" says Joy.

Joy's dad ignores her. "그리고 말이야, 우린 서울출신이야. 미국에 오지만 않았어도 당신 같은 시골 무지랭이랑은 상종도 안했어. 미국만 아니었어도 당신 아들 같은 놈이 어딜 감히 우리 딸을 만나. 아 뭐 그래. 지금은 지들끼리 잘 지내라 그래. 그래도 우리 딸은 더 낳은 사람 찾아갈꺼야. 당신 아들? 방탄조끼나 사 입혀."

Dad breathes in and out.

"We going now," says Dad.

chapter 27

we are okay

I have two hands on a wheel.

Tilt the wheel counterclockwise, and my body shifts right.

Tilt the wheel clockwise, my body shifts left.

My right foot rests on something that pushes down. When it does, I press back into my seat.

Before me is a black-and-orange-and-gray freeway dotted with pairs of red lights.

I am driving an automobile. A strong flat belt rests snug across my chest and lap. Two bright lamps help me see ahead in the dark.

Must be a new moon tonight, because I can't find any big white disc in the sky like normal. I drive in the dark and follow the lines before me.

My father, whom I call Dad, sits next to me.

My mother, whom I call Mom, sits in the seat behind him. She slips a new paper to-go cup into a cylindrical hole in the center arm of the front seat. Dad hands it back.

"I'm no drinking nothing," he says with disgust. "I'm not be intoxicated."

It's the first words anyone has said for a few long minutes.

"Dad," I say.

His voice rises. "I'm very clear mental awareness having now."

"Dad, what—"

"I'm not accepting no nothing that man's house," says Dad. "No food, no drink, nothing."

"Dad," I bark. This seems to dislodge Dad out of whatever state he's in. "What the hell happened back there?"

After Dad said, *We going now,* he grabbed his jacket, grabbed his wife (whom I call Mom), and grabbed his son (whom I call me). He pointed at our shoes in the foyer: *put these on right now.*

"Frank?" was all Joy could say. She looked terrified. I could see her six-year-old self in her eyes, and I know she could see mine, too. Something tectonic was happening. The earth was shifting and splitting apart.

All I could do was shrug in a wild panic. "I don't know," I said. "I'll text you."

And in a silent scramble we Lis went outside and into the car, like some family of lowlifes discreetly fleeing a bloodless crime.

And now I'm driving. Our car hurtles just ahead of a lightning-fast fracture unzipping the asphalt in great chunks.

"Dad?" I say.

Dad says nothing. In the rearview mirror, I can see Mom carefully unrolling the lip of the to-go cup and peeling it apart until it becomes its raw components again: a flat collar of card stock; a die-cut moon circle that she crushes in her palm.

"Dad?" I say.

"He son of bitch," says Dad finally.

"Daddy, stop it," says Mom from the back.

"You have to tell me what happened," I say.

"You trusting nobody," says Dad to no one. "Only you trusting family. Friend? No. Nothing."

I look to the rearview mirror for help. "Mom. Give me something here."

"Daddy, Mr. Song make bad joke," says Mom, ignoring me. "Why you get so mad?"

"He reveal true nature, shedding skin like serpent," says Dad. "Bible say, 'Woe to those who scheme iniquity.'"

"Bible say you have to forgive," says Mom.

"God forgiving him, go ahead," says Dad. "Not my problem."

There's a chevron of yellow-and-black barrels coming up, and I'm tempted to drive straight into them. Why can't I get a goddamn explanation?

"Mom," I say through my teeth. "What. Happened."

"Aigu," says Mom. She sighs, like *Where to begin?*

"Mr. Song," says Mom. "He making fun of Daddy, is worth it you getting shot in same place you make no money? He saying he going to give nice Daddy bulletproof vest for Christmas, Gucci brand."

Dad scoffs silently to himself.

"Well, that's a shitty joke," I say.

"Don't using bad word," says Dad absently, out of parental reflex.

"Daddy say don't making fun, I working hard," says Mom. "Mr. Song, he apologize! But Daddy keep going! He say Mr. Song business is fake, not good business, only debt he making."

I'm confused. "Huh?"

"Why you keep going mad, Daddy?" says Mom.

"Mr. Song," says Dad with theatrical calm, "he taking loan, okay? So many loan. Every day he working, office furniture business, every day he must be pay debt so many people. Maybe he miss one day? Oh boy. Whole of business collapse. So-called *house of cards*. You knowing that expression, *house of cards*?"

"I know *house of cards*, Dad."

This still isn't explaining why they blew up at each other. I ask Dad gingerly, as if talking to a bomb.

"So you're saying you're mad at Mr. Song because he's . . . over-leveraged?"

"No," says Dad. "Mr. Song pretending he superior to us. But my situation? I'm no debt having. I'm free man. I'm not be owing nobody no nothing. Mr. Song, forever in financial bondage. So he making fun our family."

"Because he's jealous of our security?" I say.

"No," says Mom from the back. "Mr. Song look down on us because we are from Gwangju countryside. Mr. and Mrs. Song are from Seoul. You know Seoul Gangnam neighborhood? Rich area. We same class during university, but always they treat us like lower-class student."

"Wait, so have they always made fun of you guys?" I say.

"Aigu, always they talk-talk-talk, make fun my accent. Daddy accent too." And Mom laughs. If you didn't know Mom, you'd think she was being a complete dick, but I know she's laughing only because she's nervous.

My mind zooms way out.

I examine all the Gatherings we've had over the years. All the parents, gabbing it up downstairs like they were having the greatest party in the world while we Limbos lazed about upstairs.

But in reality Mom-n-Dad were being needled the whole time? Putting up with mean little jokes, none ever big enough to ruin the evening? Just sucking up and putting up?

I had no idea. None of the Limbos did. I always thought of them being all in this Great American Adventure together, where just being Korean in a new country was enough to call each other family.

Now I wonder: what other dramas were happening with our parents, right under our noses?

Of course they would never tell us about them. Their job was to provide for us, and our job was to study. They would never want to distract us with their bullshit.

I understand that. I really do. But I want the bullshit. The bullshit makes me see the parents, every Gathering, in a totally new light. Suddenly I'm dying to learn who these parents really are. Because that's what kids do, isn't it? Watch their parents. Learn. See what parts of you came from them.

Right here in the car as the orange streetlamps above rapidly go *sunrisesunsetsunrisesunset*, I regard Mom-n-Dad with fresh eyes as if they were characters in a story. I see them as twangy bumpkins in some rural high school. As new lovers in a big-city university in Seoul. As a young couple in a new country. As husband-n-wife.

"So you're going to say you're sorry, right?" I say to Dad, with a lilt of hope.

But Dad remains firm. "I'm not any wrongdoing having. Mr. Song must be apologizing me first."

"Daddy, Bible say—" says Mom.

"He saying very bad thing to you, too," says Dad.

"Me?" I say. "What did he say about me?"

"Aigu, never mind," says Mom.

"He saying more better you buying bulletproof vest too," says Dad.

I squint with confusion. Joy's dad was talking shit about me too?

"I'm not be associating no more Song family," says Dad. "Everybody knowing they wrongdoing having. Mrs. Song knowing it. Joy knowing it."

My eyebrows shoot up. "Wait. Dad."

Dad says nothing.

I flick a lever, tic-tic-tic, and take our exit.

"Dad, are you saying you don't want *me* to associate with Joy?"

"I am free man," says Dad. "You free too. You going your own way."

"Are you saying you don't want me to see Joy because of your own bullshit with Mr. Song?"

300

"Frankie-ya, calm down," says Mom.

"You own-your-way you going," says Dad. "I'm not be stop you. You make your own decision, making own consequence, okay? You understand what I'm saying?"

"No, I don't understand what you're saying," I say.

"Frankie, slow down," says Mom.

"I don't get what's happening right now," I say. "Are you or aren't you saying I am no longer allowed to see Joy?"

"You own-your-way you must be going," says Dad quietly.

I've almost gone completely insane at this point.

"I can't believe what I'm hearing," I say. "You wanted me to date a Korean girl. I dated a Korean girl. I gave you exactly what you wanted. Now you're saying it's the wrong fucking Korean girl?"

"Frankie, don't using bad word like that," says Mom.

"Slow down," says Dad.

"No, really," I say. "Which girl do you want me to be with? Just tell me. Okay? Pick the hair you want, the big eyes you want, all that shit. Go ahead."

"Why you shouting?" says Mom.

"I don't fucking get you guys," I shout.

"Frankie," says Dad.

"I take one wrong step, I make one wrong move, you gonna disown me too?" I say. "I can't win."

"Frankie, stop it," says Mom.

"Are you?" I say. "Did you seriously come all the way here to this country, raise two kids, just to not fucking talk to them again ever?"

We hit a pothole. I want to hit all the potholes until this stupid car shakes apart. Dad makes a sound, like this burble, and when I glance at him, I see him wincing.

"Frankie, drive careful," says Dad. "Please."

My rage pauses at the word *please*. Dad never says *please*. Dad looks sick with fear.

"Mommy," says Dad. "Gimme cup, cup, cup."

Mom glances at the wax paper collar and the crushed moon circle. "No more cup, Daddy," says Mom. She's gripping both Dad's seat back and mine.

"Frankie, stop," cries Mom. "Stopstopstop."

I stop the car. Thankfully we're on a long stretch of empty unlit road, because when Dad kicks the door open to throw up on the ground, there are no passing cars to see it.

"Are you drunk?" I say, even though I already know he's not. Mostly I ask out of sheer confusion.

I look at Mom, but she doesn't answer. Neither does Dad. He simply shuts the door.

"I am okay," says Dad. "Going home now, Frankie."

We arrive at our house. It abuts a cinder-block wall separating it from the nearby freeway. I park in our oil-stained driveway flanked by brown stubble lawn. They say immigrants bring their aesthetic with them wherever they go, and now I know it's true. Our house would probably look like a mansion to Korean country kids from the eighties.

I step out of the car and help Mom lead Dad into the house.

"Did you eat something funny?" I say.

"I am okay," is all Dad will say.

I want to punch him, but he suddenly looks like a single punch would kill him.

We make it into the house.

"I go lying down," says Dad, and slowly vanishes upstairs.

I hear him settle into bed, and the house becomes silent. It's just me and Mom, standing among all the shoes in our foyer.

"Mom, what's going on?" I say. It's almost a whisper.

"He is okay," says Mom. She blinks. A tear hangs from her eyelash.

"Mom, is Dad okay?"

"Go sleep," says Mom. "We talking later."

"Mom."

"Don't worry about anything," says Mom. "We talking later. We are okay."

"What is this *we*?"

"Go sleep, Frankie," is all Mom will say. She ascends the stairs, leaving me alone.

• • •

When I finally begin to drift off in bed, I dream a cool hand is on my forehead. Is it Joy's? I open my eyes.

It's not a dream. There is indeed a cool hand on my forehead. It belongs to Mom.

Mom's sitting on my bed in the dark in her sweatsuit pajamas, touching my forehead. Not checking for fever or anything. Just resting it there.

My heart surges with sudden tenderness. Countless times has she come in to touch my forehead while I was half asleep.

Me, her boy, busily evolving while I slumbered to gradually grow taller, stronger, to grow up and away from her no matter what she thought or wanted.

Two bright lines flash in the dark. They are the twin streaks of her tears.

"Mom," I say without moving.

"Daddy feel so sad," says Mom.

"I'm sorry I lost it," I murmur. "I shouldn't have yelled like that."

"It's okay. Daddy love you so much."

The tenderness inside me contracts into fear. We never say these kinds of words.

"Is Dad okay?"

"They checking bullet injury, they scanning whole Daddy's chest with CT scan, PET scan, something like that."

I can only watch as Mom blinks fresh wet tracks down her cheeks. I've seen Mom cry only a few times. She has the scariest way of crying. No sobbing or sniffling. Just silent tears, like her eyes have a leak that will not stop.

"Doctor say lung is okay, bullet injury is okay, but whole of torso, little bump they finding," says Mom. "So many little bump. He say like Christmas tree. Doctor like you, he Korean yisei, second generation, speak only English."

"What are you talking about, Mom?" I say it so quiet, so scared.

"I asking him, what is so many tiny-tiny bump everywhere? Doctor say is small-cell carcinoma. I asking him, what it is, carcinoma?"

I can't say the word.

"Doctor say Daddy better start the chemo right away, so Daddy start right away."

Cancer.

"At the first time, Daddy doing okay, no symptom at all."

Cancer.

"But second time, Daddy getting sicker, sicker, sicker. Lose appetite."

Cancer.

"I making vegetable juice and Chinese medicine, hanyak. Maybe it's helping, I hope so. I hope so."

And Mom just runs out of things to say.

The heat from my forehead has made her hand hot and moist, so she switches to the other one.

"Why didn't you tell me?" I say.

"He didn't want you have to worry," says Mom.

"What do you mean? Mom, I need to know these things."

"If you worry, causing stress."

"When did you find out?"

"If you worry, hurt the SAT score."

"You found out that long ago? Jesus, Mom."

"Frankie. We protecting your future. You understand me, right?"

I do and don't at the same time. It confounds me how they managed to hide all this. They've been faking it for weeks.

"Does anyone at the Gathering know?" I say.

"Oh no," says Mom gravely. "If we say something, everybody so worry. Too much talking-talking, too much stress. We waiting first Daddy get better, then we telling everybody. I hope so. I hope so."

Mom's voice shrinks until it's nothing. I just stare at her for a long while. She's looking at something in my room. It's my night-light, which I've had since I was little. It's twin baby star angels snuggled up to sleep upon a cloud in the heavens. I always assumed they were me and Hanna. But now I think they could be Mom-n-Dad.

"Is he gonna be okay?" I say finally.

"Doctor say six month," says Mom. She nods to herself absently in the dark. "Six, maybe twelve month, yeah. Six to twelve month."

My mind goes blank.

I can see Mom's teeth flash as she bares them. "Why he get cancer? He eating so good. No smoking, no drug. No too much drinking. Maybe he working too much. But he sleep good. Why he get cancer?"

Now it's my turn to cry. Mom squeezes the tears out of my eyes with her thumbs and wipes them up on the shoulders of her sleeves.

"You praying God every day," says Mom. "I praying every day."

"Okay," I say, even though I'm undecided on prayer. I just say *okay* to say okay for Mom's sake. *Okay* is my prayer.

Dad's freak-out at the party now makes a kind of sense. There is no more room for any kind of crap from anyone anymore in Dad's life. All the room has been taken up by the one big thing. There is no bigger thing anywhere.

Mom leaves.

I lie still in bed. I feel the air drift in to fill the space created by her absence. I sink down. Something is pushing me from above. It's panic.

There's an end coming.

Once upon a time, Dad was born. A bunch of shit happened as he grew up and grew older. I know none of those details. He married Mom, moved here, started The Store. He worked every day without a single break.

And now there's an end coming.

How much of my dad do I know? He never tells me about his childhood, or his adulthood for that matter. I know some basic facts: his date and place of birth, what kinds of foods he likes, his favorite English poets, and so on. But now I realize it's not much. Then again, how much is there to really know about a person? Dad settled into his role as breadwinner, expected me to settle into my role as disciplined academic, and we both put our noses to the grindstone and never looked back up.

There is jeong, though: that time spent wordlessly bonding. So I begin to calculate our time spent together. A few minutes each evening. Sundays at The Store for the last couple summers. I do some rough numbers.

It adds up to about three hundred hours. A baker's dozen of days.

Who is this man who was my dad?

Is, Frank. He's not dead yet.

But he will be.

Panic seizes me again. I breathe faster and faster. I press into the pillow to muffle the sound of my cries, and wonder at the cold mystery of it all: cold as a statue ruin in the moonlight whose meaning has long been lost. Dad—this man whose house I live in—contains clues about myself. There are things I do and say and like and excel at that might have their origins in him somewhere, but I'll never know now.

I am panicking because I realize I've been desperate to know Dad my whole life. I learned a long time ago that such a hope was impossible with an impenetrable statue ruin like him. So I gave up. Moreover, I pretended *I didn't care* if I never knew him. I pretended I was okay living as a Limbo, belonging nowhere, a son without even the most basic connection to the man who fathered him.

But it turns out I care very much. I cared this whole time.

And now that there's an end coming, I now know that the eternal mystery of Dad will forever remain precisely that: an eternal mystery.

Should I have worked at The Store with him more?

Should I have learned Korean better?

Should I have tried harder?

And finally:

Did I make Dad happy?

It takes me hours to sleep.

When I do, I have a vivid, insane dream.

I am in a vast pulsating forest of moist black trees. They are all strung up with red pinlights. It must be a new moon, because I can't find any white disk in the sky, 0.22 inches in diameter or otherwise, sun or moon. The ground is spongy. It rises and falls slowly.

This forest is not contained by the finite boundaries of

Dad's lungs. This forest is endless, and I wander for hours and days and weeks searching for an exit. I try my best to not touch the trees. They will stain me with their wet black. After hours and days and weeks of searching, I am marked here and there with dark lines of their muck, and still remain trapped as ever.

I am alone this time. There's no Brit in a futuristic yellow dress. There's no Joy peering at me through a hole far above. Just me.

Finally I realize something. This forest is the way it is because there is no love here. Who would accept such a revolting place? This lack of love is the key. I'm sure of it. As a test, I approach a tree, take a deep breath, and wrap my arms around the trunk.

The bark is lukewarm and slimy and acrid like medicine. I close my eyes and hug harder. I feel branches begin to move around me. From all sides they come, increasing their embrace as I tighten mine. Soon, I'm covered in black limbs. They smother me with their awful warmth.

All at once, the trees pull away. I can't lift my feet. I'm rooted in the spongy ground. I am covered head to toe with tarry goo. My chest begins to glow with a point of red light. It's my heart, and it's the brightest red pinlight in this whole place. I am now a black tree in the exact center of the black forest.

I blink. Suddenly the muck has evaporated to leave the trees dry and gray and clean. I look down: I am now clean, too.

I blink again, and a sun has begun to rise.

Blink: The trees have color now and are laden with brilliant green leaves.

Blink: They've parted to form a tunnel of foliage leading to an exit. The forest is letting me go. I walk out onto a rolling meadow full of people and picnics and kids running games on warmed earth that beats with each spirited step.

Blink, and it's morning in my bedroom.

I am awake.

you

own-your-way

you must

be going

hi irony

I am awake.

The stupid sun is dancing its beams through the tree out-side my bedroom window, all chipper and shit. It feels late. How long have I been sleeping? I check my alarm clock—a vintage analog folding compact model, no bedside fartphones for me—and see it's almost eleven thirty.

I am a teenager. We are supposed to sleep the crap out of our beds. But eleven thirty seems excessive, even to me.

I get up. I shower until I'm red. I need a haircut. When I comb out my wet hair, it's long enough to tie together with one of Hanna's old hair bands. I leave it that way—why not—and change into my summer outfit: cargo shorts, Front 242 tank, wrist elastics, all in a rainbow of blacks of differ-ent hues.

Summer outfit.

Summer is almost here.

It's 85 degrees, and this being Southern California it'll stay that way until it's time for school to start again. But when school starts again, I won't be here anymore. None of us will. We'll all be somewhere else, depending on the will of the admissions gods.

Buzz-buzz.

You okay? says Joy.

Just woke up, I say. *Rough night.*

What the hell happened? says Joy. *Do our families suddenly hate each other or something?*

It's that, but it's also not that.

Yubs? says Joy.

I sit up. *It's simplicated,* I say. *I'll tell you all about it in person.*

They said they don't want me to see you anymore, says Joy. *I don't understand what's going on*

They said the same thing to me, I say. *We should talk.*

Sorry one sec, says Joy. *Shopping for dorm stuff right now*

Dorm stuff. College.

Huh.

Little early, don't you think? I say.

The only thing I hate more than shopping, says Joy, *is long checkout lines*

I wait for her to text back some more, but I guess she's busy. I head downstairs to find a pink box and some money sitting on the counter. Open the box, and behold: donuts, and a note.

You don't working at Store today OK Frankie
don't worry Daddy he will be fine. I helping
him you relax maybe go to Q house and play
game together OK? Don't worry anything I
love you.

—Mommy

I stare at the words *I love you.*

"I love you too, Mom," I say, mostly to see how saying those words would feel. It feels funny and a little embarrassing, like a phrase in a foreign language—*Je t'aime, Maman*—but I don't care.

I can't believe Dad still went to The Store knowing he has a terminal illness. But then again, he's been going to The Store for weeks. He's known for weeks. If it were me? If I had learned I had six to twelve months? I would drop everything and go skydiving, race cars, go to music festivals, do anything besides stand around at The Store.

But that's because I don't know anything about life, and am therefore an asshole.

Dad worked The Store with his two bare hands, right alongside Mom. He knows everyone who passes through its doors. Every day Mom-n-Dad work, and every night they stack up the bills on the coffee table and do the accounting.

To Dad, The Store must provide a kind of comfort I could never imagine.

Skydiving doesn't provide comfort. Neither do race cars or music festivals or blablabla.

If I found out right now that I had six to twelve, where would I go for comfort?

I look at my phone again.

I want to see you, I say.

I want to see you, says Joy, at the same time.

Jinx, I say.

Where? says Joy.

I don't care, to be honest, I say. *You decide.*

Cafe Adagio? says Joy.

Eh. Can't deal with people today.

The beach? A hike?

How about this, I say. *You just come over here.*

After what happened last night? Isn't your mom gonna be there?

She's at The Store until 3 today.

Why?

Unforeseen circumstances.

You sure, yubs?

Just come over.

I put the phone in my pocket, and the house falls silent but for the white waves of freeway traffic coming over the high backyard wall. I realize I've never recorded that sound before. I should. But I can't bother right now.

I head upstairs into Hanna's room.

The place looks like she left without much thought. Everything's the same—movie posters on the walls, shelves spilling with old compact discs and vinyl and books, all waiting for her to return and tidy things up. I wonder if Mom-n-Dad are hoping she will return someday, somehow. Maybe that's why they left her room untouched.

I lie on her bed. I can feel the weight of my phone in my pocket.

Does she already somehow know about Dad?

I can imagine Hanna learning about Dad via one of Mom's crazy mom-emails, and the mixture of terror and frustration and anger such a message would produce. I wonder if Hanna's supposed to learn something like this through an email from Mom—they don't talk on the phone anymore—or if I should tell her.

I call Hanna.

Hey, it's Hanna, leave a message.

I kill the call.

I like Hanna's room. Hanna's room feels cool. I don't care if she's probably long over it and everything it contains.

I miss my big sister.

I'm in your room looking through all your crap, I say.

Hanna doesn't text back.

I wander to the guest room, which we call the storage room since we almost never have guests. In the far back of the crawl-in closet—there, in the far, far back—is an old black spy suitcase made by Legionite, some defunct company from the 1970s.

I spin the brass combo lock wheels with my thumbs: 7-7-7 for the left latch, 9-9-9 for the right.

Inside the suitcase are artifacts from another time. Among them:

- A name tag from an extinct restaurant named
  Cup-N-Saucer etched with the gaily dancing
  eponymous cartoon characters and the
  word DIANE. Diane is Mom's English name,
  D+I+A+N+E+L+I making seven letters.
- A still-new ten-pack of ballpoint pens printed
  with the address of EAT MY KRUST SANDWICHES,
  one of the first businesses Mom-n-Dad tried out.
  The pens are so old the phone numbers on them
  don't even have area codes.
- A little wooden abacus
- A flaking book in Korean about Victorian
  literature filled with underlined passages. The
  inside cover has PROPERTY OF FRANK LI in
  Dad's panicked handwriting. Frank is Dad's
  English name. It is also mine.
- A tough old yearbook from Mom's high school. I
  open it to her picture—I've dog-eared the page—
  and see her at my age. She's pretty. She's in a
  uniform. All the kids are in uniform. Everything's
  in Korean. There are no autographs, because I
  guess back then in the Korean countryside no
  one did stuff like that to such an expensive item.
- Three marble signature stamps and a lacquered
  black compact that unscrews to reveal a
  vermillion-red ink pad

Everything about this spy suitcase makes me want to
cry, and I know why. Because it's such a small, light case—

luggage was smaller back then—and yet it contains all there is.

Dad will be gone soon.

One day Mom will be gone, too.

Maybe I'll have kids one day. They'll ask me all about my life. It'll be easy to give them answers. We will speak the same English. We will be able to look up all my shit on the Internet, if we're still calling it the Internet. We'll talk about my hopes and dreams and fears and how they compare with their hopes and dreams and fears. Then we'll openly say *I love you* and hug, because Americans are huggers, dammit.

Then they'll ask me about all the stuff in this suitcase, and I won't be able to explain half of it. Not even close. This small, light suitcase will be to them what it is to me.

A wunderkammer.

Buzz-buzz. *I parked down the street,* says Joy. *Coast clear?*

I wipe my eyes and stand.

I'll be at the front door, I say.

When I open it, there stands Joy in the outside heat in all her summer dress glory.

"Hi," I say.

Joy grabs my head and kisses it, and for a moment it's the only sound in the whole house.

"What's wrong?" she says, because Joy can tell when she's kissing a statue.

I want to tell her. But not here. I will for-sure cry. I will become dizzy with tears and fall, and my head will strike the nearby bronze figurine of a bronco bucking an astonished infant cowboy and inflict a debilitating concussion. So I say,

"Wanna see some cool old stuff?" and lead her to the spy suitcase.

"Are you okay?" says Joy.

"Yes," I say, walking. "No."

"Last night was a shit show."

I sit her down on the soft, nonconcussive carpet before the suitcase.

"Huh," says Joy. "Is this all your mom-n-dad's old stuff?"

I nod. One small suitcase. My eyes sting with tears, so I lie down and let them pool as if I were catching raindrops.

"Hey," says Joy. She leans over me and caresses my cheek. "Hey, hey, hey."

I sniff. I have the crazy urge to lay into her dad, right here in front of Joy, for talking shit about me. But I keep it cool. "What did your mom-n-dad say about last night?"

Joy jets her hair again. "Something about your dad not having a sense of humor. Dad implied it's because your mom-n-dad are from the sticks. Are they?"

I blink away the raindrops. "Apparently they are."

"From the sticks."

"And apparently, your mom-n-dad have been making fun of my mom-n-dad basically for their entire friendship."

Joy recoils at this news. "So my mom-n-dad are king dicks?"

King dick is an old joke of ours, because *king* is *wang* in Korean and *wang* is *dick* in Casual English Vulgar, and you could therefore say it *wang wang* if you wanted to. Even now, even in the state I'm in, I just have to laugh a tiny laugh.

That's Joy for you.

"Either that," I say, "or my dad's a psycho with an inferiority complex."

"What the fuck," says Joy.

"Or both," I say.

"These are our parents?" says Joy.

"Apparently," I say, and latch the spy suitcase shut. I push it away into the crawl-in and close the closet.

Joy stares at the flattened rectangle of carpet where the case had lain. "I hate them right now."

"Someone once told me you have to hate your parents in order to leave them," I say.

"That makes absolutely no sense," says Joy. "I'm just saying I hate them right at this moment, not forever, because hopefully they'll figure it out and quit being dicks."

She has on this defiant look. She can do this because she doesn't know the whole story. I wish I could be defiant, too. It would be simpler.

"My dad, he's . . . " I begin, and the tears creep back.

Joy holds me still. "Hey. Their relationship is their relationship, and it has nothing to do with ours. Okay?"

She's right, but this is not the problem really, not really at all, but she doesn't know that, and I don't want to talk right now. I can't bear the thought of talking right now.

So I kiss her. The kiss astonishes us both so much that we must kiss again to make sure we both felt the same thing, and then again and again. Each kiss washes warm water over my racing mind. Calming it.

I let her lay me down. I let things happen, as slow as they need to. There is no rush. There is no expectation. I let myself drift from sensation to sensation.

And afterward, as we both lie in a parallelogram of dusty light, I cling to her because it turns out this is what I need right now: to be naked and vulnerable but safe in her arms at the same time. We take long breaths. Before me I see the bright corona of her eyes, the wispy baby hairs at her temple, a little mole on her chest. The air in the room seems to attenuate to the rising and falling of our chests.

"So listen," I say finally. "My dad has cancer."

"What?"

"The doctor said six to twelve months."

"What?"

". . ."

"Oh no," says Joy again and again. "Oh no, oh no."

She asks what kind it is, when he found out, all that. I tell her. She says she gets it now—she gets why Dad would freak out at the party like he did. Anyone under that kind of stress would be ready to snap. She understands this quickly, because she is Joy.

"I have to tell Mom-n-Dad," says Joy.

"Don't do that," I say.

"But then they'd understand why your dad got so mad."

"My mom doesn't want anyone to know. She says it'll cause all kinds of stress."

"But—if I had cancer, the first thing I'd do is tell my close friends."

"She's afraid of burdening people with heavy news," I say.

"She says she wants to wait till Dad gets better to tell every-one."

Joy's face unfolds. "But yubs . . ."

"I know."

"Your dad isn't gonna get better."

"I know," I cry, and bury my face in her neck.

"Shh," is all Joy will say, because what else is there to say? She holds my head and rocks it for a long time. For a long moment I feel like I'll fall asleep. Joy says "Shh" and "Shh," again and again, and I never want her to stop.

Joy takes a breath as she realizes something. "I guess we should lie low for a while, huh."

Joy is right. Because imagine Dad coming home to find his ex–best friend's daughter here. He wouldn't yell, or kick Joy out, or accuse me of betrayal. Nothing as dramatic as that.

Instead, he would just get really sad. And cancer feasts upon sad. Cancer is uniquely evil in that way.

"Yeah, we should," I say.

"Just when we were done with the fake dating," says Joy.

"Hi, irony," I say.

"Should we fire up the shared calendar again?"

"Nah," I say. "We're pros by now."

Joy gives me a weak laugh. Then her face falls. It's a sad, miserable little joke.

"We'll just take it as it comes," I say. "We still have the rest of the year."

"The rest of the year," says Joy.

A whisper in my head says, *I just want to walk away from it all.* I don't exactly know what this means. But I don't dare say it out loud. Not while Joy and I lie here under this warm felled sunbeam. *I just want to walk away from it all* makes it sound like Joy is part of the problem. *I just want to walk away from it all* makes it sound like I want to break up with her, which I do not.

But it would make things simpler, though, wouldn't it, says the whisper.

Sure, I say back. *Just like living alone in a desert bunker would make things simpler.*

Joy is part of the problem just like I'm part of the problem just like Mom-n-Dad are part of the problem and so on. We're all part of it whether we want to be or not. Everyone is part of the problem, and everyone is part of the solution, and that's what makes everything so infuriating.

I think all I really want to say is *I wish things were simpler.* But I feel like I've been saying that a lot lately. It hurts a little more each time.

Summer will come and go. Dad will most likely pass on. In Korean, *to pass on* is *doragada*, which means *to go back.*

Oh my god, back to where?

Joy leaves.

Then Mom comes home, with only a ten-minute gap in between and Mom none the wiser. We excel at running down low, me and Joy.

Hi, irony.

Usually Mom fusses over me when she gets home: *you eating something, you go playing Q's house, you study for SAT,* and so on. But she just sits at the empty dining table, which we never use, and listens to the distant freeway traffic go shh, shh.

"Store so hot today," says Mom.

"Did Dad turn on the AC?"

"He don't!" cries Mom. "He so stingy."

The urge to say, *What the fuck's he waiting for?* rages, then ebbs.

"Aigu, so tired today," says Mom. She goes to the living room couch and rests her body there.

Mom takes a deep breath, holds it, and sighs one big sigh. She flops her wrist across her eyes. "Mommy so tired," she says.

I watch her begin to slip out of consciousness.

"So hot," mumbles Mom, even though it's not. "Frankie-ya, you open window?"

I open up the house to let the breeze in. "That better?" I say.

But Mom doesn't answer, because she's already still.

The white curtains from the open windows billow back and forth without a sound. Back and forth, moved by the breathing of the warm sun-swept wind.

chapter 29

thins & fats

The High School Era is slowly disintegrating into a pre-apocalyptic orgy of wanton dereliction. People ditch school to have lunch off-campus. The bell rings, but people ignore it to continue lying on the grass or whatever. There's a mandatory assembly for some presentation by the Associated Student Body to show off all their accomplishments; hardly anyone shows up. Even the school president herself is absent. Five minutes in, a flock of corn tortillas go flying onto the stage from somewhere in the audience, and the vice principal literally throws his hands up and walks away.

Mr. Soft has foreseen the coming of this proverbial tortilla storm. Mr. Soft is prepared. He hauled in his outrageous 8K projector from home—apparently he's an avid home theater product review blogger in his spare time—and is letting us watch whatever we can bring in on disc. He even brought in a little popcorn machine. Forget calculus. It's popcorn and movies at seven o'clock in the morning.

"I'm so proud of you turkeys," says Mr. Soft. "These last two months, all we're gonna do is celebrate each and every one of you as those acceptance letters come rolling in."

And roll in they do.

Naima Gupta got in to The Harvard. She found out during class and sent her laptop clattering to the floor. Extra popcorn for her.

Did I get into The Harvard? With my email notifications muted, only the mail sitting in the Bag of Holding can say.

Do my parents still care about The Harvard like they used to?

Amelie Shim got into the University of Chicago. Paul Olmo, University of California at Santa Cruz. Brit Means got into the University of California at Davis, as planned. I'm happy for her. I'll never visit her, never see her dorm room, never see her favorite spot on campus to sit and daydream. It's strange that I once wanted these things so bad.

Andrew Kim got into Yale, where his acting dreams will surely come true. John Lim and Ella Chang both got in to UCLA. They haven't come out to their parents yet. Wu Tang got into USC and will join his family pantheon of strong-jawed Trojan grads.

I force Q to ditch fourth period to tell him all about the blowup at the Gathering, and how it sent me and Joy pinwheeling skyward, and how my dad has thousands of tiny-tiny time bombs throbbing inside him. Q listens. He can only frown at the ground: the surface of the planet Earth, such an unfair place, so messy and tragic all the time.

Then Q cries. He cries until the bottoms of his glasses fill

327

up. I take them off, wipe the lenses clean with my tee shirt.

"I'm sorry I'm crying like an infant with gigantism and a poopy diaper," says Q.

"It's okay, abnormally huge baby," I say, and reach out to hold his arm.

Students walk by and glance at us, probably wondering if we're a couple who has just broken up in the last weeks of school. That sort of thing has been happening all over campus. End of Days.

"No," says Q. "I mean I'm sorry I'm giving you yet another problem to deal with. You've got enough crying of your own. Last thing you need is me piling on more."

"Pile away, old bean," I say. "There's room."

"I just," says Q with a mighty sniff, "what the fuck does any of this mean? You live, you work, you die? One day you fight with your friends from forever and then the next day you're just strangers again? Is that what the universe is telling us here?"

"I know, right?"

Q pretends to push up his glasses, but I know he's hiding his eyes with his hand. "Is that gonna happen to us?"

"Hey," I bark. "No way. Stop that noise."

Q blinks at the lockers, the shiny linoleum floor, the doors. "I'm gonna miss this infernal asylum," he says. "My mom said the last of the envelopes arrived today."

"Mine too. She's putting them in the Bag of Holding, yeah?"

Q shoots me a look. "Is your mom?"

"Of course."

"And Joy's?"

I nod. "I guess our bags are finally complete."

"And you haven't peeked."

"My boy, none of us know shit."

Q lets his head fall on my shoulder. "I love you, man."

"And I love you too, top chap."

"I'm so, so sorry about your dad—"

I raise a hand to stop Q. Enough of this sobbing. "What did the nut say to the other nut it was chasing?" I say.

"Huh?"

"I'm a cashew."

"What?"

I look straight into Q's eyes. "What did one nut say to the other nut it was chasing?"

Q meets my gaze. His irises are so dark his pupils vanish into them.

"I'm a cash—" I say.

"Puhahahahahaha," says Q. "Geehahahahakekekekek."

"Say it," I say. "Don't spray it."

• • •

An hour before school ends, me and Joy conspire to get to the somnolent Consta early to see how many kisses we can fit in before Q arrives to ride with us.

"Let's go out to Mouse World Theme Park this Saturday," I blurt.

Joy smiles, but gets cut short. "I can't. I have a Gathering."

I elevate my eyebrows as far as they will go: *Huh.*

She gives a sad shrug. "Just the Kims and the Changs."

"So it's true," I say. "Everyone's chosen sides."

Now it's Joy's turn to raise an eyebrow.

"I have a Gathering on Sunday," I say. "Just the Lims."

"Wow," says Joy with dismay.

"Whatever," I say, and reel my beautiful girlfriend Joy in for a kiss. But it's like kissing a ham.

"What's wrong?" I say.

"I don't know," says Joy.

I look at her.

Joy draws a circle on her thigh. "Here's us. Kissy-kissy. But outside the circle is all this endless bullshit. And it just sucks. It makes me feel icky and tainted."

"Like a forest covered in tar," I mutter.

"Huh?"

"I said, 'Me too.'"

I cover the circle with my palm, then place her hand atop mine.

"Can we agree not to let the endless bullshit get to us?" I say.

"Can you agree that it sometimes will, though?" says Joy. "I mean, I can't believe I have a king dick for a dad. I'm so ashamed of him. His pride. Fucking with our lives."

I raise the armrest and pull Joy closer. A brown leaf blows in from outside and lands on my thigh. The leaf's cells have dried out and turned it into lace.

How long do our parents hold power over us? I wonder. Is it only as long as we let them?

As if in answer, Hanna finally texts back on my fartphone. *You can have anything you want in my room,* she says. *Are*

you wearing my clothes too? Bad joke, I would totally support
you if you had gender issues to work out

Maybe the answer is forever: our parents hold power over us until they die and beyond.

I promise myself to call Hanna soon.

"Compose thine garmenture," says a voice. "For here approacheth anon your humble servant Q with such light step that the snowflake herself wouldst grow heavy with envy at missing—"

"Ask him who he likes," I say to Joy. "Blindside him."

Joy pops her head out the window.

"Who do you like?" she yells.

"I shall whisper the answer to that mystery upon my last breath," says Q, not missing a single damn beat. "And not a sigh ere. Motherfucker."

"Grr," says Joy. She climbs into the back seat so Q can ride shotgun. We arrange ourselves like this for a specific reason: for visibility.

As we gather the Bags of Holding.

We head to my house first. I park right in the driveway. Mom peeks out and flashes a frown at the sight of Joy in the irreproachable Consta. But she also sees Q riding shotgun, and smiles and waves like normal.

I run in, grab my Bag of Holding, and drive off.

We get to Joy's house. Joy gives my right earlobe a pinch as she hops out, heaves open the front door of her house, and disappears for a long, soundless moment before reappearing. The great door is easing closed behind her when it stops.

It reopens.

Joy's dad stands there. Impeccable. Intelligent. Penetrating.

I see Joy's dad say something to Joy. Joy says something back. He raises a cautionary finger, still staring right at me, and says something more. Then he looks at Q, and suddenly gives an absurdly cheerful wave.

Jesus, what would this guy do if it were just me and Joy without Q?

I watch Joy groan, twirl her hair into a spinning umbrella of green underglow, and hustle back to the car.

"Let's get the fuck outta here," she sighs.

So I drive. Joy's dad's eyes follow us as we leave.

"You okay?" I say.

"Yeah-but-nah," says Joy.

"I feel that," I say.

"Our parents, who wanted us to date, no longer want us to date," says Joy to Q. "Can you believe that shit?"

"Actually, yes," says Q.

We hit Q's house last. While Q runs up his four-hundred-mile-long gravel driveway, I stretch myself to the back seat to clock in a few more kisses with Joy. Hot twin sister Evon appears in one of the windows, rolls her eyes at us, and vanishes.

"That crazy wingnut has all my phone chargers," I say.

"I'll kill her," says Joy.

When we reach Cafe Adagio, it's nearly empty: no students with their laptops, no nothing.

"I guess the senioritis has hit this place, too," I say.

"Inflammation of the senior," says Joy.

We order our drinks and take over the biggest table we can

find. Q instructs us to raise our Bags of Holding laden with envelopes.

There are two types of college admissions responses: Fat envelopes and Thin envelopes. Fat is good. You want Fat. Fat means *we have lots to talk about, and we need all this space for all the words.*

Thin, on the other hand, means they need space for only one word.

"This is it," says Q. "Dump on the count of three. Joy, do not jump the gun this time."

"I won't," says Joy.

"I mean it," says Q.

"I won't, jeez," says Joy.

"One," I say.

"IgotinIgotin," cries Joy. Six envelopes now lie tumbled before her, two Thin, four Fat, and she holds up a Fat marked with the Carnegie Mellon University logo.

Q and I still stand poised with our Bags of Holding as Joy springs up and down.

"I knew you'd get in," I tell her, beaming. "I knew it. You're a rock star."

"Thank you, Frankie," says Joy, and kisses me. She gives me a look. I know what the look means, because I'm giving the same look to her, too. It's the look that says

I guess this is really happening.

"Come on, Frank, onetwothree dump," sighs Q.

"Onetwothree dump," I say.

We dump. The envelopes spill onto the table like fish.

I sift through my pile. UC Berkeley, in. Yes. I pump a fist.

Goal achieved. UCLA, in. Too close to home, but I'll keep it in my back pocket. Princeton, no, whatever, and The Harvard, no. Also whatever. I was expecting nos from those two. Plus, at the moment I could not care less.

Because now I see a big red *S* and a tree: one of the stupidest logos ever created, but to me it transforms the envelope it adorns into a priceless work of art.

It is a Fat.

It is Stanford.

The Harvard of the West.

Actually, fuck everybody: Harvard's the goddamn Stanford of the East.

"Aaaaaaaaaaaaaaa," says Joy, and leaps onto my back. I stumble to keep my balance. I feel dumbfounded, like my face has just been hit by a flying bag of marshmallows, and I slowly turn to face Q.

"We're gonna be roommates," I say.

"My man!" screams Q, and hugs my neck.

Now there are two people hanging off my body. My two best friends on the surface of this unfair, messy, and tragic planet Earth.

"Ow," I say.

Q lets go; Joy slips off as I tip backward, hitting her butt on the floor.

"Let me see yours," I say to Q. "Where is it?"

We sift through his prodigious pile—Q applied to fifteen schools—using all six of our hands to spread everything across the whole table surface.

"Where is it, where is it," I say. I'm scanning for the big red *S* and its tree. Howard, Georgia Tech, Cal Tech, Cornell, all Fats, and finally there it is: Stanford.

It's a Thin.

Everything's gone quiet. Even the baristas say nothing. They eye us nervously from behind their big coffee machines.

"Q," I say.

Q's knees buckle once and he catches himself at the edge of the table.

"I don't get it," says Q. He carefully picks up the envelope and tugs at its edges, like maybe it shrank in the wash. Then he lets it drop.

"But my uncle does research there," says Q to no one. "Even my stupid sister got in. This makes no sense."

"Oh, Q," says Joy.

Now it's our turn to hang off of him. He doesn't handle the weight so well, and falls into a chair.

"Stanford was my only West Coast school," says Q. "I just assumed."

"You didn't apply to Berkeley?"

Q shakes his head. "I just assumed."

"What's your second choice?"

Q shrugs and nudges a Fat on the pile. "Well, I guess I got into MIT, but."

My eyes go flat. "You got into MIT."

He shrugs at the envelope. It is most definitely a Fat. It's the most Fat one there.

"You got into MIT," I say.

"We're gonna be so far away from each other," he says.

Q, I decide, is the stupidest smart person I know. I take the envelope, hold it by two corners, and give it a generous backswing.

"Don't," says Joy.

"I have to do this," I say, and score a clean hit to Q's temple.

"You got into MIT," I say, hitting Q over and over again. "You got into MIT. You got into MIT."

"I guess that's something to be proud of, huh," says Q finally.

There's a pitter-patter of applause coming from behind the counter as the glamorous baristas clap their finely boned hands together.

"You kids are, like, smart," says the male barista.

"Jyeah," says the female barista through her chewing gum.

Me, Joy, and Q huddle in close for a group forehead hug.

"We did it," I say. "I'm happy and sad at the same time."

"Sappy," says Q.

"Had," says Joy.

• • •

When I get home, I flop the Stanford Fat onto the kitchen counter. Mom smiles like *I knew it.* Of course Mom knew. She's the one who's been dutifully packing the Bag of Holding in the first place. She takes the Thin from Harvard and simply rips it in half and smiles.

Dad's at The Store. I call him with the news.

"You doing good," says Dad.

You doing good means *Mom and I are so, so proud of you*

336

and all of your hard work and diligence. Don't sweat all that
Harvard stuff. We love you.

"Thanks, Dad," I say.

I go upstairs.

I flop onto my bed. I never hit it, though, because I'm as light as a toy balloon. I just kind of float an inch above the comforter. I'm an astronaut, and this is my first exciting night aboard the International Space Station, where of course they have normal beds that look just like mine.

School is done. Admissions are done. I did great. So did everyone else: the Limbos, the Apeys.

We all *doing good.*

I see the rolling meadow full of people and picnics and kids, and hey: Joy's there too. All that's left to do is be with her as long as I can until the sun sets and the streetlights come on.

chapter 30

a land called hanna li

—It's Frankie!

—Dude!

—Du-u-u-de.

—Does your portable texting device not work in Boston?

—Shut up.

—I figured if I placed a telephone call, you would pick up because you're old.

—Isn't hearing my voice nicer than texting?

—So how's Boston?

—This way we get to actually be present with each other, unlike these two Bradys here not even fucking watching where they're going? Heads up, bros, there's a whole world around you?

—Your voice sounds different. Are you getting sick?

—Are you Frank or Mom right now?

—How's Miles?

—He's the best, he says hey, and oh shit, he wants to meet

up in SF when you go to *Stanford*, what what, congrats, homie!

—Hey! That was my big news.

—Mom emailed me already.

—That makes like two whole times this year.

—It's like I'm her daughter or something, right?

—Jeez.

—Sorry.

—So, uh, did you and Mom, you know, get to talking about stuff or anything?

—Oh, Frankenstein, can we just celebrate you right now? You're a total rock star.

—Thanks.

—Rock star. You.

—Thankyouthankyouthankyou.

—So, uh, Mom emailed me about the other stuff. With Dad.

—I was gonna tell you.

—

—Hello? You there?

—Dad's really sick, huh.

—I mean it's, basically, um . . .

—I know.

—It's so fucked up.

—My doctor friend's been helping me look up a bunch of shit about small-cell and she thinks the prognosis is right.

—It's so fucked up.

—I just don't know what to think.

—I know. I don't know. I wanna say I wish you were back home in Cali.

—I wanna say that too.

—Your room's the same.

—

—Hello?

—Change of subject. How's Q? He got in too, right?

—Dude. Stanford rejected him.

—No! Is he okay?

—He got into MIT.

—Pthpthphtpt, whatever then. Tell him to come hang out with me and Miles when he gets here. What about Joy?

—CMU.

—So, summer of love and then that's it, huh.

—Change of subject.

—Joy's dad didn't pull any shit with you, did he?

—No.

—It wouldn't surprise me.

—It wouldn't?

—He's been driving Dad crazy for years.

—Huh?

—The guy's a rich prick!

—You knew about that this whole time?

—Kyung Hee told me forever ago! It's a bunch of city mouse, country mouse bullshit!

—Why didn't you tell me?

—Oh, you know what else that peg-legged pirate whore said?

—Hanna!

—Kyung Hee's all, *You've chosen a difficult path to love outside your race* and *You need to be prepared to deal with*

340

how that affects all parties around you and *Don't just think about yourself* and blablabla! She's such a fucking super-Korean!

—Hanna!

—What?

—We need to talk more!

—I know, I know, I know.

—I like talking with you.

—I like talking with you too.

—*And* you're my sister. You know how rare that combo is?

—Oh, Frank.

—Because with Dad and all . . .

—Stop.

—I just think about when we're older and stuff.

—Don't make me cry.

—Okayokay. Wanna hear a joke?

—You're my favorite person in this whole shitty world, and I love you.

—

—Frank?

—I mean, I love you too. You know?

—

—Hey, are you crying?

—No.

—What did one nut say to the other nut it was chasing?

—I'm pregnant.

—That makes no sense.

—I said I'm pregnant.

—Wait.

—

—Are you serious?

—It's only a month in, so you're not really supposed to tell anyone because anything can happen and you never know, but I really needed to tell someone, and besides, anything *has already been* happening for a super-long time now and it's been nothing but *you never know* forever. So I'm telling you.

—Oh my god, Hanna!

—We find out the sex around month three. I really want a girl.

—What the fuck, congrats!

—You're gonna be an uncle, Frank Sinatra.

—Do Mom-n-Dad know?

—Hell no.

—Want me to say something?

—Hell no.

—But don't you . . . ?

—I'll handle it. Just gotta work up to it.

—You are?

—Wull, I have to, don't I? It's six to twelve, right?

—Fuck.

—I know.

—Your room's the same.

—You already said that.

—Maybe you could come home with Miles and like stay in a hotel or something, I don't know.

—Maybe. I want to. Miles says I should.

—You could meet Mom-n-Dad at The Store or like some-place neutral.

—You know what I hate, Frankerchief?

—What.

—I hate that I miss home. And Mom-n-Dad too. I fucking hate that I feel that.

—So just come the fuck home, then.

—It's way more simplicated than that.

—I miss you. Does that help unsimplicate things?

—But you don't know. You're still in the high school bubble. Out here, love strikes whenever it wants.

—Love chooses you.

—What?

—Hanna, just come home, say your piece, and let Mom-n-Dad deal with it, the sooner the better so they have more time to get over their brainlock before—you know—before—

—I'm just saying it's extremely, extremely simplicated is all.

—Tell me about it. Me and Joy have to lie low.

—How come?

—There's enough tension between the parents already.

—Right, right.

—Kinda sucks the fun out of things.

—I wish this whole shitty world were different.

—This sounds weird, but sometimes I feel like I'm cheating on Mom-n-Dad by sneaking around with Joy. Does that make sense?

—Unfortunately, yes.

—You gonna make it home before I head up to college?

—I'll try. I don't know. Just gotta work up to it.

—Okay.

343

—Okay.

—Do you guys have any baby names picked out?

—Shit, my T's here. Probably gonna lose you.

—What's a T?

—My train. I love you, Frankie.

—Hello?

—

—Hanna?

—

—

oobleck

When we were little, we used to make oobleck.

You know oobleck: one part water, two parts cornstarch, green coloring for flair. This mixture creates a substance known as a non-Newtonian fluid. It's named after a substance in a children's book by Dr. Seuss. The Oobleck is a big ball of ruinous, sticky goo that arrives and almost destroys everything after a king, bored with his too-perfect realm, fervently wishes for something—anything—new.

It's a careful-what-you-wish-for story.

It's also an appreciate-what-you-have-before-it-turns-into-what-you-had story.

Isaac Newton was a groundbreaking scientist from the seventeenth century. But he was also super into the occult, and wrote a lot about creationism and how there must be some way to turn lead into gold.

Dr. Seuss was a groundbreaking children's book author beloved for his antifascist humanism. But in his early career, he drew a lot of racist cartoons depicting black people as savages and mocking Japanese-American internment victims. He was full of remorse for this earlier version of himself for his entire life.

Nothing is just any one single thing. In fact, what starts out as one thing can turn out to be something completely different.

If you press hard on oobleck, it feels like a solid. Same if you strike it. You can even run across a big trough of oobleck, if for some reason you (a) have a big trough lying around and (b) enough oobleck to fill it.

But here's the weird thing about oobleck: if you gently pass your fingertips through, it yields just like liquid.

SO . . .

If walls of oobleck block your way,

don't punch and slap and kick all day.

Just hold your breath and close your eyes

and simply ease yourself inside.

Walk slowly through the dark, don't fear

For someday you'll be far from here.

• • •

Dad's getting worse.

I always wondered what his last day at The Store would be like, but that day just came and went before I even really noticed. One minute he was sitting on his still-new stool at the cash register, and the next minute he got the spins so bad he had to lie down right on the floor.

At the emergency room it was determined that his white blood cell count was dangerously low from the chemo. This means his immune system is extremely weak. This means he can no longer work or be among people.

This is the trade-off. Chemo means Dad will live longer. But it also means he lives worse.

I guess it's good that Palomino High School has been brought to a standstill because of widespread inflammation of the senior, because it frees me up to do things like help Mom shuttle Dad back and forth from the hospital, help train Luis (the ex-con once jailed for a carjacking gone wrong) as a store assistant, and just sit with Dad at home, to build whatever jeong we can while we still can.

I sneak a selfie with Dad while he's asleep—he's asleep a lot—and send it to Hanna. Hanna starts to respond but never does.

I spend a lot of time at The Store with Luis while Mom mans the register. I like Luis. We put on our hoodies and move shit around in the walk-in cooler. He's openly remorseful about his mistake, and loathes himself for carjacking someone just to get approval from his gang friends. Like most human beings he was desperate for validation. Now he gets daily validation by the armload from his wife and baby. He prays before every meal, at the end of every day, and every time he gets behind the wheel of his car to go home, for forgiveness.

Being busy and in constant motion means my fartphone goes unanswered for longer stretches of time. Joy buzzes and buzzes, wondering if I'm okay. If Dad's okay.

"Your phone's blowing up, holmes," says Luis. "You got a girl or something?"

I like Luis. But it wouldn't be very cool to just openly blablabla about Joy right in front of Mom, so I tell him no, there's no girl, it's just friends calling about graduation parties.

For four weeks I barely go to school, because I work basically nonstop at The Store. It's the opposite of senioritis. I don't see Joy. I live with a weight belt strapped around my waist. Q drives all the way to visit one time, and makes a comedic attempt to help mop the floor. Out of mercy Mom sends him out to get tacos instead.

Within those four weeks Luis has mastered The Store, and has even brought in his shy, ever-smiling teenaged cousin to lend a hand. And finally, one time as I'm closing up, I notice that me and Mom have barely lifted a finger all day.

Hey yubs, says Joy. *How's The Store? Wannaseeya wannaseeya.*

I want to see Joy too. I need to get this summer of love going, stat.

"I have an idea," I tell Mom. "I'll be right back."

"Luis doing everything so good," says Mom. "Don't tell Daddy."

"That's why I have my idea," I say.

I take Mom's bank card, drive out to Tweeters & More, and buy a dozen drop cameras. When I get back to The Store, I explain the situation to Luis before installing them.

"Listen, I trust you and your cousin completely," I say. "This is not about you. This is Dad management."

Luis clocks each of the cameras with a wary eye but readily understands why they're a good idea. Still, he tweaks the angles when I'm finished.

"I need some kind of dead zone for breaks," he says.

"You got it, Luis," I say.

We craft a nice dead zone by the paper products.

"Just remember to call and ask how to do things now and then," I say.

"Uh, okay," says Luis.

"Even though you already know how to do everything, just call."

Luis stretches his eyebrows. "Ah, I get it."

My idea is perfect because I know Dad would never let someone work at The Store without him present. He's too paranoid, too proud of what he's built. But without him there's only Mom, and no way am I going to let Mom work all day by herself.

So when me and Mom approach his bedside to break the news that Luis and his cousin will be operating The Store full-time, I make sure I have a brand-new tablet all set up and ready for him.

"No," says Dad. "I never allowing full-time employee without I'm being there."

That's when I shove the screen in his face. "This lets you switch cameras. Here's a tile view of all twelve. Full-color HD, Dad."

"Frankie, no," says Dad. "Luis stacking wrong way this one. He—"

On screen, the much younger, much stronger Luis reorders and stacks three hundred cans of beer in under a minute.

"Oh, he doing good," says Dad, mesmerized.

"I told you," says Mom. "That's Luis."

"Gimme one ice water," says Dad, his eyes fixed to the screen.

"You got it, Dad," I say.

Ring-ring. It's Luis, calling Dad's phone.

"You doing good job," says Dad.

"Thanks, boss," says Luis. "So quick question, boss: when does the ice delivery come in again?"

"Thursday ten a.m.," says Dad. "You write down, remembering."

"Will do," says Luis. "Thanks, boss."

I bring Dad his ice water, and he barely notices me. I squeeze Mom's shoulder. She nods at me: *go.*

So I go to the bathroom, lock the door, and turn on the shower. As it warms up, I finally indulge myself in a little fartphone time.

New exhibit at the Henry Gallery, says Joy. *You free?*

I smile. *I'm free,* I say.

Really? says Joy.

Yes.

Heart smileys fill my screen.

The shower's hot now, but before I get in, I send a quick message to Q. It's been a while since I set up a fake date. It's high time for some Joy in my life.

My dear old bean, I say. *Your assistance is crucially needed tonight for an impromptu rendezvous.*

Confound it, says Q. *For I am encircled by familial interlopers visiting with the irritating pretense of endless pre-graduation formalities.*

Huh?

Got a bunch of relatives in town from DC using me and Evon's graduation as an excuse for a California vacation with free lodging.

Crap, I say. *So you're busy?*

I'm never too busy for you, mate. Give me a sec.

By the time I'm out of the shower, Q has responded.

Full steam ahead, my boy. The three of us are "watching" Dwarven Wars: Song of Torment.

I pump a fist. I have my in-car alibi for when I pull up to Joy's house and the watchful eyes of her dad waiting there. Thank you, Q.

I get dressed, leap down the stairs, and lean from a door-jamb to inform Mom-n-Dad, who are still huddled over the drop cam tablet.

"I'm going out to see a movie with Q," I say. I of course don't mention Joy, for the same reason I of course don't smack away ice cream from a child.

"Oh, Luis cousin doing so good job mopping," murmurs Dad to the screen.

"We should be hiring sooner," says Mom.

"We making less money," says Dad.

"But more time we having, figure it out!"

"You right," says Dad. "More time we having."

"Guys," I say.

Mom looks up. She looks like the girl in her yearbook. "Have a fun," she sings.

Then she snuggles closer to Dad and returns to the tablet.

I'm so proud of myself I could puke rainbows.

"Ninety percent of Mexicans, they stealing," says Dad to the screen, quoting his own fake statistics. "But Luis not stealing nothing."

"Not ninety percent," says Mom, armed with fake statistics of her own. "Something like seventy-five percent."

"Luis cousin no steal nothing too," says Dad, impressed.

I roll my eyes so high it hurts, and leave.

• • •

It feels good to be back to what I hope will become an old routine:

- Pick up Q
- Go to Joy's, have Q ring the doorbell
- Get in the Consta, floor it
- Go over the plot synopsis of *Dwarven Wars* just in case
- Park, then give Q a big group hug to let him know how much we love him for this
- Grow uncomfortable with guilt as Q shrugs and says, *What are single friends for?*
- Part ways for three to four hours

"What are you gonna do with yourself?" I say.

"Plan out our next big Dungeons & Dragons campaign at a cafe, maybe," says Q, shifting his heavy backpack. "Paul wants to play one more before summer ends."

"Nerds," says Joy.

We look at her like *So?*

Everything is full tonight in the warehouse district: the food trucks, the shitty Burger Mac, that brand-new Sixth Taste, everything. A woman and her daughter are grilling bacon-wrapped hot dogs illegally on a converted shopping cart—delicious, illegal hot dogs—and even *she's* got at least a forty-minute line of customers.

It's pre-graduation madness. Has to be. There's only one restaurant that's remotely feasible.

Cheese Barrel Grille.

"Shoot me in the head and stuff it with socks," says Joy.

"That's super disgusting," I say.

"Let's just go," says Joy.

They give us an LED buzzer coaster, which Joy hisses at. We head outside and down the street to see if we can get tickets to the Henry Gallery, but there's a surging line there, too.

"Maybe it'll be shorter by the time we're finished with dinner," I say.

"Grr," says Joy. "I'm getting hangry, so call me on my bullshit if I bullshit."

"Easy, wild beastie," I say. "They said half an hour."

The only thing to do is get a couple of sodas and stand around a cocktail table shaped like a barrel with a cheese logo stamped onto its side. Joy sips fiercely. I wrap an arm around her, put my straw in her drink, pretend we're an old-tyme couple in an old-tyme soda parlor, and she softens a little bit. We even kiss a little, until we discover a family of four staring at us and stop.

"Ng, party of four?" says the thin, European-American hostess with flat eyes.

The dad from Ng Party of Four triumphantly offers the hostess his pulsating coaster, and they vanish into Cheese Barrel Grille's neon-lit interior.

"We were here before them," says Joy.

"Were we?" I say.

Joy stabs her ice cubes with a straw. "Definitely."

"I don't know," I say.

Joy practically scowls at me. "Yeah, but I know. We were."

I rub her back. "Hey, look, we have only like ten minutes to go. You want another soda?"

Joy cocks her hip and eyes the hostess podium. "I'm gonna say something."

"Joy, come on."

"Not gonna sit here and just take this kind of shit."

The hostess comes bustling back, and suddenly Joy's there to intercept her.

"Hey, we were here before the Ngs, miss—Becky?"

"Joy, hey," I hiss, and slit my throat with my thumb.

Joy ignores me. "Why did they get to go first?"

The hostess gives Joy a blank look. "We seat our guests based on table availability. They're four, you're two."

"So can't you just split the table?"

"We're unfortunately unable to saw our four-tops in half," says the hostess, and begins dabbing at her podium screen.

"Are we next?" says Joy.

"I have you ready in about ten minutes," says the hostess. "Would you like another soda?"

"I don't want another soda, Becky," says Joy.

Becky freezes in midtap and just stares at Joy. Is she considering kicking us out? Because that would make this already great night even better.

I lunge forward to grab Joy. "Ten minutes is great," I say.

Back at our barrel, Joy stews. "Way to be on my side, Frank."

"You said to call your bullshit, so I'm calling your bullshit," I say. "Look at these guys over here. They're waiting like big kids. You can wait like a big kid, too."

I nod at two toddlers jammed in a stroller with a fartphone, and I can see Joy realize how petty she's being. She offers me a simpering look.

"You're just hangry, okay?" I say.

"Li, party of two?" says Becky.

"Thanks, Becky," I say.

"We had a cancellation," says Becky, and gives Joy an eyebrow.

The bread helps. It makes the hangries go away. After a prodigious delay our food finally arrives—Joy gets her plate of I-forget-what and I get my order of it-doesn't-matter, because it's all truly awful anyway. Fried something atop wax pilaf next to green mini-logs in a pool of salty milk, all easy to chew. Retiree food. We don't even bother with any of the desserts, which are insultingly huge, like some kind of gluttonous dare. We just ask for the check, and wait, and wait.

"I'm a mess without my little China girl," sing drunken voices amid the din of the restaurant.

Three huge European-American guys—fuck it, let's just call them white—are crooning at Joy.

Joy buries her face in her hands. "You gotta be kidding me."

But they're not. My heart floods. The whole world stops down to a dark halo.

I stand. "Hey. Go find a gopher hole to fuck."

"Grasshoppa mad," says one.

"Ah so," says the other.

"Hai-ya waaaah," says another, and aims a flat hand.

"I will feed your severed dicks to each other," I shout, just as there's a lull among the shocked diners.

The three bros become sober. "I think this prick really wants to do this," says one.

"Sir?" says a voice. It's Becky.

"These—assholes—are antagonizing us," I tell her.

"I apologize, but I'm going to have to ask you to leave," says Becky. "Consider the meal our treat, compliments of the house."

"Why do we have to leave?" I shout.

"Oh, both parties have to leave," says Becky. "I'm giving you a head start."

"We shouldn't have to leave in the first place," I say. "These guys started it."

"Frank," groans Joy. "It's not worth it."

And so, to the bemusement of all the dining patrons at Cheese Barrel Grille, me and Joy walk the long walk out of the restaurant. It is a bizarre walk of shame. Because what do I have to be ashamed of?

Outside, me and Joy find a stretch of wall to lean on and regain our balance.

"It's like the world is trying to fuck with our night," she says.

"I think that's a little egotistical," I say. "The world doesn't care that much about two specific people."

"Jesus, Frank, just agree with me."

"I'm joking," I say.

"No you're not," says Joy, and she's right. I'm being prickly.

"Anyway, I don't think the forces of fate are conspiring against us," I say, and shove off the wall. I lead Joy around a corner toward the Henry Gallery. Might as well keep going, I figure.

But when we reach the gallery, we see that the doors have been closed with a handwritten sign.

AT MAX CAPACITY NO FURTHER ENTRY
BY ORDER OF THE FIRE DEPARTMENT SORRY

"Huh," I say. "Maybe I'm wrong about the forces of fate."

I glance at Joy. She looks like she's fighting tears.

"Hey, come on," I say. "It's just one bad night."

"Out of how many, though?"

"Don't think like that."

"But don't I have to?" says Joy. "I haven't been able to see you in a month, and I'm not blaming you, you were doing what you had to do, but I've been waiting a month and—this—is what we get?"

"It's just one bad night. We'll have more nights."

"You are not ditching your dad to see me," says Joy. "I won't allow it. You have to see him while you can."

"I'll be able to see both you and Dad."

357

Joy wrings her hands. "Be realistic. We don't have that many nights together before summer ends. That's the reason why I'm crying like a stupid baby right now. I just realized it, just now. There's all this bullshit pressure for the few nights we have left."

"We can have a do-over."

"When, Frank? Next couple of weeks? A month? And that's *if* we can find a spare sliver of time to sneak out in, and also *if* Q can fucking chaperone us?"

I approach, then gingerly touch her shoulders before bringing her in for a hug. "It does put a lot of pressure on us, you're right. But I promise next time will be more fun. We can make it fun."

"Summers of love are supposed to be carefree and la la la lovey dovey skipping in a meadow, not sneaking around to keep your parents from going to war with each other," says Joy. She wipes her eyes. "I must look like someone just died."

"Not yet, anyway," I find myself saying.

And a strange spell must have befallen me, because now Joy is carefully kissing my face all over. "Oh yubs," she's saying. "I'm so sorry. I'm so sorry."

Buzz-buzz. When I look, there are messages waiting for me, all from Q.

I'm back at the Consta.

Ready when you are.

Oy mate, been waiting 45 minutes now.

Where the bloody hell are you two?

"Shit," I say. Me and Joy hurry back down the street to where we parked. Back away from all the couples, away from the lights, away, away to where the car sits all by itself beneath a single sad streetlamp lashed to a telephone pole.

"Q?" I say. "You here?"

Q emerges from behind the car.

"Were you hiding?" says Joy.

"You know cops shoot kids like me when they're alone on streets like this," says Q.

"Fuck," I say. I throw an arm around him. "I'm sorry. I just lost track of time."

Q ducks away, his face a mixture of irritation and fear and relief.

"We should go home," says Q. "It's late."

So go home we do.

- We drop off Joy first. Q sits shotgun, for visibility. Joy gives me a blue little wave bye.
- Next is Q. He jogs away backward to wave at me before breaking into a sprint.
- Last is me.

Everyone is asleep when I get into the house. I flop onto my bed and stare at the stained popcorn ceiling. I close my eyes and see Joy's face.

There are moments in time, and this is a moment in time for sure. Joy's face, shining with glee, with tears, with anger. Joy's face gone dim with melancholy as she waved bye earlier.

"Tonight was pretty much a disaster," I say to the ceiling. I take out my phone. My thumbs begin tapping away all by themselves.

Tonight was pretty much a disaster, I say. *I'm sorry.*

Next time we'll have proper fun.

And the time after that, and the time after that.

We will defy the fates, me and you.

Let the summer of love begin!

My thumbs finally stop. I rest the phone on my belly, satisfied, and let the glass slab rise and fall with my breath. Minutes pass. No response from Joy. Maybe she's asleep?

Buzz-buzz. There she is. I check my screen.

If you say so, yubs, says Joy.

Joy types some more. I watch the speech bubble do its little One Moment, Please dance to let me know she's typing. Finally her message appears: a cartoon character of herself in pajamas, yawning. *Good night.*

I like this idea of *If you say so.* If I say so, so it shall be.

I'm talking about *will.*

If you have the will to do something, and you keep at it, and you don't give up, you can do anything. And there's no greater will than the will to love who you want.

So I say it again: *Let the summer of love begin!*

I watch for a moment. I yawn. Joy doesn't respond. She's probably asleep.

I don't want to wake her, so I write *I love you* without hitting Send. I just know in my heart that somewhere in those sleeping circuits my speech bubble is there, doing its little One Moment, Please dance.

chapter 32

alpha & omega

THA K YO   CO FE

Graduations are supposed to be celebrations. But why? Why would you celebrate the end of close friends? Why would you celebrate leaving your academic home, bless this mess, of four years? Or your parents' home, which had its rules to be sure but also all your stuff plus free food?

Most students fake it: the smiles and hat tossing and all that.

Me and the Apeys? We're doing it right.

Look at Amelie Shim, with her phone upheld to record a tearful Snapstory.

Or Paul Olmo, sitting with a heavy arm draped over Q's shoulders.

And look at Q, just kind of examining his sneakers under his purple robe in a catatonic state, probably looking for some clue about why he never made a move with his mystery girl. Now it's officially too late.

John Lim is missing, probably bickering silently with Ella Chang behind a hedge or something. John is the letter *N* and Ella is the letter *U*.

Brit Means sits alone, staring at the school buildings with her ancient and gray and eternal eyes in a never-ending farewell gaze. She turns to me for a moment. She *observes* me. Then she's finished observing, and turns away again. Brit is the letter *F*.

Now look at me, and look at Joy. We sit on opposite ends of our aisle—that was intentional. I catch glimpses of her catching glimpses of me, but there's no way we can risk any looks longer than that. Both my mom and her parents sit close by in the audience. I want to sneak her away for one last sad and desperate make-out session by the AC units, but as of today that's officially no longer an option.

I'm the letter *T*, and Joy is a far-off *E*.

The only happy one of us is Naima Gupta, who long ago abandoned our aisle to dance around handing out sour gummy worms to everyone. I think Naima grew up until she was thirteen, decided that was enough, and just stayed there. I find myself envying that. Naima must've heard some version of *Go do you* and taken it to heart.

Naima is the other *E*.

All together our mortarboard caps were supposed to spell out the breathtakingly witty joke:

THANK YOU COFFEE

But so much for that.

The speeches end, we all stand, and me and Q just kind of toss our caps over our shoulders and walk away.

"The diploma things are empty!" shouts a voice. It's Wu, surrounded by hysterically laughing girls watching him through raised phones. "We're still in school, guys!" says Wu. "It's not over!"

We get them in the mail, I want to say, but I'll let Wu have his moment. One of the girls cannot help but run her hand down his chest, the way a dazzled child pets a big beautiful Labrador. Wu glances at me, whips a quick chin-nod. I nod back.

Me and Q head to his parents, who give me a hug.

"We're so proud of you," says Q's mom.

"Diplomas on fleek," says Q's dad with great rapidity.

Evon stops texting the world only to snap uncomfortably close-up photos of me, Q, and her own golden tassel before resuming texting the world.

Behind Evon stand fifteen of her and Q's relatives, all looking out of place in their East Coast jackets and boots. They're taking photos of everything: palm trees, the hills, grass, a seagull eating half a hot dog. Stuff I never even notice.

Q introduces me to each and every one of them. As I'm shaking hands, I notice one guy just a couple years older than me dressed in a rainbow of blacks, with black elastics around his wrist and a Ken Ishii tee shirt. He's staring at me as intently as I'm staring at him. His name is Francis.

"They say if you shake hands with your twin, the world will cease to exist," says Francis Lee, cousin of Q Lee.

"Air shake, then," I say, and vigorously masturbate the gap between us.

The formalities completed, me and Q head over to where Mom's standing, alone.

363

Mom has been live-streaming the whole event to Dad at home with her phone mounted to a colossal telescoping stick. She swings the stick, hits me in the face, then backs up to compose the shot.

"Congratulation," says Mom. She spanks the air with her free hand. "You hugging Q. Hugging-hugging."

So me and Q hug.

"Congratulation," says the tiny voice of Dad through the phone speakers.

"Thanks, Dad," I say.

"Thanks, Mr. Li," says Q.

I glance over to Joy's parents a ways away. They are watching us. They probably assume Dad was too busy at The Store to come to his own son's graduation. They're probably judging us.

Let them judge. Dad is here, just not how they think.

Mom sees me looking at them. She waves them off and laughs. "You pretending hugging Daddy," she says.

Q and I look at each other, then decide to hug invisible columns of air before us like the world's worst dancers.

"Ha ha," says Dad's tiny voice. "I hugging too."

Hanna's here too, at least in text message form.

Congrats, baby brother . . . Let me know when you get my care package

Mom swings the phone around, strikes someone at the base of their skull. When Dad begins to have a coughing fit, Mom snaps the stick closed and whispers to him close against the screen. She shoos me away.

"Go have a fun," she says. "You celebrating."

Graduations are supposed to be celebrations, so me and Q wander off to join a circle of classmates and stand around.

"It is done," says Q.

"I am the Alpha and the Omega, the Beginning and the End," I say.

"Some biblical shit right there," says a voice.

It's Joy. Her robe is stupid—all our robes are stupid—but somehow she manages to make it look sexy.

She gives Q a friend-hug, then gives me a friend-hug as well. Her touch is like giving a desert wanderer the last snort of water in an empty to-go cup. Nowhere near enough.

But I don't complain or try for more, because I can feel the eyes on me.

Joy's dad, watching me through cop sunglasses.

"Dinner? Dinner?" I say, pointing. "Everyone have their respective fancy dinners to go to?"

"Yeah," says Q. "Remington Resort."

"Dang," says Joy. "We're going to Capital Steakhouse."

"Ain't you two fancy?" I say. "I guess I'll catch up with you guys later, then."

Inside, I wonder, *How many more times will I be able to say such a thing, and with such ease?*

"Where are you going for dinner?" says Joy.

"Eh, probably just gonna stay home and order delivery," I say as casually as I can. Because it's kind of a boneheaded question, and I see Joy quickly kick herself for asking it.

"Of course," she says. "Right, duh."

I stifle the urge to kiss her embarrassment away, let her know it's okay, don't sweat it. We make do with another friend-hug. I give one to Q too, just to quell any suspicions. I hope he doesn't notice my ulterior purpose, or care.

We part ways.

Within fifteen minutes, the graduation lawn stands empty. It is done.

chapter 33

asshole light

I tell Mom-n-Dad, "Go rest. I got this." I pack away the half-finished food containers into the fridge. I load the dishwasher, squirt in detergent, and hit Start. I unfurl my graduation gown and hang it in the closet next to winter coats that never get any use.

I head up to my room, change into my reddest blacks and reddest-red sneakers, and quickly rummage to find a head-mounted flashlight. I tiptoe and check on Mom-n-Dad. They're both asleep in Dad's lazy chair. I scribble out a note.

GONE TO GRADUATION PARTY

Outside, I silently heave the Consta out of the driveway in neutral, waving hi as one of my unknown neighbors watches with his head cocked, and wait until I'm down the street to coax the engine to life.

I'm still a good climber, I think.

By the time I get to Crescent Cove, it's night. There's no official parking at this tiny local beach. Just a long shoulder flanked by blond grass tall enough to hide a car, which is good. Opposite the shoulder is a flimsy gate—easily hopped—and a fire road winding its way up.

She must be in bed by now, back from her big graduation dinner. She must be alone by now.

I want to pick up where that graduation-ceremony-appropriate friend-hug left off. I have in my bag this glass teardrop-shaped terrarium filled with moss and lichen as a gift for Joy. I will give it to her, and I know she'll love it more than any bouquet of flowers. I'm getting this summer of love started right now, despite the hour. Because I say so.

I'm talking about *will*.

I know this fire road. When the Songs hosted Gatherings, me and the rest of the Limbos would jump the balcony above and hike down to the water with flashlights dancing.

Me and Joy.

Now, years later, I am the only Limbo here. My flashlight is steady against my forehead. And instead of down, I'm heading up. The dirt road dips and rises gently; I pass through rivers of warm and cool air as I travel. When I reach the huge concrete pilings beneath Joy's house, I click my light off.

It's easier coming down than going up, because of the climb. But I remember—my ten-year-old body remembers for me—how to brace myself on the massive I-beam and shimmy up to the narrow diagonal cross support, which, once traversed on tiptoe using the square rivets for extra grip, leads me up to the only scary part: a pull-up from a bar with nothing beneath it for fifteen feet.

Jesus, I think. *We used to do this as kids?*

Anyway, turns out I can still do pull-ups.

I throw one leg over and find myself staring at acres of pristine wood deck flooring. The house lights are off. I listen. Amid the warm breeze and faintly sighing ocean I can hear the far-off blabbering of a television, which means the Songs are home.

I tiptoe along—tripping a rude cone of light.

I make a pathetic attempt to hide behind a small cylindrical planter—the Songs always were so goddamn minimalist and tasteful with their decor—and wait for my heart to go from sixteenth, then to eighth, and finally back to quarter notes as no one appears to investigate.

I duck out of sensor range, wait for an eternity for the stupid light to go off, and press myself against the back wall of the house. Twenty feet to go.

A face floats in the black glass when I get there.

It's Joy, reading a book by pinlight.

I tap as quietly on the glass as I can, just inches from her head, and give her a heart attack.

"It's me, it's me," I hiss. I turn my flashlight on myself to prove it.

Joy stops herself from throwing her book through the window. She marks her page, opens the window, and then hits me across the face with it.

"You almost made me shit the bed," she says.

"Doesn't this bring back memories?" I say.

Joy's eyes widen. "You climbed up here?"

I nod.

"Using the old way we used to?"

I nod.

"Oh, Frank," says Joy, and looks about to cry.

"Are you okay?" I say.

"We need to talk," says Joy.

She shoves a big beanbag against her door, locking it but not locking it, and perches on the open windowsill. She removes a sensor the size of a pill from the sash frame, tapes it to a corresponding sensor lodged in the side jamb, and hops outside.

"Last thing we need is the alarm going off," she says.

It's a badass bit of hackery that makes me grab her waist for a kiss. But her lips are limp. Her body is tense.

"Come on," she whispers.

She leads me hand in hand into a moonlit clearing hidden among three Monterey cypresses. They form a kind of tent, hidden to the land but open to the sea before us. I can see the white of waves tumbling below.

We duck inside and sit. If I had a fool's head full of fantasy, I would think she was taking me here to make love with this view of the ocean.

But right away I can tell this is no fantasy.

She tailor-sits, and waits for me to tailor-sit too. I look at her hand. There it is, placed right on top of mine. She painted her nails. In the dim light I can't tell what color.

I am just thinking to myself, *I need to kiss her now before she can say anything* when she says it.

"I think we should stop seeing each other."

"No," I blurt, like a child.

"Frank."

"You didn't call me yubs," I say with wonder. "I knew something was wrong."

"Frank, listen."

"This is a breakup, isn't it."

"How long do you think we can sneak around before something really bad happens?"

"Holy shit, we're breaking up right now."

I dig the heels of my hands into my eyes until the ocean sounds like it's roaring.

"You're really doing this," I say. "Our dads get into some stupid fight, and now you're really just giving up and walking away."

What is happening to my face? Whatever it is, Joy becomes slightly fearful of it. Do I look angry right now? Betrayed, and out for vengeance?

"We just graduated," I say. "We only have three months of summer. If we're just super careful and get coordinated and time things right, we can make the most of it."

A touch from Joy stops my babbling. "Listen to yourself."

"We can make this work," I say.

"This is the situation," says Joy, and clutches her hair. I'm sure it's flashing green, but again: this light is so dim. "This is my life they're messing with," she says. "It's yours, too."

"So let's just ignore them," I say. "Fuck the tribe. Let's just walk away."

"You can't just walk away."

"You can do whatever your soul wills you to do," I say. "Fuck everyone else."

"Is that really what you want?" she says. "Just fuck everyone else? Do you even know what *fuck everyone else* would entail? It's not just about me and you. I don't want our families fighting. I don't want things to get weird with my dad for god knows how long. I don't want that for you, either."

I laugh to myself. "You're saying it's not worth it."

"What's not worth it?"

I look at her. "Love."

Joy looks hurt. "That is not what I'm saying."

But I just keep looking at her—

"That is not what I'm saying," she says again.

—because it is.

"I'm only saying there are other, bigger things to think about," she says.

"There's nothing bigger than love," I say, and draw my knees in close so I can press my eyes into them until the green-and-black checkerboards appear.

Let's just be in love, I think, and all I want is for her to say, *If you say so, Frank,* and bring everything back to the way it was with a single, long kiss. But instead she's just staring at the waves tumbling and tumbling far below, preparing other words to say.

"You know how your dad had to choose between living shorter but better, and taking the chemo and living longer but worse?" she says.

I swallow to quell a rising lump of tears.

"We're not taking the chemo," she says.

I don't quite get what she's saying here—is she comparing us to cancer?—but it doesn't matter because her words gut me anyway.

"But I love you," I say. "You love me."

"We're a happy family," says Joy, in the saddest singsong ever.

"So let's just be in love," I try.

"Frank, I can't just, we—" says Joy, and covers her mouth because she's run out of words. Or is she trying to keep them in?

"I love you," I say. "You love me. It's as simple as that."

She buries her face and I hold her with one arm, then two, but she is already feeling strange to me. Some aura is slipping away. Joy is a campfire dying before my very eyes, and I am inept when it comes to campfires.

She peers through barred forearms. "The ocean is glowing—look."

I glance out. Indeed, the waves are crashing blue.

"It's peak sparkles right now," I say.

"I always wondered what causes that," mumbles Joy to no one.

"Dinoflagellates."

Joy turns her head to face me through her hair. "How do you know that?"

"It doesn't matter," I say, and the last of our embers goes out.

But I don't want them out. I stomp and stomp on them, because the moron inside me believes that stomping is the best way to stoke a fire back to life.

"You could start going on hikes," I say, mustering the fakest pep ever. "Then I could meet you down at Crescent Cove—"

"I can't do this."

"It'd be perfect because you can't even see the left edge of the beach from here."

"What would Hanna think of your plan?"

"This is not like that."

"Good night, Frank."

And Joy just gets up and leaves.

I don't watch her go.

It's easier to stare at the dinoflagellates glowing blue, their minuscule, pathetic way of raging against the waves that simply refuse to stop bullying them around.

Asshole waves.

Asshole ocean.

If I stare at the ocean, I can pretend Joy is still sitting next to me. But she's not. There's barely a mark where she had been sitting, and that mark went cold quick.

I take the teardrop-shaped terrarium and hang it from a branch to swing madly in the wind. Its contents won't last long.

Eventually I get up and leave the scraggly tent of cypresses. I walk down the hidden path, back onto the Songs' deck. Joy's window is closed. The blinds are drawn. I trip the blinding floodlight again and walk right through it.

Asshole light.

I lower myself off the edge of the deck and grasp the bar to dangle for a moment before my hand slips, and I find myself in midair. *Well, that's perfect,* I think. *I'm falling.*

It's the exact wrong thing to think, of course, because if I'm ever going to learn how to fly, I should focus my mind on something else, something entirely irrelevant, so that I'll miss the ground and soar upward instead.

chapter 34

if you say so

MESSAGES

JOY SONG

EDIT

CLEAR CONVERSATION

ARE YOU SURE?

ALL MESSAGES DELETED

The doctor finally comes in, swivels a monitor my way, and shows the inside of my ankle.

"Nothing broken," she says. "Except maybe your pride, ha ha!"

"Pthpthpthh," I say.

"I'm joking, I'm a dad-joker, so, anyway. It's an inversion sprain. Not too-too bad."

"Not broken," says Mom with relief. She punches my shoulder. "Aigu, stupid."

"We get a lot of this sort of thing this time of year among a certain youthful demographic," says the doctor.

"He going graduation party so late," says Mom. "Not even he drinking!"

"Remember RICE," says the doctor.

Racist, I want to shout.

"Rest, ice, compression, elevate," the doctor says.

"So not racist," I say out loud. Whoops.

"Someone's feisty," says the doctor, and looks me up and down. Is this mature female doctor really hitting on me in front of my own mother?

"Thank you, doctor," says Mom, oblivious. "He getting into Stanford."

"Ooh, gets real hot up there," says the doctor.

• • •

I slip an elastic bag over my foot to shower because I'm too lazy to undo and redo the brace. Then I sleep until two. I could sleep until dinner if I wanted to. I could sleep until September and wake up just in time for convocation.

Because it's summer.

Summer.

"So much for the summer of love," I say to my pillow.

I hobble down the steps, Rest with a baggie of Ice on my Compressed ankle sitting Elevated on a cushion next to Dad resting with his legs elevated too, and post a short video to Snapstory in a totally depressing cry for attention.

Within minutes, Q says, *I'm coming over.*

I also notice Joy's name among my dozen viewers of the video. I go to her feed and fling it up and down for a bit. And this, I guess, is our future.

Life got complicated, and Joy spooked. She gave up on our love. It makes me realize: love is a belief mutually held. As soon as that belief fades on either end, then poof, the whole thing falls face-flat like a tug-of-war suddenly gone one-sided.

I let my fartphone fall to the floor, then fall asleep again.

Ding-dong. I wake up. Dad's gone. I'm alone.

"Frankie-ya," says Mom. "Q here."

"Don't get up," says Q. He drops his big heavy backpack and takes a seat close to my elevated foot. "What the heck did you do? No toes missing?"

"Remember, we were at that crazy warehouse party, and I slipped on that big puddle by the thing?" I say, making my eyes as big as I can.

"Ohhhh ahhhh riiiight," says Q. "That thing was amazing."

"I check on Daddy," says Mom. We wait until she leaves to lower our voices.

"I went to see Joy last night," I whisper, and let my eyes fall.

"Oh no," says Q.

I nod.

"But—you—she—" says Q.

"We're done. Dunzo. Donut disco."

"Donut disco?"

"I don't know," I say.

"I can get you donuts. Whatever you need right now."

"I want Joy," I cry, and shade my eyes with a stiff hand.

"Oh man, come here, come here," says Q. "Let big papa Q hug it out."

"I don't want donuts," I sob. "I don't want any of this shit. I just want everyone to stay put. I don't want Joy's stupid Snapstory. I don't want you three thousand miles away. I don't want Dad to—"

"Oh man," says Q. "Get serious now, really hug it all out."

When I'm done, Q's tee shirt is all wet.

"Sorry," I say.

Q looks at the tearstains with an odd sort of pride. "Don't be sorry. You're lucky."

"Jyeah right, so lucky, look at me."

"You love hard enough to cry," says Q. "I admire that."

I just have to laugh at this, and Q joins in. "You know how weird you sound?" I say.

"You're the one all diarrhea diapers and donut discos."

I smile at my friend. My best friend. "You wanna go out somewhere?"

"You're not going anywhere with that ankle," says Q, "which you still need to explain. And besides, I have with me our completed, ready-to-play final campaign."

"You finished it," I say with awe.

Q waggles his glasses. "Last night."

From his backpack, Q draws forth his big spiral Dungeons & Dragons campaign notebook. It's titled *The Evasive Cambith of ¡P'Qatlalteiaq: Totec's Return.* It has skulls and pentagrams and everything. I don't know how he can possibly top the demigods and gem-swapping drama of our last campaign, but now I'm curious.

"Totec the mage gets resurrected?" I say. "Is Paul playing, too?"

Q nods. "He should've been here ten minutes ago, in fact. Where is Paul? I brought back Totec for that motherfucker."

We wait and wait before deciding that, in the interest of the limited time we have remaining together, we should just go ahead and get started. I play both my paladin and Paul's mage simultaneously, switching bullshit Middle English

379

accents as necessary. On paper we are the biggest losers in Palomino High School history. Two boys launching their summer vacations with a lonely game of Dungeons & Dragons.

But we don't care. Within minutes we're laughing, conspiring, cheering, groaning.

Thank you, Q.

"You eating melon," hollers Mom, scaring the shit out of both of us, and brings in a plate of honeydew wedges.

Thank you, Mom.

We do this for weeks.

I post pictures of our figurines locked in battle. I also post my ankle, which has traded in its brace for a simpler bandage. More melon. Q's intense dungeon master stare. Dad, finally eating something bigger than a piece of toast. I get my handful of pity likes from my two dozen followers. Whatever. I'm too busy to really care.

One day three curséd valkyries ambush my character while I'm reconnoitering a shattered keep on my own, and my character doesn't even get the chance to counterattack. I die alone, in this unnamed ruin.

I topple my figurine.

Q rights it again. He scrambles to ad-lib.

"Oh, uh, behold, I am the last surviving spirit protector of this ancient castle," sings Q. "I am known as—as Barbra the Good and Lawful, and I hereby reward the justness of your soul."

"What are you doing?" I say.

"I'm bringing you back to life," says Q.

"Can you do that?"

"The dungeon master can do whatever he wants," says Q. "And I say you're back."

He's smiling so big at me that I can't help but smile.

"Barbra?" I say.

Q doubles down. "Barbra the Good and Lawful."

"If you say so," I say.

chapter 35

champagne from champagne

Night. I'm in my bed alone, thinking about Paris.

The Songs went on an impromptu two-week vacation to Paris and beyond, because (a) they're loaded and (b) it gets Joy far, far away from me. Does that sound egotistical? Does that sound crazy?

There are pictures of Joy squinting in the sunlight with her little brother, Ben, before all the usual sights: the Eiffel Tower, the Sacré-Cœur, and so on. Wheels of friggin' cheese. Friggin' baguettes in bike baskets.

Joy looks gorgeous, photo filters be damned. And lost. And resigned.

Like, like, like, like, why not. I can pretend they're kisses she can't feel.

One night I post a picture of the demented little scroll crazy-man Charles gave me at The Store months and months ago, which I still have. I focus in on the drawing of the nude man and woman and the *vaginal ouroboros* and all that.

Joy comments with a little blue heart.

I guess that's gonna have to be enough.

Days later. Q and I have another rip-roaring all-day dungeon-crawling session. Minutes after he packs up and leaves for the evening, the doorbell rings.

Dad shuffles into the room, sleepy and perplexed. "Who is?"

"Maybe Q forget something," says Mom.

I look around. "Oh crap, his dice."

I'm talking about Q's velvet bag of seventy-dollar dice, hand carved from glistering opalite stone. That's ten dollars per die, nerds. Q loves these stupid dice. I hoist the bag and give it to Mom.

"So heavy," she says.

When she gets to the door, I hear murmurs in Korean.

Korean?

I see Dad shuffle over. The Korean gets louder, more formal.

So I get up to see what the commotion's all about. It takes a second—my ankle is still tender—but there they are, all standing around our shoe-cluttered foyer.

The Songs.

"Whoa," I say at the sight of Joy's dad. He's wearing a sweater around his shoulders. He is totally that guy who returns from Europe and is flustered that everything's just as ding-dang American as he left it.

There's Joy's mom and little brother, Ben, pressed together by the astonished bucking infant cowboy figurine.

And there's Joy. She's wearing a Cheese Barrel Grille polo shirt. Where the hell did she score such an artifact?

I laugh aloud, then want to cry, because an insufferably

maudlin part of me wants to believe she wore the shirt for me to say, *I will always love you.*

You know what? Fuck it. That is why she wore the shirt. That's what I'm going to believe right now. Why else would she, of all days, of all places, for me of all people?

"Hey," I say.

"Hey," says Joy.

Joy's dad hooks a finger at her mom, who dutifully presents a large fancy bag.

"We wanted to bring you a few things from our trip," he says. "Just little things."

In the bag are three fine silk scarves, a crystal brooch, a jar of Dijon mustard from Dijon, a bottle of Champagne from Champagne.

"We are so sorry we did not come sooner once we heard the news," says Joy's mom, speaking slowly and without error. "We want to offer our sincere apologies."

"It's okay," says Dad. He looks almost embarrassed to be seen the way he is right now, in the lounge sweats he's lived in for weeks, holding a trembling to-go cup close just in case he vomits. "Thanks much."

"If there's anything you need," croons Joy's dad. "Anything at all."

I keep my eyes on Joy, who can only glance at me for a half second at a time. She must have told them about Dad's illness during the trip. Her body language says it all: this whole thing is fucking weird.

"Frank," says my dad. "You take bag upstairs, put it in Mommy closet."

I reach for the bag. I look at Joy again. She's bent back a finger so far it looks like it's going to snap. She still has love for me—I can see it—but she doesn't know what to do with it.

Neither do I, but for different reasons.

"Thanks for the goodies," I call over my shoulder, and climb.

When I get to Mom's closet, I close myself in and breathe in the dark and stare at the bright line under the door growing dimmer and dimmer.

That night, after everyone's gone to sleep, I sit out in the backyard alone. I'm in brand-new lounge wear: a Stanford shirt-and-shorts combo, sent in a care package from Hanna. I post a terrible photo of the moon with the caption *Good night, backyard summer.* I get a few likes, Joy among them.

For an hour I sit there, listening to the traffic on the freeway, wondering how I must look to Mom-n-Dad and Joy's family now.

Say me and Joy had been born in Korea. We'd be Korean. We'd belong to a tribe. But that doesn't necessarily mean we'd belong with each other. Because there are tribes within tribes, all separated by gaps everywhere.

Gaps in time, gaps between generations. Money creates gaps.

City mouse, country mouse.

If there are that many micro-tribes all over the place, what does *Korean* even mean? What do any of the labels anywhere mean?

My reverie is interrupted by a rustling in the bushes at the far end of the backyard. I jump to my feet and fumble for my phone light—I've always wanted to catch a photo of a possum, or a raccoon.

The possum is huge. It has green in its hair.

It's not a possum.

"What the fuck?" I say.

"You say that a lot when you see me, you know that?" says Joy.

She extricates herself from the bushes with a graceless kick, then smooths her shirt.

"How—?" I say.

"There's a gap in the wall three houses down and the fence is all bent," says Joy. "I have like two minutes. My car's on the shoulder with the hazards on."

"You're insane."

"I just—I leave tomorrow."

Crap, she's right. CMU starts earlier than Stanford. She walks toward me as if on cracking ice.

"I just wanted to tell you that I'm sorry," she says.

She takes another step. I just watch her. She looks so lovely, I want to crush her in my arms and twirl her around, but the fist of my stomach stomps *no*. So I say nothing.

"I'm just sorry," she says.

I don't move. I just stand there with my arms folded.

"I wish I could be more brave," she says. She takes another step, then takes it back. "I wish I could be as brave as you. I feel so stupid sometimes. I'm eighteen already, I'm a freaking adult already."

Joy growls at the sky. After a moment, she looks at me again.

"But fuck all that," she says. "I just want to say I'm sorry. I'm really, pathetically, contemptibly sorry and I want you to forgive me and this sounds like the shittiest thing in the world but you have to know you're my best friend and I don't ever want to lose you."

That last part—*I don't ever want to lose you*—gets lost as I kiss her.

It's way longer than two minutes. Let her car get towed away. Let them all.

Because fuck it. I'm not going to waste my life blaming her. I'm not going to waste my life fanning embers of regret alone in the dark.

"I love you, yubs," says Joy. "I'm always gonna love you. Do you agree that we're always gonna love each other and that it was all just circumstance?"

"I do."

"I do too."

"I now pronounce us husband and wife," I say. "You may now, uh, go off to college and not see me until the holiday season."

"Grr, your stupid jokes!" shouts Joy amid the din of the traffic, and lands the best hit ever with her open palm.

"I will love you forever, Joy Song."

"I just needed to hear you say it."

"I can't help but love you, Joy Song."

"Now I'll have something to keep."

"I'll keep it, too," I say.

The traffic takes on an insistent tone, and I begin to imagine a curious cop discovering her empty car.

"Your car," I say.

"I know," she says.

"Go do you," I holler, before she heads toward the bushes again.

Joy looks back. Her smile glints in the dark. "What the hell else is there, right?"

chapter 36

life is but a dream

The final two weeks of summer pass like cats after an earth-quake. Mom-n-Dad, sensing my melancholy, tiptoe around me. Asking if I need anything. Cutting melon after melon.

My ankle feels strong now. I feel taller, as if things healed in such a way to grant me extra height. I leave the house to go for runs without telling anyone, come back whenever, fix my own meals. I've been researching the local music scene in and around Palo Alto. I'm starting to see myself there.

I tell Mom-n-Dad all about it, and they can tell I'm getting excited. It makes them sappy (sad plus happy). Because just when they thought their son was all done growing, here I go changing on them all over again. I'm becoming different.

Q notices, too. We finish up *Totec's Return* in a blaze of savage glory under my meat-headed command. I do not fight smart. I do not think it through.

"Totally insane man, I love you," shouts Q.

What neither Q nor Mom nor Dad can see is the secret little chamber in the wunderkammer of my heart, and what it contains.

Back to my campaign of reckless blood: by the time Paul finally shows up to play, we've already destroyed the Supreme Bladeling in ¡P'Qatlalteiaq's central keep, divvied out the piles of treasure, and traveled back to our homelands. Normally we would now spend time gathering resources and healing and training for the next big campaign, but there will be no next big campaign. So Q just closes up the campaign book, folds up his cardboard screens, zips his big backpack shut, and exhales.

Paul examines his figurine of Totec before slipping it into its little special bag.

"I guess we're finished," says Paul. "Isang bagsak?"

We clap.

"So when do you guys leave tomorrow?" says Q.

I look at Paul. "Mr. Olmo, what time?"

Me and Paul are driving north together. I'll drop Paul off at Santa Cruz, then keep going to Stanford.

"I dunno," says Paul. "Nine? Ten? Maybe eleven. After lunch?"

"Sunday traffic should be light," I say. "Convocation's on the Monday after—it's all good."

"I can't believe this is the last time we'll—" says Paul, unable to finish.

After a truly uncoordinated group hug that evades headbutts only by millimeters, Paul and Q leave.

Seconds later Mom hustles in. "They leaving already?"

"Yeah."

"Oh," says Mom with a sag. "I saying goodbye."

"You'll see them at Thanksgiving."

Mom starts to say something, but stops. I want to say the same thing.

But Dad won't be around then.

"Are you okay?" I say.

"I'm okay," says Mom.

"Mom, just say it. Whatever it is, I want to hear it."

"I'm okay," is all Mom will say, and leaves to pretend at laundry.

Joy and I have been texting again. We send idiotic stickers and animations and so on. She sends me a photo of her new dorm room, and a stealthy candid of her roommate, who looks eerily like an African-American version of Brit.

Joy's messages start out strong but begin to dwindle as she explores her new world. And that, I decide, is perfectly okay. It would be strange otherwise.

That night Mom makes my favorite dinner of seafood pancakes and cold mul naengmyeon noodles, and we try not to panic when Dad makes a heroic show of eating with forced gusto. He winds up vomiting most of it back into a to-go cup.

"I sorry, Mommy," he says.

"Aigu," says Mom, which means, *Don't worry about anything. It wasn't your fault.*

She gives him water to sip. He pushes it aside.

"Gimme two beer, would you, please, Frankie-umma?" he says. That word *please*. He's gearing up to something.

"Shouldn't be drinking, you sick," says Mom.

"Doctor say drink as much beer as I want, doesn't matter," says Dad.

This stops Mom cold. She sees him, sitting next to his son on his last night before college, and understands. She knows the next time I see him might be late one night, after a rushed trip back home from Stanford, in some hospital room.

So she brings the beers. She opens them. She leaves us.

"Beer is terrible," I say. "Why do you drink it?"

"It's all-natural barley water," says Dad, and we toast.

I drink, because I can't think of anything to say. I drink again. Terrible.

But it's the best drink I've ever had.

"So," says Dad. "I'm reading other day. I'm learning new word."

Dad waits for me to take the bait, so I take the bait.

"What word, Dad?"

"*Neohumanistic.*"

Dad's being cryptic. Here we go.

"What does *neohumanistic* mean, Dad?" I say dutifully.

Dad takes a sip. "I am Korean. You Korean too. But you also American boy, hundred percent. You so-called *neohumanistic*. You know *neohumanistic* what it is?"

"Sort of," I say, looking into my beer.

"Spiritual essence, so-called nucleus of soul, like particle, physical particle. You know what is quark? Nothing different. Atom? Nothing different, same-o same."

"Okay, Dad," I say.

Meanwhile, Dad winds up for another round of free-form

arcana. I gird myself. Tonight is our last night together. Must maintain.

"Anyway," says Dad. "Anyway."

He's silent.

"Anyway what, Dad?" I say.

"I very proud you," says Dad. "So, so proud. I love you, my son, okay?"

He places his hand atop mine. His skin is so thin. He has a hospital needle port thing taped to his wrist, and always will.

I can barely get out the words, they're so frozen shut. "I love you too, Dad."

I get that old floaty feeling again, but this time it's not me doing the floating. It's not Dad. It's all the crap around us. The chairs and toaster and pots and pans and thousands of kooky knickknacks atop bookshelves coming unmoored from their spots in the carpet.

It's beautiful, this constellation of ephemera.

"Anyway," Dad declares, restoring gravity with his voice. "Life is but a dream." He releases my hand with the pretense of wiping clean his sweating beer can. He's never been comfortable with prolonged physical affection. It's never been his way. And that's fine.

"Come on, Dad. Don't be morbid."

"No, I'm not be morbid," says Dad. "Life is but a dream. My dream? So beautiful dream I'm having whole my life, God giving me. Beautiful wife I having. Store success having. Beautiful son Stanford going. My daughter too, beautiful woman she becoming. You telling Hanna my dream is best dream."

"Tell her yourself," I say.

Dad laughs, which in Korean means, *I am so terribly ashamed by my own behavior.*

"Dad," I insist. "Tell her yourself. Okay?"

"Okay, Frank."

"You need to talk to Hanna. She has big, important things going on right now. You hear me?"

"Okay, Frank, okay."

I sip the bitter-sour beer. Who likes this crap? I sip it again, and again.

Thank you, beer.

"I going sleep," says Dad. "Big day tomorrow."

"Yeah."

"Maybe I'm sleeping, you waking me before you going, okay?"

"Of course, Dad."

"Also music study? No money earning, music," says Dad. "You majoring business. More better."

I just laugh to myself. Because you know what? I'll do what I want anyway. I need to. So did Dad, after all.

"Okay, Dad," I say.

chapter 37

fire hazard low

Before me and Paul hit the road, I have one pit stop to make: Q's house.

He forgot his big bag of dice again.

"Wait here," I tell Paul, and run up the three-hundred-kilometer-long gravel driveway.

When Q opens the door, he's all alone.

"Where is everybody?" I say.

"Mom-n-Dad are with Evon up in SF tooling around before Stanford starts," says Q. "She said you might want these back, by the way."

Q hands me a fistful of cables in Loco-Lime™ green, Grape-Escape™ purple, Citrus-Spin™ orange, and so on. All the colors of the rainbow, in order.

"Thanks," I say.

"What about your million relatives?"

"Mouse World Theme Park," says Q.

"Jesus," I say.

"I told them I had tapeworm."

"Nice," I say, and give Q a fist bump. "You forgot your big-ass dice."

I hand him the bag, and he presses his lips to mine.

"What—" I say, only to have him kiss me again. Curiously, his lips are softer than Joy's. More tentative. He smells like lime soda and Blazing Hot Nachitos.

When he pulls away, I see his eyes are brimming with tears.

"Please don't tell anyone," he says.

A wave surges the sea level in my chest; two new tears sting my eyes with their salt. Suddenly realizing that Q, my top chap, has been living with a secret fear—secret even to me—for who knows how long makes me want to rage out against entire stupid world.

But Q does not need rage right now. He needs the opposite.

I wipe his tears with both my thumbs and study his face. I never noticed how fine it was, how lovely in shape. I never noticed his *freckles*, even. It is a face, I realize, whose beauty shows itself only when it's ready—a face that has the grace and strength it takes to reveal the true self just beneath. It is a face someone will no doubt fall in love with one day. So I tell Q this.

"One day you're gonna make some lucky boy very happy."

"I'm gonna miss you," he says.

"I'm gonna miss you too," I say.

• • •

We know we're out of civilization when we reach the burned forest. The flames that ran through here were the same flames that started while I was breaking Brit's heart, a million years ago.

"Man, I guess the fire reached pretty far," says Paul Olmo.

"Yeah," I say. It's been an hour and a half of driving, and I'm still kind of in shock.

Suddenly I need to get out of the car. "Hey," I say. "Gotta pee."

"Take your time," says Paul. "We're frankly in no rush."

"Har," I say. "You're olmo funny."

Paul smiles a sad smile and begins flipping through photos of all of us on his phone.

When I'm done peeing, and the crinkly pattering sound stops, all that's left is silence. Total and complete silence. I realize why: with all the leaves burned away, the forest no longer makes sound. There is a brand-new sign, probably put here recently to replace the old burnt one, bearing the words FIRE HAZARD LOW.

And yet, there's a size and shape and quality to this dead forest that is palpable. It is there. Like a soft breathing. This is but a moment in the life of this colossal organism, for the trees will grow back, and everyone will forget there were ever flames hot and high enough to melt houses.

I am standing on a road leading away from home. It's strange to be here. I shouldn't be here. Because at home lies Dad with his to-go cup. Mom gets him whatever he needs, which is becoming less and less with each day. He hasn't checked the security cameras at The Store for a couple of days now. He knows it's no longer important.

Anyone else would think I was weird for leaving like this.

One day soon I will get the call. I'll slip out of lecture, or shush my dorm friends, or freeze in midstride on a quad path. I'll drive home as fast as my car will go, holding ready the one last goodbye I've saved in my heart.

For now, Mom-n-Dad would be proud to see me standing here on this road. They insisted I do this. So I'm here for them just as much as I am for me. And that makes me proud, too.

"We are okay," said Dad when I left. "Have a fun."

I take out my Tascam. I hit Record. I brace the device in the crook of a tree limb. Memory is cheap and plentiful, and the Tascam will record for hours and hours even with all the other sounds that are still on it: Lake Girlfriend, ocean waves, diners at Scudders, that samulnori quartet, and so on. Maybe someone will find these sounds, and also find delight in them.

I leave the Tascam, get back in the indomitable Consta, and head out north.

thanksgiving

after we end

I have one name.

It's Frank.

I used to think I had two names: Frank, my quote-English-end-quote name, and Sung-Mi, my quote-Korean-end-quote name.

But now, I'm calling Frank my first name and Sung-Mi my middle name. That's for a few reasons:

- Frank + Li makes a funny pun, which I used to hate but now I've grown fond of.
- Having two names is like trying to be two people at once. Who does that?
- No one ever calls me Sung-Mi, not even Mom. Dad never did, either.

Dad lasted two more months before my phone rang.

"You coming home," was all Mom had to say.

When I arrived, Hanna was already there in the room with Dad. She let him feel her belly. He took both of Miles's hands in both of his and said:

"You whole of world number one best daddy for Sunny."

Hanna and Miles are having a girl, and her name will be Sunny Lane (nine characters).

I stayed in my room. Hanna and Miles stayed in her room. Mom stayed with Dad. We lived like this for three whole days, waking up together, cooking meals together, watching television. Just being bored together. Feeling the jeong. Mom gave Miles whatever he wanted, and too much of it, which meant, *I am eternally ashamed of how we treated you and will forever be sorry for our foolishness.*

Thanksgiving came, and we had the world's simplest feast of take-out Korean fried chicken, white rice, and pickled radish. Dad even managed to eat a little and hold it down.

It was fun in a bittersweet way. I felt like a little kid again for some reason.

Then it was time for Dad to leave.

Everyone gathered on the green slope the afternoon of the funeral. The Apeys, the Limbos. Q was there, with hot sister Evon. Brit was there. Even Wu showed up. Everyone in black, not knowing where to look. Trying not to stare at me or Mom or Hanna. The ceremony was conducted in Korean, and translated in turn into excellent English by Joy's dad.

Joy was there. When she hugged me, I felt her secretly kiss my neck.

"You look nice," she said.

"So do you," I said, and melted with tears. Joy held me up. I don't know why I cried so much, or for so long. As in I can't articulate why. All I could feel was my brain exploding with a million tiny dark stars. When I opened my eyes, me and Joy were the only ones left on the green slope. Everyone else had gone to the wake.

We all sat together in a strange room, eating strange food. It was a phantom party in a dream. No one had changed—no one had started dating anyone new, everyone looked the same—but still: all of us were different now. I could feel it. At one point we all ran out of things to talk about, so we just stared at the black framed photograph of Dad flanked by dancing candles.

Hanna was the one brave enough to start the farewell hugs. Everyone else followed one by one. Q was the last in line, with an awkward bro-hug. I understood why he would give me such a hug, what with all these people present. But to hell with bro-hugs: I held him with all my might, to let him know I loved him.

And then, I was all alone.

"Bye, Dad," I said to the photograph, and felt a hand slip into mine.

"He can do whatever he wants now," said Joy.

"Probably open another store in the afterlife," I said.

We laughed at this. Then Joy began staring at me with a look I recognized. It was the look from that night when she snuck into my backyard for our last kiss. There in the funeral reception hall, Joy stood looking back and forth between my eyes and my lips. Waiting.

But the thing about last kisses is this: they are final. Me and Joy already did that. It was done.

I let her know this by giving her hand a squeeze.

"It's really good to see you," I said.

"See you at Christmas, I guess," said Joy.

"See you at Christmas," I said.

• • •

It's three days later, and I'm headed back north. Mom's insisting. Hanna and Miles are staying behind for a few more days, ostensibly so that Mom can buy them a metric ton of baby clothes.

"No way am I letting her buy a bunch of pink princessy crap," says Hanna.

"You're such a bullshitter," I say.

"She's gonna buy whatever she wants, isn't she."

"And you won't stop her," I say. "And you're gonna love every minute of it."

Hanna gives me the longest hug she's ever given me, which means, *You're right.*

And now I'm back on the road. Paul Olmo sits in the front seat, Evon Lee's in the back seat. We drive and drive. We pass a phone around and take turns playing music. We pass through the burnt-out forest again, and when I spot the fire hazard sign, I slow down and crane my neck to see if my Tascam is still there.

But the Tascam is gone.

I'm so happy to see it missing that I tear up. I'm grateful someone is listening to it right now. I'm grateful for everything:

this road, the trees that will soon bloom with life again, and all the life ahead of us.

I drop off Paul Olmo in Santa Cruz, and then it's just me and Evon alone.

"Your turn to DJ," I mumble, blindly handing her the phone.

"So my brother told you he's, uh," says Evon.

I glance at her. She peers at me from behind my phone.

"Yes," I say. "He did."

Evon nods. "He said he was gonna, so. Good."

"How long have you known?"

"Since March."

"Huh."

"He's been working up to it," says Evon.

We drive for five miles, passing endless tan hills and vast refinery lots. I glance at Evon a few more times. She doesn't know about the kiss.

"So did he come out to your mom-n-dad?" I say.

Evon shakes her head. "He was barely able to tell me, let alone them."

"And you kept his secret this whole time."

Evon just shrugs at me: *of course.*

"You're the best little sister by three seconds in the whole world," I say.

Heavenly Evon Lee smiles one of the best smiles ever.

We reach Stanford. I drop her off at her dorm. I reach my dorm, park the car, and get out to stretch.

I don't know what else to do, so I walk the campus.

I cross the parking lot to find myself in a field that dips to reveal a serpent-like wall constructed of stone. It's a famous sculpture, apparently, one that evokes sinuous change and unyielding permanence both at the same time.

I descend the bank to the wall and walk its length. I run my hand along its undulating tapered top ridge as it winds left, right, left, right, left, right, left, right.

Then the wall ends and I continue on.

acknowledgments

Thank you, Mom. I love you.

Thank you, big bro. I love you too.

Thank you, Jen Loja, for taking the time and caring with such sincerity. Thanks to your team as well.

Thank you, Jen Klonsky, my champion at Penguin. I'm beyond lucky to have as a believer someone as smart and fearless as you.

Also many thanks to:

- Shanta Newlin and her indomitable publicity team, including Elyse Marshall and Marisa Russell
- Emily Romero and her inspired marketing team, including Alex Garber and Felicity Vallence, and Erin Berger and Christina Colangelo
- Felicia Frazier and her intrepid sales team
- Laurel Robinson, Theresa Evangelista, Marikka Tamura, and Caitlin Tutterow, plus Kelly Hurst across the pond

I could not dream of more gracious, patient, and ingenious people to work with. All of you are the shinobi elite of publishing.

More thanks to my Alloy family: Josh Bank, Sara Shandler, Joelle Hobeika, and to Les Morgenstein and Elysa Dutton here on the West Coast. You guys believed in me so steadfast for so long, even when things weren't going so well, and now I'm teary-eyed.

Enormous thanks to Yoon Bai and Gemma Baek for keeping my crappy Korean straight and for your critical translation skills.

All the hats off to artist Owen Gildersleeve, for crafting a cover authors dream of.

Thanks to Jillian Vandall, because Jillian Vandall.

I would not even be here without wife Nicola Yoon. You are my love, my best friend, my weirdest friend. You are my most trusted writing partner and tough-as-nails business sounding board. I have a hard time believing we actually get to be on this creative journey together. Hand in hand. Step by step. Some mornings I wake up and think, "We are married, and we are writers!"

Thank you, Nathan Cernosek, Wendy Wunder, Gregg Rosenblum, Anna Carey, Adam Silvera, Sabaa Tahir, Ransom Riggs, Tahareh Mafi, Marie Lu, and Primo Gallanosa for your cheers and support. You know like only fellow writers can know.

Thank you Andrew Dodge, Michelle Hlubinka, Sue Jung, Christina Ma, J Chad Evans, and the rest of the original Apey crew.

Hi Penny! One day I bet you'll get to write acknowledgments too.

Thanks also to Billy Lambufonda.

Finally: thank you, Dad. You taught me more than I think either of us realized. I know you only got to hold the book in your hands, and not for very long because you were so tired, but I know you read it in your own way using your heart instead of your eyes. You can officially brag about me to your new mysterious friends. I miss you.

David Yoon is a writer and designer

who created the illustrations for the #1 *New York Times* bestselling novel *Everything, Everything*. He lives in Los Angeles with his wife, novelist Nicola Yoon, and their energetic daughter. *Frankly in Love* is his first novel.

'Heart-wrenching . . . I devoured it in one sitting'
Jennifer Niven, author of *All the Bright Places*

Read it before you see the film

nicola yoon

EVERYTHING, EVERYTHING
Nicola Yoon

LIVE LIFE IN A BUBBLE?

OR RISK EVERYTHING FOR LOVE?

Maddy is allergic to the world. She hasn't left her house in seventeen years.
Olly is the boy next door. He's determined to find a way to reach her.
Everything, Everything is all about the crazy risks we take for love.

'Powerful, lovely, heart-wrenching, and so absorbing I devoured it in one sitting'
Jennifer Niven, author of *All the Bright Places*

'This extraordinary first novel about love . . . is one of the best books
I've read this year' **Jodi Picoult**

Now a major film starring Amandla Stenberg and Nick Robinson

NEW YORK TIMES BESTSELLING AUTHOR OF
EVERYTHING, EVERYTHING

THE
SUN IS
ALSO A
STAR

nicola yoon

THE SUN IS ALSO A STAR
Nicola Yoon

THE STORY OF A GIRL, A BOY AND THE UNIVERSE.

NATASHA:
I'm a girl who believes in science and facts. Not fate. Not destiny. Or dreams that will never come true. I'm definitely not the kind of girl who meets a cute boy on a crowded New York City street and falls in love with him. Not when my family is twelve hours away from being deported to Jamaica. Falling in love with him won't be my story.

DANIEL:
I've always been the good son, the good student, living up to my parents' high expectations. Never the poet. Or the dreamer. But when I see her, I forget about all that. Something about Natasha makes me think that fate has something much more extraordinary in store – for both of us.

Did the universe bring them together only to keep them apart?

The incredible bestselling novel from Nicola Yoon, author of *Everything, Everything*.

Now a major film starring Yara Shahidi and Charles Melton